Death by Roses

Death *by* Roses

Vivian R. Probst

SelectBooks, Inc.

New York

This edition published by SelectBooks, Inc.
For information address SelectBooks, Inc., New York, New York.

First Edition

ISBN 978-1-59079-148-6

Library of Congress Cataloging-in-Publication Data

Probst, Vivian R.
Death by roses / Vivian R. Probst. – First edition.
   pages cm
Summary: "For the first time in nearly thirty years of marriage, Art McElroy Sr. buys his headstrong, disapproving wife a dozen yellow roses. Hours later, he discovers her lifeless body seated on the toilet. Mae Rose McElroy's sudden death leaves a void in her family and in the entire Midwestern farming community of Fairview. It's a void Mae Rose will attempt to fill, herself, from the hereafter, by meddling, directly, in earthly affairs. Mae Rose's meddling leads to her spiritual expulsion from heaven, and she winds up in the body of Mary Lee Broadmoor (Scary Mary), a crusty writer and director of exquisite horror movies. Mary Lee refuses to succumb to stage-4 pancreatic cancer until she gets one final shot at an elusive Oscar. Like Mae Rose, who argues with God for a return to earth, Mary Lee pleads, from her Hollywood deathbed, for more time to complete her work, as her hospice nurse, Gertie Morgan, looks on. The two women's spirits work together and Mae Rose provides her host with a new script idea: a love story, based on her life! The script earns Mary Lee her coveted Academy Award, but the movie's release shocks and disturbs Mae Rose's family. They set out to find, and confront, the woman who has somehow co-opted, and publicly revealed, their personal tragedy. Along the way, new love emerges as the reader meets a caste of crazy, eccentric, but highly memorable, characters. Death by Roses suggests that relationships don't end at death, but continue until their ultimate purpose is achieved. The universe has every resource at its disposal to get the job done. It also has an amazing sense of humor" – Provided by publisher.
   ISBN 978-1-59079-148-6 (pbk. : alk. paper)
   1. Husband and wife–Fiction. 2. Dead–Fiction. 3. Future life–Fiction. 4. Humorous stories. I. Title.
   PS3616.R626D43 2015
   813'.6–dc23
                                    2014012151

Manufactured in the United States of America
10 9 8 7 6 5 4 3 2 1

For
Cheryl Ann (Theobald) Cook
October 6, 1951–March 26, 2008
Beloved sister, teacher, and angel
after whose death, this story began.
and
Fred Howard Loeb
July 10, 1946–November 17, 2008
employer, partner, mentor, friend
whose last words to me in this lifetime were
"I think at last you have a story."

Acknowledgments

First and foremost: Thomas Henry Probst, my husband and soul mate—the man who kept insisting that I *"publish the damn book!"*; Steve Eisner, visionary owner of When Words Count Retreat; Jon Reisfeld, When Words Count Retreat; Anne Wondra, my personal life coach and consultant, travel partner, *angel*, crisis manager, tantrum tamer, protector of writing space; encourager, editing reader, sacred space holder, etc.; Kenzi Sugihara, publisher, SelectBooks, Inc.; Nancy Sugihara, editor at SelectBooks, Inc. (incredibly talented woman who made editing *fun*); Kenichi Sugihara, director of marketing at SelectBooks, Inc.; my publicist: Meryl Moss, Media Muscle & MLM Marketing; my literary agency: Irene Goodman Agency in the person of Rachel Ekstrom who has kept me sane (I think!); book cover designer: Asha Hossain; Best Friend Ever: Susie Losinske, with whom I have both laughed and wept through life's ups and downs, including meeting boyfriends who became husbands; Paul Theobald, my brother and a supporter of my writing life who accompanied me to the When Words Count Retreat Publishing Trifecta and held me up when I thought the world was crashing around me and *who so mesmerized the judges that they now want me to write his memoirs!* Mary Hunter, beloved sister who has journeyed with me through the traumas of our childhood into wholeness and my most enthusiastic cheerleader; Readers offering valuable insight, encouragement, and edits: Jennifer Kersten, Georganne Wilson, Elizabeth Price, Nancy Bauer, and Andrea Howe (Blue Falcon Editing); TheoPRO employees who have kept our consulting business going while I have undertaken the "business" of writing this novel: Lisa Kaebisch, partner; Phil Bogan, bookkeeper; Stephanie Wade, executive assistant and provider of hair, make-up, and wardrobe advice; Energy workers and healers who have kept me going emotionally, spiritually, physically, and all points in-between: Dr. Rose Kumar and staff at The Ommani Center, Dr. Boris Matthews, Sujata Sengupta, Sara Joy, Sue Katzuba, Rowynn Gilraine, Amy Martin, and Billie Jean Crawford. Coaches for life and for business: Teri Bach, Kate Beeders, and Margaret Lynch. PSST! Everyone needs a coach! Video Consultants/Web Designers: Roberto Mighty, Suzanne Evans and Hell Yeah! Studios, and Stella Orange. *Others angels in human form:* Barb Stremick, Tara Lynn Majeska, Martha Bach-Wiig, Lori Falk & Debbie Kleinschmidt, Paula Casey, and Mike Robichaud; Fellow Contestants in the When Words Count Retreat Publishing Trifecta: Roger Corea, Marc Abbot, Sharon Spies, Jan Cannon, and Zoe Fowler.

Children by birth and marriage: my daughter, Sonia Heileman; my son, Jonathan Tiegs; my step-daughters: Pamela Probst, Alyssa Probst, and Juanita Probst; my step-sons: Henry Probst, Charles Probst, and Josh Dieringer

Most brilliant grandchildren on earth (in order of age): Spencer Tiegs, Jacob Probst, Avery Tiegs, Peyton Tiegs, Logan Probst, Grant Probst, Natalia Probst, Elliana Tiegs, Brenner Heileman, Dylan Heileman, and Alona Dieringer.

Parents: Sterling and (the late) Wanita Mae (King) Theobald. *Where would I be without you?*

1

If Mae Rose McElroy had known that by evening she would be dead *à la commode* after a fit of rage at her husband, she might have made different choices. Of course, if she'd done things differently, she might not have died while sitting on the toilet.

But on that frosty March morning, as she stood by the kitchen window washing breakfast dishes, Mae Rose was preoccupied with the effects of the last night's storm. Everything glistened in sparkling crystal coats of ice that most would have found beautiful. As she anxiously surveyed the backyard trees, the barn, and the gardens and fields of their farm home, Mae Rose was far from feeling awestruck.

This was because today—of all days—her husband would be driving her meticulously restored 1974 VW Beetle to the mechanic shop where he worked. "Please be *very* careful, Art," she said without looking up from the sink, "the roads could be *very* slippery."

After thirty years of marriage, Art understood the meaning of Mae Rose's words. They meant she didn't trust him and was worrying about her precious car. Her fretting did not dissuade Art from feeling an uncharacteristic joy.

Mae Rose could tell from the noises in the background that he was indeed ecstatic. The hangers clanged merrily as he removed his coat from the closet. Even the zipper sang with an abnormal enthusiasm as he closed his jacket against the cold.

"You know I'll be careful," Art replied, planting a dutiful kiss on his wife's stern cheek. Earlier, while shaving, he had practiced saying

"I love you" to Mae Rose. Although her obvious unhappiness made him decide not to attempt it now, nothing—not even his irritation with her remarks—could suppress his buoyant feelings of hope.

It was rare for Art to drive Mae Rose's car. But once his new client at the shop saw the car's spectacular restoration, he was certain the man would confirm his intention to pay the large expense of having his own antique Beetle refurbished. And Art hoped for much more— surely his impressive sale would help to renew Mae Rose's faith in him and their marriage.

Three decades of marriage to Mae Rose had left deep creases across his forehead. Each crease could have been labeled: the upper line for shock at Mae Rose's intensity, the middle for his resistance to her relentless drive, and the lower for the wavering boundary where Art tried to keep his identity from being discarded as irrelevant.

As he squeezed his tall frame into her car, he put the keys into the ignition and waited patiently for the engine to turn over. It was understandably reluctant, but as if it knew how important the day was, the engine gave in to Art's persistence. He headed down the long gravel drive, turning left on the two-lane country road with caution.

As the sun melted the icy coating on the asphalt, Art was able to relax and enjoy his drive. Everything glistened in the soft, feathery frost—so breathtaking that Art considered it the best possible omen for a successful day. He couldn't help that his right hand caressed the leather upholstery he had so lovingly used to recover the seats of Mae Rose's car; he felt pride, perhaps even a mild flirtation, as he touched the dashboard and turned the radio dial to his favorite oldies rock 'n roll station.

He'd have to remember to turn it back to Mae Rose's country music station later, but just now he needed to mark his territory. Art loved nothing more than working on old VWs, the only car, he claimed, that possessed a personality all its own, and the possibility of working on another old VW Beetle gave him an unfamiliar sense of exhilaration.

"I'd hammer 'bout justice!" Peter, Paul, and Mary sang, and Art joined in: "I'd hammer 'bout freedom! "I'd hammer 'bout the love between," and Art, who loved to change words of a song to suit himself, sang, "A man and a Beetle, all over this land!"

As Art brought Mae Rose's car to an obedient stop at the four-way before proceeding into town, he downshifted through each gear, listening for the purr of pleasure as one cog slid into the next. But today the car growled low and mean as if to remind Art to drive straight though town instead of turning right, as he often had years ago for a cup of coffee and some fornication with Maggie Whitman. Back then, he felt justified in doing this because of Mae Rose's increasingly insufferable nagging and her proportionately deflated interest in sex.

A trip through Fairview included passing Good Shepherd Presbyterian Church, a cornerstone of the McElroy's lives. It housed times of great joy: when Art and Mae Rose had married and when they had baptized their son Art Jr., and eight years later, their son John. It radiated with the beauty of Mae Rose at the piano and organ, and more often than not, a flower arrangement she had created adorning the altar. But the church also held their deepest pain in its stone structure as the wounds of Art's affair had been exposed in quiet confidence to Pastor Frank. The hope of a happy marriage had faded into an ever-sensitive, tender scar.

Art's heightened emotions brought all these memories back into sharp focus as he drove past the church that morning. Each memory rose, crested, and fell into the embrace of his pending triumph against the stunning backdrop of the ice show that glistened in the sun. Surely today would be the lucky day he had been longing for.

The reflection of Mae Rose's yellow 1974 VW Beetle—a high school graduation gift from her parents, Dr. and Mrs. Henry Carter—caught Art's eye as he drove past display windows of the few shops in town. He smiled. It was a happy car, he decided, en route to a happy event, and yellow was a fabulous color for happiness. After all, Art had met the Carter family because of that car, and had courted both

Mae Rose and her Beetle right to the altar where he had promised to love and cherish her (or them if you included the car) until death.

All Art could think about these days was restoring the pride and love Mae Rose had felt for him in those early years of their marriage—before he became unfaithful and she became nearly impossible to live with.

After his confession of infidelity, Art had learned to spend his evenings out of Mae Rose's "range" by hiding out in the barn after dinner each night. There, surrounded by the hoard of antique VW parts he and Mae Rose had enthusiastically collected together in the early, myopic years of their marriage, he pretended he still believed in their retirement dream of restoring and selling old VWs. But most of the time he smoked and fumed at Mae Rose.

Art justified his withdrawal from his wife by claiming that even a saint would be hard-pressed to love Mae Rose. In the deepening darkness of evening, he would dispatch his wife in his imagination with an authority he could only exert in her absence. "Off with her head!" he would mutter and snicker quietly lest Mae Rose be within hearing range.

It gave him momentary relief, but of course he never, ever, considered that Mae Rose would actually die in the undignified manner that Art found her hours later.

* * *

The meeting with the customer went even better than Art expected. When the man saw Mae Rose's car and the love Art had poured into restoring it, he signed the contract and left a large deposit. Art and the shop would receive the balance when he picked up the car in six months. For once, Art couldn't wait to get home. A phone call to Mae Rose was unworthy of the occasion—he wanted to take her in his arms, share the news, and tell her he loved her.

As he prepared to leave the shop at the end of the day, his fellow mechanic Ben Strong came over with an apologetic look on his face.

Ben's distinctively bushy red hair sprouting atop his tall, lumberjack frame made it hard for him to hide himself or his tendency to spend his free time and his paycheck at the Tree Top Bar. His wife, Louise, made a career out of packing his suitcases, sending him to rehab, then unpacking them when he returned home clean and sober. Ben was a darn good mechanic and Art liked him.

"Art, you know—Louise has kicked me out of the house. Again." Ben confided humbly. He paused repeatedly when he spoke. Art supposed it was because he was used to his wife finishing his sentences for him. "I need a favor."

"What's that, Ben?" Art asked, unable to hide his jovial mood. He was sorry for Ben's problems but glad they weren't his. Mae Rose was a handful, but Louise made Mae Rose look like an angel.

"Our barn cat had kittens recently. I gotta find a home for 'em for a little while. Since I won't be at the house. The mother cat hasn't been around the last few days. We—I mean I—think she might, you know, be dead. If I don't find a place for 'em, Louise would just as soon shoot 'em. She don't understand how beneficial they are."

Art could easily imagine the one-sided conversation that had taken place in Ben and Louise's run-down mobile home as Ben begged his wife to let his barn cats live. It most certainly would have been sprinkled with Louise's favorite word that started with "f" and ended with "k."

On the rare occasion that she came into town, anyone within ear-shot would hear Louise declare, "That man will be the fuckin' death of me. My momma tried to warn me. She would say, 'Once an effin' drunk'—momma didn't believe in the "F" word—'always an effin' drunk.' But my momma also told me, 'A vow is an effin' vow. You made your effin' bed; you sleep in your effin' bed.'"

Ben continued speaking in his hesitant, halting way. "The first few months—you know—they are the most important. Can you take 'em? You've got a barn. It's just until Louise and me—you know." He stopped speaking and hung his head.

"Sure, Ben," Art replied without a moment's hesitation. "We'd be glad to help you out." While technically the barn Ben was referring to was Mae Rose's barn, since the ownership of the entire estate passed through the women in her family, Mae Rose had no use for it. She had allowed Art to house his retirement project there for years. After years of waiting for anything worthwhile to happen there, Mae Rose laughed bitterly whenever Art said he was going to "work" in the barn. "No, Art," she would fume. "You're not going to *work* in the barn. You're going to *smoke* in the barn because I won't allow it in the house. As for our 'retirement plan,' you can stop pretending that anything you do in the barn is for *us.*"

Ben gingerly placed a cardboard box on the front passenger seat of Mae Rose's car. "Just be real careful, Art," he cautioned after the kittens were situated. Art could tell from their constant mewing and the pathetic scratching of their tiny claws inside the box that the poor little felines were antsy and looking for a way out.

"These are barn cats," Ben explained, as if Art didn't know what a barn cat was. "Don't go trying to pet 'em or make friends with 'em. They've got their claws. You know. So they can kill their food. But they're not old enough to do that for themselves yet. They still have to be fed." He paused again. "Put 'em in the barn. Leave 'em alone. Give 'em some water and a little dry food in the morning and check 'em at the end of the day. That's all. Otherwise, they gotta learn to fend for themselves. I'll let you know just as soon as I can, you know, take 'em back."

Before heading to his own truck, Ben took off his Mike's Mechanic Shop hat and ran his hands through his hair. "You sure Mae Rose won't mind?" Art noticed Ben twisting his hat into odd shapes and wondered why he was so nervous.

"No problem, Ben," Art called to him as he got in Mae Rose's car. "I've always thought barn cats would be a good idea. This just might be an answer to prayer. You know Mae Rose; she's always looking for a way to help folks. Good luck with Louise. We'll be praying for you two." With that, Art headed down the road feeling pretty good about things. Mae Rose would be over the moon about his new project, and she might even change her mind about barn cats.

7

The radio in Mae Rose's car was playing "Blue Moon." Art started to sing along, replacing the title with his wife's name, "Mae Rose," he sang, "you caught me standing alone, without a dream in my heart, without a love of my own." Suddenly, Art felt what he had felt for Mae Rose all those years ago. He remembered that something besides Mae Rose's family's love of VW Beetles had drawn him to her. Maybe, just maybe, *now* they could get it back.

2

As Art took his customary route home through downtown Fairview, the local flower shop, A Bouquet Today, caught his eye. He found himself downshifting and pulling into a parking space.

Mae Rose loved flowers, and most particularly white roses. She never understood why Art didn't buy her a bouquet occasionally, particularly for her birthday or their wedding anniversary. Art would patiently explain what a waste of money it was; the flowers would be dead in a few days, and it didn't make any sense, especially at *those* prices. He never thought to put his cigarette purchases in the same category.

"You're so good with flowers, Mae Rose!" Art would exclaim. "You can whip up a much lovelier bouquet in a heartbeat, better than anything I could buy." He'd wrap his arms around her, if she'd let him, and say, "Mae Rose honey, you know how I hate to spend money." It was a silly rhyme, but it had once upon a time made her smile.

The fact that Art never bought Mae Rose flowers, that he rarely bought her *anything*, had less to do with his feelings for her than with his famous frugality. It pained him to spend money. He handled cash as if it had razor edges and would cut him if he pulled it out of his wallet. "Used" was good and "free" was best of all. Art was in heaven when he rescued something useful that was being discarded. Like barn cats.

An internal war raged inside Art as he sat outside the floral shop considering his next move. He knew he'd have some good money coming in from the VW job, and it occurred to him that it might be appropriate *just this once* to buy his wife some flowers. *But am I setting a new precedent for my marriage?* He wondered. *Will Mae Rose forever after wonder about the next time I might bring her flowers—and be disappointed every time I don't?*

Art recognized the frightening consequences his decision could have. But if he were ever going to do it—and if he were ever going to try to set things right with Mae Rose, this would be the right time. His heart softened. Eyeing the box on the passenger seat that sat quietly as if to encourage him, Art hoped the kittens were sleeping so that he could buy some flowers and get home without disturbing them. That settled it. He opened his car door, and headed reluctantly into the flower shop.

*   *   *

The owner of A Bouquet Today, Jill King, was a transplant from the Deep South who had never lost her Southern charm, her accent, or her knowledge of the power a woman held over a man. Despite being in her late fifties, Jill still looked like the quintessential Southern belle, dressing fashionably and taking fastidious care of her body, face, and hair. She was also Mae Rose's closest friend.

Mae Rose's talent with flowers was well known; her love of white roses was legendary. When Jill's shop received a large order, she knew she could count on her help. Mae Rose's disposition always improved when she was able to work with Jill—and she'd make a little money, which she put in a separate savings account that she had had since she was a child. She didn't consciously intend to keep it a secret from her husband, but her mischievous subconscious allowed her to feel entirely justified in doing so since Art felt free to spend *his* money on frivolous things like cigarettes and old VW parts.

Furthermore, Jill encouraged Mae Rose to set money aside for herself. "Every woman needs a 'rainy day' fund," she explained. "Never let a man control *all* the money. In fact, honey," she'd add with a coy smile, "don't let him control *any* of it."

It wasn't often that Mae Rose had another woman to confide in. She tried not to complain, but her sorrow about her marriage, her rage over Art's affair, and her grief over her expanded body size came out despite her best intentions. Jill understood more than Mae Rose could have imagined. She could evaluate a man in about thirty seconds and Art, bless his heart, was no match for his wife, who would be a hard woman for any man to love. She had watched Mae Rose grow from an enviable size six at the time of her marriage to a size sixteen, and knew what that could do to a woman.

Despite everything, Mae Rose was no fashion slouch. She had her own sense of style that she applied skillfully to her meager wardrobe. While her clothing came from thrift shops or as gifts from family rather than high-end department stores, she would alter or accessorize whatever she wore with such colorful creativity that it didn't occur to others that Mae Rose was wearing the same outfits repeatedly. A bright scarf, bold belt, or interesting pin could change everything.

Next to her VW Beetle, Mae Rose's most prized possession was her deceased mother's old Singer sewing machine. She drove it with great skill and enthusiasm, turning, for instance, the generous fabric of a gathered skirt into an entirely different outfit. Art would later recall that his wife had turned the yellow and white checked sundress she was wearing the day they first met into the kitchen apron she wore that last morning as he kissed her good-bye at the kitchen sink—when the words "I love you" got stuck in this throat.

In many ways, Mae Rose was as frugal as her husband. She, too, loved to save money and was quite good at it, certainly better than Art could have imagined because she didn't spend her savings frivolously. Mae Rose clipped coupons and could barter over the price of almost anything until the person on the other side of the negotiation gave in from sheer exhaustion.

*   *   *

Jill was busy wrapping up a bouquet for a customer when Art finally grabbed the metal handle of her shop's glass door and slunk inside, hoping not to be noticed. Jill, on the other hand, *did* notice and had to bite her tongue to keep from shrieking in surprise as she chatted with her customer. She watched Art as he crept stealthily along the front window where he was keeping an eye on the box inside Mae Rose's car. Jill had no idea what he was so keen about. If she'd known about the barn cats, she would have beat Art until he finally came to his senses.

When she was finally ready to acknowledge his presence, Jill put a look of surprise on her face. "Why, Art McElroy!" she exclaimed in her easy drawl. "Whatever brings you in to my little flower shop for the first time in your life? Did hell freeze over and nobody told me?" Jill loved to tease people, and Art knew not to take her seriously.

"No reason at all, Jill," Art said with a tight smile. "I just want to buy a small bouquet for Mae Rose. Nothing fancy but it has to be roses, you know, because——." He stopped talking and started to feel a little foolish.

"Well, Art," she replied pleasantly, "being the big spender that you are, I'd suggest a single rose, a little baby's breath, and some greens. Sometimes one is just perfect, especially when there's no particular occasion. One rose is five ninety-nine. I've got white or red. Mae Rose loves white, as you know." He did. Their entire wedding had been done in white flowers.

Art cringed. *Six dollars for one little flower? That was a whole pack of cigarettes!* He knew Jill could tell he was hedging. Suddenly he felt trapped. He didn't dare leave without flowers because Jill would call Mae Rose about his visit. In fact, Mae Rose would know before he got home that he had been in Jill's shop. Art had to purchase something, but one scrawny little rose didn't feel right.

"How much for a——a dozen?" he asked, gripping the counter while trying to appear casual. Then he remembered the kittens and walked to the front window to check on them. He wasn't sure but he thought the box was moving around a bit.

"A dozen roses is thirty-nine ninety-nine," Jill called to him. "It's much cheaper to buy them by the dozen; you save thirty-two dollars that way." She knew that Art despised the concept of buying more of something just because it made each one cheaper, except when it came to his cigarettes. Art was good at math in his head. This spontaneous act of love was going to cost him an entire carton of smokes! He slunk back to the counter.

Jill knew it was time to close the sale. She leaned forward and said softly, "Mae Rose would probably faint dead away if you bought her a whole dozen, Art. Wouldn't that be worth it? You know how Mae Rose loves roses. She'd come up with a way to make them last the rest of her life." Jill didn't mean anything by saying those words. She had no idea that rest of Mae Rose's life was only a few hours. But she did know that by leaning over the counter, just so, her soft, peach-colored, cashmere V-neck sweater would reveal just enough of her cleavage to help a man who was trying to make a decision. Yes, a little cleavage never hurt, just a little and at just the right time. Jill hadn't spent most of her life in the South for nothing.

"Well, she's worth that much," Art agreed, speaking to Jill's breasts while trying desperately to pull his eyes back up to her face. "And you're right about how long she'd keep them." He took a deep breath and reluctantly pulled out his wallet. "OK, Jill, let's wrap up a dozen," he said with more confidence than he felt. If he smoked just one less cigarette a day for a while, it wouldn't be too bad, and Mae Rose would be absolutely out of her mind with joy.

"What color, Art?" Jill asked as she moved to the cooler. "I've got red, pink, white, yellow, peach . . . I'd go with white," she reminded him.

"Um, I know she likes white," Art called out to her. He was back at the front window, looking at Mae Rose's VW Bug. "But I think—yellow. She likes yellow too." It made sense to Art since her car was yellow and it had just helped bring in a new project at the shop. He saw that the box in the car was rocking back and forth a bit and headed toward the door to check on the kittens.

Jill frowned, fully aware that yellow roses would not be Mae Rose's choice—especially since they symbolize joy, happiness, and

13

friendship, none of which had applied to Mae Rose's feelings about her marriage for a long time.

Mae Rose loved white flowers for many reasons, but mostly because they reminded her of her wedding day and the immense happiness she had felt. Mae Rose was a stubborn woman and she believed that the joy she had felt that day would some day be returned to her. But the momentous occasion of Art buying Mae Rose flowers for no reason could not be ignored. Mae Rose would probably forgive Art's color choice in favor of his magnanimous gesture.

"Art, guess what!" Jill called out again.

"What, Jill?" he asked with the door partway open. Sure enough, he could see a kitten on top of the box. He ran to the car to put it back inside the box, and it scratched him badly. He yelped.

"Art?" Jill had stepped out of the cooler. Then, "Good Lord!" she exclaimed when Art returned with a bleeding hand.

"Oh, it's nothing," Art replied. "Just a scratch is all. What were you trying to tell me?"

"Art, you're not going to believe this! I just found a dozen yellow roses that are a couple of days older and they've opened up a little, so I can give you a real deal. How about nineteen ninety-nine? Maybe you're right; yellow could work for Mae Rose. You sure you don't want something for that hand? It looks bad." Jill offered him a tissue to absorb the blood.

"No thanks. Just wrap up those flowers. Nineteen ninety-nine you say? That just about makes my day, but hurry if you can. I've got to get home." Art knew he had to get back to the car before those kittens found their way out of the box again.

Jill was not one to be rushed. She wrapped the bouquet carefully and chatted easily with Art. "Mae Rose will be thrilled, Art. Now, be sure to put them in some water right when you get home. I've cut the stems for you so they'll last longer. Give my love to Mae Rose."

Art grabbed the flowers and almost ran to the car, but he was too late. The kittens had managed to tip the box over. He found their furry bodies on the floor of the passenger seat. "Take it easy, fellas," Art soothed as he grabbed each one and forced the kittens back into the box, which cost him more scratches. "I just need to get you to our barn. Then you can run free."

Placing the dozen roses on top of the box, Art eyed his purchase critically as he eased into traffic, hoping the kittens would settle down again. He still wondered who in their right mind would spend so much money for something that was going to die in a few days. Then he chuckled. "Who would spend so much money for something that was going to last a few minutes and perhaps one day kill you?" Mae Rose would have retorted, referring to his cigarettes. She always told the truth.

All Art needed to do was to get home. He smiled to himself as he thought about the look of joy he would see on Mae Rose's face. A couple of scratches never hurt anyone, and to top it off, the radio was playing another of his favorite songs, "All I Need Is a Miracle" by Mike and the Mechanics. "All I need is you," he sang at the top of his lungs.

*   *   *

The Reverend Franklin Matthews, known to his parishioners as Pastor Frank, was coming out of Good Shepherd Church as Art drove by. Art lifted his right hand off the box to wave to him through the passenger window.

As if on cue, the kittens took advantage of the opportunity to tip the box over again. This time both the roses and the kittens tumbled to the floor. Before Art could get the car stopped to restore order, one of the terrified felines clawed Art's right ankle, causing him to take his foot off the accelerator. The other kitten clawed its way up his left leg, which hurt and tickled at the same time. Art was laughing and cursing as he continued to work Mae Rose's car to the side of the road while trying to retrieve the flowers at the same time. That worked until one of the kittens planted its claws into his crotch.

Howling in pain, Art almost blacked out as he released the steering wheel and grabbed for his groin, sending the flowers hurtling into the backseat. Mae Rose's car careened into a ditch just beyond the church. The sudden impact terrified the kittens, who proceeded to urinate all over Art and the car.

When Art's pain had subsided enough that he could pay attention to the world around him, he saw that the kittens had scampered over the passenger seat, tearing the original leather upholstery with their claws.

Pastor Frank ran over to the car. "Art!" he yelled. "Art! What's wrong? Art! Are you OK?"

Art had enough sense to tell Pastor Frank, "I gotta get home before Mae Rose finds out. Please don't tell her. What am I going to do?" He started weeping as he gasped in pain.

"Art, don't worry about a thing. I'll take care of this," Pastor Frank reassured him. Within minutes, Big Charlie Nelson, one of Fairview's two police officers, pulled up in his squad car. Thankfully, he had not sounded the siren. He found Pastor Frank trying to talk to Art as Art's head rested against the open driver's window.

"Hello, Art, Reverend," Charlie said respectfully. Bending over to look inside the car was not easy considering his girth.

"Charlie," Art choked, holding his bleeding hand to his groin, trying to stop the pain.

"What in tarnation?" Charlie saw the mess the kittens had made of the interior of Mae Rose's car. His nostrils took in the cat urine odor and he winced. "Mae Rose know about this?" he asked.

"Ah, no," Art gasped, wishing Charlie would be more worried about his injuries than about Mae Rose's reaction. "One of them scratched me pretty bad and clawed me you-know-where. Please help me and please don't tell Mae Rose," he begged.

"Barn cats, huh?" Charlie replied. "You'd best get over to the emergency room. Some of 'em could have rabies."

"Oh, these are from Ben's farm," Art choked. "I'm sure he takes good care of them. I just need to get home," he said, feeling miserable.

"Can you help me get out of the ditch? How does the front look? Is it damaged? Dear God," Art sobbed.

Big Charlie thought this was appropriate given how Mae Rose would react once she knew.

"I wanted to surprise Mae Rose. Ben asked if we could take the kittens for a couple of days; Louise kicked him out again. What am I going to do? I even bought her flowers," he finished lamely.

"Well," Charlie replied thoughtfully, "we can put the cats in your little bitty front trunk. I dare 'em to get out of there before you get home. It's just a teeny-weeny, little car, and it's damaged for sure, but it could be worse. Just put 'er in reverse, and I'll heave it back onto the road. If anyone can fix it up, you can, Art," Charlie conceded. Art wished that he'd thought of putting the kittens in the trunk in the first place.

Once the car was back on the road, Art lifted himself out so Charlie could take over. "Be careful, Charlie; these are some mean kittens."

When he saw the kittens on the floor of the backseat, wreaking havoc in Mae Rose's antique gardening basket, Big Charlie was angry. He had always been sweet on Mae Rose, and seeing her gardening basket in ruins was more than he could bear. While he had never gotten over Mae Rose's decision to marry Art McElroy, now was not the time to seek revenge. Art would suffer enough once Mae Rose found out.

Art and Pastor Frank watched in awe as Charlie put on his massive leatherette gloves that even cats' claws wouldn't penetrate, and dived into the car as far as his immense size would allow. It was a challenge to get a hold of the kittens, but Officer Charles Nelson would not be denied. The car rocked back and forth, lurching this way and that until he was victorious.

Once Charlie had a grip on those screaming little devils, he threw them hard into the box, tossed the box into the front trunk, and slammed the lid triumphantly. Art winced in a different kind of pain. If in addition to everything else that had gone wrong, Big Charlie had just killed Ben's kittens, Art would never forgive himself.

But that was exactly how he had always lived, never forgiving himself for anything.

Diving into the back of the car one more time, Big Charlie found the roses and placed them gently in the front seat. As Art waved a sickly but appreciative good-bye to both him and Pastor Frank, Charlie said, "Well, I got you out of the ditch, that's for sure. But I sure enough can't get you out of the hole you've dug with Mae Rose. Good luck, Art." Then he looked at the flowers again. "Mae Rose sure does like roses," he added as he waved Art off.

In the rearview mirror, Art saw Charlie shaking his head and Pastor Frank looked like he was already deep in prayer. Art was in trouble, even with the flowers, which Mae Rose would now think he'd purchased as an apology for ruining her car. He hoped Jill had called Mae Rose already so she would know the truth.

*   *   *

Jill had indeed called Mae Rose with the news the moment Art had left the flower shop. He could not possibly know the impact Jill's call had on his wife. When Mae Rose hung up their old kitchen wall phone, she was so elated that she was crying. Her tightwad husband had just purchased a dozen roses for her, *"For the first time in his life and for no reason at all,"* Jill had emphasized.

When Mae Rose heard the familiar sound of her car turning onto their long gravel driveway, she ran into the bathroom, splashed water on her face, and pulled her shoulder-length hair behind her ears, the way Art liked it. Pausing for a moment, she saw her glowing face in the mirror and reached into her makeup bag to touch her cheeks with blush and her lips with a bit of gloss. Smoothing down her blue housedress and the apron she had indeed created from the remnants of the dress she wore when she first met Art long ago, Mae Rose took a deep breath and headed out to meet her husband. She practiced her line. "For me, Art? Roses? Whatever for? Oh, Art!" Her heart pounded with excitement.

Art got out of the car like a wounded soldier returning from war. With the roses in one hand, he limped to the front trunk from which he extracted the boxed barn cats. Hunched over and bleeding, he shuffled toward Mae Rose, who might have been able to cope with one unhappy surprise, but the double-dose of her damaged car and the presence of the box of barn cats sealed her fate. Her joyous smile instantly turned into an outraged glare as she ordered Art to turn around and take those cats back where he got them. She couldn't stop screaming in horror, "My car—my *poor* car! Art, what have you done? How could you? You know how I feel about cats and you should know by now that you can't buy me off with flowers!"

"Mae Rose," Art gasped, still limping from the painful clawing of his testicles, "I was doing a favor for Ben. He and Louise are at it again and it's just for a few days. If I'd thought you would have objected, I never would have agreed, but it was for Ben and Louise. And honey, we got the contract on the VW—that's why I bought the flowers."

Mae Rose cut him off as he moved toward the house. "Art McElroy, don't you dare even think about coming into this house! Where have you been living for the last thirty years? Whenever you mentioned anything about *any* kind of cat, I always said no! That wasn't clear enough? You couldn't have called me to *ask* what I thought before you lugged them home in *my* car, which is now destroyed?" Mae Rose stood clutching the lower portion of her faded yellow gingham apron against her heart, which was pounding wildly. She felt like she couldn't breathe.

Art was too consumed with rationalizing his actions to notice that Mae Rose was struggling. "No, actually I thought you'd allow it, that you'd want to help Ben and Louise out. That's the only reason I agreed—"

This only stoked Mae Rose's rage. "So now it's *my* fault?" she cried. As she whipped off her apron, she screamed, "I've had it, Art! I can't live like this any longer. You don't hear a word I say. You don't care what I'm feeling, and you don't lift a finger to help with the work around here! All you do is waste time smoking in the barn!" She stopped and tried to inhale. "I'm not saying another word to you about this, but if you care about me at all, you'll do as I say!"

Art couldn't believe what he was hearing; he stood immobilized in disbelief.

"Get out! Get out of here!" Mae Rose gasped as she threw her apron at him. "Go find some place to clean yourself up and *get rid of those cats!* If I see one cat hair, hear a meow, or get a whiff of anything that smells like a cat, you and I are finished! And you'd better get my car looking and smelling just like new! Don't show your face here again until I say so. Sleep in the barn with all of your broken-down old cars if you have to. *Do you understand me?*" she screamed.

As she turned to go back into the house, Mae Rose stopped and faced her husband once more, tears coursing down her cheeks. "White roses, Art," she wept. "If you'd paid any attention to me, you would have known. White is my favorite color." She stumbled back indoors, slamming the door so hard that it rattled the windows

*   *   *

It was difficult for Mae Rose to pay attention to her son John as she struggled to appear calm during dinner a few minutes later. Her heart hammered in her chest and she played miserably with her food as she heard Art's truck leaving. John was eight years younger than his brother Art Jr., and had been conceived in an act of reconciliation after Art's affair.

Although both of his parents loved John immensely, his birth had not solved their problems. Mae Rose and Art had tried to keep their marital distress private from their boys, but John had obviously heard the whole scene in the backyard and Mae Rose felt bad. He didn't say a word about the fight. When he was finished, he got up, put his dishes in the sink and kissed his mother on the cheek before he left for work. She knew he would not be home until quite late because he always stopped at his girlfriend's home afterwards. "Love you, Mom," he said as he always did.

Mae Rose wept bitterly after John left. *What happened to the beautiful life I wanted to have?* she thought as she cried. *Everything I hoped for is gone! My husband buys me flowers for the first time ever as a way to placate me for ruining my car!* She moaned louder as she remembered how it had looked when Art drove up. *How could he?!* she raged. Other frantic thoughts pulled her deeper into her innermost fears. *What if John and his girlfriend are having sex? What if . . .* and Mae Rose's heart thumped with dread as she pictured Elliana as a pregnant bride.

Still feeling short of breath, Mae Rose decided she should get to the bathroom to take the medicine her father had prescribed for occasional anxiety. She was careful to use it only in extreme emergencies, and this situation certainly met that qualification.

What she really wanted was someone to talk to, but at the same time, she didn't want anyone to know how desperate she felt—because they wouldn't understand. Most of the people she knew thought she had a wonderful life—she had taught them to believe that. "Oh, it's so hopeless!" she cried as she stumbled to the bathroom. Some medication and a bath would have to do. And perhaps a prayer. *I so need a miracle!*

Mae Rose had often found solace in her fern-patterned bathroom, even though the wallpapering wasn't finished because Art hadn't gotten around to it yet. Still, it gave the impression of a feminine influence that usually relaxed her as soon as she closed the door. She would normally draw a bath and weep until a sense of peace came over her.

3

As she sat on the toilet to pee before starting her bath, Mae Rose reached into the medicine chest for her anti-anxiety tablets. She was struggling to get the cap open when suddenly she couldn't breathe. As everything began to go dark and pain consumed her, Mae Rose screamed and tried in vain to inhale. Her efforts etched her face into a horrific expression, mouth wide open, bulging eyes staring into emptiness.

In that moment, Mae Rose heard the toilet flush and a familiar voice quipped, "Shall we just leave all this *shit* behind, Mae Rose?" It was most certainly her deceased mother's unmistakable voice, sounding surprisingly terse and impatient.

"What the—?" Mae Rose gasped as she turned toward the bathroom door. Although she could see nothing, it was easy to envision her mother's hand on her hip in her own apron-clad housedress, which had always looked awkward on Josephine Carter's wide-hipped body. She looked better in slacks but Fairview had an unwritten dress code for a doctor's wife—one that Mae Rose's mother had learned the hard way.

"*Mother is that you?*" Straining to see in the darkness, Mae Rose focused on what she supposed was the tiniest sparkle of light.

"What on Earth? What are you doing here?" Mae Rose demanded angrily.

"What? You're not happy to see me?" Josephine asked pointedly. "Like I give a rat's ass," she added. Mae Rose had never heard her mother use such profanity.

"I can't see anything," Mae Rose retorted. "Why don't you go back where you came from," she hissed, "and leave me alone? You're *dead*. And I don't appreciate your foul language."

Josephine roared with laughter. "Newsflash, Merrily," she bellowed using Mae Rose's childhood nickname. "You're dead too! Welcome to the beginning of your afterlife. I'm here to help you make the transition—not that I'm happy about it. So pardon me if I'm a bit testy."

"I'm *dead?*" Mae Rose screamed. "*Dead?* That's impossible! I'm not ready—it's not my time! My family needs me—the whole town of Fairview relies on me. Have you seen my 'to do' list? This is *ridiculous!* Go away! Leave me alone and give me my life back right now!" Mae Rose was used to getting her way with her mother.

"I can't give you your life back," Mae Rose's mother explained impatiently. "It doesn't work that way. Besides, did you really want to keep living like you were? You and Art always at each other? You feeling unloved and making yourself more unlovable every day?"

"No, not really, but—" Mae Rose stopped in the middle of her reply. "Wait a minute! What do you mean about making myself more unlovable?" *How could my own mother make such a statement?* Mae Rose wondered. *Why am I yelling at a ghost—and more to the point, why has a ghost just insulted me?*

Mae Rose was livid. "How dare you, Mother—or whoever you are! How dare you judge me like that! If you saw what I suffered and what kind of man my husband became, you wouldn't be so cruel! I can't believe this! Anyone who knew what my marriage was like would *never* say something like that to me—especially *you!* I did everything I could think of to make my marriage work!"

The toilet flushed again. Mae Rose felt herself moving up and away from her body. "No, no, no!" she screamed. "I won't go! I'm not ready! It can't be over like this! My boys, my husband!" she cried out. "How are they going to survive without me? Who will play the piano at church and make the flower arrangements? Life *needs* me Mother. Surely God can change His mind? And speaking of God, if I'm dead as you suggest, where is heaven?"

"You're going to be very surprised by both concepts," Josephine replied, and Mae Rose could hear a smile in her mother's voice. "But it's time, Merrily," she added firmly. "You're the one who decided you couldn't bear to live any longer. Your rage killed you. I'm only here to help you finish what *you* started. I *volunteered* to come for you. I didn't have to—I could have stayed blissfully where I was and let others show you the way. Show a little gratitude, dear, or I'll leave you with others."

"No!" Mae Rose cried out. "Don't leave me, mother! Please don't leave me!"

"Very well, Merrily, but don't test me beyond what I can bear. I have limits, even in my enlightened state. Now you've got an appointment to keep, and I'd really like to get back to my own eternal life." Mae Rose saw a starry pattern circling hypnotically in front of her and realized that while she couldn't see her mother fully, she could see what she was supposed to do. Josephine Carter was motioning Mae Rose to get moving.

Suddenly Mae Rose shrieked in horror. "My body!" she cried out. "My big, awful body! Oh, Mother, it's sitting on the *toilet*! They're going to find me like that, and oh!" she shrieked again. "Everyone will know! I can't bear it! How are they ever going to get me looking decent in a coffin? And my face! They'll never be able to get that hideous look off it! You have to help them fix this, Mother! Please! If anyone finds out how I died—if I look bad at the funeral—I'll just—I'll just . . ." Mae Rose stopped talking, realizing there was no use completing that sentence if she was already dead.

Mae Rose felt like she had been duped about the next life, particularly when her tears began to flow. "This isn't how it's supposed to be, Mother," she sobbed. "If I'm dead, I should be happy; it should be lovely and bright here. I shouldn't be crying—the Bible says there are no more tears," she sobbed. "And I should have a mansion," she blubbered, "and a harp and crown. That's what I was taught, Mother! Look at me! I'm a mess. This isn't the way it's supposed to be."

Mae Rose felt a soothing energy envelop her.

"OK, Mae Rose," Josephine relented. "The Valley of the Shadow of Death can be a bitch. It's pulling all of your negative earthly energy out of you and, let's face it, you died pretty pissed off. I can't give you your life back, but I can let you look at my Viewing Pane. You'll be able to see how your family is doing and *what* they're doing about your body. It won't be easy to look at, but at least you'll know."

Josephine paused for a moment. "Before I do this I must warn you that the Viewing Pane is a very powerful device—a privilege in fact—that can be revoked. You'll get your own after your Reflection, but there are strict rules about using it. I shouldn't be doing this at all so I want you to understand *right now* how it works. The Viewing Pane allows you to see life on Earth, but you can't interfere with it; all you can do is observe. *Understand?* If you ever try to change something or to influence an outcome while you're in Viewing Pane mode you'll be 'vanished' from heaven."

"Don't you mean 'banished'?" Mae Rose corrected her mother, even though she was captivated by the possibility of seeing life on Earth.

"No. *Vanished* is the right word—trust me on that," Josephine replied with confidence.

"Does that mean I could disappear? Or be kicked out of heaven?" Mae Rose was aghast.

"I don't know, Mae Rose," her mother replied. "I've never seen it happen to anyone, but it's very clear in the instructions and it's very serious. If you want to know more, your Reflection Agent might be able to assist. I'm just warning you. "I'll give you a peek at how things are going on Earth, but then we simply must move on."

"OK, Mother," Mae Rose agreed eagerly. She made a note to ask about being "vanished" when she got to heaven.

As Mae Rose watched, her mother's energy created a large square outline of light and then tapped its center as if she were entering a code. Suddenly Mae Rose could see what was happening on Earth.

"Holy shit, Mother! How did you do that?" Mae Rose exclaimed. Suddenly she started giggling. "Did I just say 'holy shit'?"

Her mother nodded and smiled. "Doesn't it feel good, Merrily, to speak what's on your mind and know you won't be scolded or punished? You're getting the 'junk' out and the closer you get to the Realm of Reflection, the better you'll feel."

4

When Art arrived home several hours after Mae Rose had ordered him to leave—after his apologetic return of the barn cats to Louise and a visit to the emergency room, which he could bear more than the thought of what rabies could do to his private parts—he saw the roses lying in the driveway. He picked them up, took them indoors, and put them in one of Mae Rose's many vases. He couldn't find Mae Rose and was actually relieved. When at last he saw that the bathroom door was closed, he relaxed even more. It was typical of Mae Rose to stay there awhile to get her emotions under control. When she came out, she'd usually at least be civil.

Art knocked politely, hoping that Mae Rose had calmed down and was ready to reconcile. He had no idea how "cooled off" Mae Rose was by this time. "Mae Rose honey," he said softly. "Honey, when you're ready, we need to talk. Please." There was no response.

Art argued with himself that Mae Rose had never been all *that* clear about how she felt about barn cats. He could understand her rage about the condition of her car, but she knew he would fix it up. He'd had time to think as he waited for the doctor in the emergency room. Mae Rose had never thanked him for the roses (so what if they were yellow?) or expressed the slightest concern about his injuries. What a bitch! She had certainly gotten testier as the years had passed. Art was vaguely aware of the impact of menopause and hormonal changes in a woman. He also knew that Mae Rose was devastated by how large her body was and that nothing was ever going to be perfect enough for her.

Since confessing his three-year extramarital affair to Mae Rose, she had inflicted the pain he had caused her back on him with such viciousness that he could no longer stand up straight. His shoulders hunched forward and slumped as if he were always on guard against a physical attack. His affair might have been a wedge fracturing their marriage, but the opinion he held to himself was that Mae Rose's self-righteous, overbearing, and incessant scolding had driven him away from her in the first place. She couldn't see what she had become over the years: a tormenter—a never-satisfied, conniving, manipulative bitch who always had to have her way about everything. He recalled how unforgiving she had been when they met with Pastor Frank over the matter.

"I had to tell you, Mae Rose," he had insisted. "I couldn't keep this a secret from you any longer no matter how much I wanted to."

"Please notice how Art doesn't even apologize," Mae Rose had said through clenched teeth. "Please notice that he's not sorry for what he has done to me and our family. He just wants us to see him as an honest man by telling the truth. That's what's unforgivable."

"What do you mean, I'm not sorry?" Art had shot back. Here he was confessing a sin that he knew Mae Rose would never forgive and she dared to accuse him of no remorse.

But today she had gone too far. He had landed a huge job and Mae Rose had acted like nothing mattered except for her car. Art quickly decided that if Mae Rose wanted to lock herself in the bathroom and pout until kingdom come, it was fine with him. *Let her stew,* he fumed and went off to bed where he feel asleep quickly as the pain medication kicked in.

*   *   *

When John came in just after midnight and peeked his head into his parents' room to let them know he was home, he noticed his mother wasn't in bed.

"Dad, I'm home," he said softly. "Where's mom?" Mae Rose was usually snoring with her back turned toward Art when John came in at night.

"In the bath—" Art was instantly awake and out of bed. He screamed in pain as his injuries from earlier that day announced themselves. "Dear God, dear God, oh God!" he wailed, limping as quickly as he could to the bathroom. He tried the door again; it was still locked. Suddenly Art began screaming Mae Rose's name and pounding on the door. Overwhelmed by his father's emotions, John panicked.

"Dad? What's wrong?" he begged. "Dad?" John shouted, choking on his fear. "What's going on? If Mom's in the bathroom, isn't that OK? Dad?"

"John, she's been in there for *hours!*" Art yelled. "Dear Lord! Mae Rose!" He pounded on the door again, tried the doorknob and then threw his body against the door. "John, run to the barn and get the crow bar. We've got to get it open!" he hollered. "Mae Rose!" Art was weeping now. "Oh, God! Mae Rose!"

When John returned, tears were streaming down his face as well. "Dad—do you think?" He couldn't finish as he wedged the crow bar into the doorframe.

"John," Art choked, "I don't want to speculate about what we'll find behind this door, but I think you know that it could be bad. I don't want you to see whatever it is. Neither would your mother. Please don't look and do whatever I ask you to do. OK?" His face was grim.

"OK, dad," John wept as he pulled on the crowbar. Art slammed himself against the door until it fell open. "Get out of here!" Art growled to his son as he covered his own eyes in disbelief. "Get out of here now and call your grandfather!"

The horror in front of Art was too great to bear. He fell to his knees and whimpered Mae Rose's name, creeping toward the ashen-colored body on the toilet. This *could not* be his wife, the woman who worshipped all things beautiful.

Mae Rose's heavy body sagged against the wall; the skirt of her faded blue housedress was crumpled in her lap, exposing her heavy legs and thighs. Sobbing and screaming, Art put his arms around Mae Rose's legs. Her body was already cool.

But it was Mae Rose's face that Art could not comprehend when he finally looked up. His wife, so careful in life about how she looked, wore a macabre expression. Her head was turned toward the bathroom door, her eyes wide open and glaring at him, as if the rage she had felt when she died had frozen hard. Her mouth, which was usually set in a determined line that he knew so well, was twisted in horror as if she had seen something terrifying. Art turned away; he could not bear to look at her any longer.

John followed his father's orders and called his grandfather, screaming, "Mom's dead! Mom's dead!" over and over. Upon hearing the horrifying news of his daughter's death, Dr. Henry Carter, who was also the county coroner, acted in his professional capacity, and instructed John to go into the family room, sit down, and put his head between his knees until he got there, which was within minutes.

"It was a heart attack, instantaneous and massive," Henry told Art and John sadly, when he met them back in the family room after completing his official assessment. "She never felt much. We can be thankful for that. Anything could have triggered this. It sort of runs on her mother's side of the family, as you know. And—" He paused to shake his head in disbelief. "Mae Rose knew something was wrong. She had—she had—" he choked up, causing the three men to break down weeping together. "She must have tried to take something to relax her. I found this on the floor near her body," he choked.

As he wept, Henry showed Art and John the pill bottle. "She knew something was wrong and she tried to stop it. I think she just didn't have the strength to push the cap down to open the bottle—not that these would have saved her. Damn safety caps. *Goddamn* safety caps." Art didn't realize that he had just heard his father-in-law curse for the first time.

"It will have to be a closed-coffin ceremony," he continued quietly. "You don't want the funeral home to attempt to make her look normal—trust me on this. We'll need to get her body out of the bathroom if we can before notifying anyone—out of respect for Mae Rose. If people found out how she died, it—it wouldn't be worthy of her life." The three men agreed.

"John, once you feel up to it, call your brother to let him know. Tell him he needs to come home tonight. Talk to him on his way home. It will be good for both of you. It would be best if someone drove him." Henry Carter paused to wipe tears from his eyes. "We're going to close the door now and it's best if you don't open it. We want you to remember your mother as she was. Let me know if you need anything, OK?" John could only nod.

Art didn't know that death is sometimes accompanied by a morbid humor, and such was the case with Mae Rose's passing. Her life ended in such a bizarre way that it suddenly struck him as funny. In his shock, grief, and remorse, he began to laugh hysterically as he and Henry worked to relocate the body. More than once, Art fell apart, guffawing, weeping, and taking his shock out on the bathtub where he beat his arms and fists until Henry had to sedate him in order to enlist his cooperation. "Art, man, pull yourself together for Mae Rose's sake. We don't want to have to ask anyone for help doing this. Please, Art," he wept. The fairy tale life that Mae Rose had imagined and longed for could not have ended less happily ever after.

* * *

Josephine Carter closed her Viewing Pane. "That's enough," she said firmly. "You can watch all of this after your Reflection if you want to, but we have kept Heaven waiting too long already. Come along, dear."

Mae Rose obeyed quietly only because she hoped that if she cooperated, her mother would open her Viewing Pane for the funeral. She was, after all, still quite used to eventually getting her way. And she was relieved that her father had taken control to assure that her coffin would be closed.

5

Death unlocks memories; stories console those who grieve. Art would repeat the story of how he met Mae Rose "quite by accident" many times over the next few days as funeral preparations were made. He would often break down mid-sentence, awkwardly correcting his references to her in the present tense. Talking about his wife in the past tense hurt like hell.

Art McElroy met Mae Rose Carter at Mike's Mechanic Shop, where he had worked full time since his trade school mechanic's internship. He had already developed quite a reputation for restoring old vehicles. His first love was his guitar and soulful music. Sometimes he'd make up his own songs, but he had no aspirations to make a career out of it. Old cars were his next love, and above all, Volkswagens, especially antique ones. There weren't many of them around the farm country where Art worked, but it just so happened that Mae Rose had one since the Carters were also crazy about Volkswagens.

The day Mae Rose had first walked into Mike's Mechanic Shop, Art remembered that she was wearing a bright yellow and white checked sundress with her sunglasses resting on top of her bobbed, flaming red hair. It occurred to him now that her apron—the one she had thrown at him so recently, had come from that dress. He winced. Mae Rose was so good at making use of old fabrics. He winced again. Mae Rose *had been,* he corrected himself.

Art recalled exactly what he had been doing when he met Mae Rose. He remembered the bump on his head when she had startled him. A mechanic didn't expect to see or hear a young woman calling for help while he was in the pit, which is exactly where

Art was, repairing an exhaust system on a dark green 1958 Buick Special four-door sedan.

"Yoo-hoo," Mae Rose had called out in a singsong tone. "Can you help me?"

Art had jumped at the surprise of hearing her voice and cursed as he hit his head. When he looked up again, this time more cautiously, Art saw a pair of daisy-topped sandals featuring two pale feet with pink toenails parked at the edge of the pit. Suddenly a face peered in the opening, which meant Mae Rose had bent over. If Art had been like some of the other mechanics in the shop, he could have walked over and enjoyed a view up Mae Rose's dress, but he was unhappy about being interrupted and in pain from bumping his head. In short, Art was not at all pleased by Mae Rose's arrival.

"Yoo-hoo," she called again. "Can you help me?"

"Not sure," Art replied matter-of-factly. "What's the problem?" He put an extra measure of gruffness in his voice, still trying to resist looking at her gorgeous thighs from under the Buick.

"Not sure," Mae Rose shot back, laughing at her witty reply. "The gas tank is full, but the car lurches like it's not getting enough fuel. That's just a guess. No idea really. My father, Dr. Carter, told me that Art McElroy was the man to see. I'm Mae Rose."

Art wiped his hands on a greasy rag and maneuvered his way slowly out of the pit. Mae Rose's crisp, clean look made Art deeply conscious of his filthy uniform and the black grease caked on his hands and outlining his fingernails. "Well, I'm Art," he told Mae Rose. "I'll have to take a look." He was careful to keep his voice polite but with an edge of disgruntlement.

It wasn't *all* an act. Art hated to be interrupted when he was working on a project. Even more than that, he hated looking like a dirty louse while standing before the Goddess of Sunshine. *At least it'll keep her from getting interested in me,* he remembered thinking. He really wanted nothing to do with women—that was, until he saw Mae Rose up close after he climbed out of the pit.

From her toes to the top of her head, Mae Rose Carter was one sexy woman. Art guessed her to be in her mid- to late-twenties. He'd seen her from afar in church and at social events but never like this—just inches away. He tried to keep his eyes focused on Mae Rose's beaming face, but her quite remarkable figure, beginning with her sizable breasts, drew him like the headlights of an oncoming car. His fingers started to twitch so badly that he had to clench his fists until his fingernails pressed pain through the palms of his hands.

"I can take it for a quick spin if that'll help," he offered. "These cars have pretty simple engines, so I should be able to diagnose it in just a few minutes. Do you have time to wait?"

Art still could not take his eyes off Mae Rose because everything about her *glowed.* Happiness gushed out of her, creating an aura of joy all around her. *Why wouldn't every man in the world want to be married to such a gorgeous woman?* He figured he'd never have to answer that question for himself. His number one job was to stay out of Mae Rose's way and not be sucked in. *Like you even have a prayer of attracting a woman like her,* he told himself.

"Could you do that?" Mae Rose beamed with relief. "Do you have time? I don't want to interrupt anything, but it would be wonderful and yes, I'll be happy to wait." Mae Rose's voice was laced with just enough "desperate woman needs capable man" innuendo that Art couldn't possibly say no. He kept his distance as best he could as she dropped the keys into his hands.

The problem with Mae Rose's car *was* the fuel line, as she had suggested. Mae Rose Carter had been right, which Art would learn she always was. But what impressed him most was that she knew something about cars.

In the end—or the beginning, as it would become—all Mae Rose did was offer her hand to shake Art's, thanking him when her car was running again. It was a simple gesture, but when their hands touched, life changed for Art and he knew it. He wasn't sure if Mae Rose felt anything, but his heart started pounding on all cylinders. As they shook hands, Art's cock began to rise in a salute, and love or something like it began to pour through his veins just like fuel making an engine run.

Even after Art went back to work on the Buick, all he could see was bright golden sunshine so brilliant that he couldn't think straight for a while. Yes, Art McElroy was in love, and while he would never call it an act of God, it certainly felt divine at the time. He hated how easily he fell in love. It made him feel weak and ashamed, but he knew he was a goner.

The whole town of Fairview loved Henry and Josephine Carter, which meant that they endured Mae Rose's effervescence with an edgy tolerance. As for Mae Rose, she found many reasons to like Art. He was not demanding—instead he was as eager to please Mae Rose as she was to be pleased, and he loved Volkswagens. He was fun and good with his hands in every way that was important to Mae Rose. Yes, when Mae Rose showed up that day in the shop and shook his hand, that was it—signed, sealed, and delivered.

Seven months later, Art and Mae Rose were married by Pastor Frank in front of an enthusiastic and erroneously relieved congregation. If they had thought her marriage would completely preoccupy Mae Rose, they learned quickly that it only served to intensify her love of life and passion for telling other people what to do. Now as a wife, and soon enough as a mother, her boundless energy saturated the citizens of Fairview. It was as if love and marriage put Mae Rose's personality on steroids.

Art lacked Mae Rose's confidence and absorbed being part of her family with a thirst he had not known he possessed. He relied heavily on Mae Rose's decision to marry him and was reassured by the enthusiastic support of her family and the community. He wasn't a man to evaluate what he didn't understand, and Art didn't understand the first thing about women. He could fix the problem with a car in a red-hot second, but a woman is not a mechanical device, as Art would learn over the years.

Later he would recall standing at the front of the church in his new suit watching Mae Rose float down the aisle toward him on their wedding day and wondering where the man Mae Rose was supposed to marry was hiding. Even as he said his vows, he felt like a stand-in for someone else, someone much more worthy of Mae Rose than he.

Art and Mae Rose scooted out of town with a string of tin cans and a "Just Married" sign on her car. Art was as happy during the next few years as he would be for a very long time. But he would continue to wonder about that other man, the one Mae Rose should have married. Now as he stood with his sons at the visitation the night before the funeral and burial, he imagined Mae Rose's VW with tin cans tied to the back bumper. Instead of "Just Married," the sign read "What Happened?"

* * *

Fairview's single downtown street was deserted on the morning of Mae Rose's funeral and burial. Everything was closed as the entire town turned out to honor her. The only inhabitant not attending the funeral was Big Charlie. He had volunteered to staff the police station because he couldn't bear to witness the memorial to the love of his life and because he blamed himself for Mae Rose's death.

Sitting slumped at his desk with nothing to do but feel sorry for himself, Big Charlie mourned. His immense body shook as he wept. "If only I'd been more adamant with Art about those damn barn cats," he lamented. "If only I had phoned Mae Rose to let her know about the damage to her car. Perhaps her heart attack could have been avoided, and she'd still be alive."

While she had no claim to fame, everyone in town (exactly 9,377 people) knew Mae Rose. Her life was not newsworthy in any particular way, but the energy that had been Mae Rose was a palpable thing, a prickly security blanket the populace had wrapped around themselves for years as they took what she gave so freely while offering nothing much in return. Having it yanked without warning from their grasp left them feeling vulnerable—and guilty.

It had been easy for folks to dislike Mae Rose or to be downright jealous of her. She was attractive and sexy in those early years of her marriage and became quite an accomplished homemaker. She did everything with flair, persistence, and unbridled passion. Nothing escaped her sense of propriety or her incredible love of all things beautiful. Mae Rose never questioned her right to take control of a situation and bring it to her specifically orchestrated conclusion, which was typically exactly the right one.

6

Mae Rose had now witnessed that even in Heaven she could get her way by persuading her mother to give in to her. While this surprised her, it also gave her an unreasonable sense of confidence. Her pride swelled as she and her mother "tuned in" to the funeral. In fact, Mae Rose's self-absorbed energy so enveloped her that her mother had to keep moving away to create more space.

"If you don't stop thinking so highly of yourself, Merrily, I won't be close enough to you for you to watch your damn funeral," her mother scolded. "Really. This is *my* Viewing Pane and *your* funeral— you didn't just win a beauty contest. Show some freaking humility."

"Yes, Mother," Mae Rose replied dutifully, rolling her invisible eyes in the process. *So what if it isn't a beauty contest? It's my funeral and the whole damn town has turned out.* Snuggling as closely as she could to her mother, Mae Rose prepared to be eulogized. She had always liked Pastor Frank's tender tributes when a member of the church passed away and expected great accolades.

* * *

At the funeral, Art and his sons sat numb and disbelieving in front of Mae Rose's coffin as it was perched on the funeral bier above its burial plot. Jill King had covered it with white long-stemmed roses. "You don't worry about a thing, Art McElroy," she had wept. "I knew Mae Rose and I know how to give her what she would want on her coffin." Jill had also reassured Art that Mae Rose knew about the dozen roses he had bought her *before* he had gotten home the day she died. "I called her and told her, Art. I couldn't help it. I knew she'd be thrilled, and she was, Art. She was beside herself and so happy."

The McElroy men showed visible signs of new grief as the burial service began. Blinking often in the bright sunshine of the cool March morning, at times they wiped away tears; other times they just rubbed their eyes as if to awaken themselves from a very bad dream. Shock had slackened their faces and hollowed their eyes.

Wearing the only suit he had ever owned—the same one that he had worn as he vowed to love and honor Mae Rose until death parted them, Art pinched the bridge of his nose. Shaking shoulders alerted his sons to grasp him from either side in case the medication wore off and his hysterical howling took over.

"How are you doing, Dad?" Art Jr. asked.

"What?" Art looked up after realizing that his son had spoken to him. "Oh. I don't know. I don't know. I—I don't know ha-ha, ha-ha—how," he howled, "to live without Mae Rose." He bent forward in his chair and covered his face with his hands, ashamed of his need to laugh hysterically in reaction to Mae Rose's death. Nothing seemed to make sense without her and there was so much to regret, he couldn't bear it.

When Mae Rose's coffin began its descent into the grave, Art shot up like a canon, setting off a chain of events that would go down in history as Fairview's most unforgettable funeral.

As Art lost control, his sons launched into action to rescue him, causing all three to tumble against Mae Rose's coffin and dislodge it. The crowd gasped in disbelief as it thudded from its platform to the ground beside the grave, flipped over and sat rocking back and forth on its arched cover. Art and his sons tumbled into the grave and had to be pulled out. But the grand finale ensued when Art saw his wife's coffin upside down. He leaped to his feet and single-handedly managed to turn it upright, tipping it perfectly into the grave, before he passed out. This forced the McElroy family's absence from the post-burial luncheon and gave a new meaning to the phrase "rolling over in her grave."

* * *

Mae Rose wasn't sure she liked what she'd just witnessed. Getting her way with her mother so she could watch the funeral on the Viewing Pane had not accomplished what she'd hoped. Her mother, however, had been quite entertained.

"Merrily!" she exclaimed. "Can you believe what Art just did? I think that man truly loved you!"

Mae Rose wasn't ready to be so jovial. She'd been humiliated enough that the coffin had to be closed. Watching it flip upside down before she was laid to rest nauseated her. She couldn't wait to get to Heaven and was not happy when her mother reminded her about their stop at the Realm of Reflection for a visit with a Reflection Agent.

"Reflection Agent?" Mae Rose lashed out. "Is that like the Gestapo? Judgment Day? Could I possibly be kept out of Heaven? Mother, what's going on? This isn't at all like the Bible said it would be. Is this normal, Mother? Do I *have* to do this?"

"Of course, Merrily!" Her mother laughed, which helped Mae Rose relax. If her mother was still using her nickname and apparently having a good time, their stop at the Realm of Reflection couldn't be *that* serious.

"We all go through this process after death, especially if we didn't do it during our life on Earth. It helps us decide our future preferences. There are choices for you to make about your role in the next life, and you can hardly do that without reflecting back on your life on Earth first. We don't all just stand around, play harps, and sing praises for eternity, darling."

"We don't?" Mae Rose was shocked. "What about a crown? A mansion? Haven't I been a saint, Mother? Look at how I behaved after what Art did to me. He cheated on me, Mother, and I held it all in. I didn't tell a soul." (She failed to mention Jill King.) "Surely there's a reward for me! I stayed with him; I kept my promise to be faithful. That has to be worth *something*! Mother! Wait up!"

7

In her Beverly Hills mansion, Mary Lee Broadmoor fought with the handle on the toilet, trying to flush it herself. Discovering that she was now too weak to manage even this simple task caused her to curse. "God! What a pathetic way to live—I mean, *die!*" she muttered. "Goddamn it! Where is Gertie for Christ's sake?"

In her rage, Mary Lee forgot that she'd sent her hospice nurse to answer the front door—a somewhat time-consuming task in her large home. Exhausted from her failed efforts with the toilet, she located the buzzer that hung around her neck. "Damn it," she muttered again as she waited. "I pay you enough, Gertrude Morgan! You ought to be stationed right outside the door. You ought to know the routine by now!" Finally she heard footsteps running toward the door.

"It's about time!" Mary Lee gasped, scowling angrily at Gertie when she finally arrived. "Where the hell have you been? You know how I hate to wait for anything! Get me up and get me a cigar. I can't even flush the goddamn toilet anymore!" She laughed bitterly. "I can't even flush the crapper!"

Gertie knew better than to remind a medicated Mary Lee that the front doorbell had rung and that she'd hurried off to answer it to let Mary Lee's attorney, James Christianson, into the study. In spite of her caustic and bitter attitude toward life, Mary Lee wanted to make one last change to her will—a financial gift to Gertie who thought Mary Lee was being kind and generous to her.

She should have known better. Mary Lee was doing it to indulge herself in a final act to infuriate her daughter Natalie, who despised

Gertie. The thought of Natalie's horrified reaction when she learned of this pleased Mary Lee at this late stage of her life, and there wasn't much left that she could enjoy. Eager to make certain the attorney was comfortably situated, Gertie had been chatting (some would call it flirting) with him when she heard Mary Lee's buzzer.

Wealthy, famous, and utterly self-absorbed, Mary Lee Broadmoor was the toughest patient Gertie had ever attended. With any luck, a financial remembrance from Mary Lee, and a steady stock market, Mary Lee would also be her last.

"You'd think we were having a party here, not getting ready for a funeral," Mary Lee fumed. "I'm *dying,* for Christ's sake, and I have to pay someone to act like they care. How funny is that? You're just like the rest of 'em," Mary Lee muttered. "God, good help is hard to find! I can't seem to keep anyone for more than a month or two before they go whining off—without a reference from me, let me tell you!"

Gertie Morgan's large brown eyes filled with tears at Mary Lee's insults, even though Gertie knew that Mary Lee wasn't truly angry at her. It was common for those in the final stages of life to be exasperated by their failing health—anger took many forms at this stage. Sniffing back her tears, Gertie focused on getting Mary Lee off the toilet, into her wheelchair, and over to her dressing table. She hoped Mary Lee would forget about wanting a cigar.

"Well, I've been here *three* months, Ms. Broadmoor, in case you've forgotten," Gertie retorted proudly, sniffing again. "I hear that's a record. Now let's get you ready for your meeting with Mr. Christianson. He's downstairs but says not to hurry."

Mary Lee had to admit that Gertie was right. According to her résumé, Gertrude Morgan was thirty-seven years old. She'd been doing home nursing care her entire adult life, having elected quite early to be certified in hospice care. Gertie's graceful and gentle ministrations gave rise to her impeccable references. Mary Lee couldn't imagine any reason that a young woman in her right mind would choose such a dead-end career, unless she was desperate. She laughed out loud. "Ha! Gertie you are in a dead-end career. Get it? Ha! Now get me that cigar like I asked," Mary Lee demanded. "I don't like to waste what's left of my breath by asking twice. You know that."

"Yes, Ms. Broadmoor," Gertie retorted smartly. "But I'm a nurse, and you know how I feel about your smoking. It's not a good idea in your condition. It makes it harder to—"

Mary Lee cut her off. "Harder to what, Gertie? *Live?* Like I *care.* Get me a goddamned cigar!" Gertie did as she was told, but there were tears in her eyes once again. She would never get used to Mary Lee's harshness.

*   *   *

Mary Lee wasn't privy to Gertie's early life, which was just as well. She probably wouldn't have hired someone who had been raised in the foster care system from an early age. Gertie's mother had been a pimp-owned, drug-dependent prostitute who had died in her young daughter's arms in the saddest, poorest part of New Orleans when Gertie was only eight years old. Young Gertie had no idea who her sperm-donor father was; certainly her mother could not have known. When Sweet Candy Jane (Gertie's mother's working name) died in Gertie's arms, something like compassion was born in Gertie. She swore she would help people die with dignity whether they were rich or poor.

Sweet Candy Jane held on long enough to tell her daughter, "Gertie, honey, I ain't been a good mom to you. Can't help that. Wasn't expectin' to be a mom. But you must have wanted to live awful bad to get born, so I did that much for you. I got you born. Now I got somethin' for my sweet Gertie. Pull it out of my left pocket. I'd do it myself, but I'm too weak." Gertie tugged at a small tin sardine can and opened it. She wept at what she saw.

"I done some lookin' into things. As soon as I'm gone, you git up and git out of here. Here's some cash. It ain't much but it will get you on the bus and to a safe place. There's a piece of paper inside that will tell you where to go. You need bus number thirteen to get you to this here address, and don't you leave there, sweet Gertie, until they put you in a proper home.

"Didn't know about love, Gertie. Didn't know what it would be like to have a child. Best damn thing, let me tell you. No matter what, you're the best thing ever happened to me. But now it's up to you. Get the hell out of here, but don't leave me, Gertie. Not till I'm gone."

Gertie had waited with her mother, smoothing her tangled hair and talking quietly to her about how wonderful heaven would be. She knew about heaven because her mother had believed enough in God to take Gertie to church occasionally. Sweet Candy Jane died smiling, and that told Gertie she had made a difference. After that Gertie looked at the contents of the smelly tin can, determined to do exactly as her mother had instructed. Underneath the money and directions, Gertie found a pair of moonstone fishhook earrings that had been her mother's favorites. She moved on with her life—but not that far. After all these years, Gertie still stayed with the dying, patiently soothing them and faithfully wearing her mother's earrings.

Two other goals were on Gertie's mind as she grew up: make enough money to never depend on someone else and learn to be happy living without anything that had a penis. Gertie knew nothing about true love between a man and a woman, but she did understand the sexual acts that her mother had been paid to perform, and they disgusted her.

Beginning with her mother's passing, Gertie kept a journal that eventually became her way of memorializing the life of each of her patients. In the early years, it had been a cheap, spiral-bound notebook, but it had evolved into a beautiful hardbound book with a ribbon bookmark. Gertie would write something every day about her patient. Surviving family members would receive this touchingly eloquent journal, commemorating their deceased family member's last days. It became a wonderful closing tool; Gertie couldn't help it if her patients remembered her in their wills, which had already occurred quite often.

*   *   *

Mary Lee continued to eye her hospice nurse critically in the mirror. Gertie kept her curly brown hair cropped very short because it didn't require any care, and she wanted to be available to her patients as much as possible. She hid the trauma of her childhood memories in her plump body. No one except her mother had ever told Gertie that she was pretty, so she assumed she wasn't and dressed accordingly. She wore the same extra-large scrubs and rubber-soled shoes every day. Gertie didn't know that her gorgeous brown eyes could drive even a tough woman like Mary Lee to a softness she would never admit, or that her moonstone earrings added a touch of class to her simple attire. With a little effort, Gertrude Morgan could be a knockout.

As she blew smoke at Gertie's reflection in the mirror, it amused Mary Lee to watch Gertie automatically hold the ashtray out so Mary Lee could drop her cigar ashes into it. Such efficiency made her smile even though Gertie frowned every time. Yes, Gertie Morgan was a keeper.

What Mary Lee didn't know was that although Gertie had grown up with distinct disadvantages, she had become a savvy investor. Pure intuition guided her through her money life—that and the advice she overheard during conversations between patients and their financial counselors. For the past fifteen years, Gertie had taken the monetary bequest of her clients along with most of her normal pay and carefully invested those sums. Because her compensation always included lodging and meals, her living expenses were minimal.

Gertie's own sense of dignity came from knowing she would never have to rely on others to support her—that she wouldn't have to sell her body in order to feed a child as her mother had. She looked forward to the future with confidence. She was not afraid to be alone, and she certainly was not afraid of death. But having an intimate relationship with a man? That was what terrified Gertrude Morgan. She had never seen a man treat a woman right, except occasionally on TV or in the movies and even then, it was the exception rather than the rule.

8

After winding a turban around Mary Lee's hairless head, Gertie draped a gorgeous Hermes scarf over her thin shoulders. Mary Lee was naturally thin, and her cancer treatments had taken what precious little extra body fat she had. When Gertie had finished fixing Mary Lee up for her appointment, she sensed that Mary Lee was pleased with the effect. It made her look as if she were ready to do the tango rather than meet with her attorney over her last will and testament. Mary Lee was only sixty-two, far too young to be dying.

"Get me another damn cigar, Gertie," Mary Lee reminded her, "and bring an extra one. I can't face that man without something to do. Then check my cigar stock. Remind Chef Michael to reorder if my supply is low. He knows what to do."

Gertie reluctantly put a another cigar between Mary Lee's fingers and lit it while Mary Lee inhaled weakly to get it started. They left her room and went to the elevator, where Gertie pushed the button for the first floor.

While Mary Lee had few visitors, she loved to see their surprised looks when they saw her looking *good*. Her attorney was no exception. As he watched the wheels of Mary Lee's chair come over the threshold of her study, he boomed as if he'd been practicing for her entrance, "Ms. Broadmoor! Wonderful to see you looking so . . . so . . . wow." Mary Lee didn't look as if she was dying, which would perhaps make this meeting not as imminently necessary as it had sounded.

"Kiss my ass," Mary Lee retorted, smiling. "Don't you worry, James. I might look good, but I'm still dying, I'm told, so let's get this over with. Make it short and—" Mary Lee fumed and inhaled from her cigar, choking, coughing, and blowing smoke in his face. "And confidential. You hear me? Only you and I know about this. If I see one word in the papers or on TV before I'm gone—and who knows? Maybe I'll be able to keep an eye on you even after I'm gone—I'm blaming you and you won't get another cent from me. My publicist is keeping an eye on you too."

James had worked with Mary Lee long enough to expect these crass scoldings. The very darkness that made her movies successful had lived these many years inside her mind. He knew that she could not help being caustic.

"Ms. Broadmoor, you must know that your latest movie, *Irene's Internment*, is a huge hit. You've outdone yourself, Scary Mary! Such passion! Such magic! I always thought *Embalming Emily* was the all-time classic, but this one was . . . well, the audience could not move until the credits were finished. They were glued to their seats, afraid to move or breathe until the lights came up! Including me, of course," he gushed.

"I am so very tired of hearing your glorious reviews, James. Surely you know that by now," Mary Lee ranted as he raved. "Oh, for someone to tell me the story was drab, the directing lousy. Tell me the plot reeked of mediocrity; the acting, appalling. I am so bored with all of this! I need to find one more movie in me and go out with a bang. Then perhaps I'll get that Oscar that has so eluded me!"

With a weak wave of her hand, Mary Lee dismissed any remaining small talk. "Let's get this over with, shall we?" She tugged at Gertie's arm and smiled at her with insincere sweetness. "Gertie, light another cigar for me, would you please? This is going to bore me to tears. And bring Edgar, Allan, and Poe to me. At least my cats can entertain me while I endure this torment."

As she left the room, Gertie overheard Mary Lee saying, "Now, James, did you make that change I asked for? The one that includes Gertie? Did you get that taken care of? Where is it? Natalie will be so upset—I can't wait. Wish I could be here to see her face!" Mary Lee laughed again, which set off another coughing fit as James pulled up a chair next to her and opened his bulging briefcase. It would be hours before they finished. Mary Lee had a considerable estate and was learning at the end of her life that having such wealth was an incredible burden. At least the plan was simple: give almost all of it to her sole heir, her daughter, Natalie, and let her deal with it.

Hours later, Mary Lee heard the words she'd been waiting for. "Now if you'll just sign here," James said, offering his rather large Mont Blanc fountain pen, "Natalie will be your sole heir, with a bequest to Gertie, as you instructed. I do so hope you have another movie in you, my dear, dear Ms. Broadmoor. And I wish you better health! What would the world be without you?" James choked out these last words, becoming rather unnaturally emotional.

"Do they teach you that in law school too, James, to tear up in front of your dying clients? That performance was good enough for one of my movies." She motioned to Gertie who had returned with her cats and then sat patiently just outside the study, working in her journal. "Get me a pen that doesn't weigh ten pounds, would you, Gertie?"

As she scrawled her signature on pages that Gertie carefully turned, Mary Lee said to her attorney, "You know I wasn't able to stay awake during your entire explanation of my estate, so just look me square in the eye and tell me there will be no announcement until I'm ashes. No publicity. Nothing. I don't want that nosy Nita Winslow breathing her busybody self around here—ever. Her show *Currents* makes me sick to my stomach." She paused to catch her breath.

"And my ex-husband gets nothing. He is not to be informed of my death; he is not welcome at the burial or anywhere near my ashes. No references to our marriage in any obituary column, either. Make sure Natalie knows this. He and Natalie can console each other on some other turf—ha! As if either of them will mourn! Do you understand?" Mary Lee's bitterness was evident.

"Yes, absolutely. It is all spelled out in the documents. Natalie knows and I'm certain she will honor these requirements," James replied.

"I don't know what my daughter will do," Mary Lee said frankly. "She and I don't talk much. That's why I'm leaving this in your hands."

"Understood, Ms. Broadmoor," James replied.

"Good. Because if that bastard that I married so much as breathes in the general vicinity of my funeral or hints at deserving any of my money, so help me God . . ." Mary Lee choked on her rage. "Now are we quite finished, James? All my affairs in order? Ha!" Mary Lee laughed and wheezed, which brought on a coughing fit.

"Affairs," she choked. "I've had plenty of those, haven't I? And what man is left? Not that louse of a husband I supported for fourteen years! Who stands by my side in these days of affliction? Only people I pay to take care of me. At least my cats are sincere. You know all you need to know. Good-bye, James. Enjoy every penny you're making off of me, and I trust you to handle everything as we've discussed. Hopefully this is the last time we meet."

Gertie stepped behind Mary Lee's wheelchair as if to whisk her off to the elevator and up to her bed. But she did not move the chair immediately. Sensing hesitation, Mary Lee suspected that Gertie and James were exchanging some silent dialogue, which further aggravated her.

"Gertie! Stop being flirty!" Mary Lee cackled and laughed at her rhyme because she was quite certain that she had just embarrassed the hell out of both Gertie and James, which brought her a special delight. She couldn't help herself. Tormenting Gertie was one of her few remaining pleasures. Both James and Gertie blushed deeply as if caught red-handed.

"Ms. Broadmoor," Gertie protested, "we were not—"

"Oh, shut up, Gertie," Mary Lee interrupted. "Like I care. Now bring my cigars. We'll drop Edgar, Allan, and Poe off for their lunch on the way. They must be starving, poor things."

Gertie rolled her eyes as she walked off behind Mary Lee's wheelchair; it was one thing she could do without Mary Lee knowing.

After Gertie gave her patient her midday medication and helped her back into bed, Mary Lee immediately reached for her laptop and dragged it onto her stomach. Whenever she was in bed and not sleeping, Mary Lee was working on her next and presumably last story. She would get that Oscar or literally die trying.

Large, dark, and lavishly carved Oriental furniture pieces decorated the massive room, giving it a sense of mystery and intrigue to anyone who was permitted to enter and could stand the stale cigar smoke that hung in the air. No one came in without Mary Lee's express permission. If she was disturbed for any other reason, there was hell to pay. Mary Lee sighed with relief as she prepared to continue writing.

"Dr. Gregory will be here this afternoon," Gertie reminded her. "I'm going down to get your lunch ready. Anything else before I leave?" Gertie asked. "Are you sure you're up to more company today? I could always reschedule."

"No. I'll see them both. Just go. Leave me in peace," Mary Lee muttered with her head against the pillows and fingers poised over the laptop keyboard. She leaned back on her pillows wearily.

Gertie tugged on the cigar that hung from Mary Lee's lips and snuffed it in an ashtray. She knew Mary Lee would be asleep within minutes. Mary Lee rolled on her side and looked up at Gertie. "Thank you, Gertie," she murmured. "You've been awfully nice to me."

Gertie's heart went out to her patient. "You're welcome, Ms. Broadmoor. I'll be back with your meal after your nap. You just need to rest. You've had a big day already."

"Yes, I guess I have. Who knew that dying would be so much work?" Mary Lee turned back to her computer and tried to lift her hands to the keyboard, but she was too tired. Her hands slipped from the computer as she dozed off.

9

If anyone had asked Gertie to complete a survey on her sexual preferences, she would have marked *None of the Above*. She thought men were okay but not necessary, somewhat like a can of sardines. She could eat it if there were no other food options but only as a last resort. Only two men were remotely interesting to her—and at least one of them was gay. Dr. Eugene Gregory held the top spot on her very short list; Chef Michael Forshé took second (and last) place because he loved Gertie like only a gay man could.

Chef Michael was teaching Gertie to overcome her shyness. She hated that she felt like a fool around Dr. Gregory, who was real eye candy for women, both the living and the dying. Any woman who had to look at a face in her last moment of life would end it on a positive note if it were Eugene's face. "Why she looks so happy!" was a comment that the family would make later. Even Gertie was smitten, but she would protest that it was his mind, not his handsome features, that intrigued her. As a featured guest on the LA TV show *Currents*, a locally famous talk show that was receiving broader—even viral—national attention, "Gene" as he liked to be called, could have been out each night of the week with an up-and-coming starlet on his arm. But he preferred to hang around with death.

Gertie was besotted with this aloof man, and while she was an extraordinarily competent nurse, she usually made a complete fool of herself from the minute she greeted him at the door. He fascinated Gertie with Mensa-quality brain cells and an absentmindedness that underscored his intelligence. She loved to hear him discuss medical details with Mary Lee. Gertie was often so mesmerized by listening to him that she would be unaware when either he or Mary Lee asked her a direct question. That usually brought a smart remark from Mary Lee and a blush from Gertie. How could she ever explain that hearing Dr. Gregory talk about *anything* did something for her that she couldn't begin to understand herself?

This dilemma had been the driving motive behind the flirting lessons Gertie finally agreed to take from Chef Michael. She wanted to be interesting to Dr. Gregory, and she hated that she felt so stupid in his presence because she knew she was not.

"*Ma chére, mais oui!* Of course I can help you!" Chef Michael had exclaimed. "*Mon dieu,* you have such a caring heart. Let the world see that!" When no one else was around, and neither of them was busy with Mary Lee's needs, he tried to teach Gertie a thing or two about relating to men, things such as asking questions and listening intently before speaking. That was a tough one for Gertie and required significant practice.

Chef Michael usually talked with a sharp knife in one hand and a glass of wine in the other, since he was often preparing a meal. Everything he used was fresh and organic, which meant there was always something to slice or dice, puree, blend, or sample for the appropriate pairing from Mary Lee's vast wine cellar. At first Gertie had been terrified of his free associating with his ultra-sharp knives. But he handled them so deftly that eventually he could now approach Gertie with one in his hand, playfully remove her earrings, and deposit them neatly in her ample bosom . . . and she wouldn't flinch. She learned to trust him, and truth be known, she came to find his daring somewhat arousing.

When Mary Lee had suggested that Gertie was flirting with James Christensen earlier that day, she had been correct. But Gertie had only been sharpening her skills. James was a bumbling idiot who sweated profusely. He just happened to have the good fortune of handling Mary Lee's estate. Gertie had no interest in him except for experimentation and making sure he didn't talk Mary Lee out of leaving a small sum for Gertie. She stroked his ego for practice, although she abhorred it. But as Chef Michael had advised her, "Ma *chére*, there are more important things to stroke on a man. Don't let this small effort offend you. He is good practice, *n'est-ce pas?*"

*   *   *

Dr. Eugene Gregory was sharp and elusive, consumed with understanding the death process for reasons he shared with no one. In his early forties, Gene didn't have much of a social life, which caused people, including Gene himself, to wonder if he was gay. But while he was terrified that he might indeed prefer a relationship with a man, he was far more disturbed than anyone could have imagined.

Those peering into his life from the outside saw a successful man, well built, and good looking in a Clark Kent way. If anyone was permitted into his personal life (which no one was, except for his house-keeper), his or her observations would reveal the stark, minimalist rooms of his city condo that displayed a sterile lack of intimacy. Nothing except the most essential and functional necessities were in sight. Everything else was behind closed and locked blonde, ash wood doors of perfectly matched wood grain with pewter knobs—too neat and perfect for a normal person. But then, Gene Gregory was anything but normal.

If these doors were opened, they would have revealed amenities such as a wet bar, an entertainment center, even a desk, but there would be nothing sitting out—no papers, no "to do" lists, not even a little black book. His clothes closet contained only the perfectly arranged wardrobe of a wealthy man. Those locked doors mirrored Dr. Gregory's locked-down internal life, a perfect disguise for a deeply troubled man.

Eugene Milroy Gregory's real life was lived on a wide-open ranch several states away and miles from anywhere. Under a carefully crafted false identity as George Milford, there were none who knew and none who were welcome there as he studied death and sexuality,

51

which were intimately connected by a childhood event that he had been unable to resolve.

At the age of thirteen, young Eugene had stood transfixed at the coffin of his grandfather, numb with virgin grief and fear from viewing a corpse for the first time. Eugene was unprepared for the experience of his first wet dream that night after the funeral. In his confused psyche, death and sex became twisted bedfellows and his strict religious upbringing had taught Gene to fear both. The "coincidence" of these unfamiliar nocturnal urges and his grandfather's death were terrifying. It convinced him that he was headed straight to hell.

For weeks afterward, young Eugene awakened with nightmares, his sheets showing evidence of his physical coming of age. Sobbing, he confessed to his concerned parents that he dreamed he heard his dead grandfather screaming for help in his underground coffin. He was certain that his grandfather had died a sinner, unable to enter heaven, and Eugene was terrified that a similar fate awaited him. This became both his morose fascination and a quest to understand what happens at the time of death, because to him death was connected to his own sexual release.

Gene's father, a well-respected pharmacist, and his mother, who maintained the cosmetic counter at the same drugstore, were convinced that their son was suffering from immense grief; that this would pass as he grew up. They had no idea that their conservative "hell and brimstone" church had terrified Eugene to the point that he was convinced that he would spend eternity in hell as punishment for his sexual urges.

When Gene's nightmares worsened, a local doctor wrote a prescription to help him sleep at night. Other than that, no one appeared to be concerned that Gene was haunted and ashamed of his dreaded fascination with death. All of this he kept as carefully hidden as possible.

His study of medical science and his dual degrees as a hospice doctor and medical examiner allowed Gene to disguise his preoccupations in a cloak of research. It also allowed him occasional relief from his sexual torment and the opportunity to study death both immediately before and after, for any sign of a peaceful afterlife. He never dated, never even considered that he would be able to function normally with a woman, which only solidified his fear that he might be "sinfully" gay.

* * *

Mary Lee knew nothing of Dr. Gregory's secrets but was keenly aware of his studious fascination with incurable illness and the death process. She lived in fear that medical science would find a cure for her cancer before she died. Pancreatic cancer was good; incurable was perfect. Mary Lee had accomplished almost everything anyone could want out of life. A deep, abiding love and an Oscar were the only things she'd missed. Otherwise, she was quite bored and ready to move on.

"How much longer, Gene?" she asked when he made his visit later that day. "I've got to get this last story done. How long can you keep me going?"

"Maybe a couple of weeks, Mary Lee," he replied frankly. "Not much more."

"That's impossible!" she gasped. "I can't finish my story by then. Surely you can do something else!"

"No, I'm afraid not this time, Mary Lee," Gene replied matter-of-factly. "Next comes morphine for the pain, which you've refused so far. Test results show you're right on schedule. I'd leave this last project for someone else if I were you. Prepare for what lies ahead. Spend time with Natalie. Dear Lord, Mary Lee, you've got so many great movies to your name. You'll live on for generations."

"Not without an Oscar!" she raged. "I don't give a crap about them, but it seems to me that I've earned one somewhere along the line, and I just hate to have the headlines read, 'Reclusive Oscarless Director Dies.' I know what they'll say and how Hollywood's reverence for dead directors vanishes before the ink on the obituary dries—unless they've got that damn little statue. This is my last shot. So you keep me alive, you hear me? I don't care what it takes! You know me. I'm up for anything—even death. Just give me a little more time!" She collapsed against her pillows. "One more thing," she gasped.

"As long as it's not another miracle you're asking for," Gene responded tenderly. "Medical science isn't known for those."

Mary Lee smiled in spite of herself. "Tell me, for my last story," she begged. "What's the very worst way for someone to die naturally? This time, I don't want to use external torture. I want the worst disease that medical science can't cure. A slow, tormented end to life. What is it?"

Gene paused thoughtfully. Death was his area of expertise, and he'd seen many excruciating ones. "Well, pancreatic cancer is tough enough," he observed. "But . . . I'd say ALS, Lou Gehrig's disease, is the worst. Amyotrophic lateral sclerosis." He spelled it for Mary Lee as she typed it into her search engine. "It's been described as being buried alive. The body ever so slowly loses its ability to function, yet the mind is alert the entire time. We still don't know what causes it."

"Excellent. Thank you, Doctor." Mary Lee waved him off. "That's all for now. Just remember my request."

"I wish you only the best, Mary Lee," Gene replied as he put his hand on the doorknob to leave her bedroom. "I know you're tough as nails. If anyone can stop death at the door, it's you. I'll be in touch."

Mary Lee was already reading about ALS and didn't look up when Dr. Gregory left. Time was that precious.

"Gertie, get Max Goble on the phone! Tell him it's an emergency!" she ordered. If she wasn't going to make it to the end of her story, she'd have to leave it in Max's hands. He was the producer of her movies and had been one of her closest friends in the movie business.

Two weeks to live? Gertie hurried out to catch Gene, who was standing at the elevator. She wanted to test a little "Chef Michael" effect on him because when Mary Lee died so would any chance for her to connect with him.

"So this is it?" she lowered her voice reverently as she followed Gene into the elevator and stood beside him.

"Appears so," was his curt reply.

"Anything I need to know to help her?" Gertie asked, wanting to make conversation.

"We'll have to start a morphine drip, and titer it to control her pain," he advised. "She won't be able to stand it much longer."

Gertie nodded then moved to the elevator door so she could keep Gene in the elevator a little longer. "Will you be here—do you intend to be here—at the end?" She looked at him frankly and then lowered her eyes.

"I like to do that for all my patients," he replied, "but unless she goes into a hospice facility, I can't be certain." The door opened and Gene squeezed past her. "Excuse me, Gertie. I'll make my way out. Call if you need anything."

Gertie watched Gene walk quickly to the front door and disappear. She sighed, disappointed, and with a pouty face walked to the kitchen to talk to Chef Michael. She had tried to reach out to Gene and it hadn't worked. She also called Max and left Natalie a curt message about her mother's imminent death.

"Dr. Gregory was just here," Gertie informed the voice mail in her scolding voice. "Your mother has two weeks to live, Natalie. It would be nice if you could stop over for a visit before she dies. Oh, and she did sign final papers for her will this morning in case *that* interests you."

10

Gertie always treated Natalie as if she were a lousy daughter—as if Gertie had any idea what it was like to be raised by a self-absorbed writer of horror movies.

"Bitch," Allie said aloud to her friend Messiah Carmichael as she hit her keypad to return Gertie's call. Only her mother and Gertie called Allie "Natalie."

"Which bitch?" Siah quickly asked and laughed.

Allie smiled in spite of herself. "Dr. G has just given my mother her 'two weeks to live' notice," Allie told her friend. "That was bitch Gertie, smugly reminding me that I'm an unfit daughter. This will be quick, I promise you," she told Siah. "I'll miss my mother more than I'll miss her nurse," she added, "and I doubt I'll miss either of them."

Siah winced, knowing that Allie was far more affected by the news than she let on.

When Gertie picked up the call, Allie said simply, "I can come over after work. How is Mother taking the news?"

"You know your mother; she's writing," Gertie retorted.

"Ah yes, of course," Natalie shot back. "Shouldn't you check with her before I come to make sure she wants company?" Natalie had always played second fiddle to her mother's lifelong drive for an Academy Award.

"Normally, yes," Gertie replied. "But this is different. It's time for you to make yourself available if you care at all about your mother."

Allie was outraged. "Like I said, I can come over after work."

"Fine. Please stop by the drugstore and pick up her meds before you come." Neither of them said good-bye.

"Two weeks. Can you believe it, Siah? I hate to say it, but I hope Dr. Gregory's prediction is accurate. It's her fault that I'm here and not in Brazil, where I want to be! Am I a bad person?" Allie vented her feelings as she took another gulp of strong Brazilian coffee, an espresso-strength blend of half coffee and half sugar that she swore could wake the dead. Her addiction had developed during her years on the Amazon as a support team member to GloMed International. It was her mother's cancer that had brought her reluctantly back to the United States two years earlier.

It was easy for Siah to absorb Allie's emotions. Her intuitive ability to transform feeling bad into something good had fascinated Allie from their first meeting. A beautiful, large Jamaican woman in her early six-ties, Siah had borne fourteen children in twenty years, then resolved to help women make important life choices other than becoming baby factories. Not that babies were not important. Oh no! But Siah knew that in many cultures women did not feel they had a choice, and even in the United States many young women became unwittingly preg-nant. This had become Siah's life work. After informing her husband that she would bear no more children, Siah had educated herself and founded a home for unwed teenage mothers. She had a grace and ease that Allie could not fathom, a mature, feminine wisdom that Allie had never found in her own mother.

Siah's bracelet bangles sparkled and chimed as she lifted her own frothy latte to her lips, took a long sip, then set the cup on the outdoor coffee table. "Of course you are not a bad person, Allie! You have been extraordinarily patient with your mother's process. You could have chosen not to come back and no one who knows your mother would have blamed you. But I am entirely selfish," she laughed. If you hadn't come back, we never would have met. How tragic that would have been! But only two weeks? I am much more concerned about you, dear Allie. Are you ready to face this?"

"Does it matter?" Allie asked as she signaled the server for their check. "And just so you know, Mother isn't seeking me out; it's Gertie. Mother is busy writing, still going after that stupid Oscar! Can you believe it? I told Gertie I'd come over after work, but I know what will happen. Mother will shoo me away like she always does. And that wicked little hospice nurse will tell me it's my fault that Mother doesn't have time for me." If Mother had ever given me *any* of the attention she lavishes on her movies and Gertie, things could have been different." She sighed. "I just don't believe it. I don't believe my mother is dying. It's like one of her movies. She'll rise from the dead and haunt me eternally. Just tell me what to do, Siah. I need my friends around me now."

"Go to her, Allie, and make peace as best you can. It won't be long."

Allie sighed again as she took the check. "God, I hope not. And you're right, of course. But I don't have to like it. I'm just glad the paperwork is done and that Gertie hasn't succeeded in turning my mother against me regarding my inheritance. There is so much good that I can do with her money!"

Siah smiled. "Leaving you a lot of money could be your mother's way of saying, 'Fuck you,' Allie. Wealth can be an incredible burden."

Allie laughed. "Not to me, Siah. You know better than that. I've got plans for whatever she leaves me, to do more good than she ever dreamed of." She laughed again. "At least I can afford to pick up the check for our lunch. Thanks, Siah. I'd better get back to the office. Give my love to your family."

* * *

Most of Allie's childhood horrors had healed over, but the residual scar tissue had made for some particularly sensitive detours in life. She possessed an aching drive to bury herself in helping others, and a "do not enter" sign at the door to her heart that flashed in neon lights in case someone, especially a man, thought about hacking a way through the forbidden forest protecting her. If anyone tried to get close, Allie freaked out, even after years of therapy. Anyone, that is, except her father and her close friend Siah.

Unlike Gertie, Allie knew who her father was. He had left Mary Lee when Allie started school. Allie didn't blame him for leaving, but she had wanted to go with him so desperately that she couldn't stop the tantrum that ensued. Twenty-six years ago, mothers were granted custody. Others thought of her as a very lucky young lady with a rich mother who could give her anything she wanted. How wrong people could be when looking at the outside of another person's life!

Other than a few special summers when Allie stayed with her father in New York while her mother was working on location for a movie production, Allie had lived with her mother in a state of constant fear until she left for college. Allie loved her dad's urban life. To this day, she could feel his big arms embracing her with hugs and their walks through Central Park, down Broadway, and in Greenwich Village with her very small hand in his much larger one. Her two favorite memories were of dancing on his feet in his cigar smoke-filled study and standing beside him with her own easel as he painted. Even now, Allie spoke to her father often. He was easy to get along with, and he listened to her—more interested in knowing about her life than talking about his own. When Allie hung up the phone with him, she was happy, which was very different from phone calls she received from her mother or, these days, Gertrude Morgan.

Growing up, Allie had wondered how many other children were raised by completely self-absorbed, inattentive mothers consumed with creating horror films. Had other mothers asked their children to stand, lie bound, or be left alone in frightening situations for hours in the middle of the night so their mothers could record their fear?

"Natalie dear," Mary Lee would say as she came into Allie's room at night. "I've just had the most deliciously scary idea for my movie. Help me now. Help me see what it would look like if it really happened."

Allie had tried all kinds of excuses. One time she even threatened to jump out of her second-story bedroom window. Her mother had only laughed. "Natalie, we're just going to *play*. None of this is real. Stop acting like such a baby. I would never hurt you! Jump if you want to, but I'm going downstairs to set up." Allie always shivered in fear when her mother mentioned "Downstairs." It was the lower level of the mansion that served as Mary Lee's stage set. Allie never knew what to expect when she got there except to be told to do things she didn't want to do.

Two events from her childhood could still awaken Allie at night with the same panic she experienced as a child. First was the chainsaw incident when she was eight years old. Sitting in her Holly Hobby nightgown with the promise of a trip to the ice cream shop if she behaved appropriately, Allie had to act terrified as her mother approached her with a buzzing chainsaw. It hadn't been difficult. Mary Lee looked inhuman with her hair standing on end and a pair of goggles strapped over her eyes. Allie's honest whimper turned into a horrified scream; one take was all that was necessary.

After it was over, Mary Lee had pulled off the goggles, patted her hair down, and hugged her daughter as they went upstairs. "Excellent, my dear Natalie! You'll be an amazing actress one day!" Whisking Allie into bed, Mary Lee gave her daughter a rare hug, covered her with her blanket and said, "There now, that wasn't so bad, was it? Certainly not as bad as jumping out a second-story window!" She had laughed, and then rushed back to her writing.

The second most memorable incident had been even more frightening. Mary Lee had created a fireplace with a tomblike crawl space in the back of it. She required Allie to creep into the tiny, closed-in area and chained her daughter's arms and legs to immobile posts. Then she left Allie alone. "I'm not going far, Natalie, but you'll feel very alone. I need you to show me what it feels like to be chained all by yourself in a small space." A tape recorder and video camera had been mounted above Allie's head so Mary Lee could see and record the details of her daughter's mounting apprehension without having to be present.

Even today, tiny scars were visible on her wrists and ankles where she had pulled against her chains in an effort to free herself. The scene had actually made it into one of her mother's movies—with no credit to Allie. "I need to protect you from the public for a bit longer," her mother told her. In the end, Allie got a new outfit—one with long sleeves for obvious reasons, a short skirt, and go-go boots as her reward.

Thankfully these events ended when Allie turned thirteen and started to understand how abnormal her mother was. One of her school teachers noticed Allie nodding off during class one day and asked her if she was feeling OK. Allie innocently explained that she had been helping her mother with her movie work during the night. When the teacher probed further, Mary Lee received a letter of concern from the school and magically found other ways to accomplish her goals. But Allie never felt a mother's love, and the terrified little girl she had been still lived inside Allie's adult body.

With degrees in cultural anthropology, linguistics, and early childhood development, Allie had finally found happiness and fulfillment working with tribal natives along the Amazon River. After college she had headed straight to Manaus, then upriver to work with the poor and needy on the banks of the largest river in the world. Her mother had scoffed at the idea every step of the way, and that was putting it mildly.

"My daughter has degrees in every type of specialty that assures she will never make money or be able to provide for herself," Mary Lee told those who asked. "It also assures that she will live her life a continent away. A mother might think her daughter is avoiding her." Mary Lee both admired and resented her daughter's independence, taking full credit for her obvious strength.

*   *   *

As Allie entered her director's office at the Los Angeles Center for the Creation of Independent Families she gave thanks for what was good about being Mary Lee's daughter. First on her list was that Mary Lee had borne no other children. Secondly, Allie's last name was her father's, so most of the world would not know her association with her famous mother. She appreciated that she had inherited her mother's skinny genes and her raven black hair, but she neither looked nor dressed like her mother. And speaking of inheriting things, her mother's death and Allie's subsequent inheritance would allow her to continue and expand her work, doing good with her mother's money. Surely that would piss her mother off! Allie smiled to herself as she checked her e-mail and considered Siah's comment about her coming into money. Her friend would think quite differently when Allie provided funds to create a larger facility for Siah's work!

Several hours later, Allie grabbed purse, car keys, and phone to head to her mother's home, but not before she said good-bye to "her kids." Heading to the glass wall that separated her office from the children's indoor activity center, she laughed as several of them saw her and ran screaming with delight to the window, calling out, "Miss Allie! Miss Allie!" Flattening their hands to the glass, they squashed their faces flat on the surface because they loved Allie and knew it made her happy. When Allie did the same, the children squealed with joy. No one was ever scolded for leaving fingerprints and face-prints behind.

If she couldn't be on the Amazon River, Allie could almost be content here—except for a few matters like the absence of a river, a jungle, the more tranquil pace of life on the Amazon, and the fact that her mother was within driving distance.

During the long commute to her mother's estate, Allie was able to prepare herself for an encounter with her mother and Gertie. Visiting them was far worse than any culture shock Allie had experienced in another country; she hated that her mother enjoyed every minute of the drama between her daughter and her hospice nurse.

Allie swallowed a Xanax, anticipating a possible panic attack. Taking these had begun in her early teenage years and had not subsided completely, even after years of therapy, until she had left the country. When she returned, so had they. *Funny,* she thought. *I felt safer in an area of the world that most consider quite dangerous. Give me snakes, alligators, and piranhas any day!*

The woman who wove her VW Beetle in and out of LA traffic had no idea who she really was. She didn't understand that she was attractive and engaging, and that it was her own charisma that charmed people and her own sincerity that made her fund-raising work so successful. There were men who thought of Allie as a sexy woman—not that she would have believed it and not that she cared.

Allie's mission in life had been informed by her own experience. She knew there were women and children all over the world who had suffered trauma far more excruciating and real than her own. She was passionately determined to do what she could to bring them to a safer haven. The fact that she now worked with domestic violence victims was not a coincidence. There were subliminal ways that women and girls around the world were mistreated that no one considered unusual or abnormal. Siah called them "subtle abuses." "Dear one," she would tell Allie, "we have all suffered from the ignorant ways of others. We can help those who come after us but only if we admit and heal our own pain."

Allie's mind went to her upcoming schedule for the balance of the year to plan her return to Brazil. It was mid-March, and her mother was expected to be dead by the end of the month. *I'm planning around my mother's death as if it were a dentist appointment,* she noted to herself, feeling quite guilty. Allie was also committed to speak about her work on the Amazon at the GloMed International conference in LA at the end of May, and she did not want to miss that opportunity. She would stay until at least then to settle her mother's affairs.

Following that was the CANIF Ball the second week of October to raise funds so single parents could afford child care as they worked toward financial stability. The acronym stood for Childcare Aid Nurtures Independent Families, and it had become a popular black-tie event, including a veritable who's who of LA's high society. It was the center's most important fund-raiser and Allie knew that to leave before then would devastate her team. But to stay would devastate Allie. She sighed as she turned onto her mother's Beverly Hills street. How she longed for her home and life on the Amazon! Thankfully, the end was in sight at last. Allie instantly felt guilty again for seeing her mother's death as a step forward.

The guards at the gate of Mary Lee's home waved Allie through as the wrought iron gates opened. It was the slightest recognition of being Mary Lee's daughter. She learned from Gertie that Max was there and that they were much too busy with Mary Lee's story for her to take time to chat with her daughter. Gertie had been too busy to call Allie and let her know.

Bitch and bitch.

11

Max sat at Mary Lee's old writing desk in her bedroom, reading her story as he and Mary Lee each smoked one of her cigars. He was wearing what he always wore: a long-sleeved white shirt with suspenders and a wild bowtie. They had worked together for more than twenty years, and he was old when they'd first met. Mary Lee figured he had to be going on eighty now. She rested on her bed waiting for any sign from Max that she had nailed her last story.

It didn't take Max any time at all to know that Mary Lee's story was too freakish for Hollywood to ever produce, much less honor with an Oscar. *It has to be the drugs she's taking,* he thought. Even he didn't like her plot, and informing Mary Lee was going to be tough. *How do you tell a dying person that her quest for one more gem in her movie crown is going to fail, that she could ruin her stunning reputation and go out with a fizzle?* he worried to himself, although he needn't have. It didn't take Mary Lee any time at all to pick up Max's reaction to her most recent story. She could tell by the grimace on his face as he read it.

"Damn it, Max, it can't be that bad," Mary Lee grumbled.

"Let's not call it 'bad,'" Max replied tactfully, although it was hard to turn and look Mary Lee in the eye and say it. "Let's just say it isn't going to make the mark. I'm sorry, Mary Lee, but I've always been honest with you. No sense changing that tack at this point in the game." Max and Mary Lee puffed their cigars quietly together.

"Maybe I need a second opinion," Mary Lee finally declared hotly.

"Be my guest," Max replied. It hurt him to be so blunt, although Mary Lee already held the trophy for that. He was used to it. "I can line someone up if you'd like," he offered.

"Don't bother. I'm out of time, Max," Mary Lee reminded him. "The doctor says I've got two weeks at the most."

"God, Mary Lee, I can't stand it!" Max stood up from the desk, came over, and sat on her bed. "Two weeks! What am I going to do without you?"

"Probably find someone with an Oscar-winning movie and make it to the Academy Awards," Mary Lee fumed. "Damn it! It's not fair! I don't mind dying. It's just that I deserve a statue, Max. You know I do!"

"You do, Mary Lee; we both do. But we've worked in the wrong genre for too long. No one who writes horror fiction gets real Academy Awards. You know that!" Max had tears in his eyes.

"*Silence of the Lambs* did," she reminded him. "And my stories have been far better!" She paused. "Shoot me now, Max," Mary Lee begged. "I can't stand to live another day if there's no hope."

Max took Mary Lee's hand. "I've gotta go, Mary Lee," he told her, weeping. "I can't stand to see you suffer like this. But there's always hope, and you know it. Haven't we pulled off some great scenes when we thought we were finished? Don't you remember all the times we thought it was over, and then it wasn't? Somehow we pulled a rabbit out of our hats, remember? So I don't care if it's the last day of your life or your last breath. You get a better angle on your story and you call me. You got that, you scary old bitch?"

Mary Lee smiled and watched him snuff out his cigar. "See you later," was all he could say.

"Yeah," Mary Lee replied. Max was certain he saw tears in her eyes, but they did not fall. Mary Lee was true grit. "See you, Max. Now get the hell out of my life."

12

After the funeral scene and back on the path to the Realm of Reflection, Josephine Carter ignored her daughter's whining about deserving a crown because she had suffered her husband's faults for so long. As much as she wanted to enlighten Mae Rose about the role she herself had played in her unhappy marriage, it wasn't a mother's place to do that. Mae Rose would figure out that and many other things on her own with the help of her Reflection Agent.

Suddenly Mae Rose heard her mother exclaim, "Here we are, Merrily! Isn't it incredible?" Mae Rose was about to retort that she couldn't see a thing when magically, like a dark movie screen suddenly blazing with color, Mae Rose could *see*. The building before them was truly beyond words—a stunning Gothic-style structure that rose into infinity and sparkled as if it had been constructed entirely of pure crystal.

"This is so much more like I imagined Heaven to be," Mae Rose marveled, "but I still wish I were back on Earth. I miss my family! I want to know how they're doing. I can hardly think of anything else. Is that normal?" Mae Rose desperately wanted her own Viewing Pane.

As they passed together through the walls of the building as if nothing stood in their way, her mother empathized with her. "It's a sign of how deeply you loved them, Merrily, even though you didn't realize it on Earth. But you'll let them go as you fall more in love with your life here. I'm so thrilled for you!"

While the building's exterior had been fabulous, the stark interior bothered Mae Rose as she looked at the large empty space around her. "There's no furniture, Mother," she complained. "No place to sit or lie down. No pictures, no decorating. Why is it so stark? And why can't I see you? I can hear you and sense you, but that's it. Will that change?"

"It's because we are all pure energy here, Merrily," her Mother explained gently. "Here *you* will create whatever you focus on, just as you did on Earth although it took much longer to materialize there. Wait until you see what incredible power you have! You'll also learn that Divine Energy never stops to rest, darling; the entire cosmos would collapse if it did. We don't sleep; we don't need to eat; there are no health issues, and we don't have bodies to dress and take care of—unless we want them—and most of us don't because they are so confining. Ugh. I know it feels strange. It does to everyone at first, but once you get through your Reflection, you'll understand. You're going to *love* this process. Most of us don't even care about what's happening on Earth once we Reflect."

Mae Rose wasn't convinced. Right now she would much rather check in on Art and the boys. She sensed another energy come into the room.

"Here's your Reflection Agent now, dear," her mother announced. "Call for me when you're finished if you want to. All you have to do is think of me with the desire to see me." Mae Rose felt her mother's energy hug her and then disappear.

* * *

"Mae Rose Elizabeth Victoria Carter McElroy?" the Reflection Agent asked in an authoritative but kind tone.

"Yes, that's me," Mae Rose replied somewhat sullenly.

"You are ready for your Reflection to begin?"

"Actually I'm not." Mae Rose had decided on a direct approach. "I don't think I'm supposed to be here, you see. My mother scared me to death."

Her Reflection Agent proceeded without responding, which irritated her greatly.

"The purpose of our visit is to give you a chance to release all of the burdens of life that you have carried with you here. You can find rest, Mae Rose—you just need to be willing to let them go. We will assist you in that process."

Mae Rose was dubious, particularly because she wasn't certain that she was ready to let go of any of her grievances. She wanted to make her case, to right the injustice she was certain had been done to her. *Surely the Reflection Agent understands that,* she said to herself.

She was ignored again as the Reflection Agent continued. Mae Rose *hated* to be ignored.

"Heaven, as you call it, will come to you in phases if that concept helps. You have successfully completed Phase I: Crossing Over into the Realm of Spirit. Congratulations and welcome! Now we are going to release whatever could hinder you from experiencing the full benefit of your next phase of eternal life. This is the purpose of Phase II: Your Reflection. Your spirit still contains debris from unresolved negative vibrations that you experienced during physical life. That's quite common. In your case, however, you died in a fit of rage, which requires particular attention."

"But I wasn't supposed to die!" Mae Rose's emotions went wild. "I wouldn't be here if my mother hadn't—"

"At the end of this Reflection, you enter Phase III: The Choice. One of those options is Bliss, or Heaven as it is called on Earth. There's no hurry to decide and many people literally take 'forever' going from one choice to the next."

It was as if the Reflection Agent couldn't hear her! Suddenly a horrible thought occurred to Mae Rose. *Is it possible that my Reflection Agent can't hear my complaint? What if nothing of a negative nature can even register here?* Her thoughts tumbled on. *How can I win an argument if there's no argument? What if I can't even tell the truth from my perspective?* She choked on that possibility.

"After you complete Phase II, you will receive your Viewing Pane," the Agent confided. "It's a marvelous tool as your mother has already shown you."

Ah, the Viewing Pane! Mae Rose thought and relaxed. "I'll be able to see what's happening on Earth?" she asked.

"Of course," her Agent replied. "Earth and any other galaxy or comic realm you'd like to consider. Earth is only one of your options."

Mae Rose wanted her Viewing Pane immediately but knew that she would have to play along. The sooner she cooperated, the sooner she'd achieve her goal. "How many choices will there be in Phase III?" she asked sweetly.

"Limitless," her agent Agent replied.

"And Heaven is only one of them?"

"Very good, Mae Rose. That's exactly correct."

"That certainly isn't how the Bible explains it," she commented dubiously.

Her Reflection Agent was humming happily. A large screen with a number of buttons, knobs, and levers below it appeared suddenly, looking very much like the Review menu on a computer with categories like Comments, Track Changes, Accept, Reject, and so on.

"Here is your Reflection Screen, Mae Rose," her Agent explained with enthusiasm. "When you feel ready, you can look at your most recent past-life and make changes by using that large black knob, called the Dial. Turning it to the right permits you to create a more positive outcome; turning it left would, of course, create a more negative one. Only you can see these outcomes and both are beneficial as you "reflect." It is a very enjoyable process.

"While you are here, you can take advantage of all of our incredible benefits. Rest, relax, and soothe yourself after your life journey. Make use of our Spa of Serenity, spend time in the Library of Limitless Learning, or create your own customized world in the Palace of Possibilities. This is a magical, creative place so feel free to stay as long as you like—even forever!"

"What if I decide I want to return to Earth?" Mae Rose ventured to ask.

"Always a possibility," her Agent responded enthusiastically. "While many find it boring once they are able to see all the options here, some do go back. It's familiar and it can be much more fun after you learn how to enjoy yourself here. We don't recommend this Choice until you have rested here for an Earth century or two. It's too tempting to get reattached to old energetic issues if you return before you have your 'feet on the ground' here, so to speak."

"So reincarnation is possible?" Mae Rose was shocked to learn this, but also keenly interested.

"We don't call it that," the Reflection Agent told her, "but yes, you can return if that's what you decide to do. All of this will be so much clearer after your Reflection is complete."

Mae Rose was captivated. She truly didn't care what the Agent's advice was—as long as she could find her way back, she intended to return to Earth as soon as possible. "How interesting!" she exclaimed.

"You can't just go back and pick up where you left off, Mae Rose."

Can my Reflection Agent read my thoughts? she wondered.

"Nor would you want to," the Agent explained. "It would interfere with the lives of those you love. They have their own work to do, which no longer includes you. That's why those who reach this Phase and decide to meddle in earthly affairs run the risk of being 'Vanished.' It's that serious."

At last! Mae Rose couldn't pass up the opportunity to learn more. "What does that mean, exactly?" she asked. "I mean, how would someone know if they had been—you know—*vanished?*" Is that another word for Hell?"

"Not exactly, Mae Rose. We compare it to a spiritual eraser. Your name is removed from the Book of Records as if you never existed. You just go 'poof,'" the Agent explained. "Your energetic vibration ceases to exist in its imprinted form as 'you' are absorbed into a different energy. That's probably the best way for you to understand it."

Mae Rose squirmed. She couldn't imagine not being who she was or worse, becoming someone else. "I'm so confused," she admitted.

"I thought only good things could happen once I died and came to—here." She no longer knew what to call the place she was.

"That is exactly correct, Mae Rose! Only good things! There is so much to look forward to! Even being "vanished" is a good thing if that's what you choose!" Mae Rose's Reflection Agent's energy filled the entire space around her with love and light. "Just think! After your Reflection, you can create whatever you desire! It's *your choice!* Imagine that! If meddling in earthly affairs is most interesting to you, then being vanished is the outcome you choose. Celebrate! It's only, always and eternally good. But frankly, since everyone has to die to get here, most folks aren't interested in interfering with the energetic vibrations that are still on Earth. They are so much more fascinated by what else is possible. Speaking of which, we really should get on with your Reflection."

Let's continue, shall we?"

"This is ridiculous," Mae Rose couldn't take it anymore. "None of what you're saying makes any sense. All these phases and choices? Being vanished? Something's wrong here and I intend to find out what it is!" she affirmed.

Completely unaffected by her outburst, the Reflection Agent was ready to sum things up. "There you have it, Mae Rose. Let's get started with your Reflection, shall we? You are going to enjoy this *so much!*" Mae Rose watched her Reflection Agent turn the Dial on the panel below the screen.

"Watch closely, Mae Rose. See how you can scroll through your life and watch events and use the Dial to change outcomes?"

"Yes," Mae Rose replied. "Why is this necessary?" I thought I would be rewarded here for all the suffering I experienced on Earth. What point is there to dialing a different outcome now, after my life is over?"

"Ah," her Agent replied. "As I suspected, you have Sainted Suffering Syndrome."

Before Mae Rose could ask what the *hell* that was, her Agent went on. "Let me explain. Contrary to a popular interpretation of your Bible, 'Heaven' is not more available to those who endured greater suffering on Earth, particularly if it was self-induced as yours was. Many people are confused about that. They thought they would be rewarded for suffering, but it's what they did with the suffering that was the most important."

"I'm not sure I understand," Mae Rose countered.

"Your mortal experience was meant to prepare you for Bliss, Mae Rose. If on Earth you learned to find Bliss even in difficult circumstances, then you are ready for Bliss here. If, however, you focused on suffering and enduring it rather than learning from it, Bliss is too foreign a concept for you to experience it here without more preparation."

The Reflection Agent stopped and said quietly, "As below, so above."

"Don't you have that backwards?" Mae Rose relished the thought of the Reflection Agent's making a mistake.

"That would not be possible here in the realm of Absolute Truth," came the response. "It did, however, get turned around on Earth but without consequence. Great truths can be reversed and still maintain their integrity. 'Believing is seeing; seeing is believing,' for example. It doesn't matter which way you say it; both are required for anything to materialize.

"Let's get on with the Reflection, Mae Rose. I believe you're ready, and it will help you so much. Just one more caution before we begin.

"I sense that you are very eager to receive your Viewing Pane so I must caution you once again that it is not to be misinterpreted as a global command station from which you can change or manipulate the world you have just left. Remember these rules, Mae Rose—and the consequence of being vanished if you misuse your Viewing Pane privileges. It is for observation and information *only*. You are not permitted to make your presence known or to interfere with what you are observing on Earth *in any way*—unless of course, you truly want to be vanished."

"Is it even possible to interfere with what's happening on Earth?" Mae Rose asked, utterly intrigued. "How could my presence be felt, much less affect, what's going on there?"

"I'm certain you are now aware of how very thin the veil is between these two planes of consciousness, Mae Rose," her Agent explained. "It takes only the slightest focus of attention and emotion to interfere on the Earth plane where souls are the most vulnerable. If you get involved in what is occurring on Earth, you can get pulled back into that lower vibration before you're ready, which causes you to be absorbed, as we have discussed. But let's get through your Reflection now and then see if you still have any questions. Ready?"

Mae Rose kept her thoughts to herself. Hearing about the Viewing Pane so captivated her that she now wanted nothing more than to begin her Reflection. Once she got that over with, she'd have access to Earth; she couldn't wait. "Yes," she replied enthusiastically. "I am ready to begin."

13

Looking back at the Reflection process after she completed it, Mae Rose understood why her death had not been the glorious homecoming she had hoped for. As she moved toward the Spa of Serenity for a delightful whirlpool treatment, she pondered why she had so greatly misunderstood life after death. As she had recently learned, you can't live and die pissed off and expect to start your next life blissfully. You had to deal with your shit one way or the other, which she had. Mae Rose found she loved using all of her words.

She also learned that she had misinterpreted the effect of being forgiven for her "sins," which were called "misunderstandings" here. Her Reflection Agent had clarified. "Mae Rose, all of your misunderstandings had been 'forgiven,' as you call it, but you used that knowledge as a free pass to behave in a very unloving way toward others. And," the Reflection Agent told her as gently as possible, "as you grew older, it got worse." Mae Rose couldn't disagree, especially after watching her life on the screen in her Reflection Room. It had been shocking! Her mother had been right when she had told Mae Rose that she was making herself more unlovely every day!

Easing in the Whirlpool of Wonder and settling in for a long, fragrant soak, Mae Rose continued to enjoy remembering her Reflection. She laughed every time she thought of her death and funeral, completely understanding why her husband couldn't stop laughing at first, in spite of his shock and grief. It was damn funny that she, of all people, had died on a toilet.

A series of Miracle Massages had released Mae Rose's propensity for suffering and eventually drew her into her Reflection. She had learned to enjoy playing around with the Dial on the Reflection screen and recreating the movie of her most recent life. She had scrolled through those awful scenes of her rage and unforgiving spirit, realizing that she could have made a different choice about her behavior if only she had chosen to see her life differently. It would have been so easy!

It was in those many painful scenes that Mae Rose learned the true magic of the Dial. How she had wished that she and *everyone* could have access to these tools during their lives on Earth, not just after! Then her Reflection Agent reminded her that everyone did. "Life is all about dialing up outcomes, Mae Rose," her Agent reminded her. "On Earth, they show up as thoughts and feelings. In fact, the whole magic of Earth is that life *outside* of yourself is a mirror of what is occurring *inside.* When you fix the inside with your thoughts and feelings, it automatically shows up outside. Isn't it amazing?" Mae Rose agreed, still wishing that had been clearer during her lifetime. She could have had a wonderful life if she'd known!

Based on the highs and lows of her life chart, Mae Rose had been able to select situations or time periods to review. Once she hit the Play button, the scene would show up like a movie. At first, Mae Rose felt twinges of shame for her unkind moments. If she got stuck there, her Reflection Agent was immediately on the scene, showing her other wonderful aspects of who she had been. As a result, Mae Rose developed love and compassion for herself. Once that happened, everything else realigned itself.

Mae Rose roared with laughter each time she reviewed a scene from her life. With the Dial, she could make each one dramatically more positive or negative. In one instance, she and Art had a disagreement over handling discipline of the boys. When fights between them started, they were always worse than anything their kids had dreamed up, except that since Art and Mae Rose were adults there was no scratching, punching, or tattling, or so Mae Rose had thought. Now that she could see her thoughts and feeling, Art had taken a real beating. She had been so viciously unhappy.

In another instance, when Art Jr. was a teenager, he had started smoking with his dad and they had both agreed not to tell Mae Rose. When she found out, Mae Rose was more furious than she had ever been until the day of her death. The actual monologue had gone something like this: "How could you hide that from me? It's the same as lying! Do you have any idea what that says to the boys about us—about our marriage? About how they should treat their wives when they grow up? That it's OK to LIE and keep secrets? You told me that you were quitting smoking and all that time you were smoking with OUR SON! I don't know why I married you! You've never ever done one thing to build up this family. I'm the one who does all of the work. You refuse to fulfill your role as the head of this family—you spend money we need on cigarettes so that all we ever do is scrape by. Years! And then you pull this! I can't bear it!" It was one of the times Mae Rose had marched off to the bathroom to console herself. Now she knew that other options could have worked.

When Mae Rose turned the Dial counterclockwise, the scenario deteriorated into kicking Art out of the house, threatening Art Jr. with his life if she ever smelled smoke on his breath, and ultimately showed Mae Rose's picture as she was arrested for murder. She had laughed her ass off (as a manner of speaking since heavenly beings don't have bodies of course).

If Mae Rose turned the Dial clockwise, however, it led to interesting options. She could have created a smoking lounge for Art in the barn (really?), learned how to smoke so she could join him occasionally (shocking!), joined him in counseling to allow any other lies or deceits to be dealt with, or asked him to leave if he couldn't stop lying (unbelievable!). But in all of it, Mae Rose saw that as she worked on whatever was going on inside of *her* more than what was going on in her marriage, the better her marriage became. It had incredible possibilities.

* * *

Mae Rose's most priceless afterlife experience with Bliss occurred as she adjusted a scene from her mostly miserable sex life with Art. It was a night when she and Art were going to bed and she knew Art would want to have intercourse. She had stopped calling it "making love" after his affair, but she still believed her husband had the right to her body. After all, that's what the Bible said, or so she had been taught.

In the scene she was watching, Mae Rose winced as she saw Art turn to her and start rubbing her back. That was his sign. She saw herself dutifully remove all of her clothes and get under the covers alongside him. As his hands started to wander around her large, unhappy body, his mouth covered hers, begging it to open for a French kiss. Mae Rose had hated that. *This won't take long,* she used to tell herself. *I know his routine by heart. I won't say anything; I'll just suffer through it.* Sure enough, after only a couple of minutes, Art was inside Mae Rose, thrusting away, never knowing the pain Mae Rose suffered by his indifference to preparing her body with loving foreplay. He never saw the tears she shed, but then, she had never told him how she felt either. She knew that was what had finally killed her.

In the beginning of their marriage, Art was good with his hands and not just when he was working on cars. He'd give Mae Rose a "tune-up" that would make her roar with pleasure. But then she'd gotten pregnant and had a baby. She had also come to know Art's faults intimately, which created a toxic drip of disappointment that began to course through her veins. It was little things at first. But as life became more demanding, so did she. Then her weight crept up ever so slowly, in direct relation to her unhappiness.

The scene on the Reflection screen had been almost impossible for Mae Rose to watch at first. Art finished his orgasm, gave his wife a hug and a kiss, and said, "Thank you," as he headed to the bathroom to clean up. Mae Rose had always thought that was pretty strange, like he was being polite about it. When Art crawled back in bed, Mae Rose took her turn in the bathroom, often soaking in the tub as she wept. Art would be snoring by the time she returned.

Determined to see this particular scene in the most positive light possible, Mae Rose had turned the Dial all the way up. She watched in absolute amazement as she and Art danced to a slow love song. They were so aroused that the sexual energy was palpable even from her Reflection room.

Art's touch caused Mae Rose to tingle all over as she watched his hands wander down her face to her neck and then to her breasts, where his fingers drew tiny circles around her nipples. A throbbing ache gathered deep inside her, and before she realized it, she was overwhelmed with desire, moaning in absolute ecstasy. It became her favorite scene to replay. Mae Rose knew each time she reviewed it that this was bliss. She also knew in her innermost being that she and Art could have loved each other like that, and that if they had Art would never have had the affair. And she wouldn't have died of outrage. Even that last scene in which she had thrown the dozen roses at Art and marched off to her death—what a tragedy that she couldn't see what Art had really been trying to do.

Learning all of this made Mae Rose yearn desperately to return to Earth and to her family. She wanted Art to know what she now understood—she felt everyone in the world needed to know that it was worth giving love a chance before death claimed them. She felt she couldn't really move on to another Choice until she fixed this one.

Her Reflection Agent cautioned Mae Rose about making her Choice too quickly and for the wrong reasons. "If you return too soon, some of your unresolved aspects might show up even more forcefully than before," she was told. "And returning does not assure that you would make contact with your past-life family. It is far more likely that you would enter into an entirely different set of circumstances. Mae Rose pondered these factors carefully until her Reflection Agent added, "It would be unprecedented for someone to return to Earth so quickly after crossing over." Mae Rose had always loved to be considered unprecedented.

With her Reflection complete and her Viewing Pane in hand, Mae Rose had moved to the Palace of Possibilities. Here she would make her Choice about the next phase of her eternal life. One thing was clear to her: she would be unable to decide her future until she checked in on her family. She turned on her Viewing Pane to see how Art and the boys were doing. Perhaps that would settle the matter.

14

Beer and the boys. Somehow Art made it back into his life in Fairview one day at a time, although it often felt like one breath at a time. John's decision to stay home with his father, thereby honoring his late mother's desire that he and his fiancé not live together before marriage, was an encouragement that Art had not counted on. A double blessing was Art Jr.'s return home in mid-May to intern at the nearby hospital. Having his sons with him comforted Art, but nothing eased his suffering. The process of grieving and regretting was exhausting. Memories played on the screen of his mind with aching precision so that he learned to hate consciousness.

As the numbing shock of loss faded into reality, Art entered a world of ever-deepening pain and a dark depression settled over him. He could not believe how he ached for Mae Rose. Whatever he had found intolerable about their relationship while she had been alive became a searing wound because he realized it could have been different if he had seen her the way he viewed her now. Much like barn cats, agony clawed its way through his psyche any time he was quiet and alone. Sleep eluded him. If he did lose consciousness, he would wake up weeping. He could not function, and he couldn't bring himself to care about anything, especially working on VW Beetles.

Ben Strong, sobered by Mae Rose's sudden passing and the part the kittens might have played, became a true friend and was a changed man. He covered for Art, often working on his projects so Art wouldn't lose his job. Even Louise was impressed with Ben's transformation. "Where's my fuckin' no-good husband—the man

I married?" she would ask when she came to town. "Must have been a fuckin' UFO took him off and performed a procedure on him." Then she would laugh, a new experience for her and the citizens of Fairview.

The church folks had stopped bringing meals to Art and the boys. These three men who had never cooked a meal when Mae Rose was alive now had to invent their own. Pizza, fast food, frozen dinners, chips, beer, and more beer were their main menu options. Mae Rose would have turned over in her grave if she'd known. More likely she'd have risen up, marched right into the house, and thrown one of her famous fits.

Thankfully Jill King still made it a habit to check on the McElroy men every couple of weeks. She'd whip through the house, cleaning, organizing, and leaving their home sparkling with a fresh energy, her endearing fragrance lingering in the air. Jill always brought a bouquet with her, but never a dozen roses, and never yellow. Her care did more to encourage Art than the therapy he was receiving. When he thanked Jill or tried to pay her, she'd say, "Now don't you be silly, Art McElroy. I'm doing this because I loved Mae Rose and she'd want to make sure someone was looking after you." Then she'd add with her subtle smile, "And it's a good thing I show up. Mae Rose would go ballistic if she saw how you boys are living."

It was as if Jill had a private line to Mae's Rose's activities. The night Mae Rose chose to use her Viewing Pane to check on her family was a typical McElroy men's night. A haggard Art Jr. walked into the house after a three-day stint at the hospital smelling of blood, sweat, and the distinct lack of time to shower. It was about 6:30 p.m. John had the night off and was sitting with his dad in the family room.

"Hi, Dad, John," Art Jr. said as he sagged toward them. He looked beat, eyes bloodshot, dark blond hair askew. He'd had only brief naps in the past seventy-two hours, he told them. Art Jr. was not a big man, but he was well built and resembled his mother more than his father. What he lacked in height, he made up for in charisma, so he always seemed taller than he was. Most important, Art Jr. was emotionally strong. He had handled his mother's death the best of any of the three men; at least that was how it looked to his father.

"Art, man, you look whipped," Art Sr. said to him as he set down his guitar. "There're some leftovers in the fridge; let me warm them up for you." He jumped up to offer his chair as he headed to the kitchen, but John was already off the sofa, en route to the bathroom. Art Jr. opted to stretch out on the couch. Outside the bathroom, John stopped suddenly.

"What is it?" Art asked him as he put old pizza in the microwave to warm up for Art Jr.

John stood there, dazed and shaking.

"John?" Art asked again. When he still didn't respond, his dad went over to him. "John? What is it? What's the matter?"

John came slowly back from wherever his thoughts had been, still shivering. Finally he spoke. "It's—Dad, it's—I don't know, but it feels like Mom was just here." He burst into tears. "I could feel her, Dad. She was getting ready to give me a good-night kiss. And she said . . . she said . . ." He could not go on.

Art put his arms around his son, holding him close for a few moments. He was relieved that John was expressing his feelings. He had always been the more emotional of the two boys, but lately he had closed down, as if he were trying to be strong for his dad.

"She said . . . she said to tell you, 'Thanks for the flowers.'" He sobbed.

Art gripped his son's shoulders and moaned. John finally broke their embrace. "Gotta go, Dad. I really gotta go." He headed into the bathroom and closed the door. Art went back into the family room to talk with Art Jr. but watched for John to come out.

Art Jr. yawned, oblivious to what had just happened. His father felt it inappropriate to bring it up. "Good to have you home son," he said quietly.

"Good to be home, Dad. It was a tough three days. Now that the weather is warming up, so are the crazy people who haven't been on their motorbikes, in their boats, or cruising in their convertibles for months. It's like everyone has to learn how to behave again." After a

81

moment, he added, "Some of them don't get another chance. We had two in today: motorcycles, DOA. Too young to die."

"Art," his father asked, "is it OK with you, you know, to face death like this so soon after losing your mother? How are you handling it? You seem fine . . . almost too fine."

"Oh, I'm OK, I suppose," he replied and yawned again. "Death is a fact of life, Dad. It was just more personal with Mom. At least she wasn't doing anything stupid that caused her death."

"She was married to me," Art replied without thinking.

"Jesus, Dad! Cut the crap!" Art Jr. scowled. "Mom loved you! I know you two disagreed with each other a lot, but Mom was no angel either."

"Actually, she was." Art moaned. "But I didn't get that until too late."

"I'm glad you're seeing a therapist," Art Jr. replied then added. "You and Mom—it seemed like you lost touch with each other as we were growing up, but I've seen worse; believe me."

"Really?" Art replied, still listening for the bathroom door to open. He headed back into the kitchen and over to the microwave, which reminded him of how he and Mae Rose had loved running into town the day before trash pickup to see what was on the curb. They had treasured finding that microwave, which still worked! When the microwave buzzed, Art grabbed the plate of leftover pizza with a dish towel and headed back to the family room.

"Just come and sit in the emergency room for a few hours sometime, Dad," Art Jr. told him. "Watch how family members treat each other in some of life's most devastating situations. You'll fall on your knees to thank God you and Mom had each other."

Art was thrilled to hear that his son had a somewhat positive impression of his parents' relationship, although neither of the boys knew about the affair. Art and Mae Rose had agreed that they should not be part of that pain.

As he put dinner in front of Art Jr., John came back into the room just in time to hear his brother say, "Oh, and by the way,

Mrs. Whitman was asking after you for the umpteenth time. She plans to visit one of these days."

"You mean *Maggie* Whitman?" John asked.

Art's heart plunged to his toes. Maggie was a staff nurse in the emergency room at the hospital, yet to Art, she had become much, much more.

"The very same," Art Jr. replied.

Art put his arm around his younger son and started to pull him into a hug, but not before he saw John's face darken.

John scowled. "Why would *her* name come up?" he asked, suddenly testy.

"She just keeps asking after Dad and she's planning to visit is all," Art Jr. replied, his mouth full of pizza.

"Maggie Whitman in *our* house?" John objected loudly and suddenly. "Mom would have a fit! She never, ever, liked her. Dad, you can't let that woman—"

"Now, John," Art interrupted, trying to calm his son down, "it wasn't that your mother didn't like Maggie. It was just that your mother had certain preferences in people." Art was suddenly in an awkward position, downplaying his wife's clear hatred of the woman with whom he had committed adultery for three years.

"Preferences, my ass!" John hollered. He wasn't one for foul language; it suggested a particular emphasis that his father noted with concern.

John continued with his voice raised. "Dad, are you stupid or what? Maggie Whitman was always flirting with you, *even around Mom!*" he yelled. "Mom *hated* her! Why can't that woman leave us alone? Don't you *dare* let her into this house—*ever,*" he growled darkly as he grabbed a piece of the heated-up pizza.

"That's for your brother," Art reminded him.

"Don't the two of you worry," Art Jr. cut in, sitting up and taking a slug of his beer. "I've got the situation under control." He stood up, belched, then apologized automatically, just as Mae Rose would have insisted. "OK, I'm off to bed, and I don't want to be wakened for *anything.* I've got three whole days before I have to work again, and

I have only two things on my mind: catching up on sleep and cleaning the barn. Good night."

John went from rage to laughter in seconds. With his mouth full of food, he asked, disbelieving, "He's going to clean the barn? Seriously? I've got to see that!" He headed back into the kitchen and grabbed a beer from the refrigerator then froze with it in his hand.

"You put that beer right back where you found it, John McElroy!" he heard his mother order. "There will be no underage drinking in this house." John started shaking again. Then he heard her say, "Not even over my dead body. Put. It. Back." John did just as he was told, and while it gave him the creeps, it also made him laugh. "OK, Mom," he whispered, certain he was losing his mind.

Art had returned to his chair and picked up his guitar, but he wasn't playing anything except scenes in his mind full of a terrible possibility. *Why was John reacting so strongly to Maggie? Was it possible that he suspected something?* He watched, puzzled, as John came back in to the family room empty-handed. He had heard the refrigerator door open and close. "Where's your beer?" he asked.

"Mom said to put it back, Dad. I'm telling you, *she's here* or I've lost my mind."

The two men finished their pizzas in silence. Finally John got up, gathered their plates and beer bottles, and took them in to the kitchen. His father watched him with concern.

"Thanks, Son," Art called after him. He heard John run water to rinse the beer bottles before putting them into the recycle bin. The under-sink cabinet door squeaked open, which could only mean that John had gotten the dishpan out to start washing dishes. John was behaving as he had when his mother was still alive and issuing regular commands to her family.

Later, as John walked past the family room on his way out to visit his sweetheart, Elliana, he poked his head in. Art had just started to strum his guitar again. A song was forming in his head, a possible tribute to Mae Rose. "Dad, I'm dead serious about Maggie Whitman," he said, looking at his father with such intensity that Art had to look away.

"Gotcha, Son," Art told him, feeling like a complete louse. "Are you sure you're all right? Anything you want to talk about?"

"I've said all I'm going to say. Good night, Dad. Don't wait up for me." John moved toward the door.

"Good night, John," Art called after him as calmly as possible. He wanted to add, "Don't get Elliana pregnant!" but restrained himself.

* * *

Mae Rose was outraged as she closed down her Viewing Pane. Her boys were living like slobs, and somehow Maggie Whitman—*that slut*—had the audacity to think she should visit Art and the boys in Mae Rose's own home. She seethed with a dark rage that emanated from her aura in a black cloud. Suddenly she heard sirens. Before she knew what was happening, her Reflection Agent encircled her with radiant love.

"You came dangerously close to meddling," the Agent told her.

"I was devastated by what I saw," Mae Rose confessed. "My family needs me. That bitch that my husband had the affair with is getting too close. She needs to be stopped!"

"Not this way, Mae Rose," her Reflection Agent rebuked her gently. "Trust me when I say you're not ready. If you want to experience hell, this is the surest way to do it. The problem is that it's not just you who would suffer. Think of your family; you could destroy them by interfering. Is that what you want? They are not yours any longer, Mae Rose. They must have the freedom to make their own choices."

"I only want to help them," Mae Rose cried. "I love and miss them so much!"

"Ah, then you simply must leave them alone, Mae Rose. You're doing such incredible work here and you will soon know the best Choice for your future. In the meantime, you've been warned. If you get this involved again, you could be vanished. Understand?"

15

"Let's go, Dad." Art Jr. downed a glass of milk as smoothly as if it were his favorite beer, setting his empty glass in the sink with such enthusiasm that his father flinched. Pulling the back door open, Art Jr. ran his hands through his hair and grinned sleepily. He knew his father would rather have a root canal than face the barn.

"You goin' out like that?" Art asked his son. Art Jr. had on a pair of wrinkled sweat pants and a T-shirt that looked as if he had slept in them. In short and indeed, he had just gotten out of bed.

"It's the barn, not a date." Art Jr. laughed. "Did you want me to dress up for the occasion? Rent a tux?" The eldest son of Art and Mae Rose McElroy was enjoying his father's lack of enthusiasm immensely. "It will be great, Dad; trust me," he insisted. "I have a perfect plan for how to approach this. I'll explain it on the way. *Let's go!*"

Shaking his head in disbelief, Art gulped his coffee, put his empty coffee cup much more gently in the sink, and followed his son reluctantly through the back door. It slammed violently behind them, pulling Art back into the day it had slammed behind Mae Rose as she had left him bleeding beside her ruined car.

"Unless you have some miracle potion or you're going to drug me so I don't give a rat's ass, I don't see much hope for this project," Art whined.

His son laughed. "Whatever it takes, Dad," he retorted. "I know some pretty decent medications and I've got legal access, so don't push me. Remember that I'm going out to LA next week to attend that GloMed conference. I want this project well in hand so that you can work on it while I'm gone."

The idea of his son leaving the United States to work in some impoverished country was hard for Art to accept, but it was a good cause and he was proud that Art Jr. was thinking so seriously about his future. If Mae Rose were alive, she'd be crying in her husband's arms at night and beaming at her son by day.

"OK, this is it." They had arrived in front of the barn door. Art Jr. paused momentarily, his eyes still twinkling, just like his mother's used to when she couldn't contain her delight.

"OK, I'm with you. I'll give it a try, Son," Art conceded. "But it won't be the same without your mother here to enjoy it with me."

"I think I understand a little," Art Jr. said softly, putting his hand on his father's shoulder. "I've only got a few hours before the guys come to pick me up. We're going to close the bars tonight."

"You meeting up with any girls?" Art never asked his son about relationships. While John was already in a committed relationship at his young age, Art Jr. had never mentioned any particular interest in women.

"Dad," Art Jr. laughed. "Who has time for girls? I've got a career to think about and trust me, too many of the guys who get involved while they're in medical school don't make it, especially if they have children. You're going to have to cut me some slack on that one," he added. "Let John go first."

"Where'd you get to be so smart?" Art teased his son with pride. "Are you really my son, or did someone pull a fast one on me?"

"Well, that's a good question, and actually I've given it some thought." Art Jr. got a serious look on his face. "You know what I've decided? That you and Mom were at two different ends of life on just about everything, so I learned where the best of each of you was, and I figure that's what I got. So you get half the credit. Now let's dig in to this mess," he said as he heaved the barn doors open.

"After you, Dad," Art Jr. said and bowed low, sweeping his arm toward the inside of the barn. Art couldn't help laughing as they walked inside.

At three o'clock that afternoon, Art Jr. waved to his dad and indicated he had to get going. "We're off to a great start," he said and Art agreed. The two men high-fived each other. "I'll be back later, Dad. Don't wait up for me. That was fun. Honest. If you want to take a load to the recycle plant, they're open until four."

Art decided his son was right and headed up to the house to get the keys to his truck. He felt the best he had in a long time, just to be starting on this. Mae Rose would have been so happy. She would have worked right alongside him if he would have allowed it. He knew there was a time when Mae Rose believed in him. He remembered when she'd say things such as, "You're the most talented man I know," then she'd whisper, "and the sexiest." But that had been years and years ago.

As he drove to the recycling plant, Art turned on the radio, which was playing the same song he'd been singing months ago on his way home from the shop in Mae Rose's car. "Blue Moon, you knew just what I was there for. You heard me saying a prayer for someone I really could care for . . ." he sang along. Then he broke down because Mae Rose could have been sitting right there next to him. *Oh, Art, just think of all the fun we'll have spending time in the barn together. I'm so excited!* That's what Mae Rose would have said.

Art had to pull off to the side of the road because the tears wouldn't stop and he couldn't see to drive. On the other hand, there were things he could see much more clearly. He sobbed. *Can you see, Mae Rose? I feel like you're right here with me, and God, I miss you so! I wish you could come back so we could make it right! I want a second chance!*

Propping his forehead against the steering wheel, Art gave in to his grief.

"You OK, Art?" a woman's voice interrupted.

"What?" Art looked up startled. "What? Oh, Maggie. I was just . . ." Art took off his glasses to wipe them dry and wished with his whole heart that anyone but Maggie had shown up.

"I was just coming in to drop off my spring gardening refuse," she offered to fill in the silence. "It feels so good to get rid of things

I don't use anymore. Saw you sitting here in your truck and thought I should check to see if anything was wrong," she explained.

Wrong? Art thought. *You mean like the affair we had?* Maggie was a decent person. She was just a terribly lonely widow with whom Art had fallen off the wagon of fidelity back when things were really bad between him and Mae Rose.

"I'm fine, I guess," he mumbled, looking down at his steering wheel and tracing its outline with his hands to give them something to do. "Just going through what's normal after losing a spouse, I suppose." Art sniffed and choked as he spoke. "You'd probably understand that. Art Jr. got me into the barn to clean things up a bit. That's what brings me to the recycle plant."

Art put his truck in gear. All he wanted to do was get away from Maggie Whitman. "I'd better get there before it closes," he told her so she wouldn't feel too bad about their conversation being cut short.

"Oh, Art, I just feel so sorry for you—for us—all of us." Maggie shook her head sadly. "I know what we did was wrong, and then Mae Rose found out. In a way, I feel responsible for her death. I think she just couldn't stand living after she knew." Maggie had tears in her eyes.

"You know, I don't think this is good for either of us," Art said firmly, amazed at his ability to speak so definitely to a woman he had been intimately acquainted with. "It's all in the past and it needs to stay there." He started to pull onto the road but stopped. He knew he had to put an end to any contact with Maggie, even after all these years. John had insisted on this and with good cause, Art realized. She was probably full of hope now that Mae Rose was dead, which suddenly angered Art and made him feel the need to be cruel.

"When Art Jr. told us that you were planning to stop by to see how we were doing, John had a strong objection. He senses something; he was adamant that you should stay away from us and I agree. Don't come over, Maggie. Ever." Art had never been more serious in his life. "It will only lead to more trouble and sorrow, and I've had my share for this lifetime. I think if you care at all for me and the boys—and the memory of Mae Rose—you'll stay away. It's funny how I see her now that she's gone. I see all the good that there was or could have been between us. Wish we could go back and start over. Gotta run."

Maggie looked at Art with the same hurt that she felt when he ended their relationship. "Nice to see you, Art," she said with tears running down her face. "I don't think it's an accident that we met up like this. You take care now. See you at church." She patted his hand and turned to cross the road back to her vehicle.

Suddenly she stopped in the middle of the road and ran back to Art's truck. She pounded on the hood to make him stop and yelled through the closed driver's window, "Mae Rose was part of the problem, Art! It wasn't all *our* fault!" Before Art could respond, Maggie ran to her car and didn't look back.

Art headed right back to the barn as soon as he got home. He stayed there until dark, sorting through bits and pieces of things, knowing that it was also time to recycle Maggie.

As she closed her Viewing Pane, Mae Rose was glad that she'd set it to alert her whenever Maggie Whitman was near her family. More than ever, Mae Rose wanted to go home.

16

The day Art Jr. left for the conference in LA, his father faced the one project he knew he had to finish now that the barn had more open working area. Mae Rose's ruined VW sat forlornly, still untouched. Over two months had passed since her death, and in his grief counseling sessions Art had been encouraged to either restore the car or dispose of it. Intuitively, Art knew that working on it was the only way to heal his grief.

Wearing a face mask and taking frequent outdoor breaks to deal with the stench and his private pain, Art began his task. The cats' claws and urine had destroyed any chance that anything could be salvaged, but Art sensed that starting over was a good thing. Since he still had plenty of parts from the seven old VWs he and Mae Rose had gathered so many years ago, he had almost everything he needed, including seats. It gave him considerable satisfaction to think about how much he was going to save and he sensed that Mae Rose would be overjoyed to know he was using them. New parts for an antique VW would cost a fortune now, if they even existed.

In order to pull the backseat out of the car, Art had to remove Mae Rose's famous gardening basket and its contents, which had been scattered by the accident. He reached for the few items left in the basket. Sorrow rose up inside of him like a tidal wave, causing Mae Rose to be so touched by what she was seeing in her Viewing Pane that she couldn't help making contact with her husband.

Art shuddered as he heard Mae Rose's voice whisper, "I love you, Art McElroy. Always have, always will. I like what you've done with the barn." He decided it was a hallucination, but one he was willing to participate in. There was no one else around to catch him pretending Mae Rose was with him. "I love you too, Mae Rose," Art replied softly. "Always have, always will. And I miss you. God, how I miss you." Then he broke down weeping. "We had so much didn't we, Mae Rose? I just couldn't see it, and I want it back so bad that it feels like I can't go on living without you. I am so sorry about cheating on you. I want another chance to be us!" There was no reply but it didn't matter to Art. At least he'd finally been able to declare how he felt.

Mae Rose's gardening basket had been particularly special to her because it had belonged to her great-great-grandmother Lily, the woman who had changed the family's dynamics by using her wealth to assure that the women in her family had their own financial strength.

From the day she had received her car, Mae Rose carried that precious basket, attempting to model her own life after a woman she had never known, but whose presence in life had made a profound impact on her family. Mae Rose had become known for that basket which she used for gathering flower cuttings, arranging them in small vases she kept handy in that same basket, and dropping arrangements off to someone in need. Teacups and saucers sometimes rattled merrily among the basket's other contents, and perhaps a book of poetry to read to an invalid.

Near the bottom of the basket, however, Art found two items that changed him forever. First was a slender silver case etched with her initials, *MRLVCM*. Art had given it to Mae Rose on their wedding day. He instantly realized that she had kept it with her every day thereafter, and his heart ached. Inside was a photo of Art and Mae Rose on their wedding day. On the back in his wife's writing, it read *Til death do us part*. Art couldn't breathe. He wondered how many times Mae Rose, even in the most trying times of their marriage, had held that picture in her hands as she honored that vow.

The second and last item in the basket was a little bank book. Art was stunned when he read the cover titled "Our Rainy Day

Fund—Saving for Our Future." *Was it possible? Had Mae Rose accumulated her own money?* When he looked inside, the shock brought Art to his feet, stumbling and gasping in amazement. She had indeed: $62,734 with interest continuing to compound! The last recorded deposit had been the day before Mae Rose died. Art was shocked that his wife had kept such a secret. Then he smiled, certain that Mae Rose was beside him again, whispering in his ear. "Use the money, Art. Do something wonderful for our family—no cigarettes and no VW parts," she warned, laughing. "Oh, Art, I'm sorry for so many things. I always meant well, but I was such a bitch!"

Art chuckled at Mae Rose's confession. She certainly had benefited from a heavenly perspective! But then, perhaps, so had he. Art would never smoke another cigarette. If he was asked, he said, "I want to honor Mae Rose's request. Better late than never."

17

Mae Rose had been enjoying her Viewing Pane reunion with Art when her mother showed up.

"Mae Rose," she heard. Not "Merrily." Mae Rose sensed trouble.

"Mother," Mae Rose answered.

"What are you doing on Earth with your Viewing Pane?" Josephine demanded.

"Don't you mean what *on Earth* am I—?" Mae Rose suggested helpfully, only to be interrupted.

"When are you going to stop trying to turn the tables when I talk to you? It's disrespectful and annoying. I mean what I said. What are you doing *on Earth* with your Viewing Pane?"

"I was just watching Art and the boys for a little while. That's all, Mother." Mae Rose tried to tell the truth inside the boundaries that had been clearly set for her.

"You think *we* don't know exactly what you're up to? Do you think you can hide *anything* in an omniscient place?"

"That's ridiculous, Mother! Of course I don't. But I also think that we have free will to do what we believe is right, especially here." Mae Rose tried to defend herself. "I'm not *hiding* anything. I'm just enjoying my family."

"You were doing more than that; you were becoming emotionally involved on Earth. You could lose it, you know," her mother warned, pointing at Mae Rose's Viewing Pane. "Perhaps worse if you don't stop."

Mae Rose inhaled as if to respond, but Josephine went on.

"I know you, Mae Rose. I know exactly what you're up to. You think I don't, because you don't know how much alike we are. Trust me when I say that Art and the boys need to learn to live without you. They will only suffer more if you interfere. Is that what you want?"

"No. But I had to let Art know what I've learned—about how awful I was to live with and how sorry I am. Surely that much is OK, isn't it?" Mae Rose was sincerely distraught.

"It's never OK to interfere, no matter what you think you're accomplishing."

"It wasn't like that. We apologized to each other, equally."

"Oh, so you *communicated?* You and Art *talked* to each other? What about the boys?"

"Just a little," Mae Rose confessed.

"You've crossed the line," Josephine Carter scolded. "You could be vanished, Mae Rose! In fact, I'm surprised you're still here!"

Mae Rose couldn't help herself; she had done what she felt was right and she was being scolded for it! "Why don't you go back to Bliss and mind your own business? And maybe I *want* to go back, Mother. It's one of the Choices, isn't it? Stop meddling and leave me alone!" Mae Rose could not believe she was standing up to her mother. She felt extraordinarily powerful when Josephine Carter's energy disappeared.

18

The last thing Art McElroy Jr. expected to do at a medical conference in Los Angeles was to fall in love. But the divine art of matchmaking must be one of God's favorite pastimes—the chance meeting, the exquisite timing. Either that or Mae Rose was abusing her Viewing Pane again.

Art Jr.'s father had been correct about his son's nonexistent love life. His passionate resolve to become a doctor was all-consuming. He was not as reclusive as his father had been when he met Mae Rose, but, like his father, all it would take for Art Jr. to fall in love was a touch or, in his case, a right hook, a knee to his groin, and a lot of explaining. For the rest of his life, Art Jr. would enjoy telling the world how he met his wife. He would never know that his mother had been so concerned about his reticence around women that she had risked her eternal life for him.

The conference convinced Art Jr. that he was on the right track, that he wanted GloMed International in his future. He attended every session he could, often wishing he could clone himself and go to all of them.

The conference ended with an evening gala featuring food from around the world and several keynote speakers, mostly men and women of world renown. Art was intensely psyched but also tired. He had a few drinks during dinner, and was only slightly conscious when the last of the speakers stepped to the podium.

Allie Schwartz, a name he did not know, had apparently worked for a number of years with tribal people of the Amazon Basin. While it was not a war-torn area in the normal sense of the term, tribal groups were being terrorized into cultures that were foreign to them. As their jungles were razed, their way of life was being torn from them as well.

Art Jr. was enjoying how this woman looked—until her closing remarks challenged Art to the core of his being. "Charity has its limitations," she said. "There will always be people in desperate circumstances, but we need to see beyond what appears obvious. We must set our sights high and ensure that we are not creating helpless, dependent cultures.

"The most important test of the success of charitable work is that it moves on. Dependent people are not the goal; self-sufficiency is. May we always remember this as our ultimate quest."

The crowd roared to its feet with approval while Art Jr. sat dazzled and immobilized at his table, his head full of Allie, her face, her words, her glow, the way her strapless gown would be so easy to remove and what he might find beneath it. He began to twitch with desire and a mounting need to "fuck or flee." Mae Rose was watching everything on her Viewing Pane and knew she needed to assist. If her son was at last besotted with a woman, she would see to it that they met even if it meant she might lose her Viewing Pane privileges—it was *that* important. What happened from there would be up to her son unless he failed to act. Mae Rose went to work.

Lost in a turbulent sea of passionate feelings, Art Jr. was distracted as he moved out of the ballroom. For a reason he would never be able to explain, he tripped and began to fall forward. As fate, fortune, (or his mother) would have it, he reached his arms out to save himself by grabbing whatever was nearest to him. This "just happened" to be the body of Allie Schwartz. Not understanding the circumstances that had caused what she perceived as an attack, Allie reacted as any strong, self-defense-trained woman would when someone grabbed her from behind. She turned, planted her fist into Art's jaw and her knee into his groin, which was particularly painful because Art McElroy Jr. had not yet been able to subdue his aroused state.

Art Jr.'s descent to the floor felt like a slow-motion time warp. When he finally met the carpet, he curled into a ball of pain, not realizing that he had succeeded in virtually undressing Allie. Several people fell over him as general chaos ensued.

This was, however, a conference of doctors and people who were comfortable with crisis. A sense of calm quickly fell over the crowd. When he dared to open his eyes, Art Jr. saw several men standing over him. Allie was grabbing her dress in an attempt to hide her sexy undergarments as she pointed her finger angrily at him. It was the most exquisite torture Art Jr. had ever known as his pummeled penis garnered enough energy to attempt to rise again. He was in love.

Art Jr. felt himself being lifted and carried out of the ballroom; he saw Allie Schwartz out of the corner of his eye, glaring at him. Art Jr. might not yet know much about romantic love, but he knew all about glaring from watching his mother and father interact. *Glaring was good,* or so he thought until a police car appeared at the curb. He was handcuffed and forced into the back of the squad car like a common criminal.

* * *

Except for a class tour he had taken in the third grade and his friendship with the cops in Fairview, Art Jr. had never been to a police station. He wasn't sure how he would get out of this predicament, especially in LA, but he had to, just as he had to see Allie Schwartz again.

While Pastor Frank loved to remind his congregation that "the truth sets us free," Art Jr. wasn't absolutely certain that would apply in this case. In his favor, Art Jr. had no prior arrest record and his explanation was simple. But Allie Schwartz was obviously well known and highly respected. If she pressed charges, it could have a devastating impact on his future.

The one phone call Art Jr. was permitted to make was to his grandfather. It was the middle of the night in Fairview, but it wasn't difficult to rouse a doctor—even one as old as Mae Rose's father. Henry Carter listened carefully to Art Jr.'s uncharacteristically desperate voice. He couldn't quite make sense of the events leading up to Art's arrest, but that didn't matter.

"Please don't tell Dad until I know how this is going to go, Pop," Art Jr. pleaded. "If I can save him some heartache and embarrassment, I'd like to. Can you help? I'm wide open to ideas."

Henry had never heard Art Jr. sound so miserable. "Oh, my poor, poor grandson!" he exclaimed sympathetically. "This is just unbelievable! It's the middle of the night, but you know I'll do whatever I can. Let me find out who's on police duty in Fairview tonight. They might have a contact with the LAPD."

"I'm sure you're right, Pop. Thanks." Art ended the call sounding like a lost little boy in the middle of a deep, scary forest. But it just so happened that Big Charlie was on call and *he* would not let anything happen to one of Mae Rose's sons.

* * *

Allie had been both shaken and stirred by the events of the evening—shaken by being undressed in public and stirred by the absolutely innocent and awestruck look on Art Jr.'s face as he was whisked off to the police station. She couldn't sleep. Every time the scene replayed in her mind, she felt worse. First of all, she had done physical damage to a young man. Secondly, she had been surprised by her almost violent reaction; she could have killed him. Finally, she had a charitable image she didn't want tarnished.

A panic attack in the middle of the night forced Allie to finally called Siah. It was difficult for her friend to figure out what Allie was so very distressed about. The story was simply too bizarre and too unimaginable.

"Siah—my god—Siah, I assaulted a man at the GloMed International Conference tonight!" Allie sobbed. "It will be all over the news tomorrow morning. Help me, Siah." Allie was truly desperate.

Siah was dumbfounded but managed to reply, "A man undressed you? In public? Dear God! Of course you protected yourself! Good for you! Are you going to press charges?"

"I don't know," Allie told her friend miserably. "I don't have enough facts. I can't believe it was an intentional act, but I really felt like I was being attacked. Can you believe I'd do something like that?"

"You're a strong woman, Allie. Nobody messes with you. Who else is going to look out for you if you don't?" Siah defended her friend's actions.

"Everyone will admire you, so there is no shame in this," she added. "Do you understand? That guiltiness I hear, that's your mother's voice in your head talking to you." Siah's voice grew louder. "You hold your head high, understand? But yes, you need more information in order to know what to do and you won't get the truth from the morning paper. You're not sleeping so you might as well go to the police station and see if you can talk to this man—for both your sakes. It will be safe to confront him there." She paused and Allie could hear the smile in her voice. "It sounds like you left quite an impression, my friend."

19

When Art Jr. hung up from that call to his grandfather, he requested a meeting with Allie Schwartz to explain what had happened. It was a long shot, but he was pretty sure he had just met his future wife and she would probably want to know *before* she ruined his life.

Allie was in her car, already headed to police headquarters when she had called her father in New York. "I am so proud of you, my darling daughter," he had yawned into the phone. "What courage you have shown! But I also agree with your thought process now that the drama is over. What man in his right mind would intentionally attack you in such a public gathering? You are the epitome of compassion and fair-mindedness. By all means, get the facts." Then he said those words that Allie could not resist: "S'il vous plaît, ma petite fille."

The entire staff at the police station was stunned when Allie walked in at 3:00 a.m., only fifteen minutes after Art Jr. had made his request for an interview with her. She was shown his blank rap sheet; she saw his college records and work history and his résumé for GloMed International. He was twenty-eight years old, which made him four years younger than Allie. She also saw a picture of the man who had attacked her. Even with a bruise on his jaw, he looked pretty wholesome—attractive actually. There was a light in his eyes that captivated her, but she wasn't about to trust him.

With a security guard beside her and a glass wall between her and her assailant, Allie decided she could at least listen to what Art McElroy had to say for himself. It wasn't much. Art had a bit of a limp when he came in and sat gingerly on the hard plastic chair he was offered. He hardly mentioned himself at all, and he didn't defend himself. He simply told the truth, apologized, and asked Allie if she was OK. That surprised Allie as he was obviously in pain. She had expected a defensive man, desperate to save himself from being arrested. But mostly he talked about Allie's speech and her work. That, in the end, was what caused Allie to change her mind about Art McElroy Jr.

On the other side of the bulletproof glass that separated them, Art Jr. watched Allie talk with the fascination of a man in love. He noticed how her eyes lit up as she spoke about her work and her vision. Her long raven hair framed her animated eyes and her earnest mouth. Her face softened and when she finally smiled, Art saw that she was even more beautiful than he had originally thought.

In the end, Allie couldn't think of a good reason to put Art Jr. in trouble with the law; she even offered to give him a ride back to his hotel. As Allie drove, both could sense that something was going on between them. By the time they arrived at Art's hotel, Allie and Art Jr. couldn't keep their hands off each other.

* * *

Just as things were getting interesting between her son and Allie, Mae Rose's Viewing Pane went blank. She knew instantly what that meant. There was no such thing as a power outage in the afterlife since energy was always abundantly present.

* * *

Mae Rose might be in trouble in paradise, but Art Jr. and Allie were on their way to heaven on Earth. It had started with their handshake at the police station. Much like Art Jr.'s mother and father, when his hand touched Allie's, he was no longer the shy young man who was too busy for women. Right in the hotel lobby,

Art Jr. took Allie in his arms and kissed her with a passion that made everyone else who was watching either jealous or horny. It was a kiss that said, "You're not going anywhere but up to my room because I want you *now.*"

Allie could not believe that she returned his ardor. She felt drawn in by a force she could not understand or resist. For the first time in her life, Allie gave in to a desire that took over her body and possessed her soul. It was a need—a hunger so intense that she was oblivious to the risk she was taking with a man she had no real reason to trust.

As soon as Art's hotel room door was closed, he and Allie melted into each other's arms, unable to get out of their clothes fast enough. Art's groin knew no pain as he stood Allie against the wall and entered her. Wet with desire, Allie wrapped her legs around him like a seasoned lover and moaned with a pleasure she had not known before. It was a glorious, first sexual encounter for both of them, and it was over within minutes.

Art and Allie stared at each other like the almost complete strangers they were, not knowing what to do next. If there had ever been an appropriate moment for Allie to entertain a panic or an anxiety attack, this would have been it. But Allie only knew she wanted more. Neither of them spoke; they knew that words would break the spell. Instead they eased themselves onto Art's bed and made love much more slowly and seriously, exploring each other's bodies intimately. For Art Jr., who had never been close to a naked woman who wasn't his patient, it was an exquisite trip. For Allie, being explored was a gift she had never been given before. Each sensation was liquid pleasure. They drifted off to sleep in each other's arms as if it were the most natural thing in the world.

When Art woke up, the bruise on his jaw was ugly but he was smiling. He had missed his plane—not that he cared. What perturbed him was the fact that Allie was gone, until he found the note she had left for him with her e-mail address. *I don't know what that was—do you?*

* * *

Things did not bode quite so well for Mae Rose, who sat quietly in her room, her Viewing Pane still on the blink. Her mother's presence came into her room.

"Well, well, well," Josephine Carter said.

"Well, well, well, *what?*" Mae Rose replied sullenly.

"I've got to hand it to you, Mae Rose. You certainly know how to make a mess of things! You obviously didn't hear one word I told you—imagine my surprise," Josephine's voice dripped with sarcasm. "First you torment your husband with your rage until it kills you. Then you interfere with your son's love life and think you're doing him a favor? When will it stop, Mae Rose? You're manipulating other people's lives from here after you were expressly warned about the consequences of doing so. That won't happen again. You're being vanished—and you know I don't mean banished, since we've already had *that* discussion," she added.

She paused. "I wish I could do something about this. The thought of never having my daughter's energy around me—of forever losing the imprint of *you*—could make me sad. But it was your Choice, Mae Rose and we all honor that. I won't leave Bliss for you—not ever again. I won't be sad; I won't suffer. You are on your own, whatever that means, from now on." Before Mae Rose could open her mouth to defend herself, she heard a toilet flush again, and felt herself swirling downward, realizing at last that being *vanished* had a literal interpretation as well.

20

When Art Jr. looked at his clock, it was 11:22. Allie was well on her way home, rapturously absorbed in remembering the events of the past couple of hours and unaware that her mother was in the final stages of life.

Gertie was keeping vigil, watching as Mary Lee's fingers rested on her keyboard. She was propped up on massive pillows and dressed, as she had been every day, in her familiar white shirt and black pants. Her bald head was bare since she wasn't expecting company. Today, however, she had been fussy about wearing the right shoes, her red spiked heels, as if she were dressing up to go out.

Mary Lee gasped, causing Gertie to look up from her journal writing. It was the death rattle, and there were usually two or three more of these exhalations before the end of life.

"Ms. Broadmoor?" she queried. There was no response.

Suddenly Mary Lee sat up in bed and started swinging at something invisible. Gertie trembled with fear as Mary Lee somehow found the strength to take her shoes off and throw them at whatever it was that Gertie couldn't see.

"Not yet!" Mary Lee cried out. "My story—I need more time to complete my last story! It's got to be my best and certainly Oscar material!" There was a brief pause. "I don't care what Max says about it, and I'll be damned if *anyone* is going to interfere!" Mary Lee's face was pure rage. Gertie shuddered as she waited for whatever would happen next.

"Over my dead body!" Mary Lee thundered.

Gertie couldn't believe what she was seeing and hearing. *A fist fight? Mary Lee arguing with Death?* But then, how like her to be fearless and determined even now. No confessions, no acknowledgment of any wrongdoing in her life because surely Mary Lee had always lived by her convictions. Whatever she was not—a devoted mother and loving wife, a charitable and generous woman—she made up for in her passionately relentless drive for perfectly horrific cinematic art.

Mary Lee was listening to something. After a moment, she gasped breathlessly, "Is there an Oscar?" she demanded to know. "Will . . . we . . . win . . . an . . . Oscar?" Gertie watched as Mary Lee scowled, falling back against her pillows, laughing bitterly. "So even *you* can't predict it? Then I give up. Who gives a damn anyway?"

And that was it. How fitting that Mary Lee's last words were dramatic and edgy; she appeared to be disappointed with *God*. That, however, was nothing compared to what was to come. It would be Scary Mary's ultimate triumph; it would deserve an Oscar.

The bedroom clock chimed 11:30. Smiling at what she had just witnessed, Gertie was certain that God would find Mary Lee vastly entertaining. In those sacred moments as Mary Lee's body settled into what such an experienced hospice nurse knew was the death process, Gertie prayed for the soul of her employer. She moved quietly to Mary Lee's bedside to check her pulse. But before she took Mary Lee's lifeless right hand in hers, God forgive her, Gertie pressed the delete key on Mary Lee's computer. She knew what Max thought of Mary Lee's recent story and believed she was doing the world a favor. Then she checked Mary Lee's pulse, which confirmed that her life was over.

Almost mechanically, Gertie entered these facts into Mary Lee's medical file. Then, as she did with every patient, she picked up her journal and wrote out the death scene in her heartfelt prose. Gertie wasn't sure Natalie would find the details to be the treasure that most family members did. In fact, Gertie wasn't sure she would even allow Mary Lee's daughter to see anything that she had written about her mother's final days—that thankless and inattentive Natalie.

It's over at last, Gertie wrote. *Mary Lee Broadmoor died at precisely 11:30 a.m. after a conversation with God that sounded more like a negotiation. I have never witnessed such a dramatic death scene! There had to be an entity that Mary Lee was talking to. Whoever or whatever it was, she faced the end like the strong and passionate woman she had been, asking God for more time to finish her story. I will miss Mary Lee Broadmoor.*

Placing her journal's white-ribbon marker at this last page, Gertie closed it and allowed herself to weep for this tough woman whom she had truly loved and whom she knew had loved her too in her cynical, brusque, and acrimonious way. She also wept with relief. The stock market had been good enough to her that she could take some time off, and yes, if she wanted to, the rest of her life.

The toilet in Mary Lee's bathroom flushed, which startled Gertie back into reality. There were people to call, first Natalie, of course and then Mary Lee's publicist.

Gertie tucked her journal under her arm, moved to the phone, and pressed Natalie's speed dial number, half hoping that she wouldn't answer. Now that the time had come to let Natalie know about her mother's passing, Gertie suddenly didn't know *how* she would tell her.

Natalie's voice came on the phone. Startled to hear her answer in person, Gertie began to tell Natalie the news.

"Natalie, dear, it's your mother," Gertie began sympathetically. "She's . . . she's—"

At that precise moment, Gertie watched in utter disbelief as Mary Lee sat up and screamed. This caused Gertie to do the same. The phone and her journal slipped out of her hand as she fainted.

On the other end of the phone, Allie heard the commotion. "Gertie!" she demanded. "What is it? I hear screaming. Gertie! Is Mother . . . did she . . . ? Gertie? Damn it, Gertie! What's going on?"

Allie's mind quickly went over the evidence. Gertie had never, *ever* called her "dear." That and the sympathy oozing from Gertie's voice had given Allie every reason to believe that her mother had just died. The silence on the other end of the phone puzzled Allie then made her angry. She had never trusted Gertrude Morgan. Something very strange was going on, and she intended to find out what.

Racing to her mother's house as fast as traffic would allow, Allie's emotions were understandably running wild. She had just made love to a man she hardly knew, not once but twice. Now instead of going home to process that exquisite experience, Allie had to set it aside and turn her attention to her mother. It pissed her off.

Screaming and cursing as she drove, Allie beat her hands on the steering wheel. "Why can't you die quietly like normal people, Mother?" she yelled. "Damn it! Why does everything you do have to be such a drama?" Allie Schwartz had had enough. "When is it my turn? I just fucked my brains out and *you* still get the headlines!"

Allie's cell phone buzzed. It was a text from Art Jr. that read, *2 prsus 4 wrds. Whn cn I C U?* She laughed out loud at his play on words and settled back into herself. "It won't hurt him to wait a while," she decided. She had no idea how persistent a desperate man in love could be. She would have thirty-seven missed calls and text messages before she was able to respond. If anything would see Allie through the next few days, it was knowing this—and not much else—about Art McElroy, Jr.

21

"What the *hell?*" Mary Lee roared as she felt her own living spirit squeezed by an overwhelming energy as Mae Rose's spirit entered her body.

Hearing Mary Lee's voice alerted Mae Rose that she was inside the body of a living person.

"What the *hell?*" they both cried out in unison. Mae Rose remembered that she had been vanished and that she was now being absorbed into someone else's energy. Mary Lee, on the other hand, was certain she was being punished for bartering with God. Both women, now inside one body, wondered if indeed this was hell.

"Mother!" Mae Rose yelled in desperation, causing Mary Lee and her body to jump in fright. "Mother! I know you said you'd never help me again, but this can't be right! I'm in someone else's body and I'm still *me*! Could you *please* get them to fix this? *Mother!*"

Meanwhile, *Mary Lee* cried out, "Okay, I don't need an Oscar. Just get me out of here! No one said anything about demons; no one mentioned hell! I don't want to be possessed! I've changed my mind. Just let me die!"

Mae Rose was suddenly captivated. "Wait a minute," she ordered. "Who are you and what's this talk about an Oscar? About changing your mind? Were you bargaining with higher powers? That's pretty ballsy."

"If I'm still alive, I'm a writer and producer of horror films," Mary Lee replied quietly. "Quite famous, actually. My name is Mary Lee Broadmoor in case you've heard of me. I'm supposed to be dead, but yes, I bargained with *someone*—I thought it was God—to live longer because I wanted an Oscar before I died. Now that you're here, I'm pretty sure it was the Devil, pretending to be God. He'd know I wouldn't be able to tell the difference."

Mae Rose couldn't help but laugh. "Well, I haven't heard of you," she replied. "My name is Mae Rose McElroy. I'm not famous for anything in particular, but I'm not the Devil, although I'm sure there are folks from my hometown who would suggest otherwise. I've been vanished from heaven. I hear it's fairly unprecedented. Maybe I'll become famous too!" She giggled.

"Don't you mean 'banished'?" Mary Lee asked. "How does one get 'banished' from heaven?"

"Actually the correct word is *vanished;* they have a potty theme going on. I suppose I was vanished due to what they consider inappropriate meddling in earthly affairs."

"Really?" Mary Lee was intrigued. "I didn't know that could happen. What on Earth—I mean—what did you do?"

"I helped my son meet a woman that I'm pretty sure got him laid for the first time in his life," Mae Rose bragged. "That young man is just too shy and busy becoming a doctor, so I saw him getting interested in a woman and arranged for them to meet. It was apparently a violation of heavenly protocol. I'm not sorry I did it, but I sure am sorry to be intruding on your life like this," she finished.

Mary Lee was fascinated. "You know, we could use some of this material in my latest movie!"

"Oh, I don't know, Mary Lee—have I got your name right? None of this was particularly spooky—except the expression on my face when my mother showed up to escort me to higher realms. It was so bad that my coffin had to be closed for the funeral," she added. "It didn't help that my body had been on the toilet for hours before it was found."

"The toilet? That's perfect!" Mary Lee enthused. "We've got some work to do, but with any luck and my Max Goble, we can make this a hit! Tell me more, Mae Rose," she begged.

"Not that much to tell. I thought my life after death would be glorious and free. I had no idea that I'd still have to work on my issues." Mae Rose's spirit showed signs of dejection. "I mean, what is salvation for if you still take all your imperfections with you into the next life?"

"I'd be the last person to ask," Mary Lee replied proudly. "I've never thought about 'issues' in my entire life. Those were things other people had—not me. I've always told the truth, no matter what; I've always lived life on my own terms. Ask anyone who knows me."

Mae Rose intuited that Mary Lee probably wasn't quite as perfect as she sounded. "How lovely for you," Mae Rose replied with a touch of sarcasm and a full ration of jealousy. "I have never lived life on my own terms—not that I didn't try. In fact, the harder I tried, the more people appeared to resent me. I felt so rejected. Now I've gone and overdone it even in my afterlife. Talk about feeling totally dissed! I was even rejected from what is supposed to be the realm of unconditional love."

She fell quiet for a moment then added. "If you want to write horror fiction, you need to write about being rejected like that. Nothing in life is more horrible than not being loved." Mae Rose started to tear up. "I tried so hard to be likable. I worked so hard to please people." She sniffed.

"Really?" Mary Lee replied, feeling surprised and thoughtful about Mae Rose's suggestion. "I've written stories about the most torturous ways to die," she added, "and dying unloved was not something I'd consider to be so bad. There certainly won't be a large crowd at my funeral, whenever that happens. Even my daughter and I don't talk to each other. It doesn't bother me at all."

Mae Rose could not believe what she had just heard. This woman obviously had no heart. *How could I of all people end up in this body with such an unfeeling person?* she wondered. *What sense is there in being vanished if I become part of someone that is worse than I ever was?*

Mary Lee had turned her attention to other matters. "Now we'd better see about my body. Since there are two of us, we're going to have to *cooperate* to get around. I want to get to my computer and start taking some notes. Oh, this is going to be *good*, Mae Rose. Just you wait and see!"

*   *   *

Both Mary Lee and Mae Rose had to focus their attention on the external world simultaneously in order to make Mary Lee's body move. "I wish we had instructions for how to do this," Mae Rose muttered. "If she wanted to, my mother could get us out of this mess. Damn it!"

It took some practice at cooperation, which was a tough concept for these two women, but eventually they found a way to share their energies. Mary Lee's body resumed consciousness to the sound of the phone line beeping. It would have been quite hilarious if anyone had been able to see two women managing one body. It was Mae Rose who first saw Gertie passed out on the floor.

Compassionately, Mae Rose nudged her gently to revive her. "Yoo-hoo," she called softly to Gertie. "Yoo-hoo."

"That'll never work," Mary Lee told her. "I'll show you how to get Gertie's attention." Mary Lee threw her right arm out and found Gertie's hair which she tugged as she yelled, "Gertie, get your ass up off my floor!"

Gertie moaned in response, rolled onto her side, and sat up, which brought her face to face with a living Mary Lee. In the next instant, Gertie started moaning, weeping, and shaking all over so violently that Mary Lee had to quickly grab her computer to record it for her story.

"Gertie?" she asked as she pressed the computer's power button. "Are you OK? What happened, Gertie? You don't look so good. Do you want to lie down for a while? That was the most amazing nap!" Mary Lee laughed. "I dreamt that I argued with God—or the Devil—I'm not sure which one. But Gertie, guess what! I have time to complete my story *and* it might win an Oscar! No promises, though. *Isn't that funny?* Apparently *no one* can predict the outcome of the Academy Awards! But I could have died; I thought I *had* died. Are you sure you don't want to go lie down?" Gertie nodded affirmatively, unable to convince her body to get up and walk to her own bedroom.

"It's OK, Gertie. You can lay here on my bed until you feel better," Mary Lee offered, shocking Gertie with her kindness.

Once her computer screen was ready, Mary Lee tried to locate her story document. Nothing appeared. She started to rummage in her saved documents and grew pale as she searched. "Where's my story? Goddamn it! Where's my story?" Looking upward, she screamed as she shook her fist, "You *promised!* What a fool I was to believe you—whoever you are!" She heaved her laptop across the room and threw a tantrum with Mae Rose in tow.

As Gertie watched, now even more horrified because of what she'd done with Mary Lee's story, Mary Lee's eyes rolled back in her head. *Oh God, is she going to die again?* Gertie started moaning but this time she was able to get to her feet, certain that Mary Lee needed her help.

Suddenly Mary Lee's body settled down. Mae Rose was now in charge. She blinked her eyes, looked around the room and then right at Gertie, and raged, "Whose cats are these? I *hate* cats! They destroy everything! Get these awful things away from me, and do it now!" Then she got out of bed, picked up the laptop that had miraculously survived it's impact with the floor, and started writing on the blank screen. Suddenly she stopped and scowled, obviously offended by something.

She sniffed. "What's that smell? Is that cigar smoke? In the bedroom? Dear Lord, how am I supposed to work in this putrid environment?" She looked upward, "Really? Is this necessary?" she asked. "I hope you're not enjoying this!"

Gertie had no idea who Mary Lee was talking to. She watched in complete amazement as Mary Lee ran to the windows and threw them open before taking up her task again. Her fingers flew across the keyboard in a way that even on her best day, Mary Lee would never have been able to accomplish—before she rose from the dead.

Gertie could take no more; she had to get out of Mary Lee's room whatever it took. As she called the very offended cats to come with her, she saw her journal on the floor. She tried to appear nonchalant as she bent to pick it up, still encouraging the cats to follow her.

"What's that, Gertie?" Mae Rose, using Mary Lee's eyes, missed nothing.

"J—just a notepad . . . in—in case I need to . . . to . . . ah . . take notes, Ms. Broadmoor," she lied. "Let's *go* Edgar, Allan, and Poe," she called. "Ms. Broadmoor's orders. On the double." Cats, of course, know nothing about hurrying unless there's an incentive. "Lunch!" Gertie reminded the cats, who were then quite motivated to follow her anywhere.

"Who would name their cats after a horror fiction writer?" Mae Rose asked. Then she paused a moment and giggled. "Oh yes, I guess that would be me, wouldn't it? Since I write horror fiction." She found it so funny, she couldn't stop laughing. It was going to be a challenge to remember that she was now part of Mary Lee. This was Gertie's cue to get out. Mary Lee never laughed about *anything*. Gertie observed the strange contradictions in Mary Lee's behavior and made a mental note to contact Dr. Gregory.

"I like notepads too, Gertie," Mae Rose called after her, her shoulders still shaking with glee. "But that's far too nice of a book for notes. Something tells me you've got more in there than a shopping list." She was thrilled that she could now meddle and get away with it.

She looked Gertie squarely in the eyes. "I wonder, Gertie, if you've got secrets. You really should write something more interesting in such a beautiful book, even if you have to make it up." Mae Rose turned back to her typing. Gertie was in shock. She had never seen Mary Lee show interest in anything of hers, and this was not a moment that she wanted Mary Lee's curiosity to blossom.

A wave of nausea overwhelmed Gertie as she escaped the room. The hallway around her started to look very dark. Just in time, the elevator door opened and Gertie escaped inside, the cats just ahead of her. But she would not feel safe, not for a very long time. She promised herself that she would not tell anyone what she had witnessed. Not *ever.*

22

Allie arrived at 12:27 p.m. Gertie met her at the front door, looking haggard and on the verge of hysteria, which confirmed Allie's suspicion that something very strange had happened during Gertie's call to her. When she told Gertie she was concerned about her mother, Gertie didn't argue. In fact, Gertie didn't say anything. She simply motioned Natalie to go upstairs.

Allie was stunned by what she saw. Her mother didn't acknowledge her at all; she just typed away on her laptop, snickering from time to time and obviously enjoying herself. The typing part was normal. The joy was not.

How can this be my mother? Allie wondered. *She's so different!*

Everything was different: the open windows; the way Mary Lee appeared to dislike the room when she looked up from time to time, sniffing the air and frowning. Allie couldn't concentrate on anything else, not even the distant memory of her mind-blowing sexual encounter with Art . . . *what was his last name anyway?* Finally Mae Rose looked up and saw Allie. She saw that the young woman looked like her son's lover. What would *she* be doing here?

"Don't I know you?" she asked carefully. She felt as though she should know this young woman, but couldn't place her. The effects of being vanished were already at work.

"I'm your only child, Mother," Allie replied carefully. "How are you?"

"My, you're beautiful," Mae Rose replied.

"Thank you, Mother," Allie replied calmly. "I believe that's the first time you've ever said that to me. Are you feeling OK?"

"I feel just wonderful, dear. What's your name, sweetheart?"

"I'm Allie to everyone but you, Mother. You insist on calling me by my proper name, Natalie."

"Why would I do that?" Mae Rose queried.

Before Allie could come back with a choice response such as "because you're a selfish, cold-hearted bitch" or something similar, Mary Lee's eyes rolled back in her head, and her body thrashed wildly on her bed.

"Gertie!" Allie yelled. "Gertie! Something's wrong with Mother!"

Gertie had been keeping her distance, desperate to avoid any questions that Allie might throw at her before she was ready with answers. But Gertie could ill afford to fail in her duties now, no matter what was going on.

"She's had one of these seizures today already," Gertie told Allie truthfully. "T-that's why I called you." Gertie lied and felt dreadful about it, but she couldn't tell the truth because she didn't know exactly what it was yet. "I thought she was dying . . . and then she wasn't." Her eyes filled with tears, thankful that it was close enough to the truth that she could weep. "You have no idea how terrified I was. I think your mother needs to go into the hospital for observation. Her — her behavior, her personality is not normal."

You should talk, Allie thought.

Mary Lee's own energy reappeared and saw Allie sitting beside her bed. "What the *hell* are *you* doing here?" she demanded. "I'm not dead yet." This was the mother Allie knew.

Allie looked at her mother then at Gertie and back at her mother. "You know, something just isn't right," she said to both of them. "Someone is not telling me the truth about what's going on here and I want you to know that I know. You either start filling in the missing details or I'll take matters into my own hands." She was certain there was something only Gertie knew, and Gertie—never before at a loss for words, flirtatious, wicked little Gertie—wasn't talking.

Before she pursued the matter further, Allie needed a medical opinion of her mother's health. She placed an emergency call to Dr. Gregory, not because she thought her mother was dying, but because she was pretty sure her mother looked as if she were going to *live*. When he arrived and confirmed Allie's observations, Gertie excused herself, went down the hall to her room and threw up before she passed out on her bed.

* * *

With Gertie gone, Mary Lee waved both Allie and Dr. Gregory out the door. "You know how I hate to be interrupted while I'm at work. I lost everything I was working on during my illness and now there's real pressure to get this done. Surely you have better things to do than sit here and watch. Besides, it distracts me. I *hate* that. Allie, go downstairs and tell Chef Michael to get Max on the phone right now! Tell him I want to see him as soon as possible— *like today!* And I'm starving. See what Michael can do for me while you're down there. Have him bring up a bottle of wine and my cigars. Otherwise, shoo, both of you." Mary Lee turned back to her laptop.

When they were safely out of hearing range, Allie turned to Dr. Gregory. "Gene, I've never seen my mother like this. That seizure was terrifying. Shouldn't we have her evaluated?"

"I'm a hospice doctor, Allie. She'll need a different doctor to work with on this. By all means, get another opinion. It's good that Gertie's here; she'll keep us informed."

Sure she will, Allie said to herself. To Gene she said, "I think I'll feel better if I stay at the house for a few days. I know Gertie is capable, but this feels like something she can't handle. Did you see how she looks? She's pretty strung out and has behaved strangely all day. When she called me earlier today, I was certain she was about to tell me that Mother had died. She even called me "Natalie dear" in the most sympathetic tone. Then I heard screaming, and the phone went dead. I headed right over. It's peculiar, isn't it, Gene? How could my mother suddenly be so *alive?*"

23

With no one else in the room, Mae Rose and Mary Lee felt at liberty to have a heated discussion inside Mary Lee's body, which to anyone walking by, appeared to be sleeping.

"I can't work in your bedroom!" Mae Rose hissed at Mary Lee. "It smells awful and the decor is so depressing!"

"Maybe you should ask for a different assignment," Mary Lee shot back. "I've smoked cigars all of my adult life, and I'm not going to stop just for *you!* And I spent a fortune on decorating that room just like I wanted it. How dare you insult me and my taste just because it doesn't suit your pansy-assed preference!"

"No wonder you write horror fiction; it suits your decorating style perfectly!" Mae Rose retorted.

As the two women snorted like bulls locking horns, they suddenly felt Mary Lee's body shaking and shrieked as they rocked back and forth. Without realizing it, they were holding onto each other as Mary Lee's body continued to tremble.

"Listen, shhh!" Mary Lee hissed. "I think I hear something."

It was Gertie's voice. "Mary Lee, Max is here. Mary Lee, please wake up. Please!"

"I'm taking this," Mary Lee told Mae Rose. "Max is *my* friend, and I trust him. He'll tell me the truth about what you're writing. I've seen it and it might be a decent story but not my style at all. You wait here; I'll be back." With that, Mary Lee's energy was gone.

* * *

"Max," Mary Lee greeted her old friend.

"Mary Lee!" Max replied, smiling broadly. "I thought you were dead for sure! But look at you and—*mon dieu*—look at the story you're writing! Amazing!" He motioned to the laptop, which he had clearly been reading while Gertie was trying to rouse Mary Lee. "What happened? You must have gone somewhere and had a personality makeover. You've never written anything like this before. It's perfect! Certainly worthy of a look by the academy!" Max was dancing around the room. "Think of the publicity! 'Scary Mary writes a love story!' You'll be the toast of the Academy Awards, or my name isn't Max Goble. I didn't think you had it in you." Mary Lee knew that Max had no idea what she had inside her these days.

"I'm glad you like it, Max. It does feel strange to be writing something like this; it's so different for me. In a way, it feels like I'm not writing it at all. It's like someone else has control of my laptop." Mary Lee was pleased that she had been able to explain the new story to Max in a believable way.

"Bravo!" Max cheered. "Now, when can you have it finished? It's May but if you can get it done by the end of next month, I think we could push it out this year. It would take everything we've got, but you and me, we know how to produce under pressure, don't we?"

"I have to think about it, Max," Mary Lee replied honestly. "Like I said, in a way it doesn't feel like it's my story, so I can hardly say when it will be done. Do you really think an Oscar is possible?"

"More than possible! Just keep writing." Max looked years younger; his eyes were shining with enthusiasm.

"OK, Max," Mary Lee said. "Anything for you."

A somewhat humbled Mary Lee approached Mae Rose after her talk with Max. "Max loves your story," she conceded, "but it's not my style at all. Everyone will know I didn't write it."

"Only if you tell them," Mae Rose replied. "We might as well cooperate, at least until someone can get us out of this mess."

"I don't think that *you* writing a story *I'm* going to take credit for is *cooperating*," Mary Lee advised. "What will I do while you're busy on the story?" she grumbled.

"Get a life, Mary Lee," Mae Rose suggested enthusiastically. "You've got a daughter; you've got money. Stop living in such darkness. Really, look at how you dress." Mae Rose had a hard time controlling her criticism once she had an audience.

"What's wrong with how I dress?" Mary Lee shrieked. "Good God! You move in here like you own the joint and decide everything about me is wrong. You obviously need some of your own medicine or you wouldn't be here! This is *my* body we're sharing. You could show a little gratitude!"

"I didn't say I was perfect, and I'm only trying to help," Mae Rose shot back. Suddenly she was weeping. "I can't help who I am!" she sobbed. "There are just things I know. I can't help it if it hurts people! I'd leave you and your sorry ass behind if I could. Believe me. But what if we're stuck like this for the rest of our lives?"

The two women looked at each other and screamed together at the thought.

"We're going to have to get along, aren't we?" Mae Rose observed. "I'm not sure I know how to do that."

"Me either," Mary Lee agreed. "But we've got to try. If you could keep your insults to one at a time, it might work better." The two women laughed.

"You can be introduced to the world as the 'new' Mary Lee Broadmoor, which would be fabulous based on your history," Mae Rose suggested. "This could also get me off the hook as well. Let's try it, Mary Lee. Let's cooperate and see what happens. I'll handle the story. You do the redecorating or just go have fun. Agreed?"

"OK, deal," Mary Lee agreed and shook Mae Rose's hand, which didn't work very well. Neither did the high-five they attempted.

"I like your daughter," Mae Rose complimented Mary Lee.

"Thank you," Mary Lee replied, genuinely pleased.

"She wants you to call her 'Allie' like everyone else does," Mae Rose offered.

"She can kiss my ass," Mary Lee replied and smiled broadly.

24

When Allie finally made contact with Art Jr. later that evening, she had some explaining to do but she was careful not to give him too much information—such as who her mother was. "Oh, Art, things have been a nightmare! My mother has been quite ill for a long time, and suddenly took a turn for the worse, which then happened to be a change for the better. She's improved so dramatically that it feels like a miracle. We've been watching her closely and I'm staying at her house. I *believe* the worst is over, but we don't know for certain. I hope you don't think I just up and bolted on you. Of all the things in the world I wanted to do, looking after my mother was not one of them, believe me. We don't get along. I wanted to think about what happened between you and me and try to make sense of it. Are you angry?"

"I don't know how to describe what I've been going through; it's nothing I've ever experienced before," Art Jr. replied, so glad that they were talking. "Every time my phone rang or I got an e-mail and it wasn't you, I could hardly stand it."

"I'll give you credit for your persistence," Allie offered, smiling.

"And I'll forgive you for not contacting me in light of the situation you've been in. But I have to see you again, Allie. I can't stop thinking about us. I'll drive to LA if I have to. Just say you want to see me again as much as I want to see you."

"Hopefully the next time we meet we can find a little time to talk, too," Allie teased. "You need to know that the experience we had was a first for me—a big first."

"Me, too, Allie," Art Jr. replied thoughtfully. "I guess we were supposed to meet even though it was a rough first encounter."

"Are you better now? Any long-term damage?" Allie asked.

"Not if I can see you again soon," Art Jr. replied. "I want to know everything about you."

"OK. For starters, I despise LA," Allie told him. "Let's find a place to meet somewhere that's quiet and private."

*   *   *

Later that night, Gertie was startled awake. Had she dreamt that Mary Lee had died and come back to life? With a sense of dread, she pulled her journal out of her smock pocket and studied the last entry. It instantly confirmed what she didn't want to know: that Mary Lee had died. How could she be so alive now? The shock of the day consumed whatever was left of Gertie's resources as an icy dread wrapped her it its chilly embrace. She would not remember that she tucked her journal into her nightstand drawer as she slid into unconsciousness. But she would awaken haunted with knowing that Natalie was staying in the guest suite down the hall. Snoopy, nosy Natalie.

25

"I don't believe it!" Anchorman Jack Riley was nearly speechless as the Best Director Award was announced at the Academy Awards in Los Angeles. "Mary Lee Broadmoor wins a whopping *second* Oscar tonight for her movie, *Something Like That*! And look at old Max Goble, grinning and—I think the old man's crying! That pair are the *last* ones I'd have expected to see on stage tonight! Donna, you're down on the floor. Tell us what it's like!"

"Sure thing, Jack! The applause is absolutely deafening." She faced the camera, her long blonde hair tangled from making her way through the crowd.

"It's going to be tough for the academy to ever outperform tonight's spectacular event. Not only was the reclusive Scary Mary out in public, looking elegant on the arm of her handsome and considerably younger escort, Dr. Eugene Gregory, who, by the way, looked terrified, but she looked fantastic in *both* gowns—one for each Oscar. Did you notice how different she looked in each of them—almost like two different people? It was breathtaking!

"What has everyone astounded is the nature of the movie and its electrifying impact. Known for her Edgar Allan Poe-ish approach to drama and her lifelong aspiration to scare us to the brink of insanity, *Something Like That* is not only the most unexpected film of her career, but one with a huge influence. The film has couples all over the country rekindling the dying embers of their love in the hope of saving their relationships before one of them passes away. It's tender and hilarious, but with touches of Mary Lee's ability to still terrify us. I'm taking my husband to see it this weekend—not that we have anything to fix—but it can't hurt to get the message while you're still in love. Right, Jack? Back to you."

"Sounds like a chick flick to me, Donna," Jack replied with a professional touch of good-humored sarcasm.

"Well, if it *is* a chick flick, as you suggest," Donna retorted with equally devilish good humor, "it's the first one where as many men as women are in the audience. Unfortunately, rumor has it that Mary Lee won't be doing the talk-show circuit. Wouldn't we love to see her on *Currents* with our own Nita Winslow? Sounds like she's headed right back into her hideaway. This is Donna Murray, live from Hollywood. Back to you, Jack, and if I don't see tears in your eyes after you see this movie, you have no heart."

"How much do you want to wager that Nita will be able to get Mary Lee on her show? I've never seen anyone able to resist her for long. She's interviewed the most famous people in the *world*." Jack laughed. "And Donna, can you imagine the dough that this one movie is bringing in? *That's* what really touches me." Jack pulled his hankie out of his suit coat, touched his eyes playfully, and sniffed. He burst out laughing as the station went to a break.

＊　＊　＊

Whatever had happened to Mary Lee Broadmoor, it became the center of attention after the Academy Awards. By not talking about her experience, rumors made their way around the talk-show circuit. Getting Mary Lee on a show would be the crowning achievement of some lucky TV station. Nita Winslow, as if possessed by a devil, determined it would be hers. Mary Lee was as reclusive as she had ever been, which only made Nita more determined.

26

Mae Rose and Mary Lee became inseparable as the best friends that neither of them had truly experienced. They argued about things from time to time, but mostly they shared their ideas and found that it expanded their interests. Mary Lee decided to redecorate her house and accepted some of Mae Rose's suggestions. She also let Mae Rose pick out some of her own favorite clothes to wear. They would watch old movies after dinner, laughing and crying together. At times, they laughed so hard that sharing one bladder was a challenge.

Alcohol or Mary Lee's drugs would affect both of them so they had to be cautious. Getting two people to control one body while under the influence of alcohol was disastrous, as they had learned after they had returned home to celebrate after the Academy Awards. Thankfully, Gertie was still out partying as Mary Lee's body made its way home.

Thus far, Mary Lee's proudest moment was when she taught Mae Rose how to smoke a cigar, which meant that from time to time there were two cigars in her mouth instead of just one. They smoked and played Gin Rummy late at night, when they could have privacy. Anyone present would have seen each of Mary Lee's hands holding cards, as if her right hand were playing against her left hand. That and two cigars in her mouth would have led to questions that neither woman wanted to have to answer.

It might be said that neither Mae Rose nor Mary Lee was the person she had been before they "met." Mae Rose became very engrossed in her abundant life. Whatever had caused her to meddle was totally forgotten. She now lived for the next outfit, the next hairstyle, the next decorating project. She and Mary Lee were deeply engrossed in their next movie and far too busy for Mae Rose to be bothered with the past.

The cast and crew of the movie *Something Like That* had certainly noticed a very different Mary Lee. She was every bit as demanding but not so *mean* or so horrible to work with. Her calmness was startling; her serenity, unfathomable; her confidence, unmatchable. The most shocking thing, they claimed, was how she looked, although her entire personality appeared to have gone through a psychic makeover. Unbeknownst to the rest of the world, she and her body partner, Mae Rose, were having the time of their lives spending Mary Lee's money and playing dress-up.

When she had hair, before her bout with cancer, Mary Lee had always worn it short and spiked. The first day she had reappeared ready to begin shooting *Something Like That,* no one was prepared for the fashion statement that presented itself. At first, no one believed it was Mary Lee at all and they would have been quite correct. Mae Rose had talked Mary Lee into a whole new look.

With her dark hair growing out, Mary Lee's choice of hair color and style became the talk of the studio. In the ensuing months, it would be streaked with honeyed gold and subtle red tones, or recolored to be totally blonde or whatever her hairdresser decided. She wore a different style each day as well. Poor Gertie had to learn to do hair along with a variety of tasks to which she ardently objected. Mary Lee would silence her with money and nighttime trips to haute couture shops.

Mary Lee still routinely wore pants, but traded her formerly famous black jeans for pants of every style and color; her formerly famous white shirt also never appeared again. In a *The Devil Wears Prada* way, she wore a different outfit every day. Whoever was dressing Mary Lee (it was a swooning Mae Rose, given carte blanche) was trendy and hip in a mature, classy way. Not knowing what was going on drove the public mad as they raced to copy her style.

Rather than ranking among the worst-dressed women in Hollywood as she had in the past, Mary Lee began to appear on the covers of various magazines. Her mystery increased her popularity. One magazine carried an entire section called "The Resurrection of Mary Lee Broadmoor." But Mary Lee never posed; she never even saw what the world was seeing, mostly because she didn't care and she despised the media as much as or more than she always had.

Precisely because Mary Lee still didn't give a damn about what anyone thought of her and her work, she claimed the highest honor in show business: being talked about. But her reclusiveness finally drove her publicist over the edge. She resigned after Mary Lee had said "no" to every possible media event. "You don't need me," she declared. "You just need a message recording on your phone that says, 'If you're calling for a media event with Mary Lee Broadmoor, the answer is NO. If you'd like an interview, the answer is THAT WILL NEVER HAPPEN. If you want to know what her next movie is about or when it's coming out, please dial this extension: GOOD LUCK WITH THAT."

While this made it even more difficult for the press to find Mary Lee, some—like Nita Winslow—refused to give up. Gertie learned how to manage the calls that came in and added "receptionist" to her résumé. She was well dressed and well heeled, but her hospice nurse career was over.

27

Chef Michael had finally gotten used to Mary Lee's early-morning visits to the kitchen for a glass of organic orange juice, a protein smoothie, and a large mug of coffee to go. He still woke up wondering when she would get over her *joie de vivre*, so he prepared himself each morning as if that day were the day Mary Lee would become her formerly sour and hateful self.

One morning when he arrived in the kitchen, Mary Lee was already there, prowling for her morning juice. It was only five-thirty, but she was ready for the day and looked good—very good. He whistled. "No one looks that good this early in the morning, Ms. Broadmoor. No one."

"Good morning, Michael," she replied, almost swooning with delight. "Another beautiful day in Beverly Hills! I hated to wake you, so I thought I'd find things for myself. You're going to have to show me where you keep everything. You've got three refrigerators and more cabinets than the president! Get it? Ha!"

Michael smiled tentatively at Mary Lee's humor and set a place for her at the breakfast bar. It had to be the drugs she was still taking that made her so upbeat, he decided. Just then the phone rang. She picked up the phone as she winked at her chef.

"Hello?" she said in a thick Southern accent.

"Hello, I'd like to speak to Mary Lee Broadmoor, please," a woman's smooth voice replied into the phone.

"Who may I say is callin', hon?" Mary Lee queried.

"Would you tell her Nita Winslow is on the phone and—"

"Oh my Lord!" Mary Lee cried into the phone. "You mean *the* Nita Winslow? Are you that talk-show host everyone talks about? Why, I am just speechless! Wouldn't dear Ms. Broadmoor be thrilled to hear from you! But, honey, Ms. Broadmoor is on an extended sabbatical visiting remote areas of the world for her next movie. She's not expected to return for *months*, darlin'." Mary Lee was pleased with her acting skills, and even Michael was smiling. "Do give us a call back in six months or so if you still want to try for an interview. Or you could just give up! Bye now! Oh, and we just *love* your show!" she squealed before slamming the phone down.

"Damn that woman!" she cursed. "Won't she ever give up?" Michael saw a trace of the old Mary Lee; surely one day, she would be her old self again.

Just then Gertie came yawning into the kitchen.

"Why don't you just give in and let her have an interview?" she suggested as she came over to the breakfast bar with a cup of tea and sat beside Mary Lee. "After all, Nita Winslow is well known and respected, like a younger Barbara Walters. It would be a great honor, don't you think?" Gertie knew she was pushing Mary Lee, but just like Michael, she expected Mary Lee's angelic phase to come to an end. It was as if they were both anxious to get it over with.

"Good grief, Gertie! You sound like my publicist—my *former* publicist," Mary Lee exclaimed. "Once I start that, everyone else will think they're also entitled. It will never end. The only way to live in any relative peace is to keep to myself. All of this will blow over. I've just never seen anyone work so hard to get through to me. I'll give Nita Winslow that much. But let's change the phone number again."

Gertie had spent the last ten months working up the courage to tell Mary Lee that she was a hospice nurse, not a secretary, but she hadn't had the heart to tell her she was leaving—not yet when all this drama was going on. Gertie did not know that Mary Lee had plans for her, although the rejuvenated Mary Lee had kept her hopping ever since that day Gertie thought she died. Her generous paychecks made Gertie feel somewhat guilty unless she was being deliciously blackmailed to postpone retirement. *Things could be so much worse.*

"Remind me not to pick up the telephone ever again when it rings." Mary Lee made a face. "I just hate publicity!" she insisted and shuddered.

"Well, I like Nita Winslow," Gertie said, then brightened. "Maybe *I'll* accept the interview on your behalf." She lowered her voice and said dramatically, "And now, ladies and gentlemen, prepare to enter the inner sanctum of the life of Mary Lee Broadmoor. We have with us this evening her former hospice nurse, Gertrude Morgan, who will share with us smoldering secrets of the life of this reclusive woman." Gertie smiled mischievously.

"You just stick to that vacation you're working on for us and schedule those meetings with the design crew for renovations to the house," Mary Lee said dryly but with a soft smile. "I want it redecorated before the holidays. I can't believe how drably I used to live!"

"Ms. Broadmoor, I'm a nurse, not a—" Gertie started to explain.

"Well, I don't need a nurse now, do I?" Mary Lee retorted in her fake Southern accent and smiled. "But your talents go vastly beyond helping the dyin', Ms. Morgan. I think you know that. Besides, I like havin' you around. Don't you, Michael? My own daughter is far too busy and important to visit her own momma, so that makes you all the family I've got," Mary Lee cooed far too sweetly. "Now, Michael, where's my coffee? And pack up my protein drink too. I need to get to the set early today."

"She's definitely breaking," Michael observed after Mary Lee left. "More of her old self coming through and perhaps a bit of dementia? There's no movie; there's no set. Where the *hell* is she going?"

Gertie nodded but kept quiet. She wasn't sure how she felt about whatever Mary Lee was up to, but she'd rather agree with Michael than disagree. He was so testy when someone challenged his opinion, and she wanted to continue her flirting lessons. She leaned toward him and let her bathrobe come loose in order to begin.

28

"Damn that woman! That was Mary Lee herself who answered the phone, or my name isn't Nita Winslow!" She ended the call and slammed her phone on the desk of her LA office, causing her new assistant, Cheryl Lewis, to jump. Cheryl had been deeply engrossed in setting up Nita's next TV interview production. She scowled at being startled out of her editing.

"Well, your real name *isn't* Nita Winslow anyway," Cheryl laughed. "Why don't you just give up? She might be a new woman and res-urrected from the dead, but that part of her hasn't changed a bit." Cheryl's voice was calm and easy. "She hasn't given an interview in over twenty years. Do you really think she's going to start now just because she won a couple of Oscars and her cancer is in remission? She's probably even more determined to stay out of the spotlight."

"Yes, and that's why I want her on *my* show," Nita shot back. "What a coup that will be, and it *will* happen, Ms. Lewis. Mark my words."

Her voice dropped to the whisper pitch she was so good at, the one that caused audiences listening to her interviews to hold their breath. "Something *very* strange has happened to our 'Scary Mary,'" she cooed.

"Think about it. Go back through all of her movies, and look for any of them that are remotely similar to *Something Like That*. There's something very suspicious going on here, and my instincts tell me there's a story." They huddled closer as Nita took Cheryl into her confidence.

"Now, I know Mary Lee Broadmoor appears to have literally been raised from the dead after her diagnosis," she continued. "That does appear to be truly miraculous and maybe that's why she is delivering such different movies. But—and this is the investigator's job—where did she come up with this story? It's too real, too wonderful. She's either discovered a ghostwriter, been handed a new script by God herself, been sent this story by someone else, plagiarized some unknown author, or who knows what? But something's up and we're going to find out!" Nita growled the last words as she slammed her left hand on her desk for emphasis, her ring finger obviously bare. There was no time for a man in her quest for the ultimate story.

Nita pushed her half glasses down on her nose and peered over them. "So as soon as you're finished with this upcoming show, I want *you* to get on *this* story. You're a former detective. I want you to find every woman who has died of a heart attack in the past ten years between ages fifty and sixty, just like the movie. I want a widower in the Midwest; look for towns named "Fair" anything. The man should be some kind of a collector with two twenty-something sons. Miracle? My ass. Resurrection? Hardly. If Scary Mary is not going to tell us what's going on, we're going to find out ourselves, and then she'll talk. Just watch!" Nita put on her phone headset to do what she did best. The investigation had begun.

Cheryl smiled and returned to her work, now anxious to get the current show on its way to wrap-up. *The Scary Mary Query*, as she decided to call this new project, would be so much more interesting.

29

One year had passed since Mae Rose died, one year exactly. Art and his boys were at her grave with her favorite flowers; Jill King had made up the bouquet. Art Jr. was a resident in internal medicine at the regional medical center and had completed his application process with GloMed International. He was almost always on the phone with Allie, who remained somewhat of a mystery to the rest of the McElroy family. Every so often, Art Jr. would disappear for a few days. It was always a secret place but he'd come back more in love than ever each time. Art knew that his eldest son's girlfriend wanted to go back to her work on the Amazon; he half expected Art Jr. to end up there as well.

John, on the other hand, had married his high school sweetheart, Elliana, at the end of last year after completing his two-year associate's degree in computer science. He was such a wiz that he already had enough clients to start his own business. Elliana was a receptionist at Fairview's Domestic Crisis Center and planned to devote her career to helping women who were victims of domestic violence. The young couple chose the cemetery visit to announce that Art's first grandchild was on the way. It was both a sad and joyous occasion.

For Art, there had been no other woman since Mae Rose. It's not that they didn't exist; it was simply impossible for any one of them to fill Mae Rose's shoes. Folks around town suggested that he get out more, and he did try. But mostly he sat at home in the evenings, composing a love song to Mae Rose. He'd been working on it for months. He had titled it "The Richest People in the World."

If every raindrop were a dollar and every grain of sand pure gold,
It would not begin to measure the love for you I hold.
And it doesn't make a difference no matter what I'm told.
I was the richest man in the world.

He already knew that the second verse would be sung by a woman. He couldn't imagine anyone singing with him but Mae Rose, except that she'd never been able to carry a tune.

"Still miss her, Dad?" Art Jr. asked as they looked at Mae Rose's simple grave site marker with their arms around each other.

"You know, she's every bit as alive today as she ever was," Art replied. "And I understand her so much better than I did when she was. Sad but true. I miss her like hell. Love it if she could see the barn now," he added, smiling. "If she could know that there's a baby being born in our family, well . . ." Art stopped and reached into his pocket for a hankie to wipe his eyes.

John put a comforting hand on his father's shoulder. "Hey, Dad, what are you doing this afternoon?" he asked. "Elliana and I are going to a movie. Sounds like a sappy chick flick to me, but you two would know how women are when they're first pregnant. It's better just to give them whatever they want. Want to come along? I could use some male support." He grinned. "Supposed to be absolutely life-changing. Won a couple of Oscars last month. It's called *Something Like That*. Strange name for a movie if you ask me."

"Nope, thanks son," Art replied. "You know I'm not much of a movie man, and if there's any love or romance, it would be too difficult. I'm going to spend the afternoon in the barn. There's plenty of work to do on that 'retirement project' I've got going."

"OK, Dad!" John laughed. "We'll check in with you later."

The barn was now Art's own VW restoration shop. Since he had officially retired, he spent most of his time there, still working on the seven VWs he had collected while Mae Rose was alive. Everything that Mae Rose saw in Art, all the creative work she always begged him to do, had come alive. He didn't understand why he couldn't see all of this when Mae Rose did. Slowly but surely those seven VWs were taking shape, although in the end it would be only six as one of them disappeared as parts for the others.

30

Art was in the barn hours later when the shop phone rang. He picked up the phone and heard John's voice, which sounded as if he'd seen a ghost.

"Dad," he said in a vacant, hollow tone.

"John, what's wrong?" Art asked as thoughts of Elliana and the baby came to mind.

"Dad," John said again as if he didn't even hear his father. "I think I should come over and see you for a few minutes. Elliana agrees. Mind if I stop by?"

"No, Son, sure don't. But you sound sort of strange, and I don't want you driving over here if something's wrong. Is Elliana OK? The baby? Want me to come over to your place?" Art asked. "Let me clean up. Say, half an hour?" Art suggested as he wiped his hands off and headed for the house. "You take it easy; I'll be right there."

"Thanks, Dad," John said.

John and Elliana lived in a large, old Victorian house on the north side of town. It was a small lot but a nice enough house. Art had helped with some of the remodeling over the past year since they purchased it; Elliana was doing a wonderful job with the gardens. It comforted Art to see the two of them settling happily into married life; it was also painful. He remembered those joyful early days of married life with Mae Rose and how quickly they had passed.

Art hurried up the steps and before he could ring the doorbell, John opened the front door, looking pale and grave—like he had been crying.

"Dad, come in," John said. He motioned his father into the living room. There was no hug or welcome, as if two of them were complete strangers. "Let me call you back. Dad just got here," he said into the phone. Art assumed correctly that Art Jr. was on the other end.

"Son, you want to tell me what this is all about?" Art asked as he took off his jacket. John went to his overstuffed recliner but didn't recline. Art sat in the middle of the matching sofa and leaned forward.

"Dad, I don't even know where to begin," John said as he put his head in his hands in anguish.

"I can't help much if I don't know what the topic is," Art offered kindly.

"I took Elliana to the movies today," John began.

"I know," Art offered. "Was it a good show?"

"It was great, Dad, honestly. It made you rethink your marriage in a very real way. I mean, it was more than just a movie; it was more like an experience. Except . . ."

"Except what?" Art asked.

"Dad, I have to ask you a personal question," John said, and Art could tell his son was choking up. "It's about you and Mom."

Art could feel his own heart pause as time warped into slow motion. This had to be about the affair. He didn't know how his sons had found out, but he knew they knew. Art was instantly sick to his stomach.

"Sure, Son," he replied, clearing his own throat and suddenly wondering what to do with his arms and legs. He'd been sitting with his right leg over his left, leaning forward on the sofa with his hands in his lap, fingers crossed slightly. Now everything felt staged. He shifted uncomfortably as the scene unfolded.

"Dad, did . . . did you ever. . . I mean . . . you know . . . were you ever—? God, I can't even ask this." John set his jaw then forced the words out of his mouth. "Were you ever unfaithful to Mom?"

"Yes Son, I was," Art replied numbly. He wasn't going to lie about it. "Your mother and I agreed that it didn't concern you boys, so we didn't tell you. You want to tell me how you found out?"

"Dad, this movie . . . I can't explain it, but it was about our lives, Dad. *Ours.* Or at least yours and Mom's. The woman died on the toilet, Dad." John's voice started to break, "after a horrible fight with her husband. It was almost like someone was looking in on our lives and recording it. The barn cats, the yellow roses. I was there when it really happened. The only piece in the movie that I didn't recognize was that the husband has an affair, and that's what finally makes his wife want to die." John stopped speaking for a moment, his weeping too strong for words. Finally he took a deep breath and continued. "And I can't—can't bear it, Dad. Because if the rest of the movie was about our family, this has to be true too. And I hate you for it."

John straightened up and when he looked at his father, there was a glare in his sad eyes, a hauntingly familiar glare. "I had to know, Dad, because I remember her." John sniffed and pulled a hankie from his jeans. "Maggie Whitman. How Mom hated her! Maybe there was a reason I wasn't able to face it at the time. Now I have to." He continued to glare with tears streaming down his face.

"John, there's no way to go back now. If I could, believe me, I would." Art's voice broke. "You have no idea how many regrets I have about your mother and me. You don't know how I've suffered. Part of me is glad you know, even if you hate me for it. I deserve it."

"How long? How long did it last?" John lashed out.

"Three years," Art replied with his head in his hands.

"My God, Dad!" John yelled. "*Three years?* It's just like the movie, I tell you! Someone has taken our lives and put it on the movie screen. Except in the movie, the woman gets reincarnated and returns to fix what went wrong when she was alive. Wouldn't that be nice?" he added bitterly.

Art fumbled miserably with his keys. "John, it was a very long time ago and there's nothing I can do or say that will help you or your brother with this. There has never, ever been another woman in my life before or since. I live full of regret every day. I don't know what else to tell you, and I only hope I've done the right thing now. God, how I wish your mother were here! She'd know how to handle this."

"Well, she's *not*, is she?" John retorted. "You know what I think? I think your affair killed our mother! In some way, between that and your stubborn insistence that you were right about everything—the way you opposed her, even about barn cats—you killed her, and I hate you for that, too! I hate how you never, *ever* gave her credit, and now we've got two issues to deal with, maybe three. Number one is Art Jr. and I have to get used to this. How do we do that? Number two is that somehow we have to find out who wrote this story and how it made it onto the movie screen. *It won two Oscars,* Dad! It's got to be illegal to take someone's life and put it into a movie without their permission. Number three, we have to have a way to respond to this because others are going to ask questions. It's too much like our real lives. This could get public, and it could get messy."

John paused, too stunned to speak for a moment, then went on. "Fairview is a small country town. The VW is in the movie, the flower shop, the barn cats—and Mom dying on the toilet. Dad, we have to stop this regardless of how we feel." His voice faltered as he choked on his sobs. "Please, if you ever loved her, if you care about us, help us find a way through this."

Art was instantly angry. "I loved your mother, John, and don't you ever think otherwise! She was tough to love, but I gave it everything I had. I was just as hard to live with, but we loved each other the best we could. Don't you *ever* judge something you don't understand!"

Leaning forward on his thighs with his head still in his hands, Art studied the threadbare weave of his jeans. "Son, none of this changes how I feel about you boys or about your mother," he said carefully, each word awakening his grief. "After all is said and done, I realize how much I loved her, and that's been a hard lesson to face when it's too late to do anything about it. I'm old enough now not to care what the world thinks of *me*, but I sure don't want you and Art Jr. to be hurt."

"Too late, Dad," John retorted.

"Maybe we should talk to Pastor Frank and then decide what to do," Art offered. "Right now I'm going to go home to talk to your mother and God. That's all I know to do. I am so sorry, and that doesn't begin to describe how I feel." Art stood up to leave.

"I'm assuming this won't come as a surprise to him," John commented.

"No, he knows everything," Art told his son honestly. "He sat with us as your mother and I made the decision that we would not tell you boys about this."

"Who else knows?" John asked.

"Well, Maggie, of course, and she's been very faithful as far as respecting this decision." Art wanted to defend her to his children.

"Poor choice of words." John seethed, clenching his fists. Art wished he would go ahead and hit him.

"Perhaps," Art said sadly. "But I know she's not the source of any leak, if there is one. I have no idea."

"Grandpa Henry?"

"No, no one else," Art replied.

"That you know of," John retorted. "Secrets are just that way, I guess. It always comes out one way or the other. But you know what? I'm glad I know because it really explains a lot. Whatever you and Mom thought you were saving us from, just know that you didn't. It would kill Grandpa if he knew, you know. But now *I* know, and that means *I* have to hide this from him unless I want him to suffer too. Just great, Dad." John shook his head.

Art could not stand the judgment from his son, as though no one else on Earth had ever committed such an act. "I hope you and your brother will accept that there are things that happen in life that are best kept private—like where and how we found your mother when she died. You have to able to live with that."

"Even that's not a secret any longer since the movie came out," John spat.

"Except that so far no one knows that piece, except *us*, John." The silence between father and son was marked by the ticking of the antique mantle clock Art had restored and given John and Elliana as a wedding present.

"I suppose Elliana knows?" Art asked as he cleared his throat.

"Of course she does!" John retorted. "We don't keep secrets from each other! If you see the movie, you'll understand why the question regarding the affair came up. Like I said, *it's all there—every awful detail.* The only thing they changed were the names—to protect the guilty, I guess," he finished.

"OK, well, I guess I should be on my way, then," Art said as he headed to the door.

John did not move to embrace his father, to tell him good-bye, or to see him to the door.

"I hope we can meet with Pastor Frank for all of our sakes. In the meantime, I really don't want to see you," John said evenly with clenched fists.

Art shut the front door behind him and walked slowly to his truck. He knew that life as he had accepted it, without Mae Rose, but centered on his sons' love and care, had just ended. He put his head on the steering wheel and went limp.

"Touché," he said to whoever had brought this to light. Payback was a bitch. He turned on the engine and somehow found his way home. A light rain made the roads wet enough to be hazardous, but there were no cliffs to accidentally drive off, no trees to slam into, and no unnavigable curves, in short, no way to end his life without it looking intentional. Whatever was left of Art's heart was broken. Whatever dignity he thought he had still possessed after Mae Rose died now lay in pixels on movie screens all over the world.

31

Pastor Franklin Matthews had been the lead minister of Good Shepherd Presbyterian Church since he graduated from seminary. Now in his mid-sixties, he had watched his flock grow from only a handful of parishioners to a fully packed service twice each Sunday morning.

As he sat with Art in the same room and the same brown leather chair as when he had met with Art and Mae Rose over two decades earlier regarding the affair, Pastor Frank ran fingers through his wiry, chestnut brown hair that was now heavily streaked with gray. As he had listened to Art's painful retelling of the prior day's events, he knew that nothing in his ministry had prepared him for an issue of this potential magnitude except for his deep, abiding faith in God, who he now leaned on heavily in prayer with Art.

"And now, Lord, we resist Satan and his wicked influence in our lives. We give You the glory and the praise. We claim victory for this man, his family, this church, this community, this country, and the world, for all things work together for good to them that know You. In Jesus's name. Amen."

Art had always found comfort in Pastor Frank's deeply earnest voice, especially when he was in prayer. It was as if Pastor Frank and the Lord knew each other in a personal way, almost like golf buddies. Art echoed the "Amen" and sat quietly observing the man who had counseled him all of his adult life.

It was Pastor Frank who broke the silence that followed. "How would you feel, Art, if instead of pursuing this thing legally, we simply did some research on our own? While I concur that legal counsel could be advisable, I think it's a long shot to expect to have grounds to sue a movie director who has had no contact with you or your family. I respect John's concern that this could become public and affect your family negatively, but the movie is already world-renowned. It might be best just to see what happens."

Pastor Frank paused for a moment as if checking in with God before making the next comment. "It also might interest you to know that while you see this as an indignity to your family, the film is so magnificently done that even in our own church, I've had calls from couples who want counseling to set things right between them. Not one of them has mentioned any similarities to your own family, Art. *Not one.* They are completely focused on their own relationships. I believe what really needs focus is your relationship with Art Jr. and John. I'm certain that's our real priority."

"OK. Sure." Art agreed, feeling great relief that he didn't have to take any sudden or drastic legal action. "That makes sense. It's just an awful way for my boys to hear about my . . . my indiscretion. I would have told them myself years ago if I'd had any idea this could have happened. Mae Rose would have agreed one thousand percent."

"Yes, I know she would have," Pastor Frank reassured Art and smiled as he remembered Mae Rose. He had always enjoyed her, even when she took an all-out assault on an issue, whether it was how her boys were doing in school, the affair, or "What are we going to do for the Tilson family now that Herman is out of work?" Mae Rose always made certain that people in need were taken care of when things went wrong.

"Will the boys come to see me?" His earnest compassion was Pastor Frank's most endearing trait; his interest in the lives of his parishioners was legendary. Sometimes, like now, he was so focused on what was occurring that he didn't realize his glasses had slid down his nose and he had to peer over them, which made him look even more . . . godly? His bright blue eyes sparkled with compassion.

"I think so," Art replied. "They don't want to talk to me right now, so . . ." Art choked. "I think it's best if you contact them directly. They're pretty upset that you've known about the affair all this time too. They don't understand and I can't blame them. I'm totally discredited, but I think they'll talk to you because you were not part of the problem."

"Any contact with either of them since yesterday?" Pastor Frank turned halfway around in his chair, looking for a book on the library shelf behind his cluttered desk.

"No. Not from either of them." Art's voice broke. "I don't know if they'll ever speak to me again." He sighed deeply as tears fell from his eyes. It was unutterably awful to have lost his wife. To have his sons turn against him now was beyond bearing.

"Why, oh why couldn't I see things then the way I do now?" he begged Pastor Frank. "Why didn't I see all the good and beautiful things that Mae Rose tried to do, and how her passion was essential to who she was, instead of my letting it drive me crazy? Now that she's gone, I'm doing all the things that would have made her so happy. What was it that came between us so that we never really saw each other? I don't know how to live without her, and if I lose my sons over this, how do I carry on?" Art was too overcome to speak further. Great gasping sobs consumed him.

"Art, brother," Pastor Frank walked around his desk to put his hand on Art's shoulder. "I do understand your suffering," he said. "It's the plight of the shepherd to feel the woes of his flock, you know. My heart is with you—all three of you." After a moment, he returned to his desk and his bookshelf. He laughed softly, causing Art to look up.

"That wife of yours was something else, Art," Pastor Frank told him. "Most of us watched the two of you and wondered how you endured her strong will. Oh, I agree that she was right about so many things, but she sort of flattened the rest of us in the process. It was like the two of you had to build boundaries around yourselves in order to survive each other. But the one thing that we all got was the *love*. No matter what, you loved each other; that was plain as day. Always focus on what was good about your marriage, Art."

Pastor Frank paused for a moment, still searching his bookshelves. "I would prefer that the boys talk to me before we take any further action, if that's OK with them and you," he said over his shoulder. Art took comfort in the sense of authority emanating from Pastor Frank, as if he were taking charge of this delicate and wounded situation.

Art wiped his eyes and face with his hankie and stood up to smooth out his jeans. "What about Maggie?" he asked. "I sort of feel like she should be aware of what's going on now that the boys know and all," he explained.

"Do what your heart tells you, Art," Pastor Frank replied. "I'm also going to suggest a family counselor for you and the boys."

"Thank you, Pastor," Art said.

Pastor Frank turned to face Art, his glasses on the tip of his nose again. "And thank *God*," he reminded Art. "Always thank *God*."

*   *   *

Art Jr. and John sat in Pastor Frank's office three days later. Neither of them was comfortable in the crowded space. The only times they'd been in the office together was when their mother thought they needed counseling for some reason and most recently to make funeral arrangements for her—all memories they would rather put behind them.

"How are you doing, boys? And I want it up front and honest," Pastor Frank began. "I've known both of you all your lives, and I think that makes for a special relationship. What's on your minds?"

"I think you know what's on our minds without us going into very much detail," John snapped bitterly. "We feel like Dad's been dishonest with us, and we're pretty upset with what we've learned about him and Mom. I guess we always thought that no matter what, Mom and Dad stuck together and stayed true. Now we know that was not the case and that changes the dynamics of our relationship with Dad. Right now I hate him and I blame him for Mom's death." John's emotions didn't allow him to continue.

"Art?" Pastor Frank turned to the elder of the two boys and waited.

"Well, I feel pretty much like John does," Art replied. "I don't like my dad very much right now. But the more immediate problem is that movie. I haven't seen it yet, and I'm not sure I want to, but I'm concerned about how the people who know us will respond. It feels like someone who knew us pretty well has betrayed us."

"I think it was Maggie Whitman!" John suggested angrily. "She's the only one who knew Dad well enough and would have had a motive to want to hurt Mom. Someone ought to question her." He added, "She doesn't deserve to live."

"That's a pretty strong statement, John," Pastor Frank said candidly, "but I'm glad you're able to express how you feel here. Have either of you been approached by someone who's seen the movie and suggested that it's about your life?" Pastor Frank asked.

Both boys shook their heads. "But it's just a matter of time," John lashed out. "I'm afraid to even go out in public now."

"I believe you can both rest a bit easier on that score," Pastor Frank encouraged. "If no one has done that by now, I don't think they're going to. Plus, I don't believe it could have come from Maggie. She wouldn't know intimate details about your family, and she is an honest woman."

"Bullshit!" John hollered. "I guess she knew our dad pretty intimately, though. Fuck this bullshit!" He stood up and paced the small room. "I don't know if I can take any more of this," he said evenly as he seethed.

Pastor Frank sat quietly, asking God for wisdom. "Whatever you think of how your parents decided to handle this, it was because they loved you that they did not tell you." He leaned over his desk toward them. "That is the most important thing for you to know. It's not uncommon for adults to spare their children from the uglier details of these hurtful aspects of life. It's just that in this case, somehow or other, God arranged it that you were meant to know."

"I don't think God had anything to do with our father's actions," John retorted.

"We're not looking for excuses, John," Pastor Frank replied quietly but firmly. "We're looking for a way through this so that you and your father can find a way back to each other. Your mother would be devastated to know what has come about. She was the one who was so very firm in her belief that you should be spared."

"Art, why aren't you saying anything?" John blew up at his brother. "You're as messed up about this as I am!" He turned to Pastor Frank. "I'd be in some sort of counseling if I were in a relationship that caused me to even consider doing what Dad did!" He stopped talking and put his head in his hands.

Art spoke in the silence. "I've seen some messed-up families in my medical career," he said. "I just never imagined that ours could be one of them. I think we all need help to get through this."

"You are such a pansy ass!" John yelled at his brother. "'I think we all need help to get through this'?" he mimicked his brother. "How can you just sit there like that and say such meaningless crap?"

"Maybe because I'm older and I've seen some pretty tough stuff in my career, little brother. Put a lid on it, or I'll take you outside! Sit down and grow up!" Art Jr. had had enough of John's rage.

"Would you be willing to go into counseling with your father?" Pastor Frank asked when he sensed both boys had settled down. "It would be with someone whose work I respect," he added. "Here's a book he wrote. I think it's perfect for what you're going through."

Art Jr. took the book from Pastor Frank titled *The Disillusioned Family: When Our Most Intimate Relationships Fail to Live Up to Our Expectations.* "I'll look at it," he offered. "But our relationship with our father is never going to be the same."

Pastor Frank cleared his throat and said, "You're right, Art. But you can also think of it as a new beginning. He's more human to you; that's not necessarily bad. The truth does set us free, no matter how ugly it looks or how painful it is. In spite of everything, your father is relieved of a great burden of hiding his affair from both of you.

"I hope you can forgive your father," he went on. "He lives each day conscious of his unfaithfulness and will for the rest of his life. Let me know how you want to proceed."

"What about the movie?" John asked. "What are we going to do about that?"

"I've already done some preliminary research on the Internet. Kind of interesting," Pastor Frank said.

Both young men looked at him in surprise. Pastor Frank was not the technological type. He and their father had a lot in common when it came to computers and the web: they both knew nothing.

Pastor Frank smiled. "I guess you could say I've come out of the Stone Age just for your family. The woman who wrote, directed, and produced the movie is Mary Lee Broadmoor. She's famous for her horror films, her horrible personality, and has never written anything like this. Also, she has late-stage pancreatic cancer, which appears to have gone into remission. Pretty miraculous, they say. She doesn't like publicity, sort of a hermit type. Lives alone. Won't talk to anyone about the movie, but the same rumor mill says she's been changed by it. That's about it. I think it would be tough to build a case against her, and it could cause more attention—exactly the opposite of what you'd be hoping to accomplish."

"Well, I intend to find out how she got this story anyway," John announced. "And whoever it was is going to be in trouble, no matter what you say about it, Pastor Frank. You can't take someone's life and make it into a movie without their permission. Thanks for your time."

John and Art got up, shook the Pastor's hand, and left together.

Pastor Frank put his head down on his desk and cried out to God. It was thirty minutes before he lifted it back up and dialed Art with the news that the boys had been in.

32

It was time for Mary Lee's one-year checkup. She sat with her feet dangling off the side of the doctor's examination table, wearing nothing but a skimpy piece of cloth they had the audacity to call a "gown." It amused her that even the most famous people in the world did this, including the president of the United States, the Dalai Lama, George Clooney—they all wore this attire at one time or another. She burst out laughing.

The door opened and Dr. Roberta Greyson walked in. "Glad you're in such a good humor," she said as she looked at Mary Lee's chart. "You must already know the good news that your cancer is still in remission. You've passed the one-year mark, so congratulations, Mary Lee. You are a survivor of one of the toughest cancers on record. *Always* fatal at stage IV," she added as she looked at Mary Lee and smiled. "You're a walking, talking miracle, Ms. Broadmoor, which means that you get to go to the head of the class in my Comeback Club."

The Comeback Club was a group of patients that Roberta managed and observed as they progressed out of the critical stages of these rare cancers. She monitored all aspects of their lives, calling attention to their successes in their "recovery journey," while looking for clues to the puzzle of cancer and what it was that enabled each of these few but amazing Comeback Club members to overturn a terminal diagnosis. Simple cancers did not interest her, only the impossible ones, for she knew that even these would eventually fall to the scientific discoveries being made every day. She planned to be on the team that found the answer to cancer. Roberta had studied pancreatic cancer since she was a child and lost her mother to it when she was only seven.

In her mid-forties, Roberta could have been a reasonably attractive woman, but the stress of her career and her care for the suffering of others was etched deeply on her face, causing her to look much older. She cared nothing for her appearance or how the world perceived her. Perhaps it was the relentless pursuit of a cure that aged her, or perhaps it was reaching beyond medical science into complementary aspects and living in that strange, tense place in between. Her alternative approach isolated her from traditionalist colleagues who remained steadfast to the science in which they had been educated. She knew that throughout history, every new discovery met with disdain and resistance before it was accepted. It was no different now. She was tough enough to endure it, but it didn't do much for her social life.

"You know, I don't even think of that diagnosis anymore," Mary Lee commented. "As far as I'm concerned, it was just a bad dream and it's over."

"And that's why we will continue to schedule these appointments, Ms. Broadmoor," Dr. Greyson retorted with a scolding look over her black-framed glasses. "It's our job to make certain that optimism doesn't overtake reality, although I am convinced that it certainly has an impact on the results."

"Why don't we want optimism to overtake reality, Roberta?" Mary Lee asked. "Would that be so bad? Personally, I think *dis*ease, as we call it, comes from our bad attitudes, and I should know. It's as if our bodies breed illness through our negative thoughts at the cellular level. I'll just bet you that in ten years, 'thought science' will be a cutting-edge theory, and I intend to be here when it is."

"Speaking of which, we could all use another one of your uplifting movies, Mary Lee. Anything in the works?" Finished with her exam, Roberta made a few notes in Mary Lee's file then leaned against the examining room counter and crossed her arms with

Mary Lee's folder against her chest, looking as if she had all the time in the world.

"That's confidential of course," Mary Lee replied, smiling. "However, I might need your help with this one—a reference per- haps. My latest story will take a journey into our concept of the disabled in our society. I'm learning how atrociously ignorant we are about these amazingly different but precious people. Even the word we use to describe them is insufferable! *Dis*abled, my ass! I call them 'dis-labeled.'" She smiled. "With any luck, the movie will come out in a couple of years, but there's a lot of work to be done, especially on the research side. No one knows about this endeavor, not even my house staff. I'm working offsite on it. They see me leave early in the morning and they know I'm going somewhere, but they have no idea where; it's *that* confidential. I even change the location and my driver from time to time."

"That's incredible, Mary Lee!" Roberta replied enthusiastically. "I'd be honored if I can help in any way. We all need to look at life differently. And you're right. There are plenty of people who appear 'normal' who are more *dis*abled than those we call by that word." Roberta walked over to Mary Lee and, in an undoctorly way, put her hand on top of Mary Lee's. "Go and write another miracle. Remember that you are a walking one, and come back to see me in a year, sooner if you have any symptoms that become a concern. Promise?"

"Oh, I promise," Mary Lee replied, smiling. "Just don't expect anything but boring, consistent reports of my continued health and well-being. See you in a year, Roberta, and make a mental note that the year after that you'll be attending a social event: my next movie's premiere. Please mark your calendar. You'll be invited, of course. Consider this an early invitation so that you can pull your nose out of your research for an evening. And bring a date, would you?"

Roberta laughed, looking years younger for a brief moment. "Which reminds me." She stopped with her hand on the doorknob. "Dr. Gregory looked incredibly interested in you at the Oscars—

couldn't take his eyes off you! Is there anything I should know about that? Love is a powerful cure," she added.

Mary Lee scoffed. "I'll stick with laughter as the best medicine. And no, there's nothing whatsoever going on between Gene and me."

"You mean Dr. Gregory, of course," Roberta laughed.

"Whatever his name is." Mary Lee smiled deceptively. "I needed an escort, and I don't know that many decent men—probably because there aren't any. Ha! It seemed a fitting tribute since he took such good care of me during my hospice phase. And he was smiling at me because he was terrified to look anywhere else. He's so shy! That's all there was to it. So how's *your* love life, Roberta?" Mary Lee shot back at her doctor. "Gene would be perfect for you."

Dr. Greyson laughed and left the room.

* * *

Mary Lee dressed slowly and easily. There was a luxury in knowing the difference between illness and health, which she now understood completely. She appreciated everything she used to take for granted, even simple things such as putting on her clothes. The feel of the fabric against her skin was divine. Her old work attire had been packed up and shipped off to Natalie's family shelter, where she expected her daughter would ensure they were auctioned for a goodly sum as "The Working Attire of Mary Lee Broadmoor." *That's my Natalie!* Mary Lee thought proudly. Something poked her in the ribs. *It's Allie!*

These days, Mary Lee—the delightful blend of Mary Lee and Mae Rose—was all about color, mostly soft hues and subtle prints, but clingy, sumptuous, and trendy. Even her undergarments had to feel and look sensuously perfect. Her clothing budget had shot up, especially since she had taken Gertie under her fashion wing.

Mary Lee enjoyed dressing Gertie up, and Gertie, who was still plump, appreciated the fashion-savvy shopkeepers who took care of that issue nicely. While Mary Lee typically invited Natalie along, her daughter always protested Mary Lee's newly discovered frivolity. Plus, she abhorred the thought of shopping with Gertie in tow while watching her mother spend ridiculous sums of money. Allie emphatically lived what she believed. And *that* was another attribute Mary Lee was quite certain she had imparted to her daughter.

Yet the new Mary Lee continued to do everything in absolute privacy. Not only did she shop in the dark but now that her movie was complete, all of her beautiful clothes were worn only at home or on the new movie set, for she refused to go out where the public could see her. She wasn't sad about it or bitter about being alone. Her life was so complete, so full, and exciting that there really wasn't room for others—unless you counted Mae Rose's spirit separately.

The all-consuming enjoyment of writing her next script, the secrecy of it, and her discovery of all things beautiful was more than enough to keep Mary Lee captivated. House renovations were under way, and Gertie was authoritative—and flirtatious—enough to handle the workmen. Mary Lee smiled, for she was quite certain that Gertie was enthralled to have so many men at her command. She was Mary Lee's friend, helper, and shopping partner—almost like a daughter without the complex emotional aspects. Yes, Mary Lee's life was almost perfect.

As she approached the nurses' station, Mary Lee tensed slightly, hoping to make her way past without being seen. She hurried her step and, lost in her thoughts, collided with Eugene Gregory.

"Ms. Broadmoor!" Gene exclaimed. "Were you going to leave without saying good-bye?" He was wearing a classic white polo shirt with gray trousers, and he looked gorgeous.

"Why, Dr. Gregory!" Mary Lee replied, surprised but happy to see him. "Whatever are you doing here amongst the living? I thought you only hung around with those of us who were knocking insistently on death's door!" She laughed easily.

"I'll admit that I missed our visits so much that I asked Dr. Greyson to let me know when you were in for an appointment. I hope you don't mind. You are one of the very few of my patients who have ever left our wing of the hospital and returned to the living. That makes you—" he folded his hands together, touching his index fingers to a point, which he directed at Mary Lee, "fascinating. Everything going well for you?" he asked.

"Yes, and I intend to keep it that way," Mary Lee replied firmly. "If I can just keep public attention away, all will be well. I deplore it when people fuss over me, as you well know," she said loudly enough for the staff to hear.

"Are you leaving?" he asked.

"Yes," she laughed gaily, "and I'm not planning to return for another year, although I know how stunning health bores the medical community. Poor Dr. Greyson and I had very little to talk about."

"Then allow me to escort you downstairs," Gene suggested as he took Mary Lee's elbow and guided her to the elevator.

"Thank you, Doctor," Mary Lee replied with a teasing touch of formality. "That would be most gracious of you." Their dialogue felt so much like a stage set that she expected to hear someone say, "Cut. Let's do that again and make it look a little more real. It sounded too much like you were reading the script."

The door to the elevator opened; Gene held it back while Mary Lee stepped inside. When the door closed, Gene turned to Mary Lee and put an arm on the wall behind her, almost like an embrace. "How are you really doing, Mary Lee? I miss our visits. You've gone hermit again. I hope our little excursion into the limelight didn't offend you. You looked well in command that night, and I thought it would draw you out. Instead it seems to have sucked you deeper into the darkness." His voice took on a ghostly tone, which made Mary Lee smile.

"The public holds no interest for me, Doctor," Mary Lee replied, giggling. "You of all people know that. And you're one to talk! It took two Oscars to get you out of your apartment for an evening! Fame is such a shame," she lamented. "It makes me visible when my work requires me to be alone and left to my imagination. I can't create if I'm plagued with social engagements, interviews, and the like."

"My dear Ms. Broadmoor," Gene whispered quietly as the elevator stopped at the lobby level, "we are like two peas sharing a pod;

both of us prefer isolation. Surely you would want the pleasure of some understanding company from time to time. I am so glad for your health except that I don't get to visit you any longer. You know my work is confined to the dying," he said in such a chill whisper that Mary Lee shuddered deliciously, wondering if Dr. Gregory were coming on to her in some strange way.

"Perhaps something can be arranged," she replied with a wink as the door opened. They stepped off the elevator, looking like the perfectly civil doctor and patient. "You'll be the first to know." He gave her his arm, and they headed toward the main entrance visitor parking area, where Mary Lee's limo would be waiting.

As they stepped companionably outside, cameras clicked, flashed, and hummed. Insistent voices called out. "What's the report, Mary Lee?" "Is it scary?" "How's your health?" "When is your next movie coming out?" "Please smile, both of you." "Ms. Broadmoor and Dr. Gregory, please look this way." "You were together at the Oscars." "Are the two of you involved in a romantic relationship?"

Gene's strong arms pulled Mary Lee back into the building and walked her quietly to a bank of chairs. She heard a voice suggesting that she sit down. Stunned and shaking, she said, "I hate crowds. Have I ever told you?" She turned to place her hand on Gene's arm for support, but he was no longer there. She looked around a bit frantically and saw him at the information desk, issuing instructions as he pointed toward the door. Unfamiliar feelings of panic began to set in.

Nevertheless, a voice responded, "No, you haven't told *me* anything yet, Mary Lee Broadmoor. Don't you think it's time?" She knew that voice. As she looked up, Nita Winslow set down a copy of *People* magazine.

"What on Earth are *you* doing here?" Mary Lee asked angrily.

"Believe it or not, I'm here to save you Mary Lee," Nita replied quietly. "The whole world wants to know your story, and I'm the best one to let you tell it your way. Those people out there? They're not going to stop until you talk. Even then, it won't stop, but I can help you control it. Reporters turn into cannibals when they can't get their story, as you've just witnessed. Even worse, they start to make things up. That's not my style. I want to make a deal, fair and square. It will be good for both of us. If you don't talk to me and clear the air, this—" she waved her arms toward the lobby entrance, "will only get worse."

Gene returned with a cup of tea for Mary Lee. "Hello, Nita," he said evenly. "That your idea?" He nodded toward the hospital entrance. "The police are on their way. You know there are rules about how these matters are handled."

"Gene, really—you know me better than that!" Nita scolded easily. "I've had my staff or myself on duty here for days, waiting to get a chance to talk to Ms. Broadmoor. We figured she would have to show up sooner or later. We've tried to cover our tracks by telling hospital staff that we were doing a series called *Those Who Wait*, which we *will* produce. I'm protecting Ms. Broadmoor from those savages outdoors.

"Mary Lee—Ms. Broadmoor," Nita spoke directly to her again, "I understand your reluctance to allow the media into your life. Most of my interviews are with others who, like yourself, do not want our relentless attention. If you value your privacy and truly desire all of this frenzy to settle down, you must act on your own behalf. Otherwise this will only get worse and," she paused, "it's not just you who will suffer. I want to help you and I can." Nita smiled in her famously reassuring way before continuing.

"In exchange, I want something from you. You have won two Oscars, and your movie is changing intimate relationships for many people. Perhaps it's time for you to reconsider and tell your story. Here's my card with my direct cell phone number. So lovely to have met you at last." Nita stood and extended her hand.

Mary Lee shook it, still speechless yet impressed with Nita's smooth and unruffled style.

"Gene, good to see you too," Nita said with practiced articulation as they shook hands. "Watch for our segment called 'Those Who Wait.' You'll appreciate it." She headed out to the main door to take care of the media problem. Gene jogged to catch up with her and they stood side by side on the other side of the sliding glass doors, dismissing the reporters. *What a lovely couple,* Mary Lee thought as she took another comforting sip of her tea.

"You have no idea, do you?" Gene asked Mary Lee when he came back inside. He took a seat next to her and leaned forward, staring at her intently. "You think it was just the academy that gave you a couple of statues and that life can go back to the way it was, don't you? Have you read the papers lately?"

"Never!" Mary Lee replied.

"Watched the news?" he asked.

"Absolutely not!"

"So you don't have any idea how deeply you've touched the world, do you?" Gene's voice turned into an insistent whisper. "And you avoid the public as if it frightens you. What are you so afraid of, Scary Mary? I thought nothing terrified you! You've even looked death in the face and scoffed. What don't you want the world to know about you? This interests me greatly." Gene's look was so intense that Mary Lee was forced to look away.

Gene laughed, stood, and gave Mary Lee his arm again. "I see your driver pulling up to the door. We'll remember this for next time so we can whisk you away instead of leaving you to face a stampede. And I meant what I said in the elevator, Ms. Broadmoor."

"How about dinner at the newly renovated Broadmoor estate?" Mary Lee suggested. "Say, three weeks or so? But I must warn you; it will be a black-tie affair. I like to play dress-up," she whispered. "Better come prepared. Even Gertie wears a gown to dinner, and she looks quite lovely."

Mary Lee stopped suddenly, stunned by an idea that occurred to her. "Perhaps we should invite that Nita Winslow woman. You know her and it might just be a way to get acquainted. I'd like to hear what she has in mind. What do you think, Doctor?"

"You, Nita, Gertie, *and* Chef Michael? Whoa, that's far too much feminine influence for me at one time. But . . . hell yes as long as Michael stays in the kitchen!" Gene laughed. "Most of the ladies I see have to be dying in order to get a visit from me. I would hardly know how to behave with several gorgeous and healthy ones all in one place!"

"High time you got some experience then," Mary Lee replied, feeling much better and enthusiastic about her idea. "Gertie will take care of the details and let you know when your presence is requested. Seriously though, thank you for helping me out here, Gene. It would have been a disaster without you. You're an angel."

"See you soon, I hope," Gene replied. "Keep the female count low if you can," he called to her as she left. "I'd be content with just you," he added.

As her car pulled away, Mary Lee lowered her window and yelled uncharacteristically, "If it helps at all, I'll try to get Nata—I mean Allie, to come and bring her boyfriend. I haven't met him yet, but if my daughter likes him, he must be worth a look. That will add another man to the count."

Gene laughed and waved her off. He'd made his preferences known, but he was a patient man, and this was a start.

33

Allie listened to her mother's request that she bring Art Jr. to dinner on a Saturday evening in three weeks. Mary Lee would pay all the expenses, of course. She knew very little about Art Jr., and Allie was not anxious to change that just yet.

"I'll check, Mother, but he's terribly busy right now," Allie hedged. The timing would be perfect, but any ideas that came from her mother were immediately suspect and automatically resisted.

"Yes, of course you should meet," she replied to her mother's insistence, "but I'm still getting to know him myself. I'll have to let you know if we can make it." Postponing her mother's gratification always lifted Allie's spirits.

"No, Mother," Allie said at last when Mary Lee suggested that Allie come alone if Art Jr. couldn't make it. "Don't count on me if he can't come. It sounds like you'll have plenty of guests." That did not meet with Mary Lee's approval.

"Yes, it would be lovely to meet Nita Winslow in person," Allie conceded, "but her focus will be on *you*, and my presence could be distracting. She can always contact me later if she wants to regarding the humanitarian work we do here. Yes, I understand how important this is to you. But you'll have Gertie and gorgeous Dr. Gregory with you . . . Yes, I'll let you know as soon as I can."

Allie pondered once again how much her mother had changed since her cancer went into remission. She seemed so—cheerful—but still pushy, and Allie still felt awkward around her strange new energy.

When her phone rang again, Allie was certain it was her mother with another reason Allie and Art should come to dinner. Allie answered, "*What, Mother?*" in her terse, warning tone that suggested the call was not appreciated.

"Whoa, Allie, it's me, not the Big Bad Wolf." Art Jr. laughed. "Is that your 'you're in trouble' tone? I'd better make a note of it. Wouldn't want to get on your bad side. Oh, I forgot, I've already been there! The bruises have healed nicely, thank you for *not* asking. Actually I just had a few minutes and thought I'd say hello."

Allie laughed as she listened to Art Jr.'s teasing voice. "Sorry, Art. My mother wants you and me to join her and a few others for dinner in three weeks. She even volunteered to fly you out. My mother is a very private person *and* persistent. Used to getting her way. I mentioned your name a few times, so she thinks I've got a boyfriend that she should meet. There's always such drama with her!" Allie added.

"Hmm, your mother wants to meet me?" Art hesitated long enough to make Allie nervous. "That sounds serious." Then he laughed easily before becoming more sober. "It would be quite an honor to meet her, and I'm undeniably curious. You haven't told me much about your parents," he added. "I mean, I know they're divorced and that you and your Mother aren't close, but I'd like to meet them both. Gotta run, gorgeous. Let's talk later this evening."

"I'll catch you up on the sordid dinner details then," Allie replied with a smile in her voice. "I always look forward to your calls," she added with whispered hesitation, "but I much prefer seeing you in person."

"Me too," Art Jr. said with an excited tone to his voice. "I hope I can see you soon—all of you!"

The call from Art put Allie in a better humor, the kind she was usually in. She knew Art would call later. He was absolutely true to his word. Allie hadn't told Art Jr. much about her mother for the same reason she had also not seen her mother's movie. She was saving both for a day when she and Art Jr. could go together because she needed to be with him when that happened. How he responded would be very important to the future of their relationship. Returning to her work in Brazil was still her top priority. Art McElroy Jr. could still be traded for an airplane ticket to Manaus or maybe, if she was lucky, he could be persuaded to join her.

34

Three weeks later, Art Jr. was headed to LA. It was as much of a vacation as he had ever taken or would have for a long time. He relaxed in his first-class seat, compliments of Allie's mysterious mother. Such special treatment was foreign to him, and he planned to keep it that way. Money could be put to a much better use than having a comfy place to sit for a few hours.

Art Jr. was incredibly weary. He had just completed a seventy-two-hour stint at the hospital followed by a long drive to the airport. Knowing he was on his way to see Allie had kept him awake. Once he was on the plane, he closed his eyes and didn't open them until the plane's wheels jolted him to consciousness when they hit the tarmac.

When at last Art Jr. and Allie saw each other, they kissed each other with such passion that bystanders made room for them in case they decided to make love right in baggage claim. They would have a few blissful hours before they headed off to dinner. Art Jr. felt like exploring Allie from head to toe and Allie had replaced the *No Trespassing* sign with one that read *Exclusive Permit for Dr. Art McElroy Jr.*

* * *

At six-thirty p.m., three black limousines made their way to Mary Lee Broadmoor's estate. In the first one, Nita Winslow and Cheryl Lewis discussed strategies for the evening.

"Not a word about an interview," Nita insisted. She was wearing a black silk designer pant suit. White and gold floral stitching graced the jacket from the left hip and wandered upward across the rib cage then over the lapel, ending at the right shoulder.

"Got it," Cheryl confirmed. "Keep it social." She could do that as long as Nita was in charge. Cheryl had dressed the best she could on her salary with a tea-length purple gauze dress and faux silk bolero jacket sporting a few sparkles.

"How's your research coming?" Nita asked.

"It's pretty depressing, actually," Cheryl replied. "I now know more than I ever wanted to about women and heart attacks. I'm combing obituaries from the past ten years just to be safe. Looking for that VW junk-dealer husband should bring it all together. Something will show up unless it's a cover for something criminal. I'm having fun."

"I'm so glad for that stint you pulled as a police officer, Cheryl. It should get you access to the data we're looking for far more easily," Nita suggested.

"That stint was twenty years, Nita—more like a career." Cheryl was tired of Nita's ability to make it sound like she had been play-acting for two decades of her life. "My career until 'cutbacks' last year, that is." Cheryl looked out the window as the car turned in to the Broadmoor estate.

"Thank God for cutbacks," Nita replied.

Black wrought iron gates denied access to Mary Lee's home until a security attendant addressed their driver, and made a call to the house. Except for the letter *B* that was cast in the center of each gate, there was no way to determine who lived at this address; the house was not visible from the drive.

Nita and Cheryl were impressed by the beautiful gardens that lined the drive as they moved toward the house. Far from the morbidity they had expected from the queen of horror films, the grounds sparkled with white flowers in bloom, flowing fountains, and a statuary of angels and goddesses placed in softly lit areas. The evening twilight brought such an ethereal beauty to the approach to the home that Cheryl almost expected to see fairies in delicate white gowns walking among the trees.

The next car brought Gene Gregory to the home he had visited many times. No official entry screening was required for his car and driver. The attendant simply opened the gate and waved them through. Gene, too, was impressed as he observed the transformation of Mary Lee's landscaping. She had always scoffed whenever flowers were delivered in those months before her miraculous recovery. "I'm not dead yet," she used to say with a scowl.

Without realizing it, Gene had braced himself for the smell of stale cigar smoke that always met his arrival. Mary Lee was a chain cigar smoker with zero tolerance for cigarettes. "Those things can kill you," was a favorite line of hers. As he stepped over the threshold into the house, the smell of jasmine and lavender stunned his senses. The beauty of the renovated entryway, full of natural light and living plants, made him gasp, and Gene Gregory didn't gasp at *anything*.

Art Jr. and Allie arrived in the third limo. Art Jr. was not fond of these vehicles since the last and only time he had been in one was for his mother's funeral. Allie apologized profusely when the chauffeured car met them at the hotel, just as she had when she handed Art Jr. a tuxedo. "Mother won't have it any other way," she explained. "You're a guest and no guests have ever arrived in anything but a limo, except for me on those rare occasions that I visit. If she entertains, which she rarely does, it's a black-tie affair."

Allie and Art Jr. held hands on the way to the estate and talked very little. Art Jr. was jet-lagged and sensually saturated. That, combined with acute nervousness about meeting his girlfriend's mother left him quite speechless. Allie was wearing the same strapless sheath gown she had worn for the GloMed conference. Her hair was pinned up elegantly. *She's so beautiful*, Art Jr. thought as he appreciated that she had not invested more money in dressing for her mother's party.

"Notice that my gown is intentionally strapless," Allie teased. "But don't go thinking I like dressing this way," she warned. "It's just that Mother has gotten, well, rather particular in her old age. The miracle is that she is having this dinner at all. There will be other people there, so you won't feel like all the attention is on you. If you don't watch TV, you haven't seen the show *Currents* and you won't know who Nita Winslow is. She'll be there, trying to convince Mother to appear on her show. Mother despises the media, and that's putting it lightly."

Art Jr. smiled as he listened to Allie's chatter. He knew that she was nervous too. Allie had never spoken fondly of her mother; it had been more like she tolerated her from a distance. Their limo pulled up to the wrought-iron gates of an elegant estate. He immediately noticed the *B* set into the ironwork. Something shifted inside of him, setting him on edge.

"Allie, what does the *B* stand for?" he asked. "I thought your last name was Schwartz." Art turned to look at the lovely woman seated next to him as the gates opened and the driver swung the car into the garden-bordered driveway.

"Well, Art," Allie explained, watching him closely now that the moment of confession was upon her, "the *B* stands for Broadmoor. It's time to tell you that my mother is Mary Lee Broadmoor, the woman who wrote and directed scores of horror movies and has recently won two Oscars for her movie *Something Like That.* I had to wait to tell you until I felt ready. My mother's fame can affect how others treat me. I didn't want that to happen to us. Does that make sense?"

Allie's eyes searched Art Jr.'s face for his reaction. He understood and tried to act impressed and excited for Allie's sake, but a blanket of dread slid over him as a sudden chill sucked the breath out of him. He shuddered in shock. All he could say was, "Whoa."

The car pulled up to the door of the mansion, and the driver walked around the back to assist Allie out of the car. Art Jr. had no time to absorb the information he had just received and found himself unable to get out of the vehicle. Part of him wanted to run; another part of him couldn't believe the opportunity that was before him. To meet Mary Lee Broadmoor face-to-face, to find out for himself and his family why she wrote the story and *how* took his breath away and put padlocks on his knees.

Allie waited for Art, disturbed by his immobility. She leaned back into the car. "What's wrong, Art?" She frowned and chastised herself mentally for springing so much on him at once.

Art had learned how to face life's most difficult moments and move through them, but this time he wasn't sure he could pull it off. For the first time in his twenty-eight years, his charisma failed him, and the light went out of his eyes.

"N—nothing, Allie," he finally stuttered. "I—it's just a lot to absorb. Meeting your mother. Whoa. Learning that your mother is Mary Lee Broadmoor. Double whoa. Wearing a tux for dinner. Triple whoa. You had me at the first 'whoa.'" He smiled a little hoping it would help Allie relax while he battled a degree of anxiety he had never known.

She laughed. "Don't you worry about a thing, Dr. Art McElroy. Mother is going to love you!"

The problem was that Art Jr. already knew he would not—could not ever—offer the same feelings to Allie's mother and that changed everything for him. This was no longer about meeting his girlfriend's mother. It was about meeting the woman who had destroyed his relationship with his father and made his family's life public. Allie would be a conduit; perhaps that was all she would ever be to him. He could hardly bear it. As he heard the entrance gates closing behind them and he stepped out of the limo, he felt the gates closing on what he had hoped for with Allie. His lovely Allie—the daughter of the monster who had forced his family's story onto the cinematic screen—how could he love her at all?

35

Mae Rose was in trouble the moment she saw Art Jr. As she peered through Mary Lee's eyes, the memory of her family careened like a galleon broadsiding the ship of her placid life and ripped her back into the woman she had been—the wife of Art McElroy, Sr. and the mother of two sons, one of whom now stood in front of her. She remembered everything including her death and being vanished. Mae Rose was suddenly aware of how intertwined she and Mary Lee had become—the result that her Reflection Agent had predicted. She knew she had to break away before it was too late although to do so at this exact moment seemed to be incredibly poor timing. The entire group witnessed Mary Lee's eyes rolling back in her head as her body went into a convulsion and she fell to the floor in a dramatic faint.

Before anyone could respond, the Mary Lee without Mae Rose revived. "What's everyone staring at?" she demanded. "I'm *fine*. Could someone help me get up off of this fucking floor?" Gene Gregory was the first to respond and Art Jr. finally joined in.

"Thank you," Mary Lee said without a drop of gratitude in her voice. "I guess it's been too long since I entertained," she added, attempting to recover her poise.

Before retreating, Mae Rose had seen how shocked her eldest son was that Allie's mother was Mary Lee Broadmoor, and she understood why he would not be at all pleased to be spending the evening at the Broadmoor estate. It was her own fault, of course. She had put the story of her family's life on movie screens all around the world for

Mary Lee. Her son couldn't help questioning his love for Allie as he connected her to Mary Lee.

Desperate to save her son from his agony, Mae Rose felt she had to intervene, but just now, she didn't know how. She knew what her priorities were. She had to let Mary Lee have control for the evening but she would work behind the scenes. As Dr. Gregory and Art Jr. helped Mary Lee to her feet, Mae Rose carefully restrained herself, but her heart ached for her son.

The group around the dining room table numbered seven. It had been laid with the finest white linen and a low, twining bouquet of hydrangeas, roses, and willow branches graced the center as a tall silver candelabrum provided soft light. Mary Lee's new, mono-grammed china and stemware whispered a quiet elegance that impressed everyone, most significantly her daughter who had never seen her mother create anything remotely beautiful.

Except for her momentary lapse early in the evening, Mary Lee was an amazingly perfect hostess who chatted easily with everyone except Art Jr.

Allie was horrified by her mother's rudeness to her boyfriend. It was as if, at the time when she most needed to believe that her mother had truly changed, Mary Lee had become her old self again except that she was drinking heavily something Allie had never seen her mother do.

Sitting on her right, Art Jr. was also incredibly uptight—not at all like the man she thought she knew. Yes, she had intended to shock him and study his reaction to her mother. While she had accom-plished her goal stunningly, she hadn't been prepared for the loss she felt as she watched him and her mother ignore each other. The evening was turning into a disaster.

If Art Jr. had been himself in those moments, he would have noticed how similar Mary Lee's landscaping and interior décor were to his mother's taste. He would have observed that the dining room would have made his mother swoon—that it was elegant in every way that Mae Rose would have loved, down to the floral centerpiece that could have been crafted by Mae Rose herself.

He would also have recalled how his mother had lived to entertain in their home. While she never had a sparkling gown to wear or an elegant mansion in which to entertain, she made every excuse to invite others over, proudly pulling out her wedding china and stemware and laying on their stained and scarred dining room table her antique lace table linens. Yes, given other circumstances, Art Jr. might have noticed so much that could have reminded him of his mother, but it was lost on him in his locked-down emotional state.

Thankfully there were others to create a privacy screen behind which Art felt he could hide. Nita Winslow entertained everyone with stories of some of her most embarrassing moments on the world's stage. She admitted to accidently belching at the microphone during a dinner speech honoring Hillary Clinton and to catching her high heel in the sidewalk and twisting her ankle on her way to meet Tony Blair. Her mind had gone blank during her interview of Jon Bon Jovi; she hadn't been able to recall his name. It was the reason people loved her. Beneath a deep need to be the center of attention, Nita could appear to be touchingly human.

As special bottles from Mary Lee's spectacular wine collection were poured, the stiffness in the group softened as if starch had been removed from a shirt. Nita chatted gaily with almost everyone, while never losing focus on her ultimate goal. Not once during the evening would the discussion of an interview come up; Mary Lee would find herself slightly, and surprisingly, disappointed.

*   *   *

The dinner's main course was over and had earned Chef Michael rave reviews. As Mary Lee's guests waited in eager anticipation for dessert, a comfortable lull born of sated appetites and slight inebriation forced her to turn at last to the quietest guest of the evening. Mae Rose withdrew completely and let Mary Lee handle the conversation, hoping she wouldn't make a complete fool of herself. Without Mae Rose's steady presence, Mary Lee relished the opportunity to humiliate her daughter.

"Art . . . McElroy, isn't it? You've been pretty quiet this evening, Doctor," Mary Lee finally spoke to him directly. "Thank you for joining us for this occasion. You must be weary from your travel."

Art Jr. looked briefly at Mary Lee, then at the others around the table. He worked at forcing his lips into a smile as he cleared his throat. "Thank you for inviting me," he responded cautiously. "Allie has kept you a mystery, Ms. Broadmoor. I must confess that a certain curiosity to meet Allie's mother convinced me to make the trip." He paused and cleared his throat again. "I had no idea of your celebrity, and it puzzles me that no one has mentioned your work this evening. I'd like to hear more about that." Had anyone looked closely, they would have seen the thumping of Art's jugular vein in his neck, a sure sign of mounting tension.

"I detest talking about anything having to do with my work," Mary Lee replied with a slight slur, and failing to cover her irritation. "Since my daughter apparently had not told you who I am, she also may not have mentioned that I avoid the subject of my profession as much as possible. It's so much easier to live out of the limelight." She paused. "I believe we'd all much rather hear about how you met my daughter," she added maliciously.

"Yes. Natalie, please tell us how you met Dr. McElroy. I have personally never seen you with a man and it's so very interesting." Under the influence of alcohol, Gertie's voice betrayed her lack of love for Mary Lee's daughter.

Gertie knew she looked delicious in her black pantsuit with its low-cut halter top. Her Swarovski crystal earrings and necklace sparkled in candlelight. All were provided by Mary Lee, of course. Her expertly manicured nails were certain proof that her nursing days were over; her hair was smoothed into a chunky, angular cut, slimming her face. Gertie's focus had been on Dr. Gregory all evening, her flirting subdued and almost refined. He had failed to respond, which only encouraged Gertie further.

Art looked at Allie and prepared to reply. But he couldn't get any words out. Instead, he felt a surgeon's scalpel cut his heart open. A huge, sucking grief forced him to grip Allie's hand so tightly that it frightened her.

"We met at the last GloMed Conference, mother," Allie finally spoke. "We sort of bumped into each other quite by accident and hit it off." A smile played around her mouth as she looked imploringly at Art, who attempted a smile, but his jaw stiffened. He knew he must ask his question.

"It is as Allie has said," he replied carefully against tears that suddenly begged to be released. "You have a wonderful daughter," he added. "But it appears that we have a conflict of topics on the table. I have not seen any of your movies, but I have heard about the last one and would rather talk about that. I'd like to ask this one question: How *did* you come up with such a story? I heard it was quite out of your normal range of subjects."

As he spoke, Art's intense green eyes locked at last with Mary Lee Broadmoor's. He had asked the one question she could not answer and done it in front of her guests. *How dare you!* she thought as her eyes bored into his.

Nita Winslow watched the sparring dialogue with interest. This young man was not one for small talk. If he could get Mary Lee to open up and respond to this question, the rest of the night promised to be very interesting. She saw Art's face drain of color, a sure sign that there was something troubling him. Suddenly she knew she needed to add him to her list of topics to be researched.

"Why Dr. McElroy!" Nita exclaimed, "You must be one of the few people on the face of the planet who hasn't seen the movie! Is it possible?"

"No, I haven't seen it," Art replied, his words achingly correct, the syllables too distinct. "My brother and his wife did, however, and told me a little about it." He paused. "I don't have much extra time on my hands, and—and it sounded like a chick flick to me." As an afterthought, he added, "With all due respect to the writer and director of the movie . . . and the academy's high regard for it."

Allie continued to try to help Art Jr. through the awkwardness as she struggled to free her hand from his. "I haven't seen it yet either, Mother," she confessed. "I wanted to see it with someone special.

That's why I've waited. Art and I are planning to see it together tomorrow before he leaves to fly home. Right, Art?"

It wasn't only Art's mouth that felt immobilized; it was as if his entire body were made of rusted tin. Clearly Allie knew that something about her mother's film bothered her boyfriend. Art Jr. asked to be excused and pushed away from the table. He had to find a restroom before he made a fool of himself in front of everyone.

Meanwhile, Mae Rose's spirit was in agony. Of course, her family knew about the movie and that meant—dear God—the boys now knew about Art's affair! She was able to get Mary Lee's attention to have her stand up to excuse herself. "I need a break as well," she announced. The dinner guests sat speechless as both Art Jr. and Mary Lee disappeared from the table.

Mary Lee marched angrily into her study with Mae Rose's spirit in a vice grip. "You want to tell me what the *hell* is going on?!" she demanded of Mae Rose.

"That's my son in there!" Mae Rose sobbed.

"Whose son? In *where*?" Mary Lee demanded.

"Dr. Art McElroy, the young man with *your* daughter, the guy who's drilling you about the story."

"Your son is banging *my* daughter?" Mary Lee was incredulous. "How—?"

"It's not important right now, but I can't bear it. My boys have seen the movie, so they know that their father had an affair while we were married," she wept.

"How is that your problem now?" Mary Lee asked.

"I just can't bear the thought of how they are suffering. I can see it in Art Jr.'s face. Plus, he's trying to make sense of how you got our family's story. That's why he's challenging you. Don't make me go back in there, Mary Lee," Mae Rose begged. "I can't bear it!"

* * *

Inside Mary Lee's beautifully appointed green and white fern-patterned guest bathroom, Art ripped off his jacket, tie, and shirt, and dropped to the floor. On his knees, he wept his grief over the loss of his mother, his rage at his father, and his fear that meeting Mary Lee Broadmoor would end his relationship with Allie. His normally well-kept ash blond hair fell forward into his eyes. The emotional reaction was long past due.

Shaking in its aftermath, Art Jr. sat back against the wall and reached into his tuxedo jacket pocket. He pulled out his cell phone and called the only person he felt he could trust to guide him. It surprised him how desperately he needed to hear the voice that he hoped would answer at the other end of the line.

36

No one called Art in the middle of the night. As he pulled on his plaid bathrobe, he remembered that John and Elliana were expecting a baby. They wouldn't call him with news at this time of night—unless it was bad. Hurrying now, he made his way to the phone.

"Art, what's wrong, Son?" Art asked when he heard his voice.

"I've met her, Dad," Art Jr. said quietly.

"Met who? The woman of your dreams?" Art was impressed with his attempt at humor, although his sense was that it fell as hard and flat as a rock launched from the top of the Empire State Building.

"Dad, I met *her*," Art Jr. sounded impatient, which was completely out of character. "The director of the movie about us."

"Who? How? Where are you? You're not making sense." Art strained to get the fog out of his brain.

"Dad, I'm in LA, remember? I came because Allie asked me to come out and meet her mother. We're at dinner at her mother's place. I found out there. The movie director, Allie's mother, is Mary Lee Broadmoor!"

"Your girlfriend Allie? *Her* mother?" Art struggled to comprehend.

"Yes, Dad," Art said again. "My girlfriend, Allie Schwartz." Art Jr. enunciated each word as if he couldn't believe it himself.

After a long pause, Art replied, "That—that's just not possible."

"Neither is a movie based on our lives, Dad," Art Jr. countered. "I—I just thought you should know in case. In case of whatever. That's all. Something told me to call you."

"Thanks, Son. When do you come home?"

"As soon as possible, Dad. I don't think I can take this." He paused. "We should probably let John know and then decide what to do." Art Jr.'s tone suggested that he was already thinking through their options. "I've checked and there's a direct flight out early in the morning. I'm planning to be on that plane."

"Should I come and get you at the airport?" Art Sr. asked. He couldn't help being hopeful that somehow he could make himself useful and reconnect with his son.

"No, Dad, I've got my car. I'll be fine."

"Should I call John now to let him know? Just tell me what to do," Art Sr. pleaded.

"No, don't bother him tonight. I'll tell him in the morning," Art Jr. replied. "It's just that I wanted you to know. That's all."

"Anything else that I should know?" Art asked.

"Not really, Dad. But Mary Lee Broadmoor is an interesting woman and seems very much like Pastor Frank told us. Keeps very much to herself. I get the impression she thinks everyone is making too much of the movie, and she absolutely won't talk about it. When I asked her how she had come up with such a story line, she couldn't answer me. Her reaction was strange, as if she was angry at me for asking. She refuses any publicity about it. Allie hasn't even seen it yet. She told me she wanted to see it with me tomorrow, but I don't think it's a good idea. This could be a game-changer for me. How can I love someone with a mother like that?" His voice broke.

"Don't be hasty Son. You've had a shock." Art advised, loving the touch of intimacy with his eldest child, even if for the briefest moment.

"I want to come home, Dad. I've had the surprise of my life— next to Mom's death. I feel sick and just don't think I'm ready to take this any further. Allie knows nothing of the connection our family has to the movie, of course, so I don't blame her at all that this has happened. It's just too much. I'll leave her a message at the hotel desk in the morning. I just have to pack up my things."

"She might never speak to you again, you know," Art Sr. told his son carefully. "Make sure you think this through. Certainly you should consider leaving early. But you should tell her, not just leave a message, unless you don't ever want to see her again. If I had pulled a stunt like that when I was dating your mother, it might have changed the course of history. Maybe that wouldn't have been such a bad idea, though." Art congratulated himself on adding a little humor to the situation. He wanted his son home, but he felt he had to give him a different vantage point.

When Art Jr. didn't respond, he continued. "I think you're finally facing some of the feelings you've kept inside about your mother's death, but you're the doctor, not me. It's as if seeing this Mary Lee woman has pulled some emotion out of you and that's what's making you feel ill. She can't help who her mother is, Son. Don't be too hard on her."

"Like you said, Dad, I'm a doctor," Art Jr. replied, testily. "I understand what could be causing my illness. It just feels weird that it's happening to *me*. But Allie is no fool. The whole group here senses that something about the movie is bothering me. Allie felt bad that she hadn't told me after she saw me react the way I did, but she'd wanted to surprise me."

"I believe she accomplished that," Art responded with a light laugh. "Let me know when you get in. Have a safe flight, Son. It will be good to have you home."

When he hung up the phone, Art thought about calling Art Jr. back and saying, "I love you," but changed his mind. Then he picked up the phone to call Pastor Frank but changed his mind about that too and decided it could wait. But he also remembered not that long ago when he had waited too long to check on Mae Rose.

Instead of going back to bed, Art Sr. went into the family room and picked up his guitar. Right then and there, he knew the second verse to his song, a verse that Mae Rose could have sung—if Mae Rose could have carried a tune.

If every blade of grass were emerald and every snowflake diamond bright,
They would pale against our love dear, when held up to love's light
'Cause they can't say "I adore you" in the middle of the night.
I was the richest woman in the world.

And then he wept for all the hurt and pain that his sons were going through without him and for the glorious fact that his oldest son had called him.

37

Art Jr. heard a tentative knock on the bathroom door. In a concerned voice, Allie asked, "Art, are you OK in there?"

"Couldn't be better," Art Jr. called out brightly. "I'll be right out. Wait for me." Somehow talking to his father had provided relief, as if he had successfully traversed a torrid whitewater into a quiet river. As he washed his face and combed back his hair, Art Jr. knew he was in a different space inside. He gazed into his eyes and saw his mother's. He was no longer afraid of what he knew he had to face.

Mary Lee was back at the table when he returned. She did not look happy.

Gene Gregory snapped to life as if on cue. "I'm glad you've rejoined us, Dr. McElroy. I believe we have an answer to your most provocative question." Looking directly at Art Jr., he announced, "Mary Lee created this story just like every other one she has ever written. She has an amazing mind and is one of the most incredible storytellers alive today. Asking a writer where a story comes from is an impossible question to answer. Writers and artists usually don't know; that's part of the thrill of the creative process. Surely in your own profession you've come to understand that many things are simply unexplainable."

Mary Lee nodded her head in agreement. "It's the one question I have asked myself over and over. I was so medicated in those days that it's all a blur. But I was writing—Gertie, you can also attest to that—and when I woke up out of the nightmare of pancreatic cancer, well, it was as if the story had written itself. It's difficult for me to give you any more details. I don't remember much, and I can't explain that any better than I can explain how it is that I'm here instead of being in an urn somewhere." She paused and lifted herself regally as she spoke directly to Art Jr. "And I refuse to make these personal matters public." Mary Lee then looked over to Nita, whom she found was nodding in agreement.

Only Gene Gregory took note that Gertie had stopped flirting and sat unusually quiet with her eyes averted. His mind wandered back to the days before Mary Lee *almost* died. He knew she had been writing a story; he had seen the evidence. He also remembered her asking him about the worst natural way to die, and he'd told her. But there had been no mention of that in her latest movie. Rather than writing about the most horrible physical way to die, as she had originally led Gene to believe, Mary Lee had written about the most tormented kind of death, when issues between lovers were unresolved—when one of the partners died enraged, leaving the other full of regret. *What caused her story line to change?*

Then there was the question of Mary Lee's miraculous recovery and her personality change. Gene glanced over to Allie, who now gazed with wide-open eyes at him as if reading his mind. *Exactly the question,* her eyes said back to him. Gene knew the facts. No one had ever gone into stage IV pancreatic cancer and lived to tell about it. Some had been lucky in earlier stages of the disease but never when it was so far advanced. *Never.* Dr. Gregory looked back, first at Gertie again then to Allie. Then both he and Allie turned their focus on Gertie, who refused to meet their gazes. *She's the only one who would know,* he thought.

Suddenly Dr. Eugene Milroy Gregory was genuinely interested in Gertrude Louise Morgan, but it wasn't her skilled flirting that attracted him. His thoughts continued as he stared from the sparkling crystal hoops dangling from Gertie's ears to her low-cut halter top. *Mary Lee should not be alive, and only Gertie knows what happened in that room.* He decided then and there to probe more deeply into Gertie's obviously troubled psyche—a distasteful task at best, but essential. He spent the rest of the evening subtly responding to Gertie's overtures when they resumed.

The conversation was spared any further consideration as dessert arrived. Chef Michael set a pear crème brûlée in front of each guest. The crackled, caramelized surface was topped with three tiny dark chocolate and hazelnut truffles; a drizzle of blackberry sauce finished the creation. Everyone focused enthusiastically, albeit regrettably, on breaking open their own exquisite work of art while Chef Michael poured a Muscat Canelli into dessert wine glasses and took orders for coffee. No further mention was made of the movie. Even Art began to relax.

Nita Winslow was captivated, making mental notes and missing nothing. For her, cracking a story was as delicious as breaking through her crème brûlée, but with a far more satisfying aftermath. Cheryl, too, absorbed subtle details with the skill of the trained detective she was, knowing a new mystery was afoot.

Art tapped the top of his dessert in a distracted, yet intense fashion, not certain what direction his relationship with Allie would take, but he was kind and attentive to her. Gertie licked her dessert spoon sensuously for Gene's benefit. He smiled in spite of the anxiety he felt. Mary Lee quietly enjoyed her own dessert while continuing to consume a large amount of alcohol.

Gene was the first to push away from the table, suggesting a close to a most memorable evening. In truth, he could not wait to get back to his condo and do some research on the Internet. He knew that in a couple of days he would call Gertie and ask her for a date. He let his hand linger against hers as they said good-bye, enjoying her blush of confusion as others who were leaving took notice of their exchange.

Inside their limo, Allie tugged on Art's arm, pulling him out of his preoccupation. She leaned over and whispered, "I am so sorry, Art. I never meant to distress you this evening."

Art smiled and grabbed her hand. "It was all a bit too much for a simple boy from the Midwest," he said. "I was stunned, jet-lagged, and inebriated, not to mention swept away by the beautiful woman at my side. Why don't we drive back to my hotel and have a coffee together?" he suggested easily. "After all, I really came here to see you."

Allie smiled and relaxed a little. "I didn't want to see the movie at all," she confided, snuggling close to him. "Then I realized that

I didn't want to see it alone." Her voice became quiet as she put her head on his shoulder and whispered. "The only person I could imagine seeing it with was you." Art Jr. didn't know what to say.

"If you don't want to see it, it's OK with me. I think we've had plenty of real drama this evening. Mostly I want to be with you as much as possible tomorrow." She was thinking that she'd like to include tonight, but after the events of the evening, she wasn't even sure if she had a boyfriend, much less a lover.

Art Jr. squeezed her hand; he knew what she was trying to tell him. But he also knew that any response from him right now would be inappropriate until he was sure of himself.

When their limo pulled in at the hotel, Allie watched as Art got out of the car. She yawned. "I'm going to head home," she told him. "You need to rest; we've got a busy day tomorrow." She waved, then turned away as tears engulfed her. She was in love and didn't know if she'd ever see Art McElroy Jr. again.

* * *

Gene Gregory didn't head straight to bed when he was dropped off at his condo. Instead, he slipped out of his dinner jacket and uncustomarily threw it over a chair as he powered up his computer. He had seen Mary Lee's personality change dramatically that evening. It made him wonder what was really going on. Was it schizophrenia born of a near-death experience or—*was it possible*—that another "spirit" had taken up residence inside of her? Was it possible that death was not a final destination—not an everlasting decision for heaven or hell? Were events in other realms possible after physical death?

The thought that he might be saved from eternal torment made Gene all the more determined to talk to Gertie. He desperately needed her help to connect all the possibilities playing in his head. But in this moment, he was so stimulated by his thoughts that he didn't make it to the bathroom where he normally and tidily relieved himself. He climaxed instantaneously.

38

A very inebriated and infuriated Mary Lee closed the door after her guests left and returned to sit in the dining room with Gertie. Her gown made soft swishing sounds as she walked, its many layers of undergarments whispering in delicious luxury.

"Well," she said as she sat down at her chair. "What the hell was that all about?! I have a dinner party and my dignity is assaulted. This is exactly why I never entertain!" Mary Lee was livid.

"Well, I disagree," Gertie replied, reeling with giddiness from her alcohol consumption and Dr. Gregory's attention. "It went well, Ms. Broadmoor. Nita Winslow will follow up for sure. She's a true professional. I like her a lot."

"God, I hope you're right! Perhaps I've had too much to drink," Mary Lee admitted as she put her head in her hands and squeezed the skin between her eyes. "What do you think of Natalie's boyfriend?"

"He certainly was uptight," Gertie said. "But I don't blame him— he didn't know who you were! Your dear Natalie threw him a curve he may never recover from! Something was bothering him, though. I couldn't tell if it was shyness at meeting you or something about the movie. I thought it was mean of him to press like he did. I'm not sure *I* like him." *Which makes him a perfect match for Natalie,* she thought. Gertie still had the good sense to keep that thought to herself. The two women sat quietly, each lost in her own concerns.

"I agree," Mary Lee finally declared. "I think Natalie should not have surprised him like she did; that's what *I* think. Oh, well. Time for bed. I hope you're right about the party, but let's not have another one any time soon. It took a lot out of me." Mary Lee felt as tired as she ever had as she pulled herself to her feet. "Dr. Gregory seemed most attentive to you, Gertie. Surely you enjoyed that."

So it wasn't just my imagination, Gertie thought. "He was just being kind in front of all those people," she said with a blush. "I'll run ahead and draw your bath. You looked wonderful tonight, ma'am." Gertie sort of curtsied and hurried down the hall to the elevator, stumbling awkwardly in her five-inch heels. Mary Lee watched Gertie's erratic run and smiled at the emotions she was quite certain were running through Gertie's mind. She sighed as she walked out of the dining room to her library, where she suddenly decided, without wondering why, to have an after-dinner cigar and bourbon before bed.

"Thanks so much, Mary Lee." Mae Rose came out of hiding once they were safely in her library. "I would not have made it through the evening after seeing my son."

"You're welcome but it's not like I had much choice. It was a tough evening," Mary Lee said matter-of-factly. "What are we going to do about your son fucking my daughter? I didn't think she'd ever come out of her tightly wound shell. It's good for her, but it feels like incest to me."

Mae Rose laughed. "My son is the best man in the world for your uptight daughter, Mary Lee. Mark my words. I can tell he thinks the world of her."

"He did until he found out that she's *my* daughter. He obviously has a problem with that."

"The problem isn't your daughter, Mary Lee. It's that I—we— put my Earth family's life on the big screen and that's how my boys found out that their father was unfaithful to me. *That's* the problem."

"Affairs happen in families all over the world," Mary Lee replied nonchalantly.

"Not in *our* family," Mae Rose replied, "and not so publicly. The whole world knows the intimate details of our family's lives. My son is devastated; I can tell. It's just that I can't do anything about it! I wanted so desperately to help them all when I was in my afterlife. When I was vanished, it seemed like I forgot everything—until tonight when my son showed up here."

"I think Gene Gregory is onto us," Mary Lee said, changing the subject because she didn't really care how Mae Rose's family felt about the very successful movie. "He knows something very strange has happened to me, and he's a notorious researcher. One of these days he's going to figure out that I'm no longer me. I don't know what he'll do about it, but my guess is that we'll make the tabloids in a heartbeat and I'll be discredited. 'Scary Mary Goes Schizoid.' I can see the headlines now."

"In the meantime, we've got the new movie to work on. That should take care of any doubt about your writing and directing capabilities," Mae Rose encouraged.

"You mean *your* capabilities," Mary Lee said without resentment. "I'm just the body; you're the brains."

"How about some Gin Rummy to take our minds off everything?" Mae Rose suggested.

Mary Lee reached for a deck of cards, shuffled them and dealt cards to both of her hands. Just then Gertie poked her head in the door. The look on her face told Mary Lee that Gertie saw clearly what she was doing. But Gertie didn't flinch.

"I just came to say good night, Ms. Broadmoor. Thought I heard voices so wanted to check. Good night." She shut the door quickly.

"Just me talking to myself, Gertie.

"Good night, Gertie," both women said in unison and laughed. *Poor Gertie would have another sleepless night.* The doors to Gertie's carefully-guarded secret had been unlocked during dinner. Ghostly images crept into her dreams, reminding her that she knew more than anyone else about what was going on inside Mary Lee, causing her to cyclically toss, turn, sweat, and freeze. What she had seen when she said good night to Mary Lee had confirmed it, Mary Lee had subdivided into two personalities. That must be what happened in her bargaining with God—*a tradeoff*, Gertie decided. Mary Lee could have success, *but she still had to pay for it.*

Gertie had kept the events of "the day Mary Lee died" locked away; her resistance to sharing her secret increased as time passed. She would look like a money-grubbing fool to bring up now what she'd seen happen more than a year ago. Everyone would think she'd gone mad, and she already had too many disagreeable traits to allow another one to be exposed. It would ruin her life.

But the evening's conversation had roused the sleeping monster whose mouth covered her head, its sharp teeth pressing into her neck when she awoke which she did often that night. She wondered why *she*, a casual observer, had to suffer for Mary Lee's sins. Gertie's rational mind fought with the memories. How would telling Mary Lee the truth (or at least what Gertie had observed), help anyone? *Mary Lee, you died—honestly you did—after bargaining with God for your life and an Oscar. Your personality split and you become two different people. That's why you don't remember writing the story—because the you that used to be you, didn't!* Or she could say, *Because, you see, the Mary Lee that started the story died, and the Mary Lee you are now, who is not at all the same Mary Lee, rewrote the entire story because, after I thought you were dead—and I promise that you were—I deleted your story.* It all sounded ridiculous!

Gertie got up, changed out of her wringing-wet pajamas, and headed to the kitchen for a glass of milk. If Chef Michael were around, she'd opt for some mind-blowing sexual maneuvers. The pressure would be on now that Dr. Gregory appeared interested, and if Gertie were going to lose her mind, she decided she might as well enjoy the process.

39

Art Jr. slipped out of the hotel just after four in the morning and took a cab to the airport. He wondered for a moment if he were making the right decision. It occurred to him that his father was right; this would probably mean the end of his relationship with Allie. She wasn't the type to allow first chances, much less second ones.

Speaking of second chances, Art Jr. thought about Mary Lee Broadmoor and how she had certainly gotten that in her life. She was a very lucky woman—almost too lucky to be real. *Wouldn't she make an interesting mother-in-law?* Art Jr. was stunned by such an outrageous thought. He wasn't even thinking about marriage, unless of course, he really was and didn't know it yet. Regardless, if he blew this with Allie, he'd never know. In that instant, Art Jr. changed his mind.

As he stepped up to the check-in counter with his bag in hand, he looked at the agent and said as matter-of-factly as a doctor would, "I need to change my ticket to depart tomorrow instead of today." He handed his driver's license over the counter.

"Yes, sir." The agent, an older gentleman with only a smile of hair around his bald head, looked at the name and typed it into his computer. "We could have taken care of this over the phone for you instead of your coming to the airport, Doctor," the agent commented, peering curiously over his half glasses.

"I didn't know until this moment that I would be making that change," Art Jr. replied.

"Very well, sir." The agent entered the new data into the computer.

"May I ask you a question while you're working?" Art asked, leaning closer to him over the counter. "Have you seen the movie *Something Like That?*"

The agent stopped and looked at Art Jr. "Yes, sir. Hasn't everyone? My wife has gone to see it at least three times."

"Well, no," Art replied. "I haven't, but my girlfriend wants me to go see it with her. Frankly, I think it's a chick flick, so I was getting ready to create a medical emergency need to fly home this morning. Would I be missing something?"

"You would go to all of this trouble to avoid seeing a movie—especially this one?" the agent asked, unable to hide his surprise. "Sounds like you've just answered your own question, young man. I'll just say this: if there's any chance you might end up marrying this woman or sharing your life with *anyone* in a love relationship, then you will spend every day being glad that you saw the movie or regret that you didn't. My wife and I are more in love today than we were before we saw it, and we've been married for thirty-six years."

"Wow! OK, thanks," Art replied. "You've been very helpful. That's why I'm not flying out this morning."

"There you go, Dr. Arthur McElroy Jr.," the agent said, reading his full name on the ticket. "It ends up being an expensive movie for you to see. This is your second ticket change and adds another $84 to the price."

"Oh, well." He gulped but stood firm. "In the long run, it could be a very small investment in the future." He smiled realizing that he was both happy and relieved.

"Best of luck to you, sir. Go and enjoy the show."

Art was so happy with his decision that he could not get back to the hotel fast enough. With any luck, Art figured he could be back in his room before Allie called, or better yet, he would call *her.* He leaned his head back against the black vinyl seat of the cab, pulled out his cell phone, and dialed his father.

"Art McElroy speaking," his dad replied the way he always did when he was at work in his shop. Art Jr. smiled. A phone with caller ID and voice mail would make a great Christmas gift for his father, but he'd never use it.

"Dad, it's Art. Sorry to have messed with your sleep last night."

"Not a problem. What's up? Plane delayed?"

"In a way. I've changed my mind about coming home today. I'm going to take your advice and take Allie to see the movie and then come home tomorrow. Who knows what I might find out about her mother too, seeing as I appear to have an inside track," Art Jr. explained, exposing every plausible reason for his change of mind except the real one.

"Well, OK, then. She must be a great woman," Art replied with a smile in his voice.

"Yes. And Dad?" Art Jr. choked up.

"Yes, Son?" his father asked quietly.

"You're the one who pointed out what I might lose, and I don't want to do that. I'm taking a big chance here but I—I have to know. So thanks." Art Jr.'s heart felt as if his feelings would burst right out through the phone.

"I love you, Son," Art said. It was the perfect moment to say it and Art, who had missed many perfect moments in his life, knew pure joy.

"I love you too, Dad," Art Jr. replied instantly then said almost fiercely into the phone, "And . . . and I don't understand what happened between you and Mom, but I don't want it to come between us any longer. Life has been difficult enough without Mom. I can't bear to lose you too." Art Jr. had tears running down his face.

"Thank you, Son," Art replied softly, also in tears. "Have a good time with this young woman, and I'll be anxious to see you when you get home."

"Ditto, Dad. Whoa, I feel so much better."

"Good. Me too. Call anytime. And bring this woman home with you someday soon. I'd certainly like to meet her. Tell you what—I imagine that plane change cost you a pretty penny. Why don't you let your mom and me cover the cost?"

"Dad, what do you mean, you and mom? You're not making sense," Art Jr. argued.

"Son, your mother may be in a different realm but I have it on good authority that she's still interested in our lives and she always managed our money. She would insist on covering this for you. That's all I'm saying." Art felt so good telling his son this that he honestly didn't mind spending the money.

"Wow, thanks, Dad. That's great. I don't know what to say." He paused, speechless.

"Nothing you need to say. Just get back to that woman of yours. Bye now." Art set the phone firmly back in its cradle.

When the taxi pulled up to the hotel, it was 6:25 a.m. Art ran in, and was ecstatic to find his room still available. He checked back in, put on his running clothes, and threw his cell phone on his unmade bed. Back downstairs, he asked for directions to a local coffee shop. After he felt that his emotions were under control, he'd call the love of his life.

Allie called Art Jr.'s room at seven. When he didn't answer, she left a message. She was still worried that she might have ruined their relationship by surprising him about her mother. But she got into the shower to begin what she hoped could be a wonderful day. If she hadn't scared Art Jr. away, Allie planned to show him where she worked and then take him to lunch. After that, she was hoping for a matinee of *Something Like That* before he had to catch his flight home. If he still didn't want to see the movie, she wasn't sure what they'd do, but she hoped it would involve getting to know each other better.

The Amazon jungle is a good place to build resilience. No one survives a life so close to the elements without tremendous mental and emotional resources. Allie had that in her favor. *We'll just figure it out as the day unfolds*, she told herself. One thing she knew for sure: she liked Art Jr. more all the time and that was a first.

As Allie was drying off, her cell phone rang. "Hello, gorgeous," she heard Art Jr. say with great happiness. "How about you and I do the town today? I'm thinking a tour of your offices, lunch at some great little bistro, a matinee, dinner, and a leisurely evening. Does that work for you?"

"I—I thought you were leaving today," Allie said cautiously.

"Well, that's *my* little surprise," Art Jr. replied gleefully. "You got yours in last night. Here's mine: I'm staying another night. I was a complete ass at dinner, and I'd like you to see my better side, if that's OK with you."

Allie was quiet for a moment as her heart thumped with joy, fear, excitement, and shock all at the same time.

"Allie?" Art Jr. asked.

"Yes, Art," Allie replied. "Yes, yes, yes." It was all she could say. They understood each other perfectly.

40

Art Sr. was happy—deeply and truly so. He was relieved that both of his boys were finding love and the reconciliation with his eldest son meant so much to him. He had to work out things with John, but Elliana was going to give the family a new baby. It was a girl, and he believed she would bring healing with her birth.

As he tinkered in the shop, finishing the assembly of the first of the antique Beetles, Art was suddenly short of breath. His heart pounded irregularly, and he fell to the floor, torn apart by a sudden wrenching pain, a profound love for his family, and an intense desire to see Mae Rose. He decided against calling 911. He could die happy right now, so he just lay there and let life decide his fate. Feelings flooded him—laughing, weeping, screaming out his pain, and embracing his joy. Then he passed out.

Somewhere he heard a voice speaking to him very firmly, but with words she would never have used in her life. "Damn it, Art, get your ass up and call 911! You've got a grandchild on the way, and I expect you to be there when she's born. Don't be a goddamn martyr. Why the hell do I still have to tell you what to do? No way you're ready to die—no way. Hold that child for me when she's born, Art. Tell her that her great-grandma sends her love." Art didn't question Josephine Carter. He did as he was told.

First he called John; then he dialed 911.

The experience of nearly dying was a finishing touch to the transformation of Art McElroy. It allowed him to transcend the narrow confines of his limiting thoughts and feelings about himself, as if the universe had coalesced its energy, splitting his soul wide open with its laser-beam light. The ever-tightening restrictions of unworthiness and self-torment Art had suffered evaporated. In that moment, he realized that everything had been created out of love—everything, including him. And if it was not human love, then it was beyond human. While he couldn't express in words what had happened, he knew it was divine.

In that moment, Art forgave himself for all of his sins and was reborn into the love that had birthed him into the world. He knew what he wanted to do with the rest of his life, no matter how long or short it would be. But first he had to get to the hospital where he found John and Elliana were waiting for him.

"Dad!" John exclaimed and raced to his father's gurney. "This is my fault, Dad," he wept. "I am a mean, unforgiving son of a bitch. I don't want you to die. Please don't die, not now, not like this! Not after Mom . . ." He couldn't continue. Elliana wrapped her arms around him and walked him to the nurses' station. Art was put into a curtained cubicle and surrounded by doctors.

Maggie Whitman was the nurse in charge that day. When she saw John and Elliana, she rushed over to them. "I'm so sorry about your father, John. He's a strong man. I'm confident he'll—" she said as she moved to put her arms around them.

"Don't you touch me!" John screamed as he threw Maggie's arm away from him and put himself in front of Elliana. "Don't you *ever* touch me! I hate you! We hate you and my mother hated you for what you did to our family!"

Elliana grabbed John from behind, putting her arms around him, as she wept pitifully. "Honey, baby, come to me. No one means us any harm here, darling. *No one.* Think of our love. Think of our beautiful baby that's coming to live with us. Give us your full attention. We need you so much!" John fell apart in his wife's arms.

Maggie stood stunned, realizing instantly that Art's sons knew about the affair. Art had never told her and she was crushed, then angry.

41

Art Jr. and Allie sat in the budget cinema matinee in Los Angeles, his left and her right hands loosely linked. Art's other hand gripped the arm of the theater seat, waiting for the movie to begin. He had had a wonderful morning with Allie. The two of them lingered over breakfast, after which Allie showed him her work at the center. Art Jr. couldn't help loving her; he was so incredibly impressed with her in every way. As the movie began, Art's nervousness caused his left knee to bob up and down. Allie couldn't help noticing, but she was pulled forcefully into the story.

Something Like That opened at a burial site where a rather large gathering was assembled. The camera slowly zoomed in from the back of the crowd to focus on one middle-aged man. Flanked on each side by younger men, he was clearly the husband of the deceased. A minister's voice droned in the background.

As the camera lens drew closer, one could see that the man's shoulders were shaking, an obvious grief consuming him. Yet as the sound became clearer, it became clear that the man was shaking, not with sobs, but with hysterical laughter. His sons put their arms around him to subdue his shaking causing the coffin to tip over on the ground beside the grave. From there, the camera began to replay the circumstances leading up to his wife's death.

It was all there in the finest detail: Art leaving the house in his wife's yellow VW Beetle, the mechanic shop where Ben approached Art about the barn cats, the stop at the flower shop, the accident, Mae Rose's rage, and the man and his son breaking down the bathroom door. "Kathryn!" the man was screaming. The camera moved closer into the scene, and Art Jr. shuddered. He reached for Allie's hand as he trembled. He had not been present when his mother had died.

"Get out of here!" the man ordered his son. "Get out of here now!" he cried, shoving his son back into the hallway before turning back into the bathroom.

"No! Not now, not like this! Kathryn! Kathryn!" he screamed. The sound went silent, and the movie action slowed. Anguish and horror were etched in the man's face as he dropped to his knees and wrapped his arms around his wife's body as it sat on the toilet.

The camera expertly began to move up the obese body of the deceased woman until it reached her gruesomely contorted face. Everyone gasped, including Art Jr. who could not bear the thought of his mother looking so hideous at death. Allie shrieked too, because this unutterably grotesque scene confirmed for her that her mother could have written it—but only this one scene. It was her finest, most exquisitely horrific success.

Art knew that his parents hadn't gotten along well—that they had lived in increasingly angry silence with occasional dramatic out- bursts. Now that he knew about the affair, he understood more about his mother's trips to the bathroom and the muffled cries from his parents' bedroom if he came downstairs at night to get something from the kitchen. But when he left for college, he had put all of that behind him—or so he thought.

As the movie played scenes from the McElroy family's life perfectly and elegantly, Art Jr. wondered again, *Who could have known? Who could have written our story so perfectly? How had Mary Lee Broadmoor gotten the story and how could it be that the love of his life was her daughter?*

Yet in the end, none of that mattered. The movie drew to a close in an old barn with the couple connecting to each other from both earth and the afterlife in the back seat of the old VW Beetle. They spoke of their love and what they had learned—of how they both hoped for a second chance. Art Jr. wept openly, partly knowing and partly only hoping that this had actually occurred between his parents. If the rest of the movie was true . . . anything was possible.

As the credits rolled, Art Jr. leaned over to kiss Allie and said, "I think I love you just like that, Allie Schwartz." She snuggled into his arms. They sat silently together until everyone else had left the theater, and then walked out arm in arm.

Basking in the afterglow of the film, hands unable to keep to themselves, Art and Allie talked for hours in the hotel bar about *almost* everything, heads bent together to hear above the crowded din. Allie talked frankly about life with her mother; Art Jr. opened the door to his own a little more. Allie already knew that his mother had died—Art Jr. couldn't bear to tell her more than that, especially now that they'd seen the movie. All of this was foreplay, the beginning of their lovemaking, which would end in Art's hotel room in the wee hours of the morning.

Allie's long dark hair covered her face as she slept deeply, lying on her side facing away from Art Jr. but snuggled tight against him. For himself, Art Jr. was awake, completely captivated by the woman sleeping beside him and what they were experiencing together. He also remembered what Pastor Frank had told him about the movie— that no one had linked his family to the story. At last, he understood why.

Staring up at the hotel room ceiling, a sigh of love relaxed Art's entire body as he turned all of his attention back to the sleeping angel by his side. He would fly home in a few hours, but his heart would stay right where it was, in love with Allie Schwartz. When he saw the same agent at the LAX ticket counter on Monday morning, he didn't have to tell him a thing. The Art McElroy Jr. who entered the boarding bridge to the plane was very different from the one who had stepped off just three days earlier.

42

"You are *not, not, not* going to believe this," Cheryl told Nita excitedly, interrupting Nita's already turbulent sleep in the middle of the night.

Art McElroy Jr. had led her on a fascinating Internet journey into his life. She now knew enough of his life story to discover that his mother had passed away, which could, of course, make a young man hesitant to see *Something Like That*. But it was *how* she died that caused Cheryl Lewis to shiver. Her access to LA police records revealed another interesting detail: Art Jr.'s near arrest from assaulting a woman who just happened to be Allie Schwartz (!) at the last GloMed convention.

Every cell of Cheryl's body went on high alert. Even before she told Nita Winslow the details of what she had discovered, she knew they were on their way to the small, Midwestern town that the McElroys called home. She shivered again as she wondered if Art's father restored old VWs and if he had committed adultery. If these facts were also accurate, she would have a direct link between the McElroy family and the movie that Mary Lee had claimed not to remember writing. But here the trail cooled off just enough to tantalize the detective that lived inside Cheryl Lewis.

While she could not yet explain *how* Mary Lee Broadmoor had made the connection to the McElroy family, it could mean that the movie was so powerful because it was *real*, as Nita had suggested some time ago. Either way or any point in between, it would make for an interesting investigation and at some point, a stunning *Currents* program.

After Cheryl detailed this to Nita, there was no more sleepiness in Nita's voice. Her own head was spinning with possible stories. "I knew it! I knew Mary Lee couldn't have written that story on her own. Didn't I tell you that? Mary Lee Broadmoor is going to have to let us interview her when we get the full details! Nice work, Ms. Lewis!

"See if you can find out more about what happened at the GloMed International conference," Nita suggested. "And charter a flight to the airport closest to this little town of Fairview for next Saturday. Bring two camera crews. Find out where the McElroys attend church, if they do. Something tells me we'll find some missing pieces and be able to rock the world. I want to be on top of it when it happens."

"OK. Got it." Cheryl signed off to take care of details. Her mind snaked around all the facts she now had, searching for clues to the mysterious connection she had discovered. If there was a logical explanation, she would be disappointed, but it was her job to find the answers. She would not let Eugene Gregory's secretive life fall by the wayside, but he would have to wait.

43

Having to say good-bye to Art Jr. at LAX had been hard for Allie. She was in love and had no idea when she would see "her man" again. For the first time in her life, Allie wanted to be with someone else more than she wanted to be alone. Art Jr. felt safe and warm to her, and she had never known that kind of caring before, except briefly with her father.

But the energy of passion also set Allie on a mission. After she said a tearful "good-bye" to Art Jr., her next destination was her "mother's" estate where she intended to confront her about the movie. Allie now emphasized the "m" word with quotation marks; she was more suspicious than ever that her own mother had somehow disappeared.

Allie's visit was intentionally unprecedented and unplanned. For the first time ever, Allie would simply drop by unannounced and see what it was like to catch Mary Lee by surprise. When the guards at the estate entrance saw Allie's car, they waved her through without asking, nor did they call up to the house to notify anyone. After all, it was Mary Lee's daughter coming to visit. Perfectly natural. Unusual and without precedence, but natural.

Mae Rose's energy was busy working on her next movie script, the story of the genius hiding inside people that the American society called "disabled." She had read everything she could get her hands on and interviewed doctors, psychologists, and agencies that specialized in helping children overcome the stigma of diagnoses of autism, dyslexia, and attention deficit disorder. Mary Lee was reading alongside her and making suggestions.

Why, both women wondered, *were there more of these afflictions now than ever before?* While it was possible that society was just more aware, it struck them both that in truth these unusual behavior patterns were simply more common. In an age of careful pregnancies and all that was known about what *not* to do, how could it be that these "disabilities" appeared in such abundance? Was it the American diet, as many suspected?. It had them completely captivated.

True to form, Mary Lee—even with Mae Rose's spirit cooperating—still hated to be interrupted when she was writing. The weather was beautiful outside and the windows in Mary Lee's newly decorated bedroom were open, allowing a wonderful breeze to refresh the air with the scent of magnolia blossoms. It was a blissful day.

Gertie was in the kitchen, practicing her flirting skills with Chef Michael. Her focus was particularly keen now that she'd had a call from Dr. Gregory, who claimed he wanted to get to know her better. They were having dinner that coming Friday at a quiet little restaurant he liked. Gertie was looking forward to the opportunity to apply her skills at arousing him, so her lesson was in earnest.

As Michael began preparations for the evening meal, Gertie sat on the kitchen counter, snuggling up next to him and making her moves. He guided her, lectured her about being overly enthusiastic, showed her how to stand just so to show off a little cleavage and make a man long for more. Gertie heard the doorbell and pouted.

"Who could that be?" she asked Chef Michael as she sat seductively on the counter with her arms behind her, crossing and rubbing her legs together suggestively.

"Doesn't matter, does it, *cherie?*" Michael responded as he took her around the waist and set her down on the floor. "You'd better answer it before our writing queen hears the doorbell again. You know how she is."

"You mean how she *was,*" Gertie corrected him as her high heels made contact with the marble floor. "She's not nearly as irritable these days. Sometimes she seems almost happy. It's getting boring around here."

"Perhaps," Michael responded, "but I wouldn't test her. Get going, girl." Michael gave Gertie a pat on her behind, which made her giggle, and pointed her in the direction of the door,. She lifted the back of her green taffeta skirt at him.

Gertie had no idea that her appearance was less than appropriate as she approached the door. The top two buttons of her sleeveless dress were missing, revealing her ample bosom; the full skirt was quite wrinkled, and her hair was messy. Her matching shoes struck the floor angrily with each step. When she opened the door and saw Allie standing there, Gertie was almost speechless.

"Natalie!" she exclaimed, "Is everything OK? This is such a surprise!"

"Hello, Gertie," Allie replied as she walked past Gertie into the house. "Everything is OK—wonderful in fact. But I'd like to see Mother. Is she available?" Allie eyed Gertie's attire and somewhat flushed appearance. "Am I interrupting something?" she queried.

"Goodness, no," Gertie replied as she smoothed her dress. "Chef Michael and I are just working on dinner. Your mother is writing and not expecting any visitors. I need to check with her; you know how she is when she writes," Gertie added.

"Ah, yes," Allie replied. "Nevertheless, I'd like to see her. I'll just go on up if that's OK with you, take my chances that being her daughter might buy me an audience. Nice dress, by the way." Allie missed nothing about the scene; Gertie was up to something. "I'd be wearing an apron over it if I were you."

Gertie frowned as she walked along with Allie to the elevator. "Your mother is not used to being surprised. You know how fragile she is these days."

"Gertie," Allie said as she stopped and turned to face the disheveled woman who benefited from her mother's newfound love of clothing and spending money, "she's *my* mother. I'll handle this and I don't want or need a bodyguard."

"I just don't want to lose my job," Gertie whined. "Ms. Broad—I mean, your mother—has strict rules, and it's my job to make sure they're followed." Gertie felt an overwhelming need to protect both

Mary Lee and Natalie from each other, especially after seeing Mary Lee playing cards against herself the night before.

"Really, Gertie?" Allie replied. "It looks like I've caught you in a moment when *you* would rather not be interrupted. Are you sure it's my mother you're defending—or is it *yourself*?" Allie pressed the elevator button, and the door opened. She stepped inside.

"Suit yourself," Gertie retorted haughtily. "Just make sure she knows you arrived unannounced. I'll be checking with the gatehouse in the meantime." She turned and headed back down the hallway. There was nothing she could do about what Allie might discover, and perhaps it was time.

Stepping off the elevator at the second level, Allie paused and heard rapid clicking, which meant her mother was indeed deep into her writing. She squared her shoulders, knocked, and turned the knob on the door.

"Gertie? Is that you? What do you want? I'd really rather not be disturbed right now."

Allie heard her mother's voice, yet it was not her voice. It was too sweet, yet not sweet—sweet like someone who was irritated and trying not to show it. Whoever this was, she was not the mother Allie knew. *Her* mother would have been outraged and would have peppered her reply with expletives.

Allie opened the door further and stepped inside the room. "Mother?"

"Allie! What on Earth? What brings you here? What's wrong?" Mae Rose's energy tried to rouse Mary Lee's.

"Mother," Allie replied, "it's just me. I think everyone assumed it would be OK for your own daughter to show up unannounced. Is it a problem for you? I wanted to see how you were doing after your successful dinner party."

"I'm fine, dear. How are you and . . . and that young man of yours? What's his name—Art? He was so fucking uptight! I'm not sure he's right for you." Mae Rose tried to put herself in Mary Lee's personality.

"Art is wonderful, Mother," Allie gushed. "I guess I really shocked him the other night—more than I intended. I think I love him, Mother." Mae Rose had to turn away as her eyes teared up. She needed Mary Lee desperately.

"Well that makes complete sense. He tried to humiliate me so you adore him. Of course!"

Allie saw that her mother looked like a queen as she sat typing at her desk. She was dressed in an elegant outfit of long, flowing, cream-colored pants and a jacket trimmed in sparkling sequins. She noticed for the first time that her mother could be quite beautiful and—*where were the cigars? Why wasn't her mother smoking? Why were the windows open?*

"So, once again, *what* the hell are you doing here?" Mae Rose continued to attempt to behave appropriately. "I'm serious. You show up unannounced. It must be something big. Are you pregnant?"

"Of course not!" Allie replied, quite offended.

"Then tell me what really brings you here, Natalie. I'm not so naive as to think that you don't have a purpose to your visit. You might as well come out with it."

"I'm worried about you, Mother," Allie admitted.

"Me? Why, I've never felt better in my whole *fucking* life!" Mae Rose was glad she'd had some bad language experience in the afterlife. She smiled.

"Yes, Mother, and don't you think that's odd?" Allie asked pointedly. "That you're so *well?* That you're writing *love* stories? That you're *kind?* That you seem to like people you used to hate and you invite them to dinner? Art and I went to see *Something Like That* yesterday and it deserves all the accolades it's received. But, Mother, surely *you* didn't write that. You had to have help. It's way beyond your reach. And when Art asked about it at dinner, you couldn't explain where the story came from."

Allie's intense gaze searched Mary Lee's face for a trace of secretive dishonesty—not that her mother had ever been dishonest. Mary Lee wouldn't have known how to tell a lie. Au contraire, she used to relish the opportunity to tell someone exactly what she thought and would sigh with relief regardless of the potentially devastating consequences.

"Where did the story come from, *Mother*?" Allie repeated.

Mae Rose wasn't certain how to respond. She'd been too focused on her son that evening to listen to much of the conversation. Then Mary Lee had consumed a large amount of alcohol after which Mae Rose's energy had passed out. "I wrote it—every word of it," she declared because she was Mae Rose and she had. "Why do you care so much? It's out. It's over and we would much rather focus on what's—"

"We?" Allie interrupted. "Who is 'we'?"

"I meant 'I,' of course. 'We' is just a general term I use for . . ." Mae Rose paused. "I thought we explained all of that Saturday evening," she finished with a sigh. "Darling, I don't know what else you want. And speaking of Saturday night, do you want to tell me why your boyfriend had to run off in the middle of dinner? Are you sure you know this man?" Mae Rose had to change the subject.

Mary Lee's energy showed up at last and took over. "How dare you just walk in here! You know the rules! Never do that again, Natalie! Now I'd like to get back to this story, the one I *know* I'm writing. For your information, it will be as touching and wonderful as the last one. Perhaps I've been changed by my recovery. Try to think of this as an act of God or *something like that*. Ha! I really don't want to discuss it any further. Get the hell out of here."

Allie sighed and stood up. "For the first time in my life, I don't believe you, Mother," she said. "I've never, ever heard you tell a lie, even in all the times I felt like it would have been merciful. Now everything about you is different, and something tells me you know more than you're saying. I don't know the woman you've become. I don't even know if the person I'm talking to is you, or if the mother I knew has traded her soul for an Oscar! And for your information, Art's mother passed away recently enough that the movie was hard for him to watch, much less meeting the woman who got credit for writing it. And you were rude to him too! *That's* why he left the table."

"Natalie," Mary Lee replied, "I can hardly believe my ears! I've never lied to you, and I'm far too old and uninterested to start now. Why would I? Try some morphine yourself sometime and see if you remember everything you said and did. And if I were going to fabricate something, don't you think I'd rather do that when I'm asked about where the story came from, than tell the truth? Wouldn't it be easier on all of us if I just made something up? I must have written the story. Pardon me if I don't remember doing it. This is preposterous!" Standing and pulling herself to her full stature, a confident Mary Lee Broadmoor faced her equally confident daughter.

"Don't bother trying to turn the tables on me, whoever you are," Allie retorted. "It's an old trick of yours, and I'm not playing. If you aren't going to tell me the truth, I *will* find out another way. Everyone is talking about it. If you can't come up with a better answer, someone else will do it for you—maybe Nita Winslow. You've been warned.

"You might look like my mother, but you don't act like her at all. You don't feel hard and crusty like her, and you're spending *her* money in ways she would not approve." Allie could not stop now that she had started to confront her mother. "Furthermore, I neither understand nor appreciate your relationship with Gertie. Why is she still here? Do you have any idea what she's doing with all of her free time? She looks and acts like she has a secret, *Mother*, like she knows something that she's not telling. I think you'd better pay attention to what's going on under your own roof. Good-bye." Allie opened the door to leave.

"Gertie is as close to a daughter as I'm going to have in this lifetime!" Mary Lee shot back. "You say I'm not your mother? Ha! *You* are not my daughter! Gertie likes and appreciates me; she does things with me that any mother would love to share with a daughter. So as long as she's willing to stay, she's welcome. Speaking of welcome, *you* are welcome to leave and do not ever come into this house again without letting the guards know. The door won't open so easily next time!"

Mary Lee hated to be so firm with her own child, but it had to be done. "I don't know why I ever thought to leave everything I have to *you*, you ungrateful bitch! I'll make certain to get my will changed, whoever I am!" Mary Lee slammed the door behind Allie and turned back to her computer.

Touché, Mary Lee said to herself and smiled. She was almost certain she was telling the truth, and it really didn't matter what the rest of the world—including her daughter—thought. She felt much, much better.

* * *

Gertie watched as Allie stepped out of the elevator. She could tell by the look on her face that the visit was over and that it had been less than pleasant. It was difficult for Gertie to mask her own satisfaction with a concerned look, but she did her best.

"I tried to tell you to let me call her first." Gertie told Allie as she moved to get the front door for Allie's exit. As she put her hand on the latch, she had to repress a knowing smile.

Allie stepped through the door as Gertie opened it, and then stopped, turned back, and said, "Gertie, the woman who lives here is *not* my mother. If I were you, I'd be on my guard. *My* mother does not buy extravagant clothes for herself or anyone else. She is unkind but she is honest. The woman who looks like her, the one upstairs, is hiding something under her sunshine exterior. I'd be careful if I were you because one of these days, the truth is going to come out, and you might just be in the wrong place at the wrong time.

"And furthermore," Allie declared as she let her eyes wander up and down Gertie's body, "live like your every move is being watched because it is. I haven't trusted you since the day you made that phone call to me to tell me my mother was dead. I know that's what you were going to say, which means you've also been hiding something. You and whoever that is upstairs will be reckoned with one day. Mark my words." With that, Allie headed down the steps to her car.

Full of rage, Gertie marched out right after her. "Well, if you think something strange happened to your mother, you could have known for yourself if you'd cared enough to be by her bedside when she looked to me like she was dying! Maybe you should consider visiting more often, Natalie, and try acting like a daughter. Your mother would love to take you shopping and share time with you. If you think she's not your mother, you should consider how much of your adult life you've spent pretending that you're not her daughter. No daughter who cared would act like you have. I think you're just jealous!" Gertie shrieked then turned, marched back up the steps, and slammed the heavy door shut.

While she was glad for everything she had finally said to Natalie, the dark cloud that had settled over Gertie on the day Mary Lee died, thickened. It would continue to damage her perspective and alter her personality.

In the meantime, Chef Michael had come into the hallway and was applauding her. "Bravo, Gertie! Bravo! It's about time someone told that snooty girl off!" Gertie figured that Chef Michael was probably ready for a break, and she was in the mood to give him one that would leave a lasting impression. She would call it the "standing ovation." With it, she earned her diploma.

44

Once Art's condition had stabilized in the emergency room at Fairview Hospital, he was moved to critical care to be watched overnight. He was glad he'd listened to the voice in his head that had told him to call 911. As the hospital settled into its night shift, Maggie came into his room.

"Art, how are you? I'm so sorry for your heart attack but not surprised. You've been under so much emotional stress this past year since Mae Rose died. But why didn't you tell me that your boys knew about us? I thought we were keeping it a secret!" She began to weep. "John did everything but call me a whore today. Why didn't you tell me they knew?" she begged. She didn't pause to let Art answer. "I feel so awful for them, but I'm deeply hurt too, Art. You should have told me. Really. I had a right to know that they knew," Maggie insisted as she wiped her tears away. "I never wanted to hurt them. You knew that."

"Maggie," Art responded wearily, "if I could go back and do everything all over again, you and I would never have done what we did, and then this never would have happened. It's been hell, Maggie. They found out through that movie that came out—what was it called? *Something Like That* or something like that. They figured the plot was about our family, and they put the pieces together about the affair. I couldn't lie to them, Maggie! They didn't speak to me for quite a while, and it was so awful that remembering to tell you just slipped my mind. I'm sorry for that along with everything else. Sometimes I wish I'd died instead of Mae Rose. Tried to do that today but didn't succeed." He smiled weakly.

He went on quietly. "I have no idea how anyone got a hold of a story so similar to our lives and made it a movie. John thought maybe it was you, but I told him I was sure you didn't know our family that well nor would you ever have done such a thing. But now I have to ask you, Maggie. Did you tell someone about our messed up family? The boys and I need to know." Art was drugged enough to put this question to Maggie without caring much how Maggie felt about it. "It was a stupid move, what we did, and now it's a stupid mov-*ie*. It won two Academy Awards. Dear God!"

Maggie started weeping as she said, "Is that all you have to say about what we experienced together for three years? That it was a stupid move? I never told anybody, Art. I've carried that secret myself for all these years, and it's been killing me, let me tell you. To lose a husband in death is one thing. To lose a living man? That's worse. Sometimes I wish I were dead too."

"Well," Art hesitated, not sure what to say, "I don't want to make things harder for you than they already are, Maggie. Yes, I wish I'd told you that the boys found out, but I didn't—it was so hard to lose them that I simply forgot. Sometimes I wish someone would stop by to tell me something I'd done right for a change, although I think the shock would kill me." He smiled. "I had a really good day today, and look where it got me."

"Art, I can't stand this any longer," Maggie said. "I've been think-ing it might be best if I were gone. Would you miss me . . . if I went away?" Maggie's voice quavered just a little at the end. "Or maybe you would be glad—"

Art heard Maggie's voice trembling again and sighed deeply. "Maggie, I can only miss one woman at a time, and Mae Rose had years on you. You understand that. I can't say what I feel about you or what it would be like if you left. Not now. It would be asking too much of anyone to do that. It's been over for years, Maggie. I might suggest that you talk to Pastor Frank about it if it still affects you so much. I wish you well. I always have. But we both need to move on. You and I are never going to be 'we.'" Art felt helpless as he finished talking.

"Thank you, Art. I appreciate your honesty," Maggie said quietly in response. "I understand. I love you and my only regret is that you are so lost in your sorrow that you can't find your way back to me. What we had was so good, Art. I will miss that. Good-bye."

When Maggie got home, she hoped God would forgive her for not wanting to live any longer. She'd thought about ending her life for quite some time, and today seemed to be a good day to die. Death was not difficult for someone who had access to emergency medical equipment and supplies. Maggie had already prepared a lethal cocktail over the course of the past few months. She would not feel much, she knew, as she laid the pills out in the right order. She expected a quiet crossing, like falling asleep; she expected she would awaken free of the deep aching hollow that was called her life.

* * *

At the same time as Maggie was preparing to end her life, Pastor Frank was paying a visit to Art, who was sleeping. With the privilege of a man of the cloth, he remained vigilant for Art, and in constant prayer. While he'd never truly felt the power of God in more than the most subtle ways, he sensed he had a solid connection. He begged God for Art's life.

He stopped suddenly in the middle of a sentence as he heard a voice say to him, *I heard you the first time. Do you know how much more efficient it would be if people just asked once and then focused on the answer they wanted like they believed I would actually answer their prayer?*

Pastor Frank half expected to turn around and see George Burns or Morgan Freeman standing inside Art's room. The voice continued. *Begging does not become you, my son. Ask, seek, knock. Too bad most people just keep asking and asking. Stop asking. Drives me nuts. That's it. Focus on the outcome you desire. So shall it be done.*

Pastor Frank felt an urgent need to burp a bubble of gas that was rising in his throat. Although he tried to be discreet, it came out quite loudly. As he allowed it to release, words formed—words that would not be heard by anyone except Pastor Frank and God.

"Be healed."

Even Pastor Frank was stunned as a deep, peaceful wave of energy flowed through the room. There was a quiet pause as all activity ceased. While in time/space reality such an event would create an instant emergency with backup generators kicking in and alerts going out to police and fire squads, none of that occurred. It was only the briefest pause that no one would notice. What they *would* remember was how good they felt and how many people had been healed that night. When reality kicked back in, Pastor Frank was gone.

At the precise moment Pastor Frank uttered the words, "Be healed," the phone rang at Maggie Whitman's home. Maggie answered it in bed, where she sat propped up on her floral-covered pillow, the death cocktail in her hand and a glass of water on the nightstand. Her only daughter, Anne, was calling from Seattle, announcing that she and her husband were expecting their second child.

"Mother, would you please reconsider relocating to help us with the children?" she begged. "I know we've asked before and you've been reluctant to leave the Midwest, but we could really use your help, especially with a second child on the way. Please, Mother. We miss you dreadfully."

Maggie began to weep uncontrollably, for she knew that God was intervening. Her daughter had to wait for her to respond, which Maggie did at first by nodding in agreement with the idea, then laughed because of course her daughter couldn't see her head shaking. Finally she said, "Yes, dear. I would love to," and she knew she would begin making arrangements the next day. All she had to do was give notice at the hospital and take advantage of the paid days off she had accumulated to get ready to move.

The only person she would contact other than the human resources person at the hospital would be Pastor Frank. She would tell him because she trusted him and wanted him to know so he wouldn't search for her when she wasn't at church. She would ask him not to mention anything to the McElroys and doubted they would even notice her absence. After she hung up the phone, she got out of bed, went to the bathroom, and flushed the pills down the toilet.

45

A wave of nausea swept over Eugene as he contemplated his date with Gertie. He had called her on Monday, knowing she would accept. Her unbridled eagerness had caused his intestinal tract to churn ever since. It was impossible not to be aware of Gertie's sexual interest in him, which notched his anxious dread to a fever pitch. He had always ignored her clear adoration and silly attempts at coyness, until now. Asking Gertie out on a date was a bizarre twist to Gene's well-ordered life. It would likely set up expectations in her mind that he would have to deal with later but he needed to know what she knew, whatever that meant. He grimaced.

Gene's weekend research after Mary Lee's dinner party took him into unusual return-to-life circumstances that had been fascinating and aroused more than his interest. Most compelling were the cases of those who had been pronounced clinically dead and had recovered. How their lives were changed interested him the most as he entered uncharted mystical territory, looking for anything that could explain Mary Lee's transformation *and* the true origin of her story. Gene wanted and needed to know more. Had Mary Lee returned from the dead with her magical story already in hand, or had some sort of "exchange" occurred in which spirits traded places? He was almost tempted to visit a psychic but he knew he had to start with Gertie.

"Howard," he had confided to the concierge at his condominium, "I need to take a woman out for dinner this coming Friday night, but I need it to be private. I don't want to be seen publicly with her. It's too complicated to explain, but is there a restaurant that could accommodate this? And I trust your confidentiality as I always have."

Howard Humphries knew his clients well after working at The Plaza for more than twenty years. He was in his sixties now and took expert care of his elite class of condominium owners. Accordingly, they returned the favor with a generous salary and tips that bought his continued loyalty. He knew that Dr. Gregory never dated and that he didn't entertain anyone in his home. Howard didn't know if the doctor had any sexual preference and wondered if his work with death had affected him so that he wouldn't want a romantic connection in his life. Howard was sympathetic and completely trustworthy.

"Yes, of course, Doctor. I can help with that," he had replied immediately in his slightly suave accent from nowhere in particular. "My recommendation would be Les Trois Soeurs, a French restaurant a short drive from here. Each table is partitioned in canopied fabric, which creates a wonderful effect and a secluded atmosphere. It would be my first recommendation, sir, although ghastly expensive," he added. "This Friday might be a bit of a challenge, sir. They occasionally have booths they will open for an additional fee later in the evening. Many famous people eat there, but of course, no one else knows who is coming and going. The staff is also very discreet."

"Perfect," Gene replied. "Please see what you can do for Friday night and Howard . . ." He hesitated. "I need you to instruct my driver to call me one hour after the time we are seated. Make it a medical emergency so that I can excuse myself and not be burdened with seeing the lady home. Can you take care of that for me as well?"

"Certainly, Dr. Gregory," Howard assured him. "I'll call you as soon as I have it arranged. Anything else?"

"No, Howard. Thank you." Eugene placed his next call to the caretakers of his ranch. "I'm flying out Friday night on the red-eye. Please have my place ready for me," he instructed. His hunch was that a disappearing act after dinner with Gertie would be wise. As he finished that call, he saw a call from Howard already coming in.

"Friday will work as long as you're willing to take a late reservation. They will open a booth at nine o'clock for one thousand dollars."

"Good God!" Eugene replied, surprised at the cost in spite of Howard's earlier warning. There was a pause. Howard heard his client take a deep breath. "But it's perfect, Howard. Go ahead and book it. Can you do it under your name? And remember to have my driver call me one hour later," he emphasized, greatly relieved. An hour alone with Gertie was about all he imagined he would be able to handle for a first encounter.

* * *

Chef Michael had taken Gertie to task about acting too eager when she accepted his invitation. "You don't say yes immediately and giggle when a man asks you out for an evening, especially Dr. Gregory," he told her as he took his anger at her out on some vegetables he was chopping for an evening stir-fry for Mary Lee and Gertie. "It makes you sound weak and desperate. Men get bored with those women. After all I've taught you? Really, Gertie! We're going to have to work hard on creating that sense of mystery that men crave. Otherwise your flirting will lead only to lots of meaningless and potentially dangerous encounters. Trust me on this," he said, waving his knife in the air to make his point.

Gertie began to wonder if Chef Michael might truly care about her. The way he reacted certainly suggested he could, in which case she didn't mind being scolded. "And we only have until Friday—*mon dieu!*" he added.

Eyeing herself critically in the full-length mirror before leaving her room for her date, Gertie's eyes dropped immediately to how she looked below her waistline. Truth be known, Gertie had a difficult time seeing her whole self. Whenever she was in front of a mirror, she saw her hips, thighs, and bottom almost exclusively and was hypercritical of those aspects. Even as a child, her foster family and kids at school had mocked her for her size, calling her "Big Birdie Gertie." It was stamped so deeply on Gertie's memory that she didn't even realize it.

Gertie might be large, but her proportions were quite perfectly balanced. She had a tiny waist that complemented her generous upper and lower parts. Normally she avoided a mirror completely, but tonight was different.

Everything she and Mary Lee could think of to impress Eugene Gregory had been done, down to the miniscule and unseen details of her preparations which included "Suck in the Gut" panties and "Trim the Thighs" tights. While they accomplished their goals, Gertie found it somewhat difficult to breathe and walk. She was used to allowing her body to be free by covering everything with her shapeless uniform. Thankfully, Mary Lee had been requiring that she dress up for dinner so she had practice wearing these breath-defying undergarments. Still, they had a strange effect. Her compressed body had to do something with the extra folds of skin, so it often crept up toward Gertie's already ample bosom.

Tonight she was dressed in a royal blue pantsuit with a flatter-ing bolero jacket. She truly did look sophisticated and almost svelte. Mary Lee knocked rapidly on the door and poked her head in to Gertie's room. "Yoo-hoo, Gertie, the doctor is in," she said, smiling, and pleased that Gertie was going out with someone Mary Lee had trusted with her own life. "You look stunning, Gertie," she exclaimed. It was obvious by the happy tone of her voice that she was genuinely impressed. "Look at you!"

Turning on her three-inch heels, which raised her height to a respectable five feet, four inches, Gertie looked at the back of her outfit in the mirror, a view that included her bottom. She frowned but had to acknowledge that this was the best she'd ever looked. When she faced the mirror again, she was certain she saw tears in Mary Lee's eyes. She twirled around again then gave Mary Lee a hug.

"Don't you go getting soft on me, Ms. Broadmoor," she whis-pered. "I'm already an emotional basket case. I can hardly breathe in this outfit. If you make me cry, who knows what could happen? I might just explode!" This, of course, made Mary Lee laugh, and she hugged Gertie.

"OK, I think the doctor has waited long enough, Gertie," Mary Lee suggested. "It's a warm evening, but take your wrap with you. It looks sophisticated and divine and finishes the outfit. Oh, to be young again!" Mary Lee clasped her hands together in utter delight. Her display of emotion was so uncustomary that Gertie could hardly believe it was her employer standing in front of her. It was then that she realized Mary Lee had become much more to her than that. She started to get tears in her eyes.

"Thank you, Ms. Broadmoor," she sniffed. "You make me feel . . . almost beautiful, and . . . and you're not *that old!*" Gertie exclaimed. "You could have any man you chose if you wanted to, even Dr. Gregory!"

"Oh, I suppose, but why bother?" Mary Lee laughed. "I am so blissfully happy these days. I think a man would just clutter up the landscape. Now get moving, girl!"

The two women walked down the hall to the elevator together. As they stepped into the cabin, Gertie became almost shy. "I don't know," she confided. "I don't know why he asked *me* out, Ms. Broadmoor. Maybe I'll just clam up and he'll have a miserable evening. What if I can't think of anything to talk about?" Gertie's worries created a disagreeable crease in her forehead, and her eyelids drooped unbecomingly.

"Nonsense, Gertie!" Mary Lee shot back. "If you can handle me the way you did when I was ill, you can handle anything! Have a drink to relax, but don't drink too much. It's a first date. Keep some secrets, dear, and have a wonderful evening. And, Gertie, please keep a smile on your face. It's so much more becoming than your frown."

Mary Lee and Gertie walked to the foyer to greet Gene, who was dressed in an evening tuxedo and looked so gorgeous that Gertie couldn't help but show her admiration—and the desire to see him naked.

"Well, aren't you looking lovely tonight, Gertie!" Gene exclaimed with a slight cough of genuine surprise. Privately he wondered what it had taken to get her into such good shape and how much it had cost Mary Lee. He had not missed Gertie's naked delight at seeing him.

"Thank you, Doctor," Gertie replied, flirtingly sweetly. "You're not looking too bad yourself."

Gene rolled only his inner eyes, thinking, *Dear God, what have I done?* He was glad no one would see them together. He put his elbow out and tucked her hand in place.

"Good night, Mary Lee," he said, making a slight bow. "Don't wait up for us."

Gertie giggled foolishly, causing Gene to grit his teeth as they left. Even with his mission in mind, once they were in the limo, he turned to Gertie and wondered what to say.

"Your employer is looking very well these days," he commented.

"Oh, she's just wonderful, Gene. May I call you that?" Gertie gushed and proceeded to propel her way into a torrent of words. "She's so changed—hard at work on her next story—all under wraps, of course, but I don't know how much longer I would have lasted if she hadn't come around like she did—she was awful—may I be frank? The worst client I have ever had!" When she paused to take another breath, Gene jumped into the conversation.

"Yes, it's a miracle to see her so happy," he agreed, hoping that "miracle" would give Gertie permission to open up. "This, of course, must take quite a bit of pressure off of you. I can't imagine what you endured when she was ill, although I must admit I found her so interesting back then. I hardly feel like I know her anymore. It's true, as you say; she is so changed."

"Well, it was awful, let me tell you, but let's not talk about that, shall we? It's all in the past. Tell me about yourself, Gene. I hardly know you at all in spite of our mutual patience with your patient." Gertie giggled at her own wit.

Gene smiled carefully. He would leave the past alone for now but not for long. And he would be very selective with what he told Gertie about himself—very, very selective. He looked up at the driver and caught his eye in the rearview mirror. He knew that after the "emergency" call, the driver would take Gertie home. Gene would be obligated only to say a quick good-bye, give Gertie a kiss on the cheek perhaps, and make the promise of a future date. That future would depend on how much he could ply from Gertie tonight. The way she was chattering, it wouldn't take much.

46

Mary Lee closed the door behind Gene and Gertie, marveling at how long it had been since she (and Mae Rose) had been alone at home. Chef Michael was out with his friends, as he usually was every night after dinner. Gertie, however, had not been out of the house at all as far as Mary Lee knew. Oh, she would run errands or go shopping, but it was always for brief periods of time. Gertie seemed content to have no social life and had no close friends or family. Mary Lee realized that it would be time to let her move on one of these days, but it made her sad, so she refused to think about it.

Heading to her study, Mary Lee sat quietly in the dark. After a few minutes, she turned on the *Currents* show to see Nita Winslow in action. She and Mae Rose had talked candidly about what had occurred with Allie on Monday. It made them both nervous, particularly because Mae Rose had let the "we" word slip. They pulled out a deck of cards and played amicably for a long time before either of them spoke. When they did, it was simultaneous. "It's time to talk to Nita Winslow." They high-fived and Mary Lee was selected to place the call.

Nita Winslow was relaxing in her room at the studio after the Friday evening *Currents* show. Tonight was another huge success. The station had finally aired "Those Who Wait" based on the waiting room interviews she had taped while spending time at the hospital, knowing Mary Lee Broadmoor would eventually show up. Cheryl expertly joined segments together so viewers could share in the drama of families experiencing both joy and sorrow.

The show opened in a waiting room of family members laughing and pacing, waiting for the birth of a first child and, thus, a first grandchild. Tears of joy and hugs of celebration made incredibly touching scenes.

Winding its way through various other life events, including everything from routine surgical procedures to one young man coming in to the emergency room with a dart embedded deeply in his chin, the show concluded with the end of life, the death of an elderly man alone in the world.

"There was no one waiting for this man," Nita Winslow's voice spoke with an ache of sorrow. "He came into the emergency room alone and left the world with no one hoping against hope that he would live another day, no one who cared enough to know what his life had meant and whether it mattered." She paused as the man's face grew larger and larger on the screen until it vanished. "May each of us have the gift of those who wait for us, who hope for us and believe that we matter." Even the studio staff had tears in their eyes at the end. The credits took over, replaying the birth scene, which magically brought everyone into a happier space.

Nita sighed as people disappeared after swarming her with accolades and invitations to regular post-show gatherings. She was used to praise and success, followed by naked loneliness. She was so incredibly popular that she could not trust any man to actually love her. After several marriages, she knew that men were exhausted by her incessant energy and her complete fascination with everything going on in the world that might make a good story. Conversely, for Nita, no man was as interesting to her as her work. Her marriages were like watching a fireworks display. The launch was inspiring; the grand finale dramatic—even newsworthy, but after that there was nothing left but ashes.

As she reached for her phone to call her driver, Nita noticed that she had a message, which intrigued her because she gave this number out to only select people. She dialed back immediately and gasped with glee at the message. Mary Lee Broadmoor was suggesting that she come to her home that very night for a private conversation—no taping. *Ooh la la!*

With a sense of renewed excitement and victory, Nita called her driver, grabbed her things, and threw them into the car. Apparently Mary Lee had watched tonight's show and felt ready to talk. Nita welcomed the opportunity to go somewhere besides an empty house or another social event. In fact, a late evening with another woman alone in quiet conversation appealed to her immensely. As she climbed into the car, she checked the time: 9:30 p.m. It was never too late to speak with Mary Lee Broadmoor.

47

Dinner at Les Trois Soeurs had gone remarkably well for Gene and Gertie. Howard's recommendation had been perfect and worth every penny. The privacy concept offered by this unique restaurant was so successful in France that the owners had decided to test the same concept in the United States. Where else but in LA could such an idea take hold? Tapestry drapes running on rails high above the dining room could be positioned into many types of arrangements, allowing complete privacy between tables for any size party. While some critics suggested that such privacy could lead to provocative or inappropriate activities, Les Trois Soeurs boasted an impeccable reputation with its "No Shoes, No Shirt, No Pants, *No Service*" policy.

The cuisine was completely French with wines, cheeses, meats, herbs, and vegetables that were all organic and flown in from France almost daily. The menu was in French with English available only upon request; prices were not given and anyone who asked was permitted to leave. No one saw other parties coming and going. Even arrivals and departures were secretive. It was a perfect place for Gene to get to know Gertie without her being seen by people who knew him. Once they were seated, he had only an hour to endure.

Gertie had behaved remarkably well—perhaps in part because she was awestruck by the impeccable surroundings of the restaurant. She sipped her wine slowly and entertained Gene with descriptions of her former clients, who remained nameless even though they were no longer living. She was actually intelligent, Gene discovered to his surprise, well read, able to discuss financial matters, and so genuine that it was hard not to be captivated. She didn't pry but Gene told her more about himself than any other woman in his life. He was not sure why.

"I live under no illusions, Gene," Gertie offered frankly as the appetizers were served. She took a delicate sip from her glass of white wine. "I don't expect a line of suitors, much less marriage. I've learned not to ask for much from others, especially men. That's not an insult to the masculine gender. It's just a fact of my life. And I like what I do. I really enjoy helping people make their way from this life to the next as comfortably as possible. Many of them open up to an interested and listening ear. I have heard confessions that would make a great novel. I have watched estranged families both drawn back together and torn further apart by death. I have seen miracles, Gene." This last sentence she said with a lowered voice.

Gene's ears perked up. "*Miracles*, Gertie?" He was glad he had used that word earlier. Now he was completely drawn in. "Like what?" Gene tried not to appear too interested, but he fixed his gaze on hers and their eyes locked.

Gertie frowned, afraid she may have said too much, but she couldn't help herself. She needed to talk to someone and share her immense burden. She proceeded cautiously—a first for her.

"Oh, I'm sure you've experienced the same types of things, Gene," she replied casually. "Like people who should have died already, but they are waiting for something to happen or someone to show up before they go. My last client was a ninety-eight-year-old man who was in a coma, but he waited until his daughter arrived from Paris. Things like that. It fascinates me. It's as if people can choose; they can wait for that, or—" Gertie smiled, leaning toward Gene, "they can wait until they are alone if they don't want others to be present. And I just love to be with them at the end. It is such a spiritual moment to share, especially if they would otherwise be by themselves when the time comes."

Gene, of course, had quite a different reaction to the death of his patients if he was present. He cleared his throat. "Well, I'm not as fortunate as you," he said cautiously. "I am surrounded by dying

people, but death comes most often when I am not present for them."
He took a sip of wine. "But there have been times when I have seen
the same thing as you have and it does speak to me—to witness someone leave this life." Gene could feel his body responding to the ability
to talk to someone else about this subject.

Gertie grew a bit bolder. "Take Ms. Broadmoor, for instance,"
she commented. "Surely a miracle occurred. How else would you
explain her recovery, Gene?" Gertie liked calling Dr. Gregory by his
first name.

"Oh, I don't know," Gene replied carefully, hoping Gertie did not
notice that he choked in surprise during his next sip of wine. "You
were much closer to her at the end than I was. What do *you* think
happened with her, Gertie?"

He said her name so softly and quietly that she wanted to tell him
everything. But she hesitated as she remembered what Mary Lee told
her in the elevator about keeping some secrets.

"Oh, Gene," she confessed, "I have no idea. It was like . . . like
one minute, I was sure she was dead, and the next, she wasn't, you
know? One minute, I was sure she had taken her last breath; the
next, she was blissfully napping. Has anything like that ever happened in your work?" she asked, eager to take the attention off of
Mary Lee. "I suppose it's not completely unheard of."

"Well," Gene replied thoughtfully, "I can't say that it has, at least
not the way you describe it. All of my patients have died, of course,
except for Mary Lee. I know it must be hard to talk about, so I won't
press you further. I hope someday we can figure this out together. It is
fascinating, isn't it?"

As he reached for her hand, Gene's cell phone rang. It was precisely one hour after their arrival at the restaurant. Gene pulled
himself reluctantly away, regretting his earlier arrangement to
escape, but he had to catch his plane, and he needed to get away
from everything for a few days and focus on his research.

When he gave his regrets to Gertie, they were genuine. Before
pulling the curtain back to leave, Gene took one of Gertie's hands in

his and pressed it to his lips. It was a gesture that he did not intend and one that surprised Gertie, awakening a fierce desire within her. It was all she could do to restrain herself from jumping into his arms.

Gertie couldn't hide her disappointment as she faced the rest of the meal alone. She was relieved to be behind curtains so others couldn't see Gene leaving, and she *was* hungry. She hoped she would see him again soon. She knew she would if she had played her cards well, and she was quite sure she had. She caressed the spot on her hand that Gene had kissed. Yes, Gertie was quite certain she had touched Eugene Gregory in a special way.

It was almost midnight when Gertie let herself into the house after waving to the guard. She noticed it immediately: the smell of cigar smoke coming into the entry hall. Gertie couldn't help but gasp in amazement. This was the second time and a sure sign that Mary Lee was becoming her old self again. As she tiptoed past Mary Lee's room, she heard the typing stop. The guard house must have notified her of Gertie's return. Mary Lee opened the door and called out, "How was your evening, Gertie?"

Gertie had taken her shoes off at the front door and tiptoed quietly upstairs. Her feet celebrated the freedom from her high heels. She had also started to remove her tight clothing and didn't want to be seen in her current state. "Short but very nice, Ms. B.," she called out. "Eugene had to leave for an emergency, but we had a lovely time and— and I think he was genuinely sorry to have to go. With any luck, I'll see him again. Good night." She said nothing about the cigar odor.

"Good night, Gertie," Mary Lee replied in a singsong voice and resumed typing.

48

As Eugene Gregory left the restaurant, he slipped the bowtie from his tuxedo shirt collar and unbuttoned the top button. He'd be on the plane to Denver in about an hour and was free for an entire week. Everything he needed except his research computer and some articles to read on the plane were already at his ranch. He would catch a connecting flight in the morning from Denver to Durango then drive the forty rugged miles to his ranch, The Double G. In the San Juan mountain range, Eugene could roam for miles on horseback on his land and see no one at all. It always soothed him and eased away the strain of his professional life.

Knowing he would always have a private retreat, a place he could go to make himself invisible was immensely important. He had selected this area particularly because of its extraordinarily sparse human population and its abundant wildlife. The town of Delores was forty miles away, and mostly dirt roads—if you could call them *roads*—separated the ranch from civilization.

Gene pulled up to his one-story log cabin Saturday afternoon, dirty and tired. Parking his dust-covered rental SUV at the back of the building, he entered through the back door and saw that the Walkers had taken care of everything. The heat was on, which was necessary at that elevation, the refrigerator was stocked, and the cabin was immaculate. There was even a fire crackling in the floor-to-ceiling stone fireplace.

After changing into jeans and a wool plaid shirt, Gene poured himself a glass of bourbon on the rocks and sat down on the worn leather sofa in front of the fire. Except for his exquisite mannerisms, his startlingly smooth hands, and his strikingly clean-cut face, which would have made him a candidate for a Lucky Strike photo shoot, one could have mistaken him for a rancher. Here, Eugene Gregory could be the very private man he was and deal with his very private fears.

Gene's horse, Spirit, lived up to his name. He was a chestnut-colored Kiger Mustang and Gene had paid well to have him raised and tamed from birth so that he could ride him whenever he was at the ranch. Otherwise, Spirit roamed the range freely with other Kiers, but was carefully tracked so that he could be located when necessary. Spirit knew who he belonged to and could sense when Gene was nearby. All Gene had to do was stand on the back porch and let Spirit pick up his scent. He knew as he sat on the couch that Saturday evening that Spirit would be there the next morning. They would both roam wild and free for days.

This particular Saturday night, Gene sat staring into the fire, fascinated with the possibility of life after death, near-death experiences, or transference in a living body. He unpacked his laptop, which was already loaded with pages of reading material about near-death experiences, reversible death, and leading research on when death actually occurred. It was a revelation to him that some people who showed every sign of being dead had come back to life, even as late as their embalming or in their coffins. He had always been taught that the death process was clear and precise. When brain activity ceased, modern science declared that life ended. Now he was no longer certain of anything related to death and dying. He cringed, wondering if at any time he might have performed an autopsy on a still-living person.

After talking to Gertie at dinner the night before, Gene felt certain that something unusual had happened to Mary Lee. It was her marked personality change and the story she had written that took him deeper than thinking that Mary Lee was just "one lucky lady."

For the next few days, Gene rode Spirit for hours, enthralled to be in such a beautiful natural setting with his new discoveries about life and death. Everything lived and died, he realized. If he could just resolve his old fear of hell and his disturbing association of sex with death, he felt he was entering a new world of possibility that could change everything for him. Each night as he fell asleep on the sofa, he imagined Gertie's breasts as she leaned over to tell him what really happened the day Mary Lee didn't die. It surprised and pleased him that he would awaken with a full erection the next morning.

49

The congregation of Fairview's Good Shepherd Presbyterian Church had been together for a long time. Mae Rose's family had been one of the founding influences of the body of believers who met in a quaint, historic lannon stone structure in the middle of town. Its sanctuary was completely original, dating back to the 1930s, and could probably have made the historic register with its curved wooden pews, gothic arched ceiling, stained-glass windows, and antique organ, which Mae Rose had played with great enthusiasm for many years. Everyone in church who had known Mae Rose missed her, even if they hated to admit it.

Today there was a hushed gasp as Art got to his feet and stepped briskly into the aisle. He was a man of few words, which didn't surprise anyone who had known Mae Rose. Art's healing after his heart attack had been so rapid and complete that he knew what he wanted to do with the rest of his life, and he couldn't wait.

Art approached the steps to the pulpit wearing the same suit coat and tie he had worn every Sunday for years. But everything else about Art had changed. Absent from the flock that morning were both Art Jr. and John, who were both working. Art also noted that Maggie Whitman was not present, probably because she was working a hospital shift, as she often did on Sunday mornings. He had no idea that Maggie had left town. Her absence from church also caused Art to give thanks, since he thought what he had to share would be easier with her not there. He and an increasingly pregnant Elliana were sharing the family pew together. Art was thankful there would be one family member present—and one was quite enough. It would be good to have a fair-minded witness.

Stepping up to the pulpit, Art cleared his throat, and said frankly, "As many of you know, I ended up in the hospital this past week—a heart attack, I was told. It happened while I was in the barn and my first reaction was just to lay there and die. I felt like a man who had committed so many sins and hurt so many people that I needed to go. Plus," Art paused to process his emotions, "I felt ready to see Mae Rose. I—I miss her so much. Her death was my fault in so many ways, and I just wanted her to hold me—and forgive me. I was ready to die." The congregation was absolutely quiet.

"But a voice came to me. I don't know whether I was conscious or not, but it told me to get up—get *the hell* up, if I recall correctly, and told me all that I had to live for, including the pending birth of our—my—first grandchild."

He took a deep breath and went on. "It's been over a year since Mae Rose died and I want you to know what I've learned from the loss of my wife." He stopped again. "I—I know now how much I loved her," he began, gripping the sides of the pulpit and looking tormented. "I—I didn't know that when she was living. She spent our entire marriage completely faithful and utterly disappointed in me, usually with good reason. And yet it was as if the day she died, I understood love for the first time because—"

He stopped to let another wave of emotion pass. "Because she took it with her. Not a day goes by that I don't think of her. There's not a moment when I don't wish I'd done for her any one thing a remotely conscious husband would do for his wife: bring her flowers, wrap her in his arms at the end of the day, tell her how much he loves her, or at least compliment her on her fine choice in husbands." Art choked to a stop while the congregation chuckled collectively. Everyone there had known Mae Rose, and not one of them blamed Art for finding marriage to her an extraordinary challenge.

"I guess what I want to say is that heaven and hell may be afterlife destinations, but I can attest to there being hell on Earth too. Our marriage was that for both of us too much of the time. In fact, I think that's what killed Mae Rose in the end. I think she died of a broken heart. I lied to her. I—I cheated on her. There came a time, slowly of course, that we could no longer stand each other. She was angry at me so much of the time, and that last day . . . I wanted so desperately to have her love me again. It just didn't go the way I had planned. And then it was too late—too late to do anything to give my wife a wonderful married life. I could have done that if only I'd seen then what I do now." Art stopped for a breath. In the pause between words, some in the congregation gasped and wondered if they had heard correctly that Art had just confessed to having an affair while he and Mae Rose were married.

He went on with gritty emphasis. "And it could have been so different. It would have been so easy if only I'd realized while she was living that I loved Mae Rose and that she often loved me with such a force that I couldn't stand it. I can argue that Mae Rose was hard to live with, and I don't think anyone here would disagree. She could see everything that was wrong, which she was quick to point out *but only so that it could be made right.* What I know now is that Mae Rose was full of love with a large dose of humanness thrown in. If I'd loved her then the way I know I do now, *if I'd known then what I do now* . . ." Art's voice trailed off.

"That's all I want to say except that if any of you here feel about your marriages the way I felt about mine, let me just say that if one of you dies, regret will become a constant companion to whoever is left behind. Every day you will think of what you could have done to make it different. That's all. Do whatever it is you think you'll do someday now—*right now.* Don't question it, and don't reason it away, because in the end, it's what you didn't do that you could have that will haunt you, and what you did do that you wish you hadn't that will break your heart. And, just so we all remember, love itself doesn't cost anything at all."

Art had never been much of a public speaker. But then he'd never felt like he was ever much of anything anyway. Being a man who now understood love had changed him. He stepped away from the pulpit and returned, full of purpose, to his pew. He grabbed Elliana's hand and hugged her fiercely. He wanted to fade into the congregation again and go quietly on his way, but this group would never forget this moment, and Art would never be the same man.

As much as his confession shocked the fellow believers, as much as they would talk among themselves about what Art did to Mae Rose, with whom, and saying "no wonder she was so unhappy—poor woman—not that she would have been easy to live with, God knows," they would look more inward than outward. When they left the service after Pastor Frank's incredible message, "Stop Asking; Start Believing," those who were in happy relationships rejoiced, and those who were not would begin to look for a way back into love.

Consumed with their own contemplations, no one noticed the two visitors dressed sedately and sitting in the very back of the packed sanctuary. Nita Winslow and Cheryl Lewis had slipped in quietly after the service began to avoid any new visitor queries. While Nita's ebony face might have been familiar to some of the congregation, certainly standing out in a mostly white-skinned group, no one paid any attention except Pastor Frank, and he was not able to get to the back of the church before Nita and Cheryl slipped out, which they did just as discreetly as they had entered, before the service ended.

Over the course of the next week, Jill King's shop would be overwhelmed with orders for bouquets; the local grocery stores that sold flowers would check their calendars, certain that they had missed an important holiday as their floral racks were emptied. But then, the floral business had been more brisk ever since that movie—what was it called?—came out. "The Sunday of Art's Confession" would never make it on to any calendar, but it burned deeply into the hearts of all who witnessed it.

*   *   *

Nita disappeared down the sidewalk, walking quietly and quickly to her waiting car. From there she was whisked to the cemetery where Mae Rose was buried. One of their camera crews, sitting in an unmarked van across the street from the church, took this as their sign to get video cameras rolling to film people from the church who might later be contacted for interviews. When Art emerged with a handshake and a meaningful hug from Pastor Frank, they zoomed in to catch the full emotional impact.

A second camera crew filmed Nita placing a bouquet of roses on a simple, almost invisible grave, then turning to face the camera. "It's Sunday and church is just letting out in this quiet, Midwestern community," her voice clipped masterfully into the microphone. "We don't expect many will think about visiting this grave, one of hundreds here. But there's something very interesting about what happened during a particular church service today, adding to our investigation into the mysterious question on the minds of many. We have reason to believe that this grave and the woman buried here are linked to Mary Lee Broadmoor's Academy Award-winning movie, *Something Like That.*

"What really happened to 'Scary Mary'? Did she truly write this story, or did someone else? While *Something Like That* might actually be a fictional plot and a surprising new story line from a woman appearing to have quite literally been raised from the dead, we reserve the right to wonder. Be sure to stay tuned to *Currents* as we take you deeper into the transformation of Mary Lee Broadmoor and the secretly scary possibilities behind her latest movie." It was so smooth, so well done, that there was no need for a retake.

Cheryl Lewis had stayed behind to follow up with some of the folks she met as they came out of church. Under the guise of research on heart attacks in younger women—a *Currents* show that would eventually run—she reached out to members of the congregation to understand Mae Rose better. She was following her hunch that there was something tangible linking the McElroys and the movie, something much more than just a coincidence.

That afternoon as Nita traveled back to LA, Cheryl followed Pastor Frank's directions to the McElroy home. She turned into the gravel driveway, thinking she was lost and needed to turn around, when she saw Art sitting on the back steps. An old shovel leaned against a rusty wheelbarrow, suggesting that he was taking a break from yard work. She couldn't pretend she didn't see him, so she waved cautiously.

People Art didn't know rarely came down his driveway unless they were lost. He got up slowly and approached her vehicle. Cheryl rolled down the window of her rental car. "I thought Sunday was a day of rest," she said.

"You lost?" he asked her. "Most folks who come into this driveway are."

"No. I mean, no, I'm not lost," Cheryl replied. "I mean, I—I heard you speak at church today. It was very moving," she added, surprised that she was nervous. "I'm Cheryl Lewis," she offered. "I just spoke with Pastor Frank, and he suggested I visit you sometime so I thought I should drive by to make sure I knew where your home was," she explained. "I'm doing research on heart attacks in women under the age of sixty," she said, "—and I was wondering if—if you would be comfortable talking to me sometime about your wife's situation. This is a growing concern. I'm an investigative reporter who wants to help get to the bottom of this."

"Who's the study for?" Art asked tentatively, frowning. "And how do you know my wife died of a heart attack? I don't think I mentioned that at church."

"Yes, those are important questions to answer. Can we talk? Is it all right if I get out of the car and can we sit somewhere? I can explain." Cheryl had not yet decided exactly how she would tell Art of her discovery or how she had come to it.

Art stood aside and let her get out of the car. "You can come into my shop for a few minutes," he said guardedly. "I've got lots of work to do, so I don't want to take too much time."

"Thank you, Mr. McElroy. I promise this won't take long. Just a few questions," Cheryl said to encourage him.

Once inside the barn, the first thing to strike Cheryl was the number of antique VWs, all in different states of repair. There was one in particular, a yellow one, that reminded her of the movie, and it took her breath away. She knew she had to explain things very carefully to this obviously sensitive man.

"I work for the director of a TV documentary show called *Currents*. It's very popular on the West Coast, although you can even get it here. Nita Winslow is the show's host. You might have heard of her. She's very well-known and respected." Cheryl hesitated to say more lest Art order her off the premises.

"Well," he said as he walked her over to his shop desk and offered her one of the broken red chairs, "I don't watch TV much, and I really don't want to be interviewed for a show, but I sure am willing to talk about my wife's experience if it will help. I still don't know how you know about my wife," he added.

Cheryl paused, remembering that the flowerbeds in front of the McElroy home were planted with the same effect as those along Mary Lee Broadmoor's driveway. She shivered.

"Are you cold?" Art asked.

"No, no. I just remembered something; that's all," Cheryl replied, her mind still rolling through details of the barn, the house, and the movie. "Mr. McElroy, I have done quite a bit of research on this matter of women dying of heart attacks at a young age. Your son, as you are probably aware, is friends with the Allie Schwartz, the daughter of movie director Mary Lee Broadmoor, the woman who wrote the story *Something Like That.*"

"Yes, I am aware," Art replied, still wondering how she would make the link to his family.

"Well, sir, to be honest, your son was acting strangely the night that he came to dinner with Natalie, and—"

"Who's Natalie?" Art queried.

"Oh, yes. I should explain. Allie is Natalie's nickname, and Schwartz is her father's name. Mary Lee is her mother."

"OK then, continue your story," Art advised and crossed his arms in a guarded gesture.

"Well, as I said, your son was acting strangely, and none of us knew him. I am a former detective from the LA police department, and my employer asked if I would run a check on your son. When I did, I learned about your wife. The Internet doesn't care much about anyone's privacy," Cheryl added. "So since I was conducting this research, my employer—"

"Who is—?" Art asked for clarification.

"Nita Winslow, sir," Cheryl clarified very much in the role of a police detective. "Nita decided we should do a documentary on heart attacks in women. Since I had learned this about your wife, I felt like it would be a good place to start. Is that OK with you, Mr. McElroy?" Cheryl looked at him hesitantly, feeling awkward and uncomfortable.

When he was silent, she continued. "What we've learned is that there are so many cases of young women dying of heart attacks these days and no one seems to know why. Our job on *Currents* is to take actual life experiences and put them in front of our audiences so that they can appreciate life beyond their own day-to-day world. And sometimes it leads to a new discovery or at least a deeper under-standing. Sometimes we can make people aware before—before it's too late," she added softly and waited for Art to speak or possibly strike her.

"Well, I won't be part of your show," Art told her. "But why don't you come in to the house and have some of my wife's tea? You're shaking like a leaf. She was quite good at blending them, and I've got some left. It will warm you up and calm you down. We can talk a lit-tle, and I can show you a picture of her." Art surprised himself at his offer. He had not been alone in his home with a woman since Mae Rose died—except for Jill King who was married and didn't count.

"Yes," Cheryl replied, "I'd really like that, Mr. McElroy."

"Come on in, then. Not much has changed since Mae Rose left us, so you can sort of see how we lived." As Art moved up the steps, he confided, "I haven't even parted with her clothes. You don't need to know that, but it might help you to get a sense of how connected I still feel to her. No note-taking or anything like that, OK?"

"Yes, that's fine, Mr. McElroy," Cheryl replied. "I would just love to know more about this woman that you are still so in love with." Cheryl, of course, would miss no details. She took in everything inside the home and was more convinced than ever that the McElroy family had been the basis for Mary Lee's story. What she couldn't understand was why Art Jr. was so uptight if his family had given the story to Mary Lee. Even though she was filling in more puzzle pieces, Cheryl felt more confused than ever.

"Have you ever been in love?" Art asked Cheryl as they sat at the kitchen table, sipping tea in the rose-patterned china teacups Mae Rose had selected when she and Art got married. Cheryl observed the cozy kitchen decorated in cottage blue and white with dried flowers and baskets hanging from the ceiling. It was very comfortable in an old-fashioned way and so much like the movie that Cheryl felt she had walked onto the movie set. If anyone had asked her where the silverware was, she would have known.

"Not like you," Cheryl replied lightly. "I've had relationships but no lingering aftereffects, if you know what I mean. Nothing like what you've experienced, that's for sure."

"Well, I didn't know how much I loved Mae Rose until the day she died. That's pretty sad, isn't it?" Cheryl saw tears in Art's eyes. "I mean, I was crazy about her when we got married, and we had some good times. But I didn't really know what love was until I lost her."

"Maybe you wouldn't have known love any other way," Cheryl observed quietly.

Art smiled. "You get it, don't you? Even though you haven't experienced it, you understand it." He set down his teacup. "Now if you're ready, let me show you around and tell you a few stories. My Mae Rose made a home out of next to nothing," he bragged. "Just look around and see what she did with some of the most natural and inexpensive things. She was great at shopping sales and getting things for free, that woman!"

Art beamed as he talked about Mae Rose; Cheryl felt drawn in to his radiance. "Of course, I had to teach her how to be frugal. She came from a pretty wealthy family and didn't know how to live economically at first. But over time, she out-saved me." He laughed and shook his head in wonder as they headed into the main part of the house. "Fact is that this house is hers—her family's, that is. It passes from female to female, so I've only got squatter's rights now. Once there's a female born to either of the boys, she'll get the house when she gets married or turns thirty, whichever comes first. John and Elliana's baby is supposed to be a girl." Art smiled as he ran his hands over a hall table in the main entrance of the house. A dried-flower arrangement sat artfully against a mirror hanging on the wall behind the table, creating a doubly beautiful effect.

Cheryl saw hydrangeas, roses, and twining patterns that reminded her of Mary Lee's home once again. She gasped. "It's beautiful," she explained to Art lest he wonder why she was so surprised.

"That was Mae Rose's work," Art explained. "She was most happy when she was arranging flowers. Of course, they were living when she put them in place. She didn't like to work with anything dried up, and that was part of her art, to let it live and then allow it to sort of stop living but still be beautiful."

As if reading her mind, Art said, "She never knew how wonderful she was. She could light up an entire room with her joy, and her artistic touch was evident everywhere she went. It was just that—"Art hesitated. "She shined so brightly that it pissed the rest of us off, I guess." He smiled, knowing he had described Mae Rose perfectly.

In one corner of the living room, Cheryl noted a guitar rested next to a pole lamp.

"Who plays?" Cheryl asked.

"I do," Art replied matter-of-factly. "Just for myself and just sometimes. I have sung more songs to Mae Rose than anything else since she's been gone. They are a great comfort for me."

"Any chance I could talk you into singing one?" Cheryl asked, full of hope.

"Nope," he replied. "They come to me and go only to her."

"You don't write them down?" Cheryl was amazed.

"Nope," he replied.

"You certainly are an interesting man, Mr. McElroy," Cheryl commented.

"Call me Art," he said and smiled.

"May—may I see that picture of her?" Cheryl asked quietly.

"Oh. Of course. And then perhaps I'll tell you how we met. It's a good story." Art headed to the bedroom to get his favorite picture of Mae Rose from his nightstand. At that moment, Cheryl heard the back door open and was surprised to see Art Jr. walk in.

Art Jr. was equally surprised, and then angry, when he saw Cheryl. "What are *you* doing here?" he asked evenly. "How did *you* find out where we live?"

Art, who was not expecting a confrontation and had avoided them most of his life, walked out of his bedroom and heard Cheryl and his son talking with obvious tension between them. He stayed quietly in the hallway for a moment.

"I came to do some research on heart attacks in women under age sixty," Cheryl replied cautiously.

"Sure you did," Art Jr. retorted. "And why would you choose here, of all the places on the planet, to do that research? How would you know that there is or has been any woman here under age sixty who died of a heart attack?" His voice grew a little louder. "How dare you invade our private space! Dad," he called out. "Dad, do you know who this is? Where are you?" He was also angry at Allie, who he suspected had told Cheryl about his mother's passing. *Anything to make money in Hollywood!* he growled to himself.

Art stepped out of the hallway with Mae Rose's picture in his hands. He had never seen Art Jr. upset like this, not even when Mae Rose died.

"Dad, this is Cheryl Lewis, assistant to Nita Winslow, who is a famous TV personality, not unlike Barbara Walters. We met at Allie's mother's house in LA. That would be the home of Mary Lee Broadmoor, who wrote the movie *Something Like That*," Art Jr. told his father. "How much have you told her?"

"Slow down, Son. Ms. Lewis has already told me all of that. I guess I'd like to know why you're so upset to see her here."

"Because I don't trust her—not her or Nita Winslow. They want a story; they want to make something out of the movie, and they'll stop at nothing. They'll hurt our family, Dad." He turned to Cheryl.

"You should leave," he told her. "Now. Just get out and don't come back to this town."

Cheryl turned to Art. "I am not here to do any harm, Mr. McElroy. I truly want to know more about your wife—her life and her death. There are things that you also might want to know someday, some peculiar similarities between her life and the movie. We've been researching this for some time now, and we believe it's only fair for you to know what we've learned."

Art Sr. looked at Cheryl kindly, a certain pain causing tears to well up in his eyes. "Please sit down, Ms. Lewis. I think it's time *we* asked *you* some questions. Art, pull up a chair. Would either of you like some—" He stopped to clear his throat as he choked on his words, "—some of my wife's tea?"

* * *

Several hours later, the three of them finally stopped talking. "I guess I need to find out for myself, don't I?" Art said slowly as he tried to get his mind around all that Cheryl had told him. "I mean, I knew there were similarities in the movie; both of my sons told me that. But this is most peculiar."

"We've still got some aspects to follow up on, sir," Cheryl explained. "But we are noticing such matches to your wife's life that I think we are reaching some interesting conclusions about this that none of us is even able to understand, much less to accept. There has to be an explanation."

"Do I need to see the movie?" Art asked.

"I don't think so, Dad," Art Jr. replied quickly, much more settled now that Cheryl had explained her insights, which informed him that Allie had not betrayed his trust. He was ashamed that he had even thought it possible. "But it's your call. It's out on DVD and available on Netflix, so it would be easy to get your hands on."

"Gentlemen, I hope you know that it is our sincerest desire to uncover the reason for this extraordinary situation," Cheryl explained as she stood to leave. "The movie has had a dynamic impact on the world, which is fantastic. We just want to understand how what appears to have been the story of *your* lives has made it to the big screen without you knowing about it. And why Mary Lee Broadmoor's personality has changed so profoundly. Frankly it feels pretty weird right now. That's all. And . . ." She paused a moment before she attempted to vindicate herself. "We *are* working on a segment about the increasing number of heart attacks in younger woman. That wasn't just a cover-up."

Art Jr. jumped into the conversation. "Do we have the assurance of your confidence in this matter, Cheryl?" he asked as he looked at his father for agreement. Art was nodding his head affirmatively.

"What I can give you is my promise that you will know whatever progress we are making each step of the way. And I agree with you, sir," Cheryl said, turning to Art. "A trip to LA could be appropriate. Besides, your son's girlfriend is there, and I know you'd like to meet her. She's a great woman—I can tell even though I don't know her personally," Cheryl added, looking back at Art Jr., who had to smile in spite of himself.

"Who said anything about a trip to LA?" Art joked as he got up to see Cheryl to the door.

For a reason that he later chalked up to chivalry, Art followed Cheryl out of the house and walked her to her vehicle. It was now dark outside. The full moon and the stars were so bright they gave the uncanny impression that one could just reach up and take a handful. Neither Art nor Cheryl spoke as they thumped down the stairs and their feet crunched the stones on the gravel driveway. They shook hands at the car, where Art said, "Perhaps we *will* be seeing you in Los Angeles, Ms. Lewis."

"Perhaps," she said. "Thank you for the visit." Then she leaned over and gave Art a kiss on the cheek. "You can call me Cheryl, Art," she added.

50

"I don't know why he hasn't called me for another date," Gertie lamented to Chef Michael in the kitchen of Mary Lee's Beverly Hills home. It had been more than a week since they'd gone out, and Gertie had expected to hear from Gene by now. She sat sullenly, slumped over the counter, watching Michael season a simmering pot of his curry and cinnamon risotto. The aroma alone usually made her happy. "We had a very nice dinner, and I could tell that we had a lot in common. He seemed genuinely interested in me," she whined.

Chef Michael smiled at a deflated Gertie and attempted to reassure her. "It's all part of the game, Gertie," he replied as he sampled the sauce. "Be patient and go about your business. If you can just let go in here—" he pointed to her head, "and here—" he pointed to her heart, "if you can just let it be and know you don't need him, it will work like magic and he'll call you. Trust me."

Gertie scowled and sat up a little straighter. "Of course I can live without him, Michael. God! I've lived alone all these years without *anyone*. It's just that for once in my life, a man shows interest in me, and I want more. God, I want more. But you're right. I don't need him or any man, for that matter. I know what I want out of life, and I'll get it. Just watch me."

"How about a little 'tune-up' for *mon petite* Gertie?" Chef Michael suggested, smiling devilishly.

"No thanks, Michael. I think you've taught me all you can," Gertie replied and headed out of the kitchen.

Chef Michael smiled as she left. "Perhaps," he muttered to himself in French. "Perhaps not."

"Perhaps what?" Mary Lee appeared at the door of the kitchen.

"Ms. Broadmoor," he replied, surprised at her presence. "I didn't know you understood French."

"I don't, Michael, but a few phrases I do know, and that's one of them. So perhaps what?"

"Our Gertie has not heard from the doctor for another date, and she is most unhappy about that. So I told her to stop thinking about it. Perhaps he will call; perhaps not."

"Well, that had to be encouraging to our Gertie," Mary Lee replied sarcastically but smiled. "Have you thought of going into motivational speaking? You'd dazzle the world." She laughed and Chef Michael joined in.

"I'm entertaining this evening, Michael," Mary Lee told him as they both settled back into their roles. "It's an impromptu visit. I'd like to know what we have for a light dessert and drinks."

The house phone rang and Mary Lee picked it up. Chef Michael watched in shock.

"Good to hear from you, Gene. Yes, she's here. I'll get her." Mary Lee put the phone on hold and pressed the intercom button. "Oh, Gertie," she called throughout the house, "you have a call holding on line one. Something about an urgent doctor appointment. Can you pick up, please?" Mary Lee replaced the phone and turned her attention back to Chef Michael. They smiled knowingly at each other.

"Tell me what to offer, and show me where to get what I need," she insisted. No one needed to know that Mary Lee had called Gene and asked him to ask Gertie out for the evening. She wasn't matchmaking; she just needed both Gertie and Michael to be gone for a few hours. Fortunately Gene replied that he'd been thinking about calling Gertie anyway.

In the living room, Gertie picked up the phone. "Hello," she said evenly.

"Gertie? It's Gene Gregory calling. I wondered what you were doing this evening," he said a little too brightly for Gertie's taste.

"I'm performing colonoscopies. You're at the top of my list," Gertie retorted smugly. "No anesthetic."

Gene could not help laughing. "Well, I certainly deserved that, didn't I? But seriously, I've been out of town and have discovered some fascinating things about a subject that I think would interest you greatly. What do you say?" he asked again.

Even if he was a doctor and the only man who had asked her out in decades, Gertie was not going to act as if she were desperate for his attention. Chef Michael had picked up the phone at the perfect moment so neither of them knew he was listening. He almost burst out laughing as Gertie gave Gene Gregory hell.

"How about if we just meet for a drink?" Gene suggested "Don't dress up. We'll go to a bar and just catch up a little. I really want to talk to you. What do you think? It doesn't have to be a big deal."

Gertie hesitated until she saw Mary Lee coming down the hall with a smile and a thumbs-up sign.

"Well, OK, I guess, but it will have to be around eight-thirty or so. I won't be off duty until then."

"Eight-thirty is perfect. Thank you. I'll pick you up." Gene hung up the phone and sat back in his chair. He knew Gertie was putting him off because she was mad as hell that he hadn't called her. He had to smile.

* * *

At her office, Nita Winslow dictated the last of the day's notes into the voice-recognition software on her computer. She looked up her last meeting with Mary Lee to go over the details before leaving. It was nearly eight o'clock, and she had agreed to meet Mary Lee at her home at nine. Tonight she was planning to surprise Mary Lee with the gift of a fine cigar and superb bourbon. If all went well, they would smoke together and exchange confidences, maybe even get a little drunk.

Their last conversation had been mostly about Nita's interview techniques. Mary Lee had wanted to know what kind of questions Nita typically asked and what kind of responses worked best for the audience. "Honest ones," Nita had wanted to tell Mary Lee, but she had kept the discussion very low-key, making a few suggestions. Together she and Mary Lee had worked up a list of nonthreatening questions.

This time Nita hoped they would get to know each other better and perhaps arrange for a practice interview. It was Nita's hope to have Mary Lee on the show just before the CANIF Ball, which was only two months away. She hoped the timing would please Mary Lee since the ball was her daughter's largest fund-raiser. She had no idea that Mary Lee and Allie were not speaking to each other. If Mary Lee showed any signs of backing out of their arrangement, Nita had brought a copy of the tape she had recorded at the grave of Mae Rose McElroy. She smiled as she thought about how Mary Lee would react if Nita had to bring it up.

A few hours later, Nita emerged from the home of the Oscar-winning director, slightly tipsy and smelling of a fine cigar. She and Mary Lee had reached an agreement at last. The interview would air three days before the CANIF Ball. The only question Nita was not permitted to ask was the only one Mary Lee couldn't answer. Nita sighed contentedly. She had several weeks to work the angle out, and time was her friend. She knew that all the pieces would fall into place and that the world would be glued to her show. The video had not been necessary tonight, but she had it in her "back pocket" in case she needed it later.

51

From the moment Gertie got into the car with Gene, she sensed something was wrong—like he was doing this because he had to for some reason—not because he really wanted to. He greeted her graciously then said nothing more. That really pissed Gertie off. Finally she said, "You know, Gene, you seem tired. You shouldn't have called me to go out if you really wanted to be alone," she scolded. "Driver, please take me home," she called to the front seat.

"I don't want to be alone. I called because I wanted to see you," Gene insisted, feeling a strange annoyance. "Aren't I being attentive?"

"Pshaw! I'd have as much fun with a corpse—perhaps more," Gertie replied as she leaned toward him the way Chef Michael had taught her, revealing just the right amount of cleavage. "I can tell the difference between attentiveness and preoccupation, same as you," she declared proudly. "You think you're the only one who gets lost on the inside, Gene?" she asked as she snuggled up to him. "Now, where are we going? Your place?"

Gene could not reply. Gertie's breasts obstructed his ability to look her in the eyes, much less think.

"Let's go somewhere interesting," Gertie suggested. "I have an idea, a place I haven't been that I'm curious about." She was thinking of a visit to Michael's gay bar hangout.

Gene had no idea where Gertie wanted to take him, but her slightly provocative moves produced just the slightest twinge of interest in his groin. "OK, Gertie, take me wherever you want to go, as long as it isn't my place. I'm not ready for company," he replied, trying to understand his physical reaction to Gertie.

Gertie gave an address to the driver, who typed it into his GPS navigation system and looked at her questioningly. She gave him an affirmative nod.

"I hope this is a quiet place where we can talk more about my research into life after death," Gene offered, hoping to draw Gertie's interest.

She laughed. "We can talk about anything you want to—if you want to," Gertie whispered into his ear. "There are other interesting topics besides death," she added.

Gene shifted nervously, trying to create some space between himself and Gertie. Gertie took offense as if she thought he was brushing off her flirting. She had no idea of the disturbance she was creating inside a man who had successfully avoided physical contact with anyone all of his life.

"You can have a 'quiet' night all by yourself," Gertie admonished. "I'm not up for any of your morbid research. It won't hurt you one bit to come with me; it might even help. Otherwise your driver can just drop me off here and I'll walk home. I could watch the stock market on TV and get more of a rise out of that."

The woman had a biting sense of humor and Gene liked that she didn't act demure and shy with him as she had when Mary Lee was on her death bed. When he smiled and took her hand, Gertie was encouraged. "Shucks, Doctor," was all she said as their limo snaked quietly in the dark through a part of town neither Gertie nor Gene had ever visited. Gertie's skin crawled with old memories of her early life. When the driver pulled up to the curb at last, a small neon sign announced in flashing letters *I Only Have Guys for You.*

Gene was horrified. "I'm not going in there," he announced.

"OK, fine," Gertie replied. "Driver, please take me back home and drop Mr. Excitement back into the hole he crawled out of."

Gene laughed again, opened his door, and got out. Gertie waited for the driver to open her door, thanked him, and took Gene's arm. "That's how I like to be treated," she told Gene.

From the moment they entered the bar, Gene was obviously uncomfortable. He slunk down and put his hands in his trench coat pockets. All he wanted to do was leave. But Gertie, who was feeling quite comfortable, walked right up to the bar and asked, "Where's Michael?"

Suddenly she heard, "Gertie! Gertie girl! Get over here! What have you got there with you? *Mon dieu!* A *man*, Gertie? Come on over, *cherie*. Bring him along so we can check him out and see if we approve. You can't go out with just *anyone*. We might take him off your hands, you know, as part of the cover charge for a real woman entering this sacred temple. God it's great to see you!" She headed over to his booth, pulling a reluctant Gene behind her.

Gertie didn't miss a thing. "For God's sake, Gene," she scolded, "they aren't going to harm a heterosexual. You're safer here than in a regular bar. Hi, boys," she said and grinned. "Besides, there's no one you would know, Gene. Everyone here is *alive*. Gene doesn't get out much," she told the men and laughed until she saw a peculiar glimmer in Gene's eyes. *Was he turned on by what he saw?* she wondered. *Was Eugene Gregory gay?*

Gene was not aroused but he was fascinated by what Gertie had just told him in front of a group of openly gay men: she considered him a heterosexual. Gertie could not have known how important this evening encounter would be to him—that for the first time in his life, he was facing a fear he had carried inside of him for most of his life and Gertie had already tagged him as if she already knew that Eugene Gregory wasn't gay.

"So, Doctor," Michael said as he sucked his drink through a straw. "What brings you to this side of town?"

Gene made a weak attempt at a sheepish smile. "Gertie. Gertie made me do it."

Everyone in the group laughed uproariously. "Go, Gertie!" they cheered and raised their glasses.

After a few minutes of listening to their banter, Gene leaned over to Gertie and took her hand. "Come on, gorgeous, time to go. My turn to pick a place."

"OK, Gene," Gertie replied with a smile of satisfaction. "It looks like you're awake now. We'll leave under one condition." She winked at the group.

"What's that?" Gene felt his stomach knotting up.

She pressed her body into his and stood on her tiptoes to whisper into his ear. "You take me to your place. Next time, *you can see mine.*"

As Gene tried to look down into her eyes, his own betrayed him as they traveled down to her breasts. "OK, Gertie." He smiled suddenly. "You win."

Cheryl phoned Nita to inform her that she had followed Gene and Gertie to the wrong side of town. She would never forget the look on Gene's face when he and Gertie came out of the bar. While this concerned her, it was also wonderfully amusing. She was laughing so hard that Nita had difficulty understanding her at first. As she followed them in their limo, however, Cheryl sobered up.

"Looks like they're headed to Gene's place," Cheryl reported. "Dear God. Dr. Death is going to make a move on Gertie!"

"Whatever it is, it's going to make one hell of a story!" Nita exclaimed. "Aren't you being a little overprotective, detective? Gene wouldn't hurt a flea!"

"My instincts tell me differently; I'm going to stay with them," Cheryl told Nita.

"OK," Nita replied. "Call me if you get anything." She clicked her phone off.

Cheryl stayed a discreet distance away. *What woman in her right mind would accompany Gene Gregory to his apartment?* Gertie, of course, would not be a woman Cheryl would consider right-minded, so she had to approach the question from a different perspective. *What wires have been disconnected inside Gertie's head? Why can't she sense the danger?* Cheryl's mind saw the story in tomorrow's paper—Gertie's body found in a trash bin several blocks away, with no clues to trace back to the criminal. That's how much she trusted Gene Gregory. She could read his sick energy, and she saw potential violence stored up inside him; it had been there for too long.

It took time for Cheryl to locate a parking spot. She had to go around the block several times before one on the street opened up. She parked the car and slid down behind the wheel for the watch. It was 10:30 p.m. Her mind traveled back to her meeting with Art McElroy Sr. She was drawn to him, and that instantly concerned her. She knew better than to allow herself to have feelings for anyone who was connected to a case she was working on. But this was different than police work; it was only for a TV show, making the ethical boundaries much fuzzier.

If Gene Gregory's love life was nonexistent, Cheryl's wasn't much better. She had always had a soft spot for men who "weren't that into her," as the book title from years before had suggested. She shot high and fell flat every time. The excruciating pain of those encounters reminded her to cut off any illusions about Art McElroy Sr. He was obviously and completely in love with his deceased wife. Even if he weren't, he was much too old for her—ten years older, based on her information. She was a detective, after all; it was her job to know these things. Having access to so much information about other people added to her difficulty in finding love. She knew too much and was highly intuitive. Cheryl could interpret human nature and what disguise it was wearing so quickly that only the most unreachable men held her interest. Dr. Gregory terrified her.

Most recently Cheryl had fallen for Jack Riley, the anchor of the TV station's evening news. He was handsome as hell and sort of important as far as title and salary were concerned. They'd gotten together a few times, and she'd thought maybe he was different; he seemed genuinely interested in her, asking her lots of questions and taking her to chic places she'd never been before.

Cheryl was a good-looking woman. She could put on her police uniform, wind her long dark hair up under a hat, and look tough enough, but out of police attire with her hair down, she still turned heads, even at fifty-two years old. Some women might choose to be cops because of a preference toward manliness, but Cheryl relished being a woman in a role usually reserved for men. She was strong and authoritative if she needed to be, but off the job, she just wanted to have fun and a family with the same man for the rest of her life.

Oh, and a big old farmhouse with a wrap-around porch to live in somewhere in the middle of nowhere. She stayed in LA because of her job and because she had sort of a life there, but her roots were shallow enough to transplant.

The very minute she began to wonder if Jack Riley was the one for her, presto! He vanished. After a week of beating herself up for trusting him, she learned that he had been promoted and transferred to New York, and *that* she learned from the news. He never called her to explain. Her shrink chalked it up to another indication that Cheryl was still deeply insecure and needy, the very thing that pushed men away. But after Jack Riley, and considering her age, she had grown tired of hearing the same message over and over again. Cheryl canned her shrink. If she hadn't made progress by this time, it clearly wasn't worth the time and expense.

Cheryl had read every book on intimate relationships known to humankind. She was intent on getting to the root of her problem and finding a happily-ever-after relationship, or at least generally happy most of the time. She affirmed what she wanted daily. She envisioned the perfect man when she lay down at night and again first thing in the morning. She slept on one side of the bed and kept half of her closet empty just in case a man wanted to move in. Cheryl had been trying to manifest a man for *years* and was finally convinced that none of it worked, not even positive thinking. She didn't believe she had any problems *that* deep—at least not enough to cause men to constantly reject her. So she had given up. Period. Until she had read about "tapping" on acupuncture points to deal with life issues. In her heart, Cheryl knew that she would never give up her dreams so she had started this new technique recently.

Sighing out loud startled Cheryl back to her current task: protecting Gertie Morgan from Eugene Gregory. She glanced at her watch and affirmed that if Gertie didn't reappear by midnight, she'd call the police. It was eleven o'clock, and Gertie had been inside the building for thirty minutes.

* * *

Cheryl had cause for concern. If she could have seen inside Gene's sterile condominium, she would have been shocked to find Gertie bound hands and feet to Gene's four-poster steel-framed bed. Having no idea what to do about her giggling and then her whimpering protests, Gene had gently taped her mouth shut so she couldn't be heard.

Gertie had been willing enough at first, but after a while she became terrified. Her eyes wild with fear, she noticed that Gene just ignored her. He would tease her then leave her. It was relentless. For a woman who had experienced very little sexual foreplay, it was a complete, single-lesson education.

When Gene had first brought his tray of scalpels to the room, Gertie was certain she was going to die. But he had been most reassuring, telling her that he did not understand women, and that he needed to try certain things on her to see how she responded. After she had gotten over her initial fear and had seen what he was doing, she could not help her body's response to being touched so tenderly, as if he had a road map to all of her.

Gene knew the human body well and it showed. He removed one piece of Gertie's clothing at a time, cutting it away with a scalpel and focusing on tantalizing that area of her body. She responded each and every time. He did not participate; he simply observed her as if she were an experiment while his fingers tweaked, pinched, and caressed. It was a most exquisite torture. In spite of herself and her fear, Gertie wanted more.

What Gertie could not know or understand was that for the first time in his life, Gene was no longer afraid that he was gay and his association of death with sexual arousal was waning. The men in the bar did not arouse him but Gertie did. He knew he'd have to pay for trespassing on her body, but he had to understand the physical aspects of a woman. He would not have had the courage had she not had the audacity to take him to the gay bar.

"Now, Gertie darling, has this been fun for you?" Gene asked gently after quite some time. "I hope so."

Gertie nodded her head with such affirmative enthusiasm that Gene could not help but be pleased.

"I have had a wonderful time enjoying you. I haven't hurt you, have I?"

Gertie's head shook back and forth. If Gene had asked if he'd scared her half to death, she would have told the truth about that too.

"I hope you know how special this has been. It's a new experience for me, and I have a lot to learn about pleasing a woman. We're almost through and then we'll get you ready to go home." Gene's eyes still looked strangely glazed over, as if an alien force possessed him.

Gertie wondered what she would be wearing when she left because her clothing was no longer whole, but the words *go home* were all that she cared about. Tears formed in her eyes as she tried to smile around the edges of her duct tape to assure Gene that this had been fun and that she'd had a good time. It wasn't that she hadn't experience unbelievable sexual pleasure. It just wasn't what she had imagined. From that moment on, Gertie would feel like an addict, wanting more and more of the pleasure Gene was obviously capable of providing.

"Now one last item remains. We just need to remove these," Gene said, referring to her thigh-shaping panties. As he sliced them away, Gertie felt her body explode out of the garment she had worn with the intention of hiding as much of her body as she could tuck into it. Her eyes welled with tears of shame; she had no desire for a man to see her expansive size. Gene didn't seem to notice as he took Gertie on an even more exquisite ride to orgasm until she was completely out of her mind. She now understood the wisdom of duct tape. Otherwise, the entire condo building would have rocked with Gertie's screams of pleasure.

No one had ever paid Gertie this kind of attention. As Gene released Gertie and gave her his trench coat to wear home, she knew she would hunger deeply for more of these opportunities. At the same time, she was not completely foolish and would make certain that Dr. Eugene Gregory got what *he* deserved later. It was time for more specific lessons from Chef Michael. She wondered what he might suggest to compete with scalpels.

Before she left Gene's apartment, Gertie heard words she had never, ever heard before, had never expected to hear in her lifetime. In that moment, she forgave almost all of Gene Gregory's sins. He took Gertie into his arms, looked into her eyes, and said, "Thank you, Gertie. You're beautiful." She knew he meant it. She couldn't believe it, but she knew he did. She smiled as she reached for her purse. Gene cinched the coat's belt around her to assure that her nakedness would not become evident on her way to his limo.

When Gertie left the building, escorted by the doorman, it was just after midnight. Cheryl's call to the police station hadn't produced the support she had hoped for, but she had convinced Ellen Crawford, one of her officer friends, to stop by on her way home. She had just pulled up in her squad car up and rolled her window down to talk. Cheryl was starting to tell her about her concern when the door of the building opened and Gertie emerged, wearing a trench coat she hadn't worn into the building, her Gucci bag slung over her shoulder. Cheryl signaled to Ellen, who backed up in front of the building.

Cheryl wanted desperately to know what had happened to Gertie's clothes, which were obviously missing. But more than that, it was the look on her face that Cheryl couldn't quite fathom. Gertie looked every bit like a hooker except that she was radiant. Stunned perhaps, but beaming as she was escorted from the building.

"Gertrude Morgan?" Ellen asked as she approached Gertie.

"Yes?" she replied, surprised to be addressed by an officer in uniform and wondering what she might have done wrong.

"We have been dispatched by a party concerned about your whereabouts. Is there anything you want to report? Are you OK, ma'am?"

Gertie froze for just a second, still puzzled, and frowned. Who would have been so concerned about her whereabouts? Mary Lee had known she was out with Gene. Who else—?

"No, I don't have anything to report, and yes, I'm fine," she replied, her eyes wide with fear. *Was this customary for women who went out with Gene Gregory?*

"Could I see some ID, please?" the officer continued.

"Whatever for?" Gertie shot back but reached into her purse and produced her photo ID. Gertie didn't have a driver's license, so she showed the officer her state identification card. "I don't understand who would be so concerned about my welfare and why you would go to all of this trouble. Don't you folks usually wait two or three days before you search for a missing person—like you did for my mother?" she snapped.

The officer looked at the ID, gave it back to Gertie, and touched her hat. "Thank you, ma'am. Sorry for any inconvenience. Just doing my job."

The limo driver had opened the back door for Gertie and presented his hand to help her in. Ignoring his offer because she needed both hands to make sure her trench coat didn't fall open as she seated herself, Gertie stepped in carefully, still wondering who would have called the police and why.

The limo driver closed the door. When at last she was able to relax, she put her head back against the softly cushioned headrest and let herself absorb the last words Gene had spoken to her. "You're beautiful. You're beautiful. You're beautiful."

Ellen sat in her police car until the limo was out of sight then turned it around and drove over to Cheryl's vehicle, where Cheryl was breathing a sigh of relief not only for Gertie but also for herself. She was now officially off "worry" duty and could go home.

"Everything appears to be OK, Cheryl," Ellen told her. "I'd say she had a bit more fun than she's used to and is a little shaken by the experience, but other than leaving without a stitch of clothing on under that trench coat, there's nothing to press charges for. Anything else before I head out? Trip to a strip club?" Ellen laughed.

"No, that will do. Thanks, Ellen." Cheryl laughed too, weak with relief. "I was probably overreacting, but I was so concerned.

I owe you big-time. Let's get together over at Jimmi's one of these nights soon. I miss hanging out with you."

"OK, that sounds great." Ellen smiled. "Still not dating after that bastard Jack Riley, I take it."

"No. I'm taking a breather from men, maybe for the rest of my life. But, Ellen, thanks so much. I'll sleep better knowing she's OK."

As Cheryl pulled her car away from the curb, she wasn't convinced that Gertie was really OK. She had looked fine—great, in fact. But if anything abnormal had occurred between Gertie and Gene that had played Gertie as a victim of Gene's warped personality or sexual conduct, she was going to find out. Cheryl still didn't trust him, and her anger at men in general only added to her intense focus. If she caught so much as a whiff of something that smelled bad about the weird Dr. Gregory, she would see Gene's license revoked and him behind bars.

52

"Dad, I have an idea," Art Jr. said to his father one evening over a rare dinner together. "Let's go to LA. Allie's charity ball is coming up, and she wants me to attend in the worst way. Why don't you come with me and meet both Allie and her mother? It could be fun and educational. You'd have to wear a tux and ride in a limousine, though," Art Jr. added and laughed at the thought.

"Would that Winslow woman be there with her assistant, Cheryl?" Art asked as he sipped his coffee.

"Oh, most assuredly," Art Jr. replied, somewhat surprised by his father's question. "Neither of them would miss an event like that. If you ever watched TV or went to the movies, you'd recognize some of the others who will be there too. This is one of those events that make the society news. Allie's connected to a number of famous people through her own charitable work and also through her mother."

"OK, then, Son. Let's do it. I'll take care of the tickets," Art replied. He knew instantly that Mae Rose would be pleased to see some of her rainy day fund used for this. But don't count on me for a tux. My suit should do just fine,"

"Are you joking, Dad?" Art Jr. Was surprised at his father's easy response. "It would be outrageously expensive." He paused and grinned.

His father smiled at the thought. "There's not much time for us to prepare for something like this, though. Do you think John and Elliana would like to come along?" Art set down his coffee cup.

"Dad, are you . . . ?" Art Jr. started to say. He was speechless.

"Yes, I'm dead serious; no, I'm not out of my mind," Art replied.

Art Jr. jumped out of his chair and pranced around the kitchen. "Really, Dad, really? That's fabulous! I'll call Allie and let her know we're coming!"

"No," his father replied firmly. "Let's not do that. Let's not tell anyone. I'd rather it be a surprise. However, you may call John and Elliana to see if they would like to take a vacation. Find someplace reasonable to stay near the ocean. What do you say? The baby will be here in a month or so; it would be nice for them to have a few days together before that. I remember well enough how different life was for your mother and me after you boys were born."

"Dad," Art Jr. stopped suddenly. "How do you define 'reasonable'? It's LA. Your definition and theirs might be very different." But he was smiling.

"I'll trust your judgment, Son. You and your brother can make the arrangements. Just let me know the details and the cost. Can you handle that?" Art felt good about this idea—very good. He wanted to spend a little more time with Cheryl, even though she was much too young for him.

"OK," Art Jr. replied. "Are you sure? You want to sleep on it?"

"Nope. I'm wide awake and I've almost never felt better," Art told him, and his smile said everything. "Your mother would be in full agreement. Can you imagine how she would be acting right about now?" It was easy for Art Jr. to imagine his mother wreathed in smiles and waltzing around the living room, dancing for joy.

Both Art Jr. and John agreed that they were going to rent their father a tux for the ball, regardless of what he said about the matter. Elliana got into the fun and they all went together to pick one out. They brought along Art's suit, which they sneaked out of the house while he was in the barn, so the tailor would know the proper measurements. As long as they got Art's suit back in the closet before Sunday, he wouldn't notice a thing. Truth be known, the only time Art went into his closet was when he needed to dress up, which these days was for Sundays only. It was also true that he opened Mae Rose's closet much more frequently than he did his own.

Allie's voice sounded edgy when Art Jr. talked to her the following Monday. He knew she was busy getting ready for the ball, which was now just shy of a month away. He kept a low profile, smiling every time he thought of how surprised she was going to be when he showed up with his family. She'd be so pleased and doubly so when he told her that the family was making a donation in loving memory of Art Jr.'s mother.

When things settled down after the ball, Art Jr. planned to pull Allie aside and tell her everything about the movie and his mother. He hoped that his father's introduction to Mary Lee Broadmoor would help pave the way. For his own peace of mind, Art Jr. had finally rationalized Mary Lee's personality change to be a result of her newfound joy at being alive. Based on the little he knew about her past, she had a lot of catching up to do on that front. He still had no idea how she got such intimate details of the McElroy family's life for the movie or why her home reminded him so much of his mother's decorating style. That was the only tricky part.

*　*　*

When Allie's cell phone rang, she reluctantly took the call from her mother. They hadn't talked much since Allie had accused her of lying, so she was prepared to continue that conversation. She braced herself for the battle she was sure she was about to face.

"OK, Natalie darling, you've put this off long enough," Mary Lee insisted. "We have got to go shopping and get you a new gown for the ball. I've got my seamstress on hold for alternations. Let's go tonight; just a few hours and it will be over."

It took a moment for Allie to put down her verbal weapons and adjust to a call about what she was wearing to the ball, not about who had written the movie. She did not tell her mother what a frivolous expense it would be. This time, she just gave in.

"OK, Mother," Allie relented easily to keep the peace. "It's just that you know I won't use it again and it seems like such a waste.

I'd rather donate the money to CANIF and wear one of my old gowns. And please don't call me 'darling.' It isn't appropriate and it makes me feel weird."

"OK, sweetheart, I understand," Mary Lee cooed. "But every so often you have to play your part and this is one of those times. Your biggest event of the year! My treat. What time do you get off work? With any luck, we'll strike gold tonight and have you looking like a million dollars in no time. Have you scheduled your hair and nails yet?"

"Of course not, Mother. I hardly have time to get dressed in the morning," Allie replied wearily.

"My, my, we're cranky." Mary Lee laughed. "I'll set that up with Arnold."

"Mother, I don't—" Allie began to once again tell her mother that she didn't want a hairdresser. She'd rather do her own hair and leave her nails bare.

"Nonsense, Natalie dear. Arnold always makes you look like a dream. Let me do this for you, sweetie. Lord knows I haven't done enough for you over the years," Mary Lee sighed into the phone.

"OK, Mother, if it makes you feel better," Allie replied, resenting the notion that her mother thought a new gown, hairstyle, and manicure could do anything to fill in the huge relationship hole she'd dug with her daughter. Allie hated to cooperate, but it would take longer to say no and argue than to just agree and get it over with. It registered with her that except for the honeyed voice, the woman on the other end of the phone sounded a bit more like the pushy broad Allie grew up with. *Could this be another sign that her mother was settling back into her old ways at last?*

"How's that young man of yours?" Mary Lee asked.

"Art? Oh, he's fine. Not much going on there right now. We're both very busy." Allie hoped her mother would get the hint and hang up so she could get back to work.

"Why don't you invite him to the ball, darling? I'd be happy to pay his way here again," Mary Lee suggested.

"No, Mother." Allie was adamant. "This time if Art wants to see me, he has to come out on his own. We've talked about my going to see him after the ball. I really need to get back to work now, Mother. I'll see you in a few hours anyway."

"OK, darling, bye for now."

Allie sensed that her mother was more than a little disappointed that Allie wasn't more enthusiastic, but she was in a quandary. She wanted desperately to go back to her work on the Amazon. Her mother was clearly going to live, which meant that Allie was free to leave. But she needed to talk to Art Jr., and she wanted to do it in person, not over the phone. She adored him but she didn't want to stay stateside much longer. He deserved to know that she'd already checked on her visa and airfare and that she was ready to go "home."

53

The next day after lunch, Nita Winslow swept into her office with the most gleeful look on her face. "Cheryl, what do you think about asking this Art McElroy guy—the father, not the son—to be on the show with Mary Lee? Sort of as a side note? He has such a good message to share with the world, don't you think? It sounds like he really wants to help other couples overcome their relationship problems, and we could tie that into the movie—a discussion with people who have lost spouses and live with regrets of a failed relationship. What do you think?"

"I don't think he'll do it," Cheryl countered immediately. "I like the idea, but he doesn't even watch TV. We can ask him, but it would take a miracle."

"Well, it never hurts to ask, does it? He likes you. He trusts you. Give it a shot. But, don't mention that Mary Lee will also be on the show. I think it would freak him out. Just talk to him about sharing his message with our audience. We've got two hours. This gives us plenty of time for both and would take pressure off of Mary Lee as the center of attention."

"You can't be serious, Nita!" Cheryl exclaimed. "You can't expect to surprise him like that on TV! Who knows how he would react to finding out that we were also interviewing Mary Lee?"

"Then write the show with him in a different location, Wonder Woman," Nita suggested. "He won't have to see Mary Lee. He won't have to watch any other part of the show. You figure it out." Nita gave Cheryl a thumbs-up and turned back to her work, chuckling at her idea. Cheryl felt the world spinning out of control.

In the meantime, Gertie finally took Chef Michael into her confidence about her encounter with Dr. Gregory. *"Mon dieu!"* he had exclaimed, launching his tirade in French so as not to offend her. *"Mon petite chère,"* he soothed. "Très horrible!" But he was so aroused by Gertie's candidness that he had to excuse himself for a few moments to bring himself back under control. He was angry that a man of Dr. Gregory's standing would frighten his little Gertie out of her underpants—not that she hadn't enjoyed it. She just needed the scales to tip back in her favor, and really, she just wanted love. Chef Michael could help with the former; the latter was not his strong suit. Gertie and he agreed that her retaliatory lessons would have to occur in a location other than the kitchen. They made arrangements for a meeting in the unused lower level of the mansion—the old "Downstairs."

The exposure of her body to Gene Gregory had caused Gertie to consider its features more seriously. He had called her "beautiful," but Gertie couldn't see it as she stood naked in front of the mirror. Despite Mary Lee's passionate quest to clothe Gertie in fashions that hid her folds of flesh, Gertie's body was plump and only she could do anything about it. She had never minded before.

After she studied herself carefully in the mirror, she requested the use of Mary Lee's exercise room in the lower level. She knew that the look she wanted would take months of dedicated effort, but for the first time in her life, she cared. And she desperately wanted Dr. Gregory to eat his heart out later after she dumped him for scaring the living daylights out of her.

When she later pumped iron and slugged it out on the treadmill, Gertie let her mind work on the suggestions Chef Michael was giving her for payback. Dr. Eugene Gregory would never be the same after Gertie was finished with him. She smiled and stepped up her pace. A new Gertrude Louise Morgan was being born. For the first time in her life, Gertie cashed in some of her stock. She sent a sum to a spa where she would spend two weeks in the lap of luxury just before the CANIF Ball as she transformed her physical, mental, and spiritual self—and took some self-defense classes.

*   *   *

Art responded exactly as Cheryl had predicted, at first. But he trusted her and he was already planning to be in LA for the ball. So with the heart of a man who wanted to help others return to love, Art McElroy said yes to appearing on the show with the condition that at no time would there be any discussion of exactly how his wife died, the affair, or that the movie *Something Like That* appeared to be a perfect image of his marriage. And that no one else would be told, including his boys.

Nita Winslow worked feverishly and privately on her upcoming interview with Mary Lee, recasting the questions subtly and training Mary Lee to open up more. She'd given Cheryl the job of getting Art interview ready.

In the last evenings before the interview, Nita was either practicing with Mary Lee, after which they might catch a drink and cigar at the studio bar, or she was following up on the myriad details she had others taking care of. In her rare spare moments, she wondered what she was going to do after this episode to create something anywhere nearly as sensational as she believed this show would be.

54

Mary Lee opened her eyes, fully aware that this was the day of her interview. She was to be at the studio in Beverly Hills by 6:00 p.m. in preparation for the 8:00 p.m. show. Every possible emotion seemed to descend on her, and in desperate need of distraction—or medication—she rang Gertie's room.

Gertie had returned from the exercise room, sweaty and ready to step into the shower when she heard the phone ring. Stark naked, she ran to grab the call, hoping that Gene Gregory had finally called again. After their last encounter, she wasn't sure he'd ever want to see her again. Her own feelings were still quite freaky so she tried not to think too much about the experience. But she wanted him to call—at least so she could tell him off—unless he wanted to schedule another date. In her heart of hearts, Gertie wanted a chance to retaliate.

But it wasn't Gene on the phone, it was Mary Lee. "Gertie, I'm going to be somewhat of a nervous wreck today," she confided, her voice shaking. Then she laughed. "I'd rather be behind a camera calling the shots than being interviewed in front of one. You know me. What can I do to pass the time?"

At first Gertie was at a loss for an idea. Then it hit her. "Mary Lee, why don't you watch *Something Like That*? It might be the perfect way to start the day and to prepare you for the interview. I need to get into the shower, but I'd be happy to watch it with you if I can have a half hour or so."

"Hmm," Mary Lee replied. "That's not a bad idea, although I think I know the story inside and out. Still . . . would you call Chef

Michael and have him prepare one of those health drinks you've been guzzling? It might help keep me alert for the evening too."

"Absolutely," Gertie replied. "And Mary Lee . . ." Gertie paused.

"Yes, Gertie?" Mary Lee asked.

"You are going to rock the world tonight. I just know it. I'll be backstage with you the whole way. If you want to watch the DVD, I have it here in my room in my nightstand drawer."

Gertie glanced at her body before jumping into the shower. It didn't look all that different to her yet, even after all the work she'd done. But she could feel the effects, and if excitement could burn calories, she'd be trim by evening. In celebration of the day, she turned on her favorite music and started to sing along with Rascal Flatts, belting out "Stand." If nothing else, Gertie had learned how to stand.

Chef Michael was in the kitchen, preparing two glasses of Gertie's health drink, wondering if it was advisable for Mary Lee to ingest something so unlike her regular diet on such an important day. If she had an allergic reaction to any of the ingredients, it could ruin everything. He couldn't hear Gertie singing, and she couldn't hear the blender whirling, but they both heard Mary Lee's bloodcurdling scream.

55

Gertie was the first on the scene in Mary Lee's bedroom, where she found her employer on the floor at the end of her bed. In her lap she held Gertie's journal in a vise-like grip. It took only a moment for Gertie to grasp what had happened. The towel wrapped around her body slipped to the floor as she bolted to recover the journal, but Mary Lee held tight.

As Chef Michael approached the stairway, he heard Gertie begin to howl, "Oh my God! Ms. Broadmoor! Oh my God! Oh my God!" She had forgotten about her old journal sitting in the same drawer as the DVD.

Never one called upon for acts of bravery, Chef Michael bounded up the stairs and then hesitated, wondering if he should return to the kitchen for a knife just in case there'd been an assault. He had enough presence of mind to call the guardhouse on his cell phone. "Code Red!" he yelled. "Code Red! Get your asses up here now!"

The sight of the back of Gertie's completely naked body unnerved Chef Michael when he burst into the room. He had never seen her so fully revealed; he couldn't help it when he heard himself yell, "Oh, dear God!" He shielded his eyes and walked blindly toward Gertie and Mary Lee, ripping off his white chef's coat to cover Gertie— wanting desperately to protect her dignity *and* the eyesight of others who might, like him, be so overwhelmed that they would be unable to focus on the real emergency.

"I died! I really *died!*" she screamed over and over, as she went into shock. She looked fascinated—then horrified. "But if that's true, then . . . oh my god. I really talked to God? There *is* a God?!"

Gertie saw that Mary Lee was losing consciousness. "You're in shock, Ms. Broadmoor. I can explain all of this. I'm so sorry!"

Mary Lee's eyes began to roll back in her head. As she slipped toward unconsciousness, she said softly, "Where's Mae Rose? I need to talk to Mae Rose!" Gertie was dumbfounded. *Who the hell was Mae Rose? Was that the name of her alter ego? The spirit that she shared cigars and Gin Rummy with?*

Chef Michael saw no blood, nothing to suggest an attack, so he couldn't understand why Mary Lee had been screaming about death. There was nothing else worthy of note except for the book both Mary Lee and Gertie appeared to be fighting over.

Suddenly the two guards charged into the room, weapons ready for any possibility. One of them was on the phone calling 911 to the house. They observed Gertie trying to console Mary Lee.

"Mary Lee!" Gertie's voice became authoritative as she put her arms around Mary Lee, coaxing her head into her ample lap. Chef Michael raced to grab a pillow off Mary Lee's bed so she wouldn't have to put her head where not even the bravest would dare to tread on Gertie's anatomy.

"Stop this! Stop this now!" Gertie ordered her. But it was too late. Mary Lee's face was ashen; her eyes closed. Suddenly the toilet in Mary Lee's bathroom flushed and triggered Gertie's memory of a past event. She had heard that same sound all those months ago when Mary Lee had suddenly come to life after Gertie had pronounced her dead and made her last journal entry.

Only it hadn't been the same Mary Lee when she had woken up! Why a toilet flush? And what did it have to do with what was occurring now? Gertie's mind was racing toward a possibility that stunned her. The flushing sound had been a big deal in the movie, symbolizing a transition to the afterlife. This had to be more than a coincidence—was Mary Lee finally leaving her body? Right now Gertie couldn't think about this—she had to get her journal back. It was even more important that no one else see it—ever!

Gertie lifted her head as she considered what to do and saw the three men standing over the two of them. With a sudden flash of insight, she leaned back over the unconscious body and hissed so no one else could hear, "Mae Rose, let go of my goddamned journal!" It worked! The journal slid easily into Gertie's hands. She spoke loudly to Mary Lee, "Chef Michael and the two guards are here, Mary Lee. They're going to lift you into your bed." She turned to them as tears coursed down her cheeks. "Be gentle. Be gentle."

Chef Michael put his arms around Gertie and walked her to Mary Lee's writing chair. He put her in the chair and wrapped a blanket around her shoulders. Gertie heaved with weeping and could not stop. Trying to be helpful, Chef Michael reached to relieve Gertie of her journal, but her iron grip made it impossible. The harder he tried, the more she resisted until at last Gertie rewarded his efforts with a right hook into his face. He dropped to the floor, screaming, "You broke my nose! Bitch! You broke my nose!"

This made Gertie cry even more hysterically, "I'm sorry! I'm so sorry!" She could not be consoled and she could not stop screaming. A second ambulance would be necessary.

One of the guards disappeared to let the police cars and the first ambulance through the gated entrance. The other, aware of the symptoms of shock, covered Mary Lee with whatever extra blankets he could find and grabbed her wrist to check her pulse, which was rapid and weak. Somewhere a clock struck 10:00 a.m.

Anyone with a police scanner or within hearing distance of the police sirens screaming down the street to the Broadmoor estate was alerted to the crisis. Neighbors began to file out of their homes, gathering to watch the commotion. The street was blocked off; the driveway to Mary Lee's home filled with emergency vehicles. By 10:30, Mary Lee was en route to the hospital. Michael, his hands covering his bloody nose, followed Gertie into the next ambulance when it arrived. Her howling quieted as medication took over her system.

As the sirens wailed toward the hospital, Chef Michael sat miserably in the back of the ambulance, nursing his nose and keeping a close watch on Gertie. Under her blanket, he noticed the journal still firmly clasped in her hands. When the paramedic turned his back for a moment, Michael reached over and feigning a tender gesture, was rewarded with her unconscious release of the book which he scooped up and hid inside his shirt, conveniently open down to the third button.

*   *   *

Gene Gregory was on rounds at the hospital, checking on one of his hospice patients who appeared close to death; she would probably go in the next several hours. Agnes Hortense breathed laboriously between words, clinging to life a bit longer before emphysema claimed her. Dr. Gregory checked her vital signs, which were right on schedule. When his pager went off, he checked the message, stood up, and ran out of the room with no explanation, leaving Agnes confused and her family upset. Agnes passed away from the shock, and while the family felt it decidedly unfair that Dr. Gregory had not been there to assist, they could not argue when they learned of the extraordinary turn of events when they saw the news a few hours later.

By 11:00 a.m. Allie had also arrived at the hospital. Both Nita Winslow and Cheryl Lewis were already at the studio, preparing for the evening event when they got the call.

Blissfully unaware of the events of the morning, the McElroy family was getting ready for a day of sightseeing activities. They had landed in LA the night before and had been settling into their suite of rooms, amazed by simple things such as the price of the bottled water, snacks, and room service, the view of the ocean, and how attentive the staff was. It took all of them to keep Art Jr. from running off to see Allie and ruining what was to be their surprise appearance at the CANIF Ball in three days.

Art was a bit jumpy, which everyone else in the family chalked up to his sensitivity to the elegance that surrounded him and an occasional consideration of what this trip was costing him. Only he knew about the interview he had agreed to that evening. He had already decided he would tell the family he was going on a walk; he preferred that they not watch the show.

While John and Elliana were relaxing in the living area, John flipped on the TV, looking for ESPN. A news announcement interrupted local broadcasting and brought the McElroys to a frozen standstill.

"This has just come over the wires," the announcer reported. "Word has reached us that Oscar-winning movie director Mary Lee Broadmoor has suffered a heart attack and is in intensive care at an undisclosed hospital location. Ms. Broadmoor is best known for her movie *Something Like That* and before that as 'Scary Mary' for her incredibly terrifying and wonderful horror films. An undisclosed source informs us that Ms. Broadmoor was to be interviewed this evening on *Currents*."

Art Jr.'s first thought was for Allie; Art's first thought was that Mary Lee had been scheduled to be on the same interview with him and he had not been informed. He was not happy.

As word of Mary Lee Broadmoor's condition spread across news wires and over the Internet, the world paused for a moment. It was not like when President Kennedy was assassinated or Princess Di died tragically, and nothing compared to when the Twin Towers in New York were hit, but the world reacted with gasping surprise and disbelief. The woman who had survived pancreatic cancer was once again at death's door.

Gertie awakened only briefly in a hazy fog and thought she was hallucinating when she saw Gene at her hospital bedside. Unbeknownst to her, her scalpel-bladed seducer had requested permission to supervise her care. Gene was surprised that Gertie had no attending physician and no apparent medical history. In truth, Gertie had never had a sick day in her life and, as she had already told Gene, she really didn't care for doctors.

Knowing that Mary Lee would want nothing but the best of care for Gertie, Gene personally selected the doctors who attended to her. He was by her side as much as possible, leaving only when one of his hospice patients was taking his or her final breaths. He was glad when death claimed them, and instead of celebrating with an enthusiastic hand job in the private bathroom off his hospital office, he hurried straight back to Gertie's room where she remained unconscious.

That evening, when he was released from the hospital, Michael took Gertie's journal with him. He was sorely tempted to read it, partly because he felt that knowing Gertie's secrets would be acceptable compensation for his suffering, and partly because Gertie was still such a mystery to him—so wounded yet so remarkably brave. He tried not to think of his efforts to cover Gertie's naked body in Mary Lee's bedroom, because now it struck him as hilarious, and it hurt like hell when his face wrinkled up in laughter. In the end, Michael's protective instincts toward Gertie won him over. He burned the book in the fireplace of Mary Lee's study, never knowing its contents and denying the rest of the world that same opportunity.

56

As she sat at her mother's hospital beside, Allie's face bore a look of deep concern. Anyone observing her would have thought she was appropriately focused on her mother's condition. In truth, Allie was brooding over the distinct possibility that once again her plans to return to Brazil were being thwarted by her mother. She no longer cared about what had caused her mother's personality change or who had really written the story. She decided that whether or not her mother survived, she was leaving as soon as her mother got past this crisis. After all, Gertie would be available, no matter what. For once, Allie was thankful for her mother's nurse.

At one point when Mary Lee's room was empty except for the two of them, Allie felt inspired to go over to her mother's bed, lean over her tenderly, and whisper in her ear, "I'm still leaving, Mother. No matter what you decide to do—no matter who you really are— I'm still leaving, and I want you to know that." Immediately she felt better.

Suddenly Allie had an urge to talk to Art Jr. She dialed his number and was amazed that he picked up her call so quickly. "Allie darling, we've heard the news. How are you?" Art Jr. could not suppress his love, which caused Allie to smile in spite of her circumstances, plus he had called her "darling."

"Oh, Art." She started to weep, "Art, I love you. I wish you were here."

"I love you too, Allie, and I *am* here," Art Jr. replied softly.

"Art, I mean I wish you were here physically," Allie explained.

"I know, darling. I am," he replied patiently.

"Here *where*, Art?" Allie asked, mystified.

"In LA. Did you think I would miss the CANIF Ball?" he nearly shouted with joy into the phone. "I brought the whole family. Just tell me where the hospital is. I'll be there as soon as a cab can get me there!" Suddenly he understood how Allie had felt all those weeks ago when she desperately wanted to surprise him about her mother and the movie.

Allie burst into tears again. "Art, oh, Art," she sobbed with relief and told him the location of the hospital. "Come quickly, please." In that instant she knew she could not, would not return to Brazil without him.

When Art Jr. hung up the phone, his father saw the look on his face and knew exactly how he felt. "You need to be there for her," he said softly as tears gathered in his eyes. "Get a cab and go directly to the hospital. The rest of us will be here. Call when you can."

"OK, Dad. Thanks," Art Jr. replied and hugged his father, his brother, and his very pregnant sister-in-law.

Nita and Cheryl wandered among the folks in the hospital waiting room until three o'clock, hoping to garner breaking news for the evening show. They then left knowing they had a two-hour slot to fill that would have an unprecedented audience and they were now without their main attraction. Working feverishly together with their staff, they coordinated some live shots from the hospital, including a doctor's update on Mary Lee's condition. Mary Lee wasn't dead, so they couldn't run a history of her life; she hadn't been an excitingly public figure, so they didn't have much in the archives. In short, they concluded that Art McElroy Sr. would become their featured guest for the entire show—if he agreed. Otherwise they were going to have to do a rerun of Mary Lee winning the two Oscars and play the video of Nita's visit to Mae Rose's grave. They didn't feel prepared but it wouldn't be the first show Nita had ever had to run on impulse alone.

With Nita pacing beside her, Cheryl called Art's hotel around four o'clock to make sure that he was available and ready to be picked up by the studio limo at six. She had braced herself for the task of persuading a man who had never been on television to absorb the limelight, but was not prepared for his anger. He had learned that Mary Lee Broadmoor was to have been on the same show.

"I don't know what you people intended, but I am not pleased to hear this. All you care about is getting a good story. I should have been told, Ms. Lewis, and I'm sorely tempted to reconsider my commitment to be on the show. I'm not going to be part of a . . ." Art hesitated because he wanted to curse, but he had never used such words in his life, not even in moments of exquisite rage at Mac Rose. He let the words "goddamned" pass through his mind and finished with ". . . a three-ring circus."

Cheryl cringed at being called "Ms. Lewis," wilted at being cast in with "you people," and crumpled in horror when Art threatened to withdraw from the show. Nita watched the conversation with a sinking heart, her fingers crossed and her eyes lifted upward.

Cheryl, being Cheryl, also knew the art of letting people get through their emotional reactions before speaking to them. Listening was a critical skill for a police officer. When Art had finished, Cheryl spoke as directly as possible to his feelings. "Mr. McElroy," she said respectfully, "I appreciate your concerns. We were indeed working on two separate segments, one for you and one for Mary Lee. But the two of you were scheduled to be interviewed in separate studios. We had no intention of creating discomfort for either of you. It's not uncommon for guests on a show not to know or even meet each other. We were being very careful," she added.

"Perhaps, but you would have played each of us off the other," Art insisted. "I've heard enough to know what you people do on shows like that. I refuse to be part of something like that." Art didn't realize he had used the same words as the title of the movie, but Cheryl caught it, and it lifted her up.

"*Currents* is not like those shows, Mr. McElroy, *sir,*" she added. "It's highly respected because we come across incredibly interesting stories and real people like you. We need you, sir—not *we* the TV show producers, but those of us who care about Mary Lee Broadmoor and the message of her movie, those of us who want to understand how love really works.

"What you have to share makes the film feel *real*. Otherwise, it's just a very good movie. But it's nothing more unless it can be used to help people in real life, Mr. McElroy. Without your true life experience, Mary Lee's movie is just an award-winning film. The purpose of our show is to make a difference." Cheryl paused. She knew that Art was listening.

"I told you I would always tell you the truth, and I have," she continued. "We had no idea Ms. Broadmoor would even agree to be interviewed until just a few days ago. The whole world wants to know about her movie and see the woman who wrote it. But she can't be here tonight—she might even be dying. If you are willing to give an account of your real-life experience—it will be the heartbeat of the entire show. *Currents* is popular because we always go for the hearts of real people, and you are very real. Are you up for that? Are you ready to tell the world what life after Mae Rose has taught you? If not, we've got a great deal of work to do and very little time, but the show *will* go on."

Cheryl paused again then lowered her voice. "Nita and I both heard you speak at church. If you can just adopt that same kind of quiet, honest attitude, tell us about your relationship when your wife was alive, how you handled her death, and what you've learned, it could be the difference I believe you want to make in the world."

Bull's-eye. Cheryl had no idea that those last few words struck Art—the new, tenderized Art—dead center. There was a long pause that Cheryl also knew not to interrupt before Art quietly and firmly replied, "OK, but I want you on the show with me, Ms. Lewis."

"Mr. McElroy—sir—I don't do live camera," Cheryl blurted. "It's not my part of the job, and I don't think the studio would—"

"I don't do *any* camera, dead or alive, so it seems to me that we're in the same boat. Besides, it's you I've talked to about the past, about Mae Rose and me," Art explained. "I think it's a great idea to have you beside me like we're having a conversation. It will certainly make me more comfortable. Those are my terms."

"OK, Mr. McElroy," Cheryl said. "I'm sure I can get a go-ahead."

When he hung up the phone, Art still refused to tell his family about the event. The less they knew, the better. He'd just disappear for a while, and then it would be over. From that point, they would focus on their vacation and the CANIF Ball. He looked forward to meeting Allie Schwartz, although he wondered how she'd be able to even think about the ball at a time like this.

The evening news carried the story of Mary Lee Broadmoor's condition as its headline. Entitled "Three Lives and Counting," the network put Mary Lee in the news even though—or perhaps because—she would not make the program that evening. Either way, it was great publicity. The show would go on, the announcer informed viewers. When he explained that the topic would be "Love Lost; Love Reborn" based on Mary Lee's movie, with guests whose lives had been changed by the movie, he knew that viewership would be at an all-time high even without Mary Lee. It was the perfect solution.

*   *   *

Mary Lee hung on to life. She had no idea that the entire world was watching and waiting for news, that flowers and wishes for her recovery overflowed the driveway of her estate—that her cats were inconsolable. She didn't know that Art Jr. had arrived, and that he and Allie were in each other's arms in her private critical care room, or that her daughter had been packing to leave the country but love had changed her mind. Allie would stay long enough to convince Art McElroy Jr. to marry her and accompany her to Brazil.

Pastor Frank always watched the national evening news. It was the only time he looked at television, and it was only to keep himself informed in case there was anything important for his parishioners. "Sermon fodder," he called it, and in a farm community such as Fairview, people appreciated that analogy.

When he sat in front of the television after dinner that evening and learned of the plight of Mary Lee Broadmoor, Pastor Frank bowed his head and asked—just one time—for her healing. He couldn't put his hands on her, and he wasn't sure that he could make a difference, but he prayed anyway. Then he remembered the McElroy family and prayed that Art and his sons not be harmed in any way by this breaking news.

*   *   *

"It's been an eventful day here in Los Angeles," Nita Winslow's voice was strong as she began the evening's segment of *Currents*. No one would know her private disappointment over Mary Lee's absence on the show, but she would openly demonstrate her respect for this woman in myriad ways.

"This evening's topic is 'Before It's Too Late: The Death and Rebirth of Love.' We delve into the fascinating world of Mary Lee Broadmoor's sensational movie *Something Like That* and give you real-world reactions to the story. Many of you have been touched by this Oscar-winning phenomenon, but you may not know its far-reaching impact. Perhaps you've been thinking that only *your* heart, or only *your* relationship has been changed."

She turned expertly to face a different camera. "Tonight, as Mary Lee Broadmoor once again fights for her life, we will take you, live from Los Angeles, into the hearts and lives of people who have been transformed by the movie. Perhaps the most changed has been Mary Lee Broadmoor herself."

Nita appeared calm and sincerely sad.

"Most of you know that Ms. Broadmoor, known for years as 'Scary Mary,' lies in intensive care at a local hospital after her collapse at home earlier today," she continued gravely. "We'll take you live outside of her home and show you the world's response to this news. We'll provide updates from the hospital and her doctors. You'll also hear from some of those whose lives have been touched by her most recent and utterly captivating movie, written by a much-transformed Mary Lee Broadmoor. We'll attempt to answer the question that so many people are asking: *How did Scary Mary, the Queen of Horror write such an extraordinary love story?* And we'll do it all without Mary Lee.

"Tonight we also have a special, special guest. You will be privileged to walk into the life of a very private, quiet man—a man who would never, ever invite the public into his home, much less his heart, unless he had a very strong purpose and he does. Ladies and gentlemen, please join me in welcoming Mr. Art McElroy Sr to our show." Art's face came on to the screen. "Art, it is an honor to have you with us this evening."

"Thank you, Nita," Art said quietly. "It is terrifying to be here tonight."

Nita laughed warmly, surprised and pleased by Art's honest humor.

"Art," she said, her full attention on him, "you have an important message for us. I'd like our viewers to know that you lost your wife about eighteen months ago to a sudden heart attack at the young age of fifty-six. What you have learned since her death has, in every way, a stunning correlation to the movie *Something Like That*, even though you have never seen it. We'll be discussing that right after we come back from this break."

The camera turned back to Nita. Art relaxed slightly, off camera. *So far, so good,* he thought. If he had to say only a few words every few minutes, he could do this, and he wanted to honor his wife, his family, and his community in this way. Cheryl Lewis, who sat silently beside him, reached over and squeezed his hand; he squeezed back.

The small world that knew Art McElroy Sr. sat stunned in front of their televisions. Art Jr. and Allie watched from her mother's intensive care room, where Mary Lee was still alive but unconscious. They looked at each other in surprise. Art Jr. put his hands up defensively, saying, "No, honestly, Allie, I knew nothing about this. Coming to the CANIF Ball was the only surprise I had in mind." He grimaced, closed his eyes, and pinched the skin between them as if trying to pull what was happening out of his mind. He had a lot of questions for his father, but they would have to wait.

John and Elliana were transfixed by what they could not yet comprehend, but their unborn daughter suddenly kicked merrily as if she completely understood and approved. Before the commercial break was over, anyone who knew Art but didn't watch *Currents* would also be tuned in to this extraordinary event, and anyone who watched *Currents* but didn't know Art McElroy would find him endearing.

The only person who was unhappy about this development was Maggie Whitman, as she sat with Al Nelson, watching the show at his home in Seattle. After recovering from the shock of seeing her former lover on TV, she asked Al if she could change the channel. She found these types of shows too depressing, she explained.

"Sure, honey," Al replied as he handed her the remote. "We'll watch whatever you want to." Then he took her hand and held it quietly. They had met at church and knew fairly quickly that they were meant to be together. It wasn't exciting like falling in love for the first time or having an affair. It was just wonderfully and comfortably perfect for both of them.

57

Two floors above Mary Lee's, Gertie was finally conscious and resting, still under the influence of strong medication. She vaguely remembered the events that had brought her here and blamed herself for Mary Lee's condition. There was significant weeping and some incoherent babbling. She needed to confess what she knew to someone and was particularly distressed because she could not locate the journal that told the truth of what she had hidden away. She never meant to do any harm; it shouldn't have happened as it had. Thankfully, the TV had been removed from her room under doctor's orders. The last thing she needed was constant media exposure to Mary Lee's condition or to see the guests on the *Currents* show.

Gertie decided she should talk to a hospital chaplain if there was one on duty. Confession was good for the soul, and she felt she had so much piled up that if she started now, she might get finished and be able to get on with her life before it was over. She expected to lose her home health care license and would probably have to start dipping into her life savings, which at that moment were approximately $3.7 million. She knew she could manage as long as she didn't have to go to jail.

A knock at the door caused Gertie to look up in time to see a bouquet of flowers waving at her, followed by the very handsome personage of Dr. Gregory. As he pulled up a chair to sit with her, she realized he had been by her side during much of the time that she was unconscious. She also knew that this man, who had helped many people over death's threshold, had probably heard more confessions than any priest, and probably had a few of his own to make.

While she hadn't quite gotten over their sexual encounter, she also knew that he would want her to keep that a secret. Therefore, Gertie decided instantly that he was exactly the one—for so many reasons—she could entrust with her confession.

Gene listened patiently, holding her hand. As Gertie wept, he smoothed back her hair, studying her face and head closely. Gertie wasn't sure if he was listening or plotting his next sexual advance. In the end, however, when she had wept her last tear and shared her last detail, Gene was able to tell her that he had researched concepts such as life extension and the possibility of spirits crossing over, trading places in physical bodies, usually at a time very close to the death of the current inhabitant. He said he didn't know if any of it was true or if it had happened to Mary Lee. Gene felt it would be a comfort to Gertie to know that she was not crazy although, to be honest, Gene's reassurance of that fact did not give Gertie the full confidence she was seeking.

While he listened, Gene knew that he, too, had his own dark secrets that needed to be brought out into the open, and his were much deeper and darker than Gertie's. While he felt quite sure that Gertie was not in a position to be his confessor, for the first time in his life, Eugene Gregory felt that he might have hope and, if he was lucky, love.

At the end of the evening, Gene gave Gertie a proper kiss on the cheek and assured her that he would check on her in the morning after he made his rounds. Hearing this made Gertie cry, which caused the doctor to order a sleeping medication to help her through the night.

Gene sat with Gertie until she was asleep and then, unable to resist the temptation, Eugene Gregory did something he had never done in his life. He pulled back some of her blankets and stepped gingerly into the bed beside Gertie. He had never slept with another person and wanted to know how it felt. Shaping his body against hers, Eugene Gregory put his arms around Gertie and slept. Gertie stirred only slightly, snuggling against him as if it were the most natural thing in the world.

* * *

In the next segment of *Currents,* brief clips of the movie *Something Like That* played. Nita then gave her undivided attention to Art. For the rest of the evening, between hospital updates and commercials, Art told the story of his relationship with Mae Rose in his quiet, unassuming way, just as he had done at church. He rarely took his eyes off Cheryl as he told his story, and he was not ashamed to cry.

Art Jr. and Allie sat in complete amazement as they watched and listened to Art. He made them laugh, and he made them cry, but most of all, he told them what he understood about love. It was easy now, he said, to look back and see how things could have been different. He gave examples of the smallest things that would have made a difference, such as saying, "I love you" more often; making small purchases that would have brought Mae Rose delight, such as a single rose from time to time; listening to his wife instead of avoiding their conflicts; telling the truth; and consulting her before buying more VW parts. But he also talked about standing up for himself, which he had not done and said could have made life much easier for both of them. "Sometimes conflict is really love that is growing into a new space," he explained thoughtfully.

Nita posed a question. "Art, we know you're not a marriage counselor, so you can't speak to problems of relationships in general, but why do you think so many people give up on their marriages? Why are there so many divorces?" Nita would want to know his answer to that question for herself most of all.

"Nita, you're right; I can only suppose, but here's what I think."

As Art spoke, Mary Lee stirred for the first time since her collapse. Art Jr. and Allie turned to see that her eyes were open. She was looking at the television with tears streaming down her cheeks. Allie was stunned. She had never seen her mother cry.

A medical team quickly surrounded Mary Lee's bed, blocking her view of the TV. Although unable to speak, Mary Lee was obviously displeased. If she could have, she would have told the doctors and nurses to get the hell out of her way. But she couldn't communicate, and they would not have obeyed her orders anyway.

For once in her life, Mary Lee had to submit to the demands of others. It was intensely unpleasant for her; all she could do was weep, which she did through the entire ordeal. Yet there was a sense of something miraculous. Mary Lee's reflexes and responses were checked and her vital signs were stable. She couldn't speak or follow any requests to move parts of her body, but it was obvious she understood everything.

Art Jr. stayed by Allie's side throughout the medical deliberation and discussion of a possible stroke. He knew exactly what the prognosis was and reassured Allie that there could be much recovery in the days, weeks and months ahead. This caused her to burst into tears—mostly for herself. She and her mother then wept together, although for very different reasons.

After the doctors left, Mary Lee used her eyes in an attempt to communicate. She looked at Allie, then at Art Jr., then up to the TV screen whenever Art Sr. was talking. She did this over and over until Art Jr. figured out that Mary Lee's eye movements suggested that she wanted to meet his father. Once it was agreed that Art would visit, Mary Lee's weeping stopped for a brief moment and she closed her eyes. But when Allie suggested this the next day, Mary Lee immediately burst into tears again. Apparently she did not want to wait that long.

Art Jr. called the station's switchboard and asked them to connect him to Nita Winslow during a break. Nita picked up the call. "Mr. McElroy," she called happily to Art Sr., "We have been advised that Mary Lee Broadmoor wants to see you as soon as possible. Cheryl, can you drive him over to the hospital after the show?"

"Can't this wait until tomorrow?" Art asked. He wanted to meet Mary Lee, but it had been a big day for both of them. He figured they both needed their rest.

"Not if you can make it tonight," Nita advised. "Mary Lee is not used to being kept waiting and you could miss an important opportunity. None of us know if she's going to pull through this time."

Art reluctantly got in Cheryl's unmarked and very plain Ford sedan. "I'm not sure how I feel about this," he said. "I wanted to meet Ms. Broadmoor on this trip but not if she is incapacitated. It can wait."

"Apparently it can't Mr. McElroy," Cheryl said quietly. "Want to take her some flowers? I know a place that's open twenty-four hours a day. Could be a nice touch. Ms. Broadmoor could become your son's mother-in-law if I don't miss my guess—and I don't." Cheryl smiled as she started the car.

"Sure, OK," Art agreed, obviously preoccupied. "It's just that—I mean, what will I say to her? She can't talk. How will we communicate?"

"Well, Mr. McElroy," Cheryl said, smiling, "TV cameras can't talk either, and you did a good enough job with that tonight. I'd suggest you not worry about what to say. Sounds like she just wants to see you, and for Mary Lee Broadmoor to want to see *anyone* is sort of a miracle in and of itself. Ready?"

"I guess so," Art said quietly then lapsed into silence. He didn't notice when Cheryl stopped the car at an all-night grocery store and disappeared inside. She returned with a dozen yellow sweetheart roses.

"This is all they had, Mr. McElroy. I hope yellow is OK with you," Cheryl put the flowers in his lap. He thanked her and said nothing more until they arrived at the hospital.

"Do you want me to wait for you?" Cheryl asked him.

"Oh—no, Miss Lewis," Art finally responded in a dazed voice. "Art Jr. and I will get a cab. Don't worry about us." He grabbed the flowers. As he stepped out of the car, he turned back and looked at Cheryl. "Thank you, Miss Lewis," he said. "Thank you for thinking of the roses . . . and everything. You pulled me through tonight."

"I doubt that, Mr. McElroy, but anything I can do to help, you just let me know." Cheryl smiled at him reassuringly. As she drove off, she saw a limo in the dark corner of the parking lot. She knew who would be in it and steered her car in that direction.

"Want me to handle this, Nita?" she asked her boss.

"No, I'll cover it." Nita smiled. "You've had some late nights recently, and I've got another successful show under my belt with no place to go and no one to celebrate with. I think I'll keep an eye on things here." Before Cheryl could drive away, Nita added, "It was our best show ever tonight. Don't you agree?"

"Yes, I do," Cheryl replied. "And I'm really tired. I didn't say a word on TV tonight, but I was scared out of my pants, and I don't scare easily."

"Welcome to stardom, Ms. Lewis," Nita teased. Then her window went up.

Cheryl pulled out into the night traffic, looking forward to getting home, where she could have a good cry. Art had retreated into himself and obviously wanted nothing to do with her except to get him through the show. She had liked him, and it hurt that he no longer reciprocated those feelings. She was used to such disappointments, but that didn't mean she was immune to how they felt.

* * *

When Art knocked on the door of Mary Lee's private room, it was Allie who opened the door. Art knew who she was and smiled broadly. "You must be the woman my son keeps yammering about." He laughed.

"Yammer? I don't yammer, Dad!" Art Jr. showed up behind Allie at the door and opened it wider. "Come on in. Yes, this is Allie. And this," he opened the door wider, "is Allie's mother, Mary Lee Broadmoor. Ms. Broadmoor, I'd like to introduce my father, Art McElroy Sr."

When Art's eyes met Mary Lee's, he stood as still as a photo, unable to move. Art Jr. watched as his father's eyes filled with tears. Allie saw the same reaction from her mother. Finally, moving slowly to Mary Lee's bedside, Art took her hands and put them together so she could hold the flowers he had brought. When their hands touched, their eyes locked even more intensely. "The roses—they're yellow. I'm sorry—so sorry—so very, very sorry." Then Art started laughing while Mary Lee beamed.

Art Jr. and Allie looked at each other and shrugged. They had no idea that Art would recognize his wife's aura regardless of what body she was wearing. They also had no idea that Mary Lee had ditched her body hours earlier, leaving it to Mae Rose when the toilet had flushed in Mary Lee's bedroom.

"Thank you," they heard Art say as he looked tenderly at Mary Lee. "Only you could have done that. What a woman!" When he started to laugh again, Mary Lee made a peculiar sound—like a dog barking—then she made it again. And again. Allie and Art Jr. looked at each other, still puzzled. What had they missed? Neither of them had seen their parent laugh in a long, long time. Finally Art spoke, not turning his face or letting go of Mary Lee's hands.

"Allie, would it be OK for me to have a few moments alone with your mother? I know it must seem a strange request but . . ." His voice wandered off, searching for the right words. "I guess you could say we feel like we have a lot in common." Art's voice betrayed intense emotion.

Allie looked quizzically at Art Jr., who shrugged. "You OK, Dad?" he asked.

"Yes, I'm fine, Son. Just fine." Art kept his eyes focused on Mary Lee.

"We'll go get something at the coffee shop and be back in a few minutes," Art Jr. agreed, taking Allie's hand. "But, Dad, in order to communicate with Ms. Broadmoor, you need to know   one blink means 'no,' two blinks mean 'yes.' Try to stick with yes and no questions; it will be easier." Art and Mary Lee watched them leave the room, arm in arm.

"Nice couple of kids," Art said to Mary Lee. She blinked four times.

"They'll leave us, you know," he added. "Go to some foreign country, I expect, and do their part to save the world." She blinked twice and shrugged.

As soon as their privacy was assured, Art laid his head on Mary Lee's chest and wept, "Welcome home, Mae Rose," he said over and over as he kissed her face. It didn't matter if her physical form had changed—Art knew his wife. He also knew it was unlikely that anyone else would believe that Mae Rose had taken up residence in Mary Lee's body, but he didn't care, and he wouldn't bother to explain. Perhaps it was better that way. And it didn't matter if Mae Rose required constant care for the rest of her life. He would love and cherish her, just as he had promised all those years ago.

"Nice work with the movie. Your idea, of course." Art's eyes danced merrily.

Mae Rose lifted her eyes upward with a significant amount of blinking.

"Ah. You had help." He laughed. His wife would stop at nothing—absolutely nothing—if she wanted to accomplish something. Apparently even God was at her service. Art laughed and laughed.

Before Art Jr. and Allie returned, Art assured a weeping but radiant Mae Rose that he would bring John and Elliana to visit her the next day. He called her "Ms. Broadmoor" and remembered to say, "It was lovely to meet you" when he left for the night.

58

When Anna Ling, the nurse on duty that night, came in for her rounds and saw Dr. Death sleeping with his arms around Gertie, she hardly knew how to respond. Her first thought was to run to the nurses' station, let the other nurses in on her secret, and start the hospital rumor mill. This would be the juiciest piece of gossip in a long, long time, and she would get credit for the discovery—a priceless trophy.

But Anna couldn't do it; something restrained her with an almost physical force. (She had no idea that Mary Lee's spirit had learned how to use her Viewing Pane). Instead, she went over to the bed and touched Gene on his shoulder, whispering softly, "Sleeping with patients is against hospital protocol, Doctor."

Gene awoke, startled, and groped for words. "She . . . needed . . . comforting," he mumbled, helpless to explain. "She has no family."

"I just thought you would want to know so that you could extricate yourself before you become a hospital headline." Anna smiled.

"Thank you," Gene said and glanced at her ID badge, "Anna. I won't forget this."

"Nor will I," Anna replied with a twinkle in her eyes. "I'll be back in five minutes to check Ms. Morgan's vitals. I suggest you not be here." She turned quickly and left.

Gene did as he was instructed but cautiously. Not only did he not want to disturb Gertie, but he discovered he had a rock-solid hard-on that would have to be dealt with.

* * *

Art kept his word. The next day, he brought John and Elliana to the hospital. He didn't tell them that he believed Mae Rose was living inside Mary Lee Broadmoor's body or that their own mother had written the movie through Mary Lee. He decided that if it were important to know, they'd figure it out. He did tell them that Ms. Broadmoor was showing signs of improvement, that he had spent some time with her the night before, and that she was a remarkable woman. He felt strongly that all of them should meet her.

John watched his wife interact with Mary Lee, but he kept his distance after they were introduced. He was very quiet but impressed with how Elliana chatted with her, carrying on both sides of the conversation. He certainly didn't miss how his father and Mary Lee kept looking at each other and smiling as if they shared a special secret. It was difficult to reconcile that his father could meet the woman who had written the story of their lives and put it on an international stage yet be so kind to her. He made a note to talk to his father about it later.

After the family left and Mary Lee was settled comfortably, Art prepared to leave. He turned to her with his hand on the doorknob and said, "Good night. I love you," with such confidence and ardor that Mae Rose in the body of Mary Lee Broadmoor swooned. Her mouth formed the words *I love you too,* although they sounded more like a dog howling. Art smiled, blew a kiss to her, and left.

*   *   *

The CANIF Ball was a huge success. Allie was animated and sparkled through her tears with Art Jr. by her side. The day before, Art had suggested that Art Jr. "get a ring on that finger before she gets away," as if somehow he knew Allie had her bags packed for Brazil. He took Art Jr. to a jewelry store on Rodeo Drive that the hotel concierge had recommended. It was no small sum that was laid out for the engagement ring Allie Schwartz wore that evening, yet its brilliance paled in comparison to the joy on Art Jr. and Allie's faces.

No one knew that a bit later that day Art returned to the jeweler and made another significant purchase, leaving the owners smiling and swearing undying devotion to the McElroy family. He had drained Mae Rose's Rainy Day account and enjoyed every minute of it.

Gertie and Dr. Gregory were noticeably but understandably absent. Gene, however, was able to sneak a bottle of champagne hidden in a huge bouquet of flowers past the hospital nurses' station that night. He and Gertie talked for hours until the combined potency of her drugs and the influence of alcohol reduced her to slobbering and eventual unconsciousness. Unknown to Gertie, Gene once again leaned over to kiss her before he left. This time he whispered something in her ear that made her smile even though she would never be able to recall it.

As they greeted the crowd at the ball, Nita Winslow and Cheryl Lewis introduced Art to as many media contacts as they could. If Art chose to, he could make a living out of telling his story. Having submitted to wearing a tux, he looked almost suave and easy in this crowd, unaffected by their accolades. His only mission was to share his vision. No one knew why he felt the joy he did. They assumed it was from all the attention he was receiving or perhaps the champagne. But Art disliked crowds and didn't touch a drop of alcohol.

Only Cheryl noticed these details. She stayed close to him during the ball, as if she knew there was more going on inside of Art. She watched carefully from a distance as Art slipped away quietly just after a midnight toast to Mary Lee Broadmoor's long life and a sequel to her movie. Cheryl knew how to avoid being noticed as she followed Art to the hospital.

Mae Rose had never seen Art in a tux. She was enraptured when he appeared with another dozen roses—white ones this time—and a small box from the jewelry store. Taking her hand in his, Art knelt at her bedside and put a sparkling diamond on her finger.

"I love you, Mae Rose," he said. "Always have, always will. Please don't ever leave me again."

After a brief pause, he added, "I'm going to have to work the rest of my life to pay you back for what I've spent on this trip. I'm afraid I spent all the money you had saved in your 'Rainy Day' account."

His confession made Mae Rose giggle through tears of joy. Art didn't know he would make back what he had spent many times over with his books, interviews, and speaking engagements. He envisioned Mae Rose at his side each step of the way, taking care of every detail, insisting on absolute perfection.

As he put his hand on the doorknob to leave, Art heard a sound from the bed. "Yoo-hoo," Mae Rose called, and he laughed, for those were the first words she had ever spoken to him. He turned to see her wave good night to him. Then she turned her full attention to the ring on her finger, leaving Art with the memory of her joy at finally knowing she was loved.

When Art walked out of the hospital, Cheryl Lewis fell into step beside him. In her official capacity as Nita Winslow's assistant, she was glad to see everything working out so well for him. On a personal level, she felt as if she had tripped and fallen in love with Art McElroy without realizing it, while he, for a suspicious reason, appeared to be enchanted with Mary Lee Broadmoor.

"Everything OK in there, Mr. McElroy?" Cheryl asked.

"Everything is just wonderful," he said. "And please call me Art. We know each other well enough, don't we, Cheryl?"

"OK . . . Art," she replied and laughed.

"Thank you. I couldn't have done it without you."

"Sure you could have; you just didn't know it. Nita wanted me to make sure you were doing OK when she saw that you had left the ball. Can I give you a ride back to the hotel?" she asked.

"Now there's an idea," Art told her. "I'll bet the fare is reasonable, maybe even free, just like I like it."

Cheryl laughed. "Something like that," she said.

59

Later that night as Mae Rose dozed lightly, she heard a toilet flush. She looked up, puzzled, and saw Mary Lee standing at the foot of her bed. It had been many hours since Mary Lee had quietly left her body. Mae Rose laughed. She wanted to spend more time with Mary Lee and Max would take care of her latest film.

"Rumor is that you're ready for Bliss, Mae Rose. Care to join me?"

"You mean I can come back? I—I thought I was vanished forever!"

"Oh no, Mae Rose. You were on special assignment—and a bit of remedial education. That's all," she replied smiling.

Mae Rose was overjoyed, and left her body behind without a word of protest. She didn't know *how* Mary Lee knew what she did, but that didn't matter. Somewhere a toilet flushed.

*   *   *

Art heard the same sound in his hotel room and woke from his sleep, thinking John or Elliana had used the bathroom. But their room was down the hall with its own separate bath. It was unlikely that he would have heard it that far away.

Suddenly he knew—he understood what the flushing meant. Mae Rose was letting him know that she was leaving. As he started to weep with grief, he saw Mae Rose standing at the foot of his bed with her hands on her hips. "Don't you go carrying on like you did the last time I died, Art McElroy," she scolded. "No hysterics."

"Why not, Mae Rose? I don't want you to go. We just found each other again. Why can't you stay?"

"Because I got what I came back for. We both did, didn't we?" she asked him. "I got to come and tell you how much I loved you, and you got to buy me *white* roses and put a proper diamond on my finger, you old tightwad."

Art couldn't help laughing. "I guess you're right about that."

"You *guess* I'm right? You *guess?*" Mae Rose bellowed and laughed uproariously. "Haven't you learned anything? I've always been right about what I know I'm right about. That's why living with me was such a pain in your ass. I was right about you, wasn't I? About loving you, about how creative you are? I knew we loved each other even if we could hardly bear each other sometimes. You remember all the good times, don't you? And weren't the bad times just so we would remember how good love was?

"But my being right didn't make you wrong, Art," Mae Rose went on. "You were right too, about so many things, about what you loved and why. You were right about marrying me. It took a man like you to put up with a woman like me. Love made us right. In spite of everything that seemed so wrong, we were perfect for each other. And just so you know, everyone else knew it too. Ha! We were probably the only ones who couldn't see it. I know you wish things had turned out differently for us. So did I for a while. But Art, there are so many things we got right; that's what we need to hold on to. All that was good!"

Mae Rose stopped speaking. Art looked up to see her energy shimmering as she began to disappear. He thought he detected a sly smile.

"If every raindrop were a dollar," she sang. Her ability to carry a tune had not improved.

"And every grain of sand pure gold," Art added, laughing.

"It would not begin to measure, the love for you I hold," they sang together.

"And it doesn't make a difference, no matter what we're told."

"We are the richest people in the world!"

Mae Rose told Art, "I'm off to say good-bye to our boys. Just remember there's so much more love waiting for you, but you have to let me go. You know that, don't you? You've got that gorgeous ring. I left it at the hospital. When you bought it, you were thinking of *her*, not me. It's time for a new love. Get my clothes out of that closet. Make room for someone else to hang hers. Got it?" The toilet flushed again and she was gone.

Both Art Jr. and John had strange dreams that night that included toilets flushing and visions of their mother looking like Mary Lee Broadmoor. With their arms around the women they loved, they dreamed their way to the answer about the movie. They wouldn't remember anything but the fuzzy edges of their dreams, but both awakened in great peace.

Mary Lee was laid to rest in accordance with her wishes. The news of her passing was not publicly disclosed until her body had been cremated. Allie and Gertie were together as James Christianson read the details of Mary Lee's will. Not only had Mary Lee left Gertie one million dollars, with the balance of her multimillion-dollar estate going to her daughter, but she had adopted Gertie, in order to make Allie and Gertie sisters. They both wept, then laughed and hugged. In spite of their differences, they were bonded for the rest of their lives, and somehow it was exactly how it should be.

* * *

It was early spring again. John and Elliana's daughter, Elizabeth Rose, was four months old and there were more surprises on the way.

If anyone had been in the barn where Art Sr.'s retirement project was still in process after all these years, they would have heard a woman's voice say, "Won't they be amazed!"

"Speechless, I'm thinking," another woman's voice replied, as they looked through the Viewing Pane they were sharing." It will leave them speechless, and I can't wait!"

"Let's do it then, since we have the power—and the permission," a third declared with authority. Together they watched as seven mechanics from Mike's Mechanic Shop miraculously finished restoring Art's seven antique VWs.

Meanwhile, Art had driven his old truck full of Mae Rose's clothes, jewelry, and things he could part with to the closest Goodwill store. On the way home, he said, "I love you. I think I knew it from the first time I saw you, but I couldn't see it because I couldn't let go of the past. I don't have much to offer. The farm will pass to Elizabeth Rose in a couple of decades, but until then, it's ours to enjoy. What do you say? Can you stand the thought of spending the rest of your life with me?"

Cheryl Lewis sat in the passenger seat. She took Art's hand. "Oh, I don't know, Art," she replied, smiling. "I saw you first, so I think *I* was the one who fell in love with you first, technically speaking of course."

"Well, since you saw me first, that would make you technically correct," Art laughed. "But the first time I saw you, which wasn't until a few hours later, I loved *you*, so that makes me right too, doesn't it?"

"Why, I suppose it does," Cheryl replied. "Now that I think of it that way, we both knew and we were both right."

Art laughed as he pulled the truck to the side of the road and stopped. They happened to be passing through town right where his accident with Mae Rose's VW had occurred. He got out, went around, and opened the door for Cheryl.

"Art, what on Earth?" she asked as she stepped out.

Right there, where his life had gone so awry, Art McElroy Sr. got on his knee and proposed to Cheryl Lewis. He'd carried the ring in his pocket, waiting for the right moment. This had to be it. He took her in his arms and kissed her long and deep. Suddenly the sound of sirens filled the air around them; the two Fairview police cars pulled up.

"Pardon us, Art," Big Charlie stated, clearing his throat and trying to appear serious, "but we've had a report of indecent exposure. You and this young lady will have to accompany us to the station."

"You're kidding, right?" Art asked Charlie. "Oh, this is payback, isn't it? For the barn cat incident?"

"Actually, Mr. McElroy, sir, I'm quoting from Section 85.7 subparagraph B of the law. I must insist that both of you come with me. Please turn around Mr. McElroy. Officer Jackson here will read you your rights while I apply the handcuffs."

"What will we do about the cats?" Cheryl asked. "We can't just leave them here; they could tear up the truck while we're gone."

"Good point," Big Charlie replied, still attempting to be serious. "Officer Jackson, can you carry their cage? I will accompany these two suspects to the station. Pardon me Ms. Lewis, could you turn around too. I apologize but we have to enforce the law on you also. I promise that the cats will be taken care of until the two of you are . . . um . . . released."

"Released?" Art exclaimed. "What do you mean, Charlie? You can't be serious. We were just kissing. I had properly proposed to Ms. Lewis. That can't be against the law!"

"We'll have to look into this further, sir. In the meantime, please cooperate." Big Charlie was nearly faint from trying not to laugh.

Cheryl squeezed Art's hand. "I think I have this under control," she assured him, winking. "You may recall I've spent some time doing police work and I do have friends at the LAPD."

As Officer Jackson grabbed the cat kennel, Poe hissed, reaching his paw through the bars as if to attack him. Charlie quickly grabbed his paw as he announced, "You're under arrest for attempting to assault an officer of the law. How do you plead?" Poe meowed pathetically. The four of them laughed as they walked to the station.

John, Elliana, and baby Elizabeth Rose, Henry Carter, Ben and Louise Strong, Jill King and her husband, and Pastor Frank and his wife were also present when the judge entered.

"All rise!" Big Charlie announced. "Court—I mean this wedding—is now in session!"

The judge turned to Art first. "In the matter of the City of Fairview versus Art McElroy under Section 87.5 subparagraph B, how do you plead?"

"Guilty," Art replied.

He turned to Cheryl. "How do you plead?"

"If he's guilty, so am I," she replied. "I stand by my man."

The judge stepped forward and joined their cuffed hands. "Under the authority granted me, I sentence you to the state of holy matrimony until death do you part. Art, you may kiss the bride." He then removed the handcuffs.

"You're sure?" Art quipped? "I won't get arrested and thrown in jail for kissing my wife?" He took Cheryl in his arms and kissed her more than properly. The group started clapping, cheering, and laughing as they left to take the party to the farm. The sound floated upward until it reached higher realms.

"Ready?" Josephine Carter asked Mae Rose and Mary Lee.

"Ready and set," the two women agreed.

"GO!" they shouted together.

As the wedding party arrived at the farm for the reception, the seven VWs started their engines and proceeded to drive out of the barn into a circle until they surrounded Art and Cheryl. Each had a *Just Married* sign and tin cans behind it.

"Would you look at that?" Art laughed. "How in heaven's name could something like that happen?" He smiled and looked skyward as if he knew.

Cheryl grabbed his arm and pointed down the driveway. "If you think that's amazing, look at this!"

Scores of VW Beetles of every vintage were lined up the road, carrying invited guests and well-wishers who were honking their horns, ready to party. There was even a VW Beetle limo in line, carrying Nita Winslow and Dr. Greyson from LA. Overhead, a helicopter was filming as the cars assembled. Art assumed this would be aired on a future *Currents* show.

"Too bad Gene and Gertie couldn't be here," Cheryl said to Art. She snuggled happily into his shoulder as the cats purred at their feet.

"Yes," he agreed. "Art and Allie either." They both laughed.

* * *

It was true that Gene and Gertie hadn't been able to make it. They were on their honeymoon in Rio De Janeiro. On their Viewing Panes Mae Rose and Mary Lee saw a lusciously tan and fit woman in a very tiny bikini sitting by a pool finishing a drink and giggling to herself as she reached into her purse and fumbled for her wallet to leave a tip for the server.

As she searched her bag, half of a pair of handcuffs spilled over the top. Unaware of this slight indiscretion, she grabbed the bag and headed up toward the hotel, a smile growing larger on her face. As she pressed the elevator button, a hotel bellman tipped his hat and said, "Hello, Mrs. Gregory. How's the honeymoon going?"

Gertie pulled her sunglasses down and winked at him. In fabulous form she said, "Let's just say I've got this all locked up," and stepped into the elevator, pressing the button for the top floor. When the doors opened, Gertie walked down the hall and unlocked the doors to a massive guest suite overlooking the water.

Setting her bag, hat, and sunglasses on the kitchen bar, she called out, "Oh, Gene, darling? Darling, are you still in bed? How wonderful! Stay right there. Turn on the stock market reports, would you? I have such a surprise for you." She pulled the handcuffs out of the bag as she untied the top and bottom of her bikini. She climbed in bed, snuggled up to her dozing husband, quickly grabbed his wrist, and cuffed him to the bedpost. Before he realized it, she had done the same with his other hand.

Gene Gregory groaned in anticipation. At least his feet were free, which gave him a fighting chance. But he wouldn't resist the torture he was about to endure.

* * *

Far up the Amazon River a boat approached a dock as dozens of native men, women, and children poured out from a village hidden in the jungle. A slender white woman stepped onto the dock, her hand shielding her eyes from the blazing sun. She looked up the hill, smiled, and opened her arms wide. Allie was home at last. She stooped to embrace the children who arrived first. *"Señora! Señora!"* came the calls as the crowd descended to the dock.

A voice behind her interrupted the squeals of pure delight. In mutilated Portuguese, Art Jr. asked, "Mrs. McElroy, where would you like your bags please?" Allie looked up in time to see Art Jr. struggling with their suitcases as he lost his balance and fell into the river. She laughed so hard, her knees wouldn't hold her; she collapsed onto the dock. She giggled as her husband climbed sheepishly out of the water and couldn't stop even when he took her in his arms and kissed her in front of the whole village. She was so glad to be home and to be in love.

"We did it!" Mae Rose, Mary Lee, and Josephine cheered as they closed the Viewing Pane they were sharing. "Yes, and without meddling this time!" their Reflection Agent added with great joy.

"It's much more fun to meddle," Mae Rose laughed. "I didn't know being vanished could be so entertaining!"

"You were one hell of a bitch," Mary Lee agreed.

"Look who's talking," Mae Rose bantered right back.

"Let me know when you two are ready for another assignment," another voice interjected. "Oh, and I've got something for you two," it added. "Take a look."

"Well, I'll be!" Mae Rose and Mary Lee exclaimed together. "Just look at us!"

If the citizens of Fairview had Viewing Panes to see into the afterlife, they would have been blinded by the brilliant light from the crowns Mae Rose and Mary Lee were now wearing. Instead, they saw dazzling ice coating everything for miles in an unfathomable beauty that would soon melt away in the bright sun.

About the Author

TJ Lambert/Stages Photography, Milwaukee, WI
www.tjlambert-stages.com

Vivian Probst (born Ruth Theobald) was raised in a small Midwestern town until the age of thirteen when her parents dedicated their lives to religious work. At the age of fourteen she was convinced that she would be given stories to write, but it would be thirty-four years before those stories began.

In the meantime, Vivian (Ruth) followed in her parents' footsteps and was trained in the studies of culture, anthropology, and linguistics, graduating from a private religious institution in 1977 with a degree in multicultural ministries. After a brief and deeply unhappy time of missionary service, she gave up everything she knew in order to find life outside the restrictive philosophy in which she had been raised.

Completely unprepared for the emotional or financial whiplash of becoming an outcast from the only life she had ever known, Vivian

(Ruth) lived in poverty until she was rescued by The Women's Center in Waukesha, Wisconsin. An opportunity to work at a minimum wage job in real estate property management eventually led her to a career as a national consultant and trainer to the affordable-housing industry. And during this time a wonderful second marriage occurred.

On March 10, 2000, the stories Vivian had long ago been told about began to appear—first as dreams, then as remarkable events that materialized into characters and plots as she wrote—without any formal training in writing or any preplanned concept or outline.

Vivian's first published novel, *Death by Roses*, began after her older sister died of Lou Gehrig's disease in 2008. She worked through her grief for five years as she wrote her novel. She then submitted her manuscript to the When Words Count Retreat's literary competition (whenwordscountretreat.com/pitch-week) and as the first place winner won the prize of having her book published by SelectBooks, Inc.

Vivian and her husband live in Waukesha, Wisconsin, surrounded by their children, step-children, and the most amazing eleven grandchildren on planet Earth (or so Vivian claims). She is happily at work, as there are more stories begging to be written.

For more information about Vivian Probst and *Death by Roses*, visit deathbyroses.com.

You can follow Vivian on Twitter @VivianRProbst and like Vivian on Facebook at www.facebook.com/deathbyroses